THE COW-HUNTER

THE Cow-Hunter

A Novel

Charles Hudson

THE UNIVERSITY OF SOUTH CAROLINA PRESS

© 2014 Charles Hudson

Published by the University of South Carolina Press
Columbia, South Carolina 29208

www.sc.edu/uscpress

Manufactured in the United States of America

23 22 21 20 19 18 17 16 15 14   10 9 8 7 6 5 4 3 2 1

Library of Congress Cataloging-in-Publication Data

Hudson, Charles.
    The Cow-Hunter / Charles Hudson.
        pages cm
    ISBN 978-1-61117-387-1 (pbk. : alk. paper) — ISBN 978-1-61117-388-8 (e-book)
    1. Travelers—History—Fiction. 1. Title.
    PS3608.U343C69 2014
    813'.6—dc23

                                                        2013032139

To Joyce, my live-in editor and fiction coach,
I dedicate this labor of love.

Deliver me from the sword, my forlorn life from the teeth of the dog. Save me from the lion's mouth, my poor life from the horns of wild bulls.

Psalm 22

As soon as the bulls caught sight of one another they pawed the earth so furiously that they sent the sods flying, and their eyes were like balls of fire in their heads; they locked their horns together, and they ploughed up the ground under them and trampled it, and they were trying to crush and destroy one another through the whole of the day.

And the White-horned went back a little way and made a rush at the Brown, and got his horn into his side, and he gave out a great bellow, and they rushed both together through the gap where Bricriu was, . . . (and) he was trodden into the earth under their feet. And that is how Bricriu of the bitter tongue, son of Cairbre, got his death.

Lady Gregory (trans.),
Chuchulain of Muirthemne, c. AD 700

I found these [cowpen] people, contrary to what a traveler might, perhaps, reasonably expect, from their occupation and remote situation from the capital or any commercial town, to be civil and courteous, and though educated as it were in the woods, no strangers to sensibility and those moral virtues which grace and ornament the most approved and admired characters in civil society.

William Bartram, Travels, 1791

CONTENTS

vii

PREFACE

This novel plays out in the setting of a little-known and long extinct American way of life, a forgotten world that was reconstructed most definitively by the historical geographer Terry Jordan in the 1980s and early '90s. Jordan made the case that the free-range cattle-herding culture of the American West was not born in the Western Plains; rather, it emerged from the womb of early eighteenth-century South Carolina. Here cattle-herding traditions from the British Isles, Spain, Africa, Jamaica, and Barbados were woven together into a culture for the tending of free-range cattle in the upland pine and wiregrass forest and swamp-cane environment of the Carolina backcountry, where these herders, always on the fringe of settled society, often invaded the very hunting grounds of Native American societies. These original cowboys lacked lariats, six-shooters, and pommels on their saddles, depending instead on flintlock guns, hatchets, long stock whips, and herd dogs. By the middle of the eighteenth century, the relentless spread of farms, plantations, and settlements had already begun pushing these frontier herders westward through the lower South and northward toward the Appalachian Mountains on their long migration toward what we know today as the American West. This cattle-herding culture adapted as it moved, making necessary changes and folding in new techniques along the way.

In these pages I have made every effort to accurately portray the historical, environmental, social, and cultural realities of these early eighteenth-century cattle herders in South Carolina. But all events and actions herein are fictional, including most of those played out by real historical persons, such as Dr. John Lining, James Adair, and Christian Priber. For readers who want to know the principal sources of my information, the meanings of archaic words, and the sources of the songs my characters sing and the stories they tell, such may be found in the Notes and Selected Readings in the back of the book.

Several archaic words need to be defined at the outset. In eighteenth-century Carolina, cattle ranches were called cowpens and cowboys were called cow-hunters. The owner or manager of a cowpen was often called a pinder, a word whose usage goes back at least to the medieval era in the British Isles and probably earlier, for the culture of cattle herding among Celtic- and English-speaking peoples is ancient.

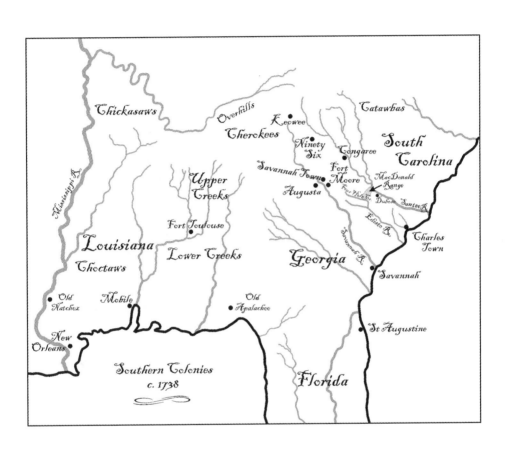

Chickasaws

Overhills

Cherokees

Keowee

Catawbas

Ninety
Six

Congaree

South
Carolina

Savannah Town

Fort
Moore

MacDonald
Range

Upper
Creeks

Augusta

Four Hole Cr.

Dubose

Santee R.

Fort Toulouse

Edisto R.

Mississippi R.

Louisiana

Lower Creeks

Savannah R.

Georgia

Charles
Town

Choctaws

Savannah

Old
Natchez

Mobile

Old
Apalachee

St Augustine

New
Orleans

Southern Colonies
c. 1738

Florida

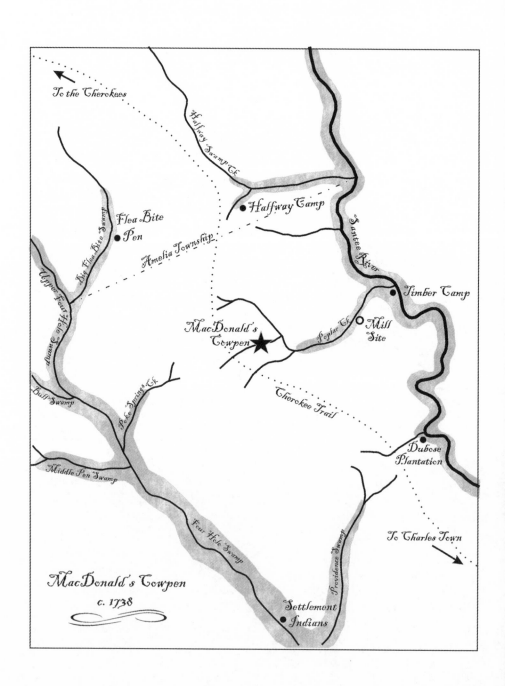

To the Cherokees

Halfway Swamp Ck

Halfway Camp

Flea Bite Pen

Big Flea Bite Swamp

Amelia Township

Santee River

Timber Camp

Upper Four Hole Swamp

MacDonald's Cowpen

Poplar Ck

Mill Site

Buff Swamp

Pole Spring's Ck

Cherokee Trail

Dubose Plantation

Middle Pen Swamp

Four Hole Swamp

Providence Swamp

To Charles Town

Settlement Indians

MacDonald's Cowpen

c. 1738

A NOTE ON CHARLES HUDSON

My husband, Charles Hudson, died peacefully of a heart attack on June 8, 2013, while *The Cow-Hunter* was in press. He had finished final revisions of the manuscript, the copyediting had been completed, and he was happy to know that the book was headed into the design and production process. Meanwhile, he was busily at work on a sequel—he had finished a first chapter and started on a second—even though he knew that with his weakening heart he almost certainly would never finish this work. Charles was like Billy MacGregor: his mind had to be engaged in an intellectual challenge in order for him to feel fully alive.

Charles was as much a writer as he was a scholar. He was a stellar scholar and a leading authority on the anthropology and history of the native peoples of the southeastern United States. The best known of his many scholarly books are *The Southeastern Indians,* which is widely used as a textbook, and *Knights of Spain, Warriors of the Sun: Hernando de Soto and the South's Ancient Chiefdoms.* One of the marks of his scholarship is his clear and lively writing style, for he placed a particular value on sparkling prose. Even with his graduate students he emphasized the value of good writing alongside the value of good research, and he spent considerable time over the years helping his students polish their own prose styles.

Charles was a natural when it came to writing nonfiction, but as he explains in his acknowledgments, he found the writing of fiction to be a tougher assignment. He rose to the challenge, however, and gave his all to the perfecting of his new craft. In the end he was as pleased with what he had achieved in *The Cow-Hunter* as he was with all the highly acclaimed scholarship he had produced in his professional career. This book is indeed a most fitting cap to his lifelong mission as a scholar. His foremost goal was to transmit to the public the discoveries he had made about the interesting array of peoples whose worlds came together in the very early South.

Joyce Rockwood Hudson
Frankfort, Kentucky

1

Mired

The New World. The first problem with this place, thought William as he shifted restlessly on a bench on the porch of the Packsaddle Tavern, fanning flies in the summer heat, is that it is so new a man must choose from a very short list of occupations. The second problem is that there are yet fewer opportunities for that same man to find even the basest employment through which he might save up enough money to stake himself in the occupation of his choice. Never mind that here money counts for less than credit and barter. If this were Scotland he could at least find work in the Atlantic trade or in service as a groomsman or gardener, draw his pay in coin, and live frugally enough to accumulate a stake. But here in South Carolina the tasks of common workers fall to slaves, and a free man of little means is left out in the cold. Had he known this before he set out across the ocean, would he still be in Scotland?

William leaned back against the wall and closed his eyes, letting his mind drift away across the sea. It seemed he had ever been faced with opportunity closing down. Even his birth among the rough and rowdy Highlanders of Scotland came just as they were losing out in their armed struggle with the Lowland Scots and their English overlords. At issue was whether the British throne belonged to the House of Hanover, as favored by the Lowlanders, or to the House of Stuart, as favored by the Highlanders. No MacGregor could stay out of the fight, including William's father, who was killed in this struggle, leaving his only child to be born fatherless into a crumbling world. William's mother, with the help of her kinsmen, raised her son as best she could. She even got him some schooling from well-meaning Presbyterian missionaries, to whom William was grateful, if not persuaded by their faith. But despite his mother's best efforts, the prospects for a fatherless lad in the impoverished

Highlands were next to nil. And so when his dead father's sister, newly widowed and childless, invited him to move down from the Highlands to her small home in Glasgow, William jumped at the chance, and his mother waved him off tearfully with her blessing.

In Glasgow he was astonished to see so many people of all sorts working at so many different occupations. Thinking back on it now, he did, in truth, almost wish that he had stayed there. Glasgow even had a university where, for a price, one could study and learn most anything. But then, as now, William had no money. To remedy this, he went to work in a tobacco factory where fortunes were being made by men in fine clothing who imported cured tobacco leaf from America, manufactured it into its many consumable forms, and sold it for a handsome profit. Though William's own job was lowly, life nonetheless seemed promising as he gained a few coins for his pocket and matured from an awkward youth into early manhood.

Then suddenly his aunt died, and to his surprise his prospects brightened. The good woman left him all she had, and though it was not so very much, it did give him a small stake with which to work toward a better future. But then her debts came in and he had to sell her house, humble though it was, to pay them. In the end he was left with no lodging and an inheritance too small to fund any enterprise into which he inquired. But he was undaunted, certain he could find a way to increase his stake. He pinched his pennies by sleeping wherever he could, and he spent from his wages only what he needed for food.

But his wages were stingy and his progress slow, so slow that as time went by he barely gained ground. How, he began to wonder, could he ever establish himself, take a wife, and father a family? His only solace was found in the company of his mates who labored beside him in the tobacco trade. He even joined together with some of them to organize a club, the Book Maggots, and together they read and discussed any books they could get their hands on and talked broadly and adventurously about the expanding world they found within those pages. It was exciting to live on the fringe of the swirl of new ideas spun out of the University of Glasgow. Because William's mother had little taste for religion—disillusioned with the divine, perhaps, by the early death of her husband—William himself had never been folded into any church, neither Catholic, nor Presbyterian, nor Church of Scotland. Instead he took naturally to a free-thinking frame of mind. One of his mates, in reading, picked up the motto "Dare to inquire." William took that motto as his own and imagined how it might be to live the life of a philosopher. But a university education remained beyond his means. He had to face the fact that as much as it would please him to do so, he could not live by his intellect alone. And so every morning he awoke to the same problem: how to escape his dead-end life, his piddling wage, his poverty? How to invest his small stake, meager though it might be, in some venture that could carry him forward?

Then came another turning point. He received a letter from his uncle, the brother of his father and aunt. Duncan MacGregor, now the last of his generation, was a tavern-keeper across the ocean in the New World colony of South Carolina, to which he had been deported when William was but a wee lad for taking up arms for the Stuart cause. More than a year had passed since William had written to Duncan to inform him of his sister's death, and now, unexpectedly, a reply came, the uncle inviting the nephew to come to Carolina to seek his fortune.

William was stunned by the prospect. He investigated the cost of passage and found that his stake would cover it. Did he dare leave his native land? His mates? His job? Poor as it was, that job filled his belly. Hard as it was, that life in Glasgow was a life that he knew. And over there, across the sea, in the wilds of the New World, what? "Dare to inquire." Was that truly his motto? Did he have the courage to live by it? Stiffening his resolve, William accepted the challenge, and in that year of 1735 he embarked on a new life in a new land.

And what had this bold move accomplished?

William opened his eyes from his reverie, sat forward, and leaned his elbows on his knees. Looking out at the street, he faced the question squarely. Here he was in Charles Town, more than two years later, in more or less the same situation in which he had been in Glasgow, except now his stake was nearly gone. With land in Carolina so plentiful and cheap, he could have settled, in a poor way, as a planter. But he knew nothing about cultivating the soil and had no inclination to learn. He wanted a life with broader horizons. And so instead he spent his first year in Carolina in the wilds of the Indian country, in the Cherokee town of Keowee, working as a packhorseman in the Indian trade. Though the initial promise of that venture did not pan out, the year was not entirely a loss. He had learned something about the Indian trade and more than a little about the ways of the Cherokees, even picking up some of their language. He had also learned more than he had anticipated about their customs of kinship and marriage, including some painful and timeless lessons of love and loss. All told, it was a hard year for him, and he was not anxious to repeat it. From a practical point of view, he had gained no more from it than a horseload of deerskins, which he sold not for money, scarce as it was in Charles Town, but for a moderate, now dwindling, amount of credit at Crockatt's store, where he and his fellow packhorsemen bought and sold.

His second year in the colony had yielded less than the first. For most of it William had been at loose ends, the problem of gainful employment pressing hard upon him. He had finally found work at Crockatt's store, but he was paid in credit, not in coin, and paid poorly at that. He was laid off whenever Crockatt's business went slack, as it was at present, and this time he had been idled far too long. He was into his second month without work. Crockatt kept promising to soon hire him back, but William was again searching elsewhere for employment.

Through the kindness of his aunt and uncle he at least had his bread and a roof over his head, a corner of a room on the third floor of the Packsaddle. He earned his keep by helping out with whatever needed to be done in the running of the tavern, but with six slaves in his uncle's household, the small chores that fell to William were not overly demanding. This left him with time on his hands and the opportunity to indulge that guilty pleasure he loved most, if intimate company with the fairer sex was not a possibility. In short, it left him time for reading. "Dare to inquire." He had not lost his hunger for knowledge. Dr. John Lining, a friend of his uncle who dined frequently at the tavern, possessed a small library of fine books, and he generously allowed William free use of it. In these books William's narrow circumstances faded while the great wide world opened up to him once more. Michel de Montaigne's *Essays* took him to French coffee houses. John Locke's political treatises allowed him to stroll the learned halls of Oxford and Cambridge. But his favorite destination had always been the playhouses of London in the company of William Shakespeare.

The most prized of the scant possessions William had brought with him from Scotland was a set of Shakespeare's plays, each work of the master in a separate, small volume of its own. There was nothing else like Shakespeare. Never mind that his elite, punning language was an impediment to easy reading. The man seemed to understand the secrets of the human heart in every part of the world, past and present. His amazing words fell from his pages like shiny new coins, forming up into glorious utterances that conveyed their truths with such clarity and precision that not a single word could be changed.

During William's year among the Cherokees he had taken along with him to the backcountry two volumes from his set—*Macbeth* and *Romeo and Juliet*. To his astonishment, the master's words, as he read them in that strange, wild land, seemed to echo the events that were then unfolding in his own life. This was especially and most painfully true of *Romeo and Juliet,* which so closely paralled that sad and difficult year, he could not yet bring himself to open the book anew and look back at Shakespeare's star-crossed lovers.

Nor, for that matter, could he make new headway in any of the master's works, given his darkened state of mind in the year since his return to Charles Town. Even now *King Lear* lay on the bench beside him, having been closed almost as soon as it was opened. He had once seen *Lear* performed on stage in Glasgow, but he had never yet read the play itself. He could recall the story but faintly: tumultuous goings on, the old king storming about, a nobleman's eyes gouged out, intrigue and armies, a tragic ending. What he remembered more clearly than the plot was the feeling of the play, how majestic and gripping the tale had been. In theory he would like to return to it. But a reader must be willing to give his all to the intricate words of the master, and William's all, on this day, was not present for the giving. Perhaps he should saddle Viola and ride out to the countryside, clear his head and shake off this darkening mood.

He rose to his feet and walked to the edge of the porch to look up at the course of the sun. Past noon. No one went out in the blazing heat of this hour unless from necessity. To do so would be cruel to his horse.

Just then William's aunt appeared in the open doorway of the tavern, and seeing him standing there, she came outside to pass the time. Mary was a handsome woman who carried her age well. The running of the tavern kept her mind sharp and her spirit bright. As she sat down on the bench where William had been sitting, she picked up the book to see what he was reading. "I have never taken to Shakespeare," she said. "What is this one about?"

"A king whose old age goes badly," said William. "I saw it performed once and thought now I might read it. But it seems not. I cannot concentrate enough to engage with it. I'm afraid I can read no deeper these days than the *South Carolina Gazette*."

"I always have that problem with Shakespeare's works," said Mary. "You should read to suit your mood, Billy. When I want to read something only a little deeper than the newspaper, I turn to Daniel Defoe. He writes his books for the ordinary man."

"I believe he learned the writing craft as a journalist," said William.

"Yes, and I'm sure Shakespeare never wrote for a newspaper," said Mary. "Who could have understood him? But Mister Defoe gained more from his days as a journalist than a talent for plain writing. I dare say he understands our world as few other men do."

"Och," William said, "if Daniel Defoe knows today's wide world, it is only by reading about it from a great distance. I read *Robinson Crusoe* back in Glasgow, like everyone else in creation. Defoe claims to know all about the wild world and its savage men. And back then, with no experience to tell me otherwise, I believed that indeed he did. But his fantastical cannibals are nothing like the so-called savages I lived amongst in Keowee. The Cherokees would no more eat a fellow human than you or I would. Their meat comes from the animals they hunt in the forest. And most of what they eat is the corn grown in their women's gardens. Their hominy grits are not so different from the oat groats we ate in Scotland. Defoe would be surprised at how like us they are. The Cherokees tell stories about witches that differ but little from the ones I heard told in the Highlands. Their houses are much like my own mother's house."

"You instruct me as if I know nothing about Indians," said Mary, getting her back up a little. "Duncan traded among them far longer than you have, and he always came home with much to tell me. What has you so on edge, Billy? You seem to be spoiling for a fight."

William shook his head apologetically. "Forgive me, Aunt Mary. I am mired again in the swamp of self-pity."

"That will get you nowhere," said Mary. "Someday you will learn that life is always more good than it is bad, even when it feels otherwise."

William sighed as he sat down beside her on the bench. "I have heard that said, but I will never subscribe to it. In my experience, life is good when it feels good and bad when it feels bad. Just now it feels bad. But if I can only find some steady work, the wheel will turn and then I will join you in your optimism."

"In the meantime, do not give up on Defoe," said Mary. "Have you read *Moll Flanders*?"

"No, I've never had that book at hand."

"Then you don't truly know Defoe," said Mary. She got up and went inside, and William could hear her go up the stairs to her bedroom, where she had a small shelf of books. Presently she returned with *Moll Flanders* in her hand. "Here," she said, sitting back down and handing it to him. "I think you might find this to your liking. It is the story of a woman who was born as wretchedly as one can imagine—in Newgate Prison, no less. Though she rose from that poor beginning, it was only to endure several reversals of fortune. But eventually she came to the Virginia colony and prospered. You will see that you would not want to follow her example in most things, but I do think she might rally your spirits. And you will see that Defoe is not so defective in his grasp of our everyday world as he is when he writes about far away places."

"Thank you, Aunt Mary," said William, accepting the book with genuine gratitude. He reached his arm around her shoulders and gave her a little hug. "I can say that life is always good when you are around."

"Now you are just humoring me," she chuckled, and she reached up and patted his hand as it rested on her shoulder.

At first William did enjoy Defoe's story about the beautiful, intelligent, and cunning Moll. She was in fact a woman of the modern world, able to survive its abrupt pitfalls and reversals, and gifted with a rare facility for stretching morality and truth to the breaking point and often times beyond. But William soon grew weary of following the details of her intricate feminine plots and machinations, and he skipped ahead to see what he might learn from her success in Virginia. Alas, she came with a good stake and settled comfortably as a planter. Defoe evidently knew no more than William himself about how a penniless wretch with no interest in planting might make a go of it in the New World. He would have stopped reading the book altogether, but now Mary was asking him about it every day, revisiting the story through his reports of it. For her sake William kept at it, though with waning enthusiasm. Finally he set Defoe aside for the present and turned back to Shakespeare, trying once again to enter *King Lear*. But still his mind would not engage, and after bogging down in the first pages, he closed the book almost in despair. What had happened to the delight he once felt for a well-told tale? Where had he lost it? Did it die back in Keowee with his beloved Otter Queen? Or was it still around here somewhere, shut up, as it were, in a closet or lost under the stairs? Perhaps if he took out his journal again, he could find it in there where he last knew he had it.

William glanced over at the intricately woven Indian basket almost buried under his other scant possessions in the farthest corner of his small, curtained-off sleeping space. His journal was inside it. Since returning from Keowee, that record of days past had felt toxic to him whenever he tried to open it. It almost made him sick to remember the naive hope with which he had recorded his observations and musings during that first, eventful year in Carolina. But now he reached once more for the small covered basket, held it for a moment to stroke the smooth surface of finely split cane woven so masterfully by Otter Queen's graceful fingers, and then he lifted off the lid and took out the journal. His stomach did not go queasy. He opened the book cautiously and found his own retelling of a scene from *MacBeth*. This was a practice he had begun as a Book Maggot back in Glasgow: he would summarize his reading in his journals so as not to lose the crux of it over time. And indeed, it was good to make a brief revisit to the Scottish tale.

He turned to the next page and there he was with the packtrain on the Cherokee Trail, carrying in their load of manufactured goods for a season of trading for deerskins with the Cherokees. They were camping overnight at Ninety-Six, a frequently used campsite that took its name from the fact that it was ninety-six miles from Keowee. He remembered reading *MacBeth* on this journey, when he was still so new to the country that he had never yet met a Cherokee nor seen an Indian town. He glanced ahead over the next few pages and then flipped past all the rest to the end of his entries. A third of the pages in the book were still blank. Turning back to the basket, he reached down into it and brought out a quill pen and a tightly corked bottle of ink. He took out his knife and sharpened the point of the quill. Then he shook up the ink, uncorked it, dipped in his quill, and took up his journal at the first of the blank pages.

Monday, August 1, 1737, Charles Town

Of late I have read almost half of Daniel Defoe's Moll Flanders. I would summarize the plot if I could hold in mind any of the details of her endless stream of so-called husbands. But each new consort blends in with the last and I cannot recollect a thing about any of them. How different it would be if her tale were told by Shakespeare. Every scene would be memorable, every character impressive. What I do find impressive is the full title of the tale, which I record here in the absence of a summary of my own. To wit, 'The Fortunes and Misfortunes of the Famous Moll Flanders, &c. Who was Born in Newgate, and during a Life of continu'd Variety for Threescore Years, besides her Childhood, was Twelve Year a Whore, five times a Wife (whereof once to her own Brother), Twelve Year a Thief, Eight Year a Transported Felon in Virginia, at last grew Rich, liv'd Honest, and died a Penitent. Written from her own Memorandums.'

It seems to me that Defoe's own life would make a good tale. He himself spent time in Newgate for unpaid debts, and one assumes he met there his inspiration for Moll. He was a journalist and pamphleteer, a political man who championed the Dissenter cause. He is especially well-regarded here in Charles Town for a pamphlet of his that was aimed at helping the Carolinians get free of the rule of the Proprietors, who first owned this colony. It was not until his later years that he took to writing novels.

I have to say this for the man. He has a heart for the struggles of those who are born without advantage. He does not condemn Moll for the disreputable actions into which she is forced by the circumstances of her life. Indeed, Moll brings a kind of respectability to her life of disrepute. And Defoe makes it clear that as hard as it is for a penniless man to make his way in the world, it is even harder for a penniless woman.

I suppose I should find comfort in that, but I do not.

2

John MacDonald

W illiam's return to his journal seemed to bring about a change of luck. Within a week Crockatt took him back again for half-time work. This was not enough to mend his fortunes, but it did improve his circumstances. He could now awake in the mornings with a job to go to and a reason to get up and get moving. The sunlight coming through the windows seemed brighter, and he found himself looking forward to what the day might offer. In short, the gloom that had plagued him for so long was lifting, and as the weeks of August slid by, he began to feel more and more like his old self.

In his improving mood, he was beginning to notice his world again. He liked to vary his walk to work, and on a particularly pleasant day in the last week of the month, he came out of the tavern into the early morning light of the city, took a left turn, and walked a short distance up King Street, past the Quaker meeting house. The light scent of wood smoke from breakfast fires in backyard kitchens mingled in the soft, warm air with the subtle fragrance of passion flower and late-blooming roses. As he turned right onto Queen Street toward the bay, he savored anew the beauty of Charles Town, with her single and double houses standing snug up against their streets, their outbuildings and gardens stretching deep behind them on their narrow lots. In her gardens as in her cuisine, Charles Town was above all an Atlantic city. Her uniqueness lay in the way she mixed together so many ingredients from all sides of that wide ocean. William especially loved the yard of a house on Queen Street that had a trellis draped with morning glory vines from South America and moon-flower vines from Spanish Florida. In the mornings the deep blue blooms of the morning glories delighted the eye, while at night, when the morning glo-ries were closed tight, the moonflowers spread open their white blooms as big as saucers, sometimes with large, exotic moths fluttering about them. Another garden on Queen Street was even more eclectic, featuring native Carolina allspice and passion flowers along with African cockscombs and Caribbean spider flowers, European tulips and Asian day lilies, a seasonal swirl of color from faraway places. There was nothing so lush and sweet as this in Glasgow.

As William continued down Queen Street toward the commercial dis-trict, passing by the new theater and the French Huguenot meeting house, he noted the rising heat. The day would be another hot one. In the distance to his left he saw St. Phillip's tall steeple reaching skyward, the highest edifice in the city. Shortly afterwards he came to Bay Street, and turning right he entered the heart of mercantile Charles Town. The western side of Bay street was lined with large buildings, many of brick, mostly English in architecture, but some with Dutch gables. Stores and warehouses were in the lower floors, with living quarters in the upper floors. The street itself was thronged with people of every station, high and low, working and transacting business.

He soon arrived at Crockatt's warehouse and went to work putting in his half day shaking out deerskins. This tedious task was necessitated by the carelessness of some of the Indian hunters in the processing of their skins, which left the skins vulnerable to maggots and rot. Each bundle had to be opened, every skin shook out, and any rot carefully excised.

When his morning's work was done and William was leaving the warehouse, he discovered his uncle just outside the door, his foot propped on a step, leaning his elbow on his knee as he talked to two acquaintances of his. When he saw William, Duncan straightened up and waved his nephew down beside him on the street. "I'll see you fellows later," Duncan said to his friends and then turned his attention to William. "I was hoping you could come with me to the grocer and help me carry some supplies back to the tavern. There's both flour and cornmeal on the list, but I figured if I had your help, I wouldn't have to bother with a horse."

"Certainly," said William. "I'm glad to be of use."

"Let's go first to the White Goose and get us a bite," said Duncan. "I like to see what the other taverns are putting on the table. I'll buy."

"I'll not argue," said William. "My stomach's been rumbling for at least an hour."

They set out for the tavern on Tradd Street, Duncan setting a leisurely pace in the hot afternoon sun. He was a stoutly built man with a pleasant countenance etched deeply into his face. His thinning hair, once dark but now streaked with gray, was shoulder length and tied behind his neck with a black ribbon. As they walked along, they encountered at least once in every block a friend or acquaintance with whom Duncan would stop to exchange pleasantries, often moving over into the narrow shade of a nearby building to escape the heat while they talked.

By the time William and Duncan had dined at the White Goose and finished their business, the afternoon was nearly spent. Coming out of the grocer's, they divided up the parcels, William shouldering the bag of cornmeal, which was by far the heaviest item. Then they walked the three blocks up Broad Street and thence a short distance up King Street to the tavern.

As they climbed the porch steps, they were pleased to find Mary in conversation with a welcome visitor. "John MacDonald!" exclaimed Duncan, setting down his load and striding over to where John and Mary had pulled their chairs to shade themselves from the slanting rays of the late afternoon sun. William followed close behind.

MacDonald rose to his feet. "The devil take me if it ain't the young MacGregor as well as the old one," he said with a grin. "You MacGregors are getting to be thick as fleas here in Charles Town."

"Och," said Duncan, "our numbers are far too spare. For the good of humanity, there's not near enough of us MacGregors anywhere." The three men laughed and shook hands warmly.

William could hardly have been more pleased to see anyone. He had first met John MacDonald on his own travels to and from the Cherokees. MacDonald's cowpen was a way station at which William and his fellow packhorsemen had spent several pleasant evenings eating meals prepared and served by MacDonald's daughters and lingering at table for hours telling histories and tales of the Old World and the New. John MacDonald was the only other soul in Carolina besides Duncan who provided William a direct link to his boyhood in the Highlands. As a young man MacDonald had fought alongside William's father for the Stuart cause and was with him on the day he fell in the 1715 Jacobite uprising. John and Duncan had later been captured together and deported to Carolina on the same ship. Because John MacDonald had been present at William's father's death, William's regard for him was inextricably tangled up with the father he had never known. But little of this could be conveyed in a handshake, and William simply smiled at him affably, shifting the bag of cornmeal from his shoulder to free up his right hand for the greeting. "Let me take this to the kitchen," he said. "Then I want to hear all about what has gone on at the cowpen since I was last there."

"Just set that cornmeal down out here for now," said Duncan. "The kitchen can wait. Let's all take a seat. We need two more chairs over here out of the sun."

William and John picked up chairs and carried them over to where Mary was sitting.

"Duncan, in all honesty," said John, as they ranged the chairs round in a circle and settled down, "I have got to tell you I've been trying to steal Mary away from you to brighten my life back at the cowpen."

"Och, that won't do," said Duncan. "Would ye deprive me of the best tavern-keeper in Charles Town? Now if it's my horse ye want, I'll give it to you, old friends that we are. But ye can't have my wife."

"You men!" said Mary, slapping playfully at Duncan. "As if I were for the taking." She rose from her chair, fluffed her apron, and went inside the house in mock anger.

"Och, Duncan, it was a great prize ye won in Mary," John said. "I only wish my Martha were still on this earth. I tell ye, it is hard facing the world alone. But how much worse it would be if I didn't have my three daughters around me."

"Thank God for those mercies he grants us," said Duncan. "Now tell me what you're doing here in town. It's too early yet for the fall cattle drive."

"We got to running short on too many things at the cowpen. First it was the flour. The timber cutters are eating enough for twice their number, more than they ever have before, I know good and well. And with the flour gone, they are starting to draw too hard on the rice and cornmeal, so that not any of it is going to last until the fall drive."

"I know you wouldn't come down to Charles Town just for flour," said Duncan. "Wheat is scarce up your way, but you can at least buy cornmeal up there to tide you over."

"And then there's the mare I lost with a breached foal we couldn't get turned. Lost the foal, too. And I was already short a horse. So now I have to buy at least one horse, and I can get a better price here in the city. Not to mention that I'm almost out of rum. If I buy in the backcountry, I've got to pay the middleman's price. So we drove ten head to market early. They're not as fat as they will be later, but I can get enough for them to buy what I need."

"Well, I'm sorry about your mare," said Duncan, "but it is a treat to have your company."

"If anybody can help me forget my troubles, it's you and Mary," said MacDonald. Then he leaned over toward William and clapped a hand on his shoulder. "And how about you, young MacGregor? How have ye been getting on? It looks like time has been good to ye."

"I am doing very well, thank you, sir," said William. "Riches still elude me, but in truth I can't complain."

"The young ones take to city life," said Duncan. "The constant clatter wears on me, but William likes it here."

"I like the backcountry, too," said William. "But Charles Town has a lot in its favor. It offers every amusement, including a new theater on Queen Street. Employment is another matter, but I've found enough to get by, doing odd jobs and working at Crockatt's store."

"And you've escaped the fevers and ague that make life so perilous here in the lowcountry," said Duncan. "You can count your blessings for that."

"I do indeed," said William.

"We all do," said Duncan, "each and every year we make it through untouched. I don't miss everything from my years in the Indian trade, but I do miss the good air of the backcountry. And I have to say, too, that I miss the freedom. You cowmen know what I mean. You don't have to endure the humdrum of city life season after season, with all its petty aggravations. Better to be on the back of a horse, riding about in God's green world, meeting new challenges with each new day."

"You've been living in town so long you've forgotten what it's like out there," said John. "You're only looking now at the pleasant side of cow herding. It's got its troublesome side, too, don't forget, and sometimes I think it is mostly trouble. Lately we have been losing too many cattle to be having a good time. Not to mention my mare that died. And the timber cutters eating me out of house and home."

"You just need a night or two at the Packsaddle, free of care," said Duncan. "You'll get your perspective back." He looked around the yard and then leaned over to peer inside the tavern door. "Where is your main man? Your son-in-law? He must be around here somewhere."

"Rufus is pitching his bedroll beneath the roof of the barn at the horse pen. With only the ten cows, we managed the drive with just the two of us."

"Rufus is not feeling sociable enough for a taven life?"

"I reckon not. It seemed like we both had burrs under our saddles on this drive. But the greater truth is that I'm short on tavern money just now. When I'm dead and Rufus is the pinder, he can have the soft bed. But until then, if there's only money for one of us, I'm taking it."

"You are starting to sound like Job with his afflictions," said Duncan. "It seems you've truly had a difficult year."

"That would be putting it mildly," said John. "I've had more of my cattle go missing than in any year I can remember."

"Is it varmints taking them?" asked William.

"We don't think so. Most of the bears and wolves and panthers have pretty well been thinned out around our range. It's a puzzle. We don't find any kill leavings, nor any drag marks. What varmint would be strong enough to carry off a full-grown cow and not leave any parts behind?"

"Two-legged varmints could," said William. "Other herdsmen lifting our cows was the worst problem we had back in the Highlands."

"It's not like that here," said MacDonald. "Every once in a while some Indian hunters will kill and butcher a cow. But the Indians stay mostly to the north of our range and seldom come south unless they have business in

Charles Town. My man Cudjo thinks it might be a *bravo* that's taking my cows."

"A *bravo*?" asked William.

"A wild bull."

"I've never heard them called that," said William. "Nor have I met up with any truly wild bulls. In the Highlands we could always track down a bull that was making trouble. He wouldn't stay wild for long."

"The Highlands don't have miles and miles of swamps that no man can penetrate," said MacDonald. "Here we do. That's why a bull can sometimes leave the rest of the herd and strike out on his own. He stops taking orders, ye might say. He enswamps himself where we can't get to him, and then he sneaks out of a night and cuts another cow or two out of the herd for his secret harem. He takes them deep into his hiding place and then comes back and gets some more. But if this is a wild bull what's been stealing from me, he's a damned sly one. No one has seen the least sign of him. Not the least. I'm at a loss to explain how that could be possible."

"It might be the devil himself," chuckled William. "And those cows in his harem might be enjoying his company. They may not want to be rescued."

"Well, my boy, you may find this amusing," said John, "but I fail to see the least bit of humor in it."

"My apologies, sir," William said awkwardly, regretting his misreading of MacDonald's mood. "I didn't mean to make light of your problems."

"I'm telling ye, Billy," Duncan said cheerfully, getting up from his chair, "we have been visited by Job himself. What we need to do is go inside and have us some wine. What is wine for, if not to dispel such dark clouds as seem to be gathering here?"

John smiled ruefully and rose with him. "Like I say, we've been on edge."

William went over and picked up the bag of cornmeal he had set down earlier and took it out to the kitchen. When he came back to the dining room, he found that Duncan had unlocked the door where the spirits were kept and was drawing a large pitcher of Madeira. They all sat down, and John MacDonald was soon into his second glass while Duncan and William were only half through their first.

"Let's give this Madeira some company," said Duncan, and he called for meat and bread. But when it arrived, only he and William partook of it. Mac-Donald was well into his third glass of wine and clearly had no wish to dilute its effect with food. Duncan gave him a long look and shook his head. "I find it hard to believe that any bovine creature, devil or not, could put you into such a temper. There must be more than lost cows that's out of kilter at the cowpen. Is all well with your family?"

"With three daughters?" asked John, his speech beginning to thicken with the wine. "How well can things be with three daughters?"

"You were just now praising them," said Duncan. "Those are fine girls you have, and ye know it well."

"I do love them, I'll not deny it," said John. "But neither will I deny that I often wish my son had survived to be a man."

"You have your two sons-in-law," said Duncan, "Rufus and the other fellow. What's his name?"

"Swan," said John, downing his glass and holding it out to be refilled.

Duncan hesitated, but then poured him another. "You have two sons in them," he said.

"Barely. If only they could be brothers to each other, as real sons would be. Brothers will stick together, but that's not so with brothers-in-law. There have been times when these two have come to blows. And more often than not, my daughters align with their husbands, splitting all of us apart. Sometimes it seems we MacDonalds are like England and France, vying for the same cowpen."

"It will work itself out," said Duncan. "Give it time."

John finished his fourth glass, and instead of asking Duncan for more, he reached out and took the pitcher himself and refilled his glass. When he set the pitcher back down, Duncan took it and set it out of reach.

"I don't see how it can ever work itself out," said John. "The world is a-closing in on the backcountry cowpens. You can hardly even call it backcountry anymore. We are getting squeezed. Amelia Township has leap-frogged over us to claim territory to the north of us. They've got German-speaking farmers up there clearing land that used to belong to all of us, or to none of us. It's the grandees here in Charles Town that want all those white settlers out there to balance against the great numbers of African slaves the planters are bringing in. Those farmers and planters don't have a bit of use for our free-ranging cattle. They take away our swamps and savannahs and piney woods and then take offence that our cows range into their planted fields, which they can't be bothered to fence. I'm telling ye, I don't see any end to it. I don't see any good end at all."

"It can't be that bad," said Duncan.

"Yes, it can," said John. "I've not even mentioned the rice planters down the Santee, always looking upriver to grab land for more rice plantations.

They keep creeping up toward us, coming closer every day. God damn their eyes. To the planters, we cow-hunters are the mud-sill of the human race. They keep squeezing us like a boil they're trying to pop. And we can't go further up into the Indian country. It goes without saying that the Indians don't want our cows anywhere near their gardens. And those devils can be murderous when they get riled."

"The Indians aren't everywhere," said Duncan. "You could find some open land somewhere out there ahead of the settlers."

"That's what Rufus says," John said wearily. He looked at the wine that remained in his glass, swirled it around, and then drank it down. "There is nothing else we can do, he says, but move our cowpen. And it's true. I could escape a host of troubles if I did. But God damn it, I am too old to move."

"Let Rufus take charge," said Duncan. "He's young and strong."

John laughed, but without any humor. "I don't trust the son of a bitch. I don't trust either of those boys, him or Swan. They're like two vultures waiting for me to die so they can feed on my carcass." He pushed his glass across the table for more wine, but Duncan ignored it. John then tried to rise from the table, but his legs wobbled and he fell back into his chair. He put his elbows on the table and his head into his hands. "Och, I wish Martha were still alive. She would know how to manage our daughters and those husbands of theirs. She could keep us all one family."

Duncan reached out and patted his arm.

The three of them sat in silence for a time. William tried to think of something to say, but nothing came to him. It saddened him to see MacDonald in such a state, so different from the last time he had seen him. When they had parted then, MacDonald had embraced him like a son and offered him work at the cowpen if ever he wanted it. But having had his fill, in his youth, of cowtending in the Highlands, William had never seriously considered taking him up on it. The only thing that had come close to tempting him toward it was the thought of MacDonald's youngest daughter, Rosemary, the one still unmarried. But William's heart at that time was freshly shattered by the loss of his Indian wife, and he had no desire to go chasing after what might bring him fresh pain. Now, as he sat with this despairing friend of his father, he second-guessed himself and wondered what would have happened if he had gone back to the cowpen a year ago instead of staying on in Charles Town. Could a "good" son have lessened this man's misery?

"If there's anything I can do. . . ," William offered.

MacDonald waved a hand dismissively and shook his head. Then he looked up and shook his head again. "I apologize to the two of you for spilling all my cares. I reckon age is creeping up on me so that all I can see around me is trouble and danger." He leaned back in his chair and sighed. "And my joints get creakier every day."

They all chuckled a little and then lapsed back into silence. The sun had gone down and the light was growing dim. They heard Mary ring the supper bell and then the sound of the lodgers coming down the stairs.

Supper was the same fare they already had at their table, a small meal of cold ham, bread, butter, and jam. Of more interest to the lodgers was what there was to drink, and on this night it was rum punch. But when a serving girl came toward Duncan's table with a bowl of it, he waved her away.

John now seemed ready to take some food, though William worried that he might not be able to keep it down. Duncan evidently had the same thought. "You might start with bread and jam," he said and broke off a piece of bread, spread it with butter and jam, and put it on MacDonald's plate.

John picked it up and ate a little.

"If there was one thing you could do to make life better at the cowpen," asked Duncan, "just with things as they are, what would it be?"

"My sorest spot is that I am short-handed. My sons-in-law are ever complaining to me and arguing amongst themselves over who needs help the most—Rufus the cow-hunter or Swan the timber cutter. It's a neverending contest, and it keeps their wives on edge, each one feeling more put upon than the other. What we need is two more slaves, one for herding cows and one for sawing timber. But where would the money for that come from? Especially with all the cows I'm losing to that devil bull, or whatever the hell it is that's taking them."

The conversation had circled back to where it began.

"What about Rosemary?" asked William, hoping to lead it off in a new direction.

"What about her?"

"You mentioned your other two daughters, but you haven't mentioned Rosemary. I'll wager that she brings you more joy than grief."

"Och, Rosemary never complains, that's true enough, but that doesn't mean that she is happy. She does bring me joy, I'll not deny it. She's as smart as a tree full of owls, the sharpest wit I ever saw in a woman. I'll grant her that." He looked for his glass, saw it empty, and in its place raised his piece of bread in tribute to her. The wine was still at work, taking him now to mellow sentiments in place of the earlier anger and self-pity. "She makes me think of Martha, my Rosemary does. She has her mother's beauty and brains, and twice her will. She is interested in everything. She has read every book I own, and most of them twice." He paused and shook his head. "But she is not at all fond of life in our cowpen, and she makes no secret of it. That is where Rosemary breaks my heart. She is a hard worker, the apple of my eye, but she is looking to marry her way out of there. She won't stay around like the other two."

"Marry?" said William and immediately felt embarrassed at how quickly he had blurted it out. He cooled his demeanor before asking, "Who is the lucky man?"

"No one yet," said John. "Her sights are set too high for the local pickings. I can at least take comfort in that. Many a backcountry traveler stopping in to lodge with us has looked at her with moonbeams in his eye. But not a one can measure up to her standard. She wants someone who can lift her to a higher station in life, and she will look at no less."

"Then her bar is set too high for me to join in the jumping," said William. Duncan and John chuckled.

William would have liked another glass of wine, but if he poured one for himself, he would have to pour another for MacDonald as well. So he ate in silence, while the conversation between Duncan and John moved from one thing to another. He eventually lost interest in what was being said, and having finished his supper, he excused himself and went up to his bed.

His journal wanting an entry, he took it out and wrote a very few words.

Friday, August 26, Charles Town
Rosemary is ready to marry. But how ready is she? How concerned should I be?

Then he put his journal away. He would have to think about that.

The next morning John left out early to conduct his business in town and then head home to the cowpen. William tried to settle back into his routine, but he found his thoughts and feelings caught in a disconcerting swirl, both John and Rosemary weaving in and out of them. Where was the John MacDonald he had first known, that strong and buoyant man who had once embraced him like a son? Perhaps it was that very sentiment that now made William feel distressed to see him in such a state. But John MacDonald was not his father, William kept reminding himself, and the man's troubles were none of his affair. And yet this in fact was his father's bosom friend, who had fought at his side that bloody day at Sheriffmuir. It was clear that what John MacDonald most needed now *was* a son—a loyal son. He as much as said so. William surely could offer his dead father's friend that much, a son's loyalty at least, to help him through a difficult time. Why not go up to the cowpen and hire on with MacDonald, take him up on that offer he had made more than a year ago? And while he was at it, he could get to know Rosemary again. He remembered well how pleasant her company had been. It was true he had as yet no prospects to offer as a husband, but she had warmed to him once before. What harm could there be in testing the waters again?

3

Bad Air

On the very day that William finally decided that he would indeed close up his affairs in Charles Town and go up to seek employment at Mac-Donald's cowpen, he arrived home from work to find Duncan sitting on the porch looking unusually tired and somewhat pale.

"It looks like you've been working too hard," said William as he came up the steps.

"It's not the work that's done it," said Duncan, "but something has. I'm feeling none too well today. Mary thinks I should take to my bed. I hate to give in to it, but I do feel spent."

"What could be ailing ye, Uncle?"

"I don't rightly know. The last few days I have been more tired than usual, and this morning I could barely get up. I practically needed help to get my clothes on."

"Then you should listen to Aunt Mary and get yourself some rest."

"I believe I will, if you'll take over for me for the rest of the day."

"You know I will," said William. "Go on up to your bed and don't worry about things down here."

Duncan was indeed ill. Before the day was out, he was shaking in his bed with a severe chill, blankets piled over him despite the summer heat, his teeth chattering. Then came a high fever. He threw the blankets off and began sweating profusely. Next came a severe headache and muscle pains. Mary was grim with worry. She was sure he was stricken with ague, the intermittent fever that was the scourge of the lowcountry, the same disease that had taken away two of her children.

When Dr. Lining came to the tavern for supper, as he often did, Mary took him up to see Duncan in his bed. After a short while the two came back down to the dining room, and William joined them to hear what the doctor would say.

"You are right, Mary, it is ague. Attend to him closely. Make sure he drinks plenty of water. And when he is able, see that he eats to keep his strength up—especially good, meaty soups."

Mary nodded soberly. She knew what to do for ague. Straightaway she went back upstairs and left William to tend the dining room.

Once Lining's food had been served, William joined him briefly at his table. "Does it seem to you to be a bad case?" he asked the doctor.

"Bad enough. But Duncan is strong. He'll be back on his feet before long."

"I don't suppose we should be surprised that he's been stricken," said William. "We are coming just now into the season for ague."

"The fact of the matter is, ague comes when it wants to come," said Lining. "Sometimes even in the spring. But the worst cases do come in fall, it is true."

"What causes it then, if not the season?"

"If only we knew. The Italians call it *mal aria,* bad air. In their land, as in ours, people don't fall sick from it everywhere. It plagues their lowlands but not their mountains, just as it does with us. The Italians reason, therefore, that it must be caused by the air that rises from wet, low-lying areas, like the miasma that wafts in from our swamps. The problem with this theory, as I see it, is that ague does not occur in Charles Town in the winter, even though the air remains much the same. So I cannot tell you the cause. It is a great puzzle, one that I would very much like to solve. This wretched disease takes away too many of us each year. It keeps our colony from thriving as it might."

William sighed and got to his feet. "What hope is there for us if the very air is bad?"

"I am not persuaded that it is the air that plagues us," said Lining. "And do not worry so about your uncle. He is strong as an ox."

"I hope he can remain strong," said William.

The chills and fever had exhausted Duncan, and he kept to his bed the next day and the day after that. Midway through the third day he suffered another bout of the same chills and fever as before, along with vomiting and diarrhea. These episodes repeated themselves every three days for more than a week. With each round Duncan grew weaker and weaker, but finally the symptoms began to taper off. Mary attended him night and day, helped by Chloe, one of the tavern slaves who had some experience nursing the sick.

Monday, September 12, Charles Town

The worst of Uncle Duncan's ague seems to be passing, but he is still not well. The chills and fevers are gone, but he is so terribly thin and weakened he can barely stir from his bed. Aunt Mary is resting easier, I am glad to say. Despite Dr. Lining's assurances, she feared greatly that Duncan would die and leave her to run the tavern alone, a prospect that fills her with dread. At times like this it seems especially tragic that she and Duncan are childless. They had only three children born to them in all. The birth of the last one, a girl, went so awry that she was born dead, and Aunt Mary was rendered incapable of having any more. Then the other two, boys half grown, died of ague. Because of these misfortunes, I am their only relative on this side of the Atlantic Ocean. I realize that this circumstance works in my favor, and I am most grateful for the kindnesses they have shown me. But it also makes me uneasy. More than once they have intimated that I might be the logical person to inherit the tavern, and I can only shake my head at the folly of my response to this. Despite my complaints about my poor circumstances, I have no desire to be a tavern-keeper. I can see my own perversity as I write, and yet my heart insists that I hold to this truth. To be tied forever to a tavern in Charles Town would mean no more ventures into the back-country with the likes of my old trading mates. No more adventures among the Indians. What I would prefer is to go to work for John MacDonald until I have earned enough to outfit myself as an Indian trader. And besides, Uncle Duncan is, mercifully, recovering from his illness. Though he and Aunt Mary are not young, neither are they yet old. They could still live for many more years, and I hope that they do. As for me, I intend to find my living elsewhere.

Meanwhile, I must make record of my latest activity in the world of letters. As things have eased up around here, I have finally engaged with Shakespeare's King Lear in the few moments of free time available to me, and I am glad to say that the story has pulled me in. It is set in a time more ancient than that of Macbeth, older than the Norman invaders, older even than the first Christians in England. It is the story of a king who ruled not from London but from Leicester, an earlier seat of power. I suppose it was originally named Lear-cester. As a tired old man, Lear wants to relinquish his cares and responsibilities, and "unburthen'd crawl toward death." But once unburthened of his duties he still wants to be called king and to be respected and honored as such. Can high position survive when power is relinquished? I suspect Lear will soon find out.

The poor fellow gets off to a bad start. As he is about to divide the inheritance of his realm amongst his three daughters, he asks them how much they love him. His two older daughters are careful to observe courtly form by extravagantly declaring their boundless love. But his youngest daughter, Cordelia, who actually

loves him most, answers his question more carefully. Whether from the inexperi-
ence of youth or from an unadorned character, she speaks as she truly thinks and
feels, with transparency and guilelessness. She has none of the "glib and oily art"
of her two older sisters, Shakespeare tells us. Blind to her purity of heart, Lear
does not take well her disregard of courtly protocol and hears it instead as disre-
spect. In a petulant fit of anger he disinherits poor Cordelia and turns her out
of his house. Standing nearby, Lear's most esteemed retainer is horrified at what
he has done and says so to his face. In his fury Lear savages him too. With these
bleak and shocking actions the play begins.

I would sit down and read it all through without stopping except for my
duties here. And because of those same duties my plans to go to the backcountry
have been delayed indefinitely. I have not yet spoken of my intentions to Aunt
Mary and Uncle Duncan, not wanting to add their cares. My greatest duty at
this time is to be of as much use to them as possible for as long as they need me.

William was now up to his ears in tavern-keeping. Though he had lived at
the Packsaddle off and on for these last two years, he had paid scant attention
to the details of running the place. But in taking on so many of Duncan's
responsibilities, he had to learn what was what.

The tavern was a typical Charles Town single house, sided with wide
riven clapboards. Though worn down here and there by human traffic, it
was, overall, a sound building. Located in a newer part of town, outside the
limits of the old town wall, it sat on a generous-sized lot about sixty feet
wide and perhaps twice that in length. Two rooms wide and one deep, the
tavern was positioned on a front corner of the lot with its narrow, gable end
facing King Street, the heavily traveled thoroughfare that led out of town
and into the backcountry. It was three stories high, including the garret,
with the two rooms on each level separated by the stairwell in the center
of the house. The ground floor held a dining room and a sitting room; the
second floor held the best guest room, which rented at premium rates, and,
across the stairwell, Duncan and Mary's private room, which served both as
a bedroom and an office where Mary kept the records and accounts. The top
floor held two low-ceilinged, "knock-head" rooms where beds were rented
at cheap rates. William lived in a curtained-off corner of one of these third
floor rooms.

A driveway led in from King Street alongside the wide porch—called by
many a piazza—that ran the length of the front on the ground-floor level. A
work yard for the day-to-day labor of the tavern lay beyond the end of the
house. Alongside this work yard was a storehouse and a detached kitchen,

where all the cooking and laundry was done, and further back was a privy, the slave quarters, and the stable. Past these buildings was a large, well-tended vegetable garden surrounded by a paling fence and bordered on one side with a flourishing rosemary hedge. William liked to run his hand through the rosemary when he walked past it, picking and crushing some of the leaves to release their pleasing herbal fragrance.

The strenuous labor at the Packsaddle was performed by six slaves, two of whom—Sampson and Delilah—were overseers. Delilah oversaw the work done inside the tavern and in the kitchen by her daughter, Susan, and the other young female slave, Chloe. Delilah, like her Biblical namesake, was a force to be reckoned with. She was small in stature, but her self-possessed manner made her seem large. Sampson was overseer of the male slaves, Cuffee and Tad. William, being a good deal younger than both Sampson and Delilah, felt a natural respect for them. Though he was master and they were slaves, he had never in his life held command over anyone, and his instinct was to be as light-handed with them as good order would permit.

Each day at the crack of dawn, before the guests began stirring, Delilah got up and cooked breakfast, while Chloe and Susan swept and straightened up the dining and sitting rooms. Once the guests were up and about, Chloe and Susan tidied up the two public rooms on the top floor, and then they attended to the guest room and to Duncan and Mary's room on the second floor. This feminine world of housekeeping was something of a mystery to William, and he did not feel competent to be in charge of it while Mary's attention was taken up with Duncan. Fortunately Delilah seemed to keep it all in hand, as she did on the day Duncan took a decisive turn for the better, and William celebrated by stealing a few moments with *King Lear* on the porch. Sitting gingerly on the edge of a chair in the shade, as if he only intended to tarry there for a moment, he was just settling into the play when he heard Susan and Chloe raise their voices in the work yard nearby.

"You been sittin on your arse in Master Duncan's room this whole time, and I been out here cleanin high and low for both of us," Susan complained loudly. "You stretchin it out and stretchin it out, like he can't keep breathin without you bein there. I see what you're doin, gettin out of your work, and I'm tired of it."

"You come try cleanin up after him," Chloe replied sharply. "Then you'll see you ain't the only one that's been workin around here. Missus Mary be up all night every night with Master Duncan, and he sick as a dog. And me tendin him hand and foot all day. I'm doin just what I'm supposed to be doin. You got no right to call me down."

William was boggled by their quarrel. Should he leave them be or step in to try to calm the waters? Before he could decide, he heard an angry Delilah come bursting out of the kitchen.

"I ain't gonna have no more of this from you two. I'm tired of it."

"I'm doin every bit of the cleanin, Mama. Chloe ain't lifted a finger in two weeks."

"You'd better watch your complainin," said Delilah in a controlled but angry voice. "You keep on like this and they'll sell you off to a rice plantation. And then where will you be? Them planters don't spare the whip. You got to wake up, girl, and see how things are. Master Duncan's lyin flat on his back, and that ain't good for us. If he don't get well, we could all get sold. You know you ain't never done no nursin, and Chloe has. That's why she's got her job and you got yours. She's helpin us all by nursin the master, so stop pesterin her this way."

"But it's not fair," said Susan, her voice trailing off. It sounded like she was starting to cry.

"Don't be a baby. It won't do you no good. Now, come on and let's tend to that laundry that's been pilin up in the kitchen." Silence fell over the yard as the three of them went inside.

Relieved that he did not have to step into that tangle of bruised feelings, William put his *Lear* away and turned back to his duties at the tavern. He was grateful to Delilah for the firm and competent way she handled the women. Around the male servants he was much more at ease.

Sampson had the skill of long experience in his management of the outside work. With Cuffee and Tad he tended to the garden, the grounds, and the stable. They also kept the fireplaces supplied with wood and the water drawn and carried to where it was needed. Everything was well organized and done on time, and William only had to oversee it in the most cursory of ways.

His greatest responsibility as a stand-in for Duncan was the task of provisioning the tavern. The firewood was carted in by a country woodcutter, who delivered it in a heavy dray drawn by oxen. The kitchen was supplied by the market for fresh food, and for stored food by one of the merchants on Bay Street, who kept a running tab of purchases. For small items William walked to the market or store to fetch what was needed. For heavy foodstuffs, he cinched an old packsaddle onto Viola and led her to his shopping, where he packed her in a rather slapdash way, unlike the elaborate packing he had learned how to do for the packhorse loads in the deerskin trade. Viola, after all, only had to carry her load a few city blocks. From an oxcart a purveyor of spirits made regular deliveries of kegs of rum, beer, brandy, and wine, all of which was stored inside a stout wooden cage built against one wall of the dining room and kept under lock and key to ward off those guests at the tavern who, prone to the drinking habit, might be tempted to pilfer.

Mary continued keeping the books. She also kept track of mail that came to the tavern, not only for guests but for some of the townspeople, since Carolina lacked a public mail service. Mary was careful to keep recent copies of the *South Carolina Gazette* punched with holes and hung up on small pegs on a wall in the dining room for customers to take down and read.

For William the hardest part of tavern-keeping was the constant requirement to be demonstrably affable toward the customers, to greet them with what passed for warmth, and to humor and caress them with light flattery. Alcoholic beverages flowed freely at the Packsaddle, as at most other taverns, and William had to be on hand each evening to make sure that none of the company got too drunk. Occasionally he had to step in and manage disputes between inebriated customers. He thought he had this well in hand until the night he rented a bed to one Benjamin Bowler, a plump planter fresh in from Barbados. At supper Bowler shared a table with Robert Allen, who was a regular at the Packsaddle and an old friend of Duncan's. William overheard their light and jocular banter while they dined, but when the alcohol began to flow, an edge came on Bowler's voice.

"I notice you speak with a burr," said Bowler. "Your r's sound as if you have a bee buzzing inside your mouth."

"Aye, it is in Scotland where we learn to pronounce our r's correctly," Allen said affably.

Bowler sniffed. "I visited Scotland last year. Very interesting. You Scots feed yourselves on what we English feed our horses."

"Very true," said Allen. "It is oatmeal that make us so strong of arm."

Bowler filled his empty cup with wine and drank it down. Then he filled it again. "My quarrel with the Scots," he said thickly, his speech beginning to slur, "is not that they eat oats, but that so many of them have turned away from the true religion of the Church of England."

"In our case that would be the Church of Scotland," said Robert Allen.

"You're a dissenter, then, are you?"

"I came into the Presbyterian fold while I was still a babe," replied Allen. "I didn't realize I was dissenting from anything until I found myself in conversation with Anglicans. Are you aware that in Carolina most of the dissenters live in the backcountry as a buffer between these settled parts and the Indians in the north? That in itself is a reason for you to love dissenters."

Bowler downed the wine in his cup and poured some more. "The problem I have with dissenters," he said slowly, trying not to tangle his words, "is that they delude themselves by interpreting their own wishes and desires as God's will. That, you see, is why they can never truly know God's will. They make themselves their own authority and thereby condemn not only their own souls to hell, but those of their children as well."

"How is that?" asked Allen, sitting up straighter, his geniality beginning to fade.

"Their invented religion is no true religion. Their children are raised up as ignorant of Christianity as the Indians are."

Allen leaned back in his chair and took a long look at his table companion. "You talk like a man who has never lived amongst men who think for themselves and speak their minds freely, as we are accustomed to do in Charles Town. Unlike you Barbados men, we in this colony accept men of all religious stripes. You may be an Anglican, if you wish to be one, and I may be a Presbyterian, and William over there may be a free thinker. We don't put one above the other."

Bowler leaned forward and slapped his hand on the table. "You might not put one above the other," he said, his voice was rising in anger, "but God in heaven does. There is true religion and there is the way of the devil. Do you think God does not *care* which way we uphold? Do you not know that he hates dissenters? And he will act, just you wait and see. The day will come when the laws of England will banish dissenters from all seats of power, banish them even from the very society of Godfearing men."

"There it is, plain for all to see," said Allen. "It is you, not I, who deludes yourself by interpreting your own desires as God's will."

"You damned heretic!" Bowler muttered, and rising up a little from his chair, he threw his cup of wine in Allen's face. "Damned oat eater! You're all alike!"

Allen took the challenge. Curses flew and then fists as they knocked over chairs trying to get at each other. A bit tardily William rose from his seat on the other side of the room and hurried over to insert himself into the fracas— as Shakespeare would say, "between the dragon and his wrath." Allen already lay sprawled on the floor, dazed from the fierce onslaught of his foe. Benjamin Bowler was surprisingly agile for such a heavy-set man, and William himself was soon flat on his back, his arms wrapped about his face as Bowler sat astride him, pummeling away. William moved his arms enough to shout, "Sampson!"

But even as he did, Sampson was already on the scene putting one of his arms in a choke hold around Bowler's neck. With his other hand he grasped Bowler's arm and pulled it behind his back. "I don't mean to hurt you, sir, but this ain't no way to behave in a tavern."

"Get your hands off me, you damned nigger!"

Sampson tightened his hold and Bowler began getting red in the face. At last he went slack and Sampson pulled him off of William, who was somewhat the worse for wear as he got to his feet.

"This is a respectable establishment, sir," William said coldly to Bowler. "You have assaulted one of our guests, and you have assaulted me. You are creating a disturbance in a public place. If you do not collect your belongings and leave these premises at once, I will call in the law, and I will not hesitate to prosecute you."

"I am leaving," Bowler said. "But I have friends in this town, and you have not heard the last from me. As for your man, he can expect to feel the full force of the law."

"Sampson was acting on my behalf," William said, "and I will answer to any further mischief you might try." Bowler turned and thumped up the stairs, went up to his room to gather up his possessions, and thumped loudly down the stairs again, slamming the door as he left.

Wednesday, September 21, Charles Town

I earned my keep this day. I had to break up a fight over a theological difference, and I ejected the blinkered Anglican who started it. He left the tavern with mayhem in his heart, though when he sobers up, I doubt he will remember much of what happened.

Despite all this excitement, it must be recorded that today I did finish at last my reading of the tragedy of King Lear. And a tragic tale it surely is. Perhaps the king's fatal flaw is that he has so little understanding of his own folly. As one of his daughters says, "He hath ever but slenderly known himself." From this all else proceeds. After his heedless, stupid cast of the die in relinquishing his power to his two oldest daughters, one can only read with dismay as his world slides headlong and relentlessly from order to disorder. Lear cannot comprehend that these two daughters and their husbands have champed at the bit during their long wait to inherit their portions of his kingdom. He cannot comprehend that they would so quickly take from him his privileges and defenses. Soon he is left naked, so to speak, at the mercy of all who are around him, and finally he is bare even to a cold rain.

We humans are clothed in the fabric of society itself, and when that fabric is rent, we suffer and perish. The social fabric around Lear is sundered particularly by Edmund, the bastard son of one of Lear's nobles, who behaves indeed like a bastard. He is without conscience. In the end, most of the principals of Lear's family and court are dead, and saddest of all, this includes Cordelia, his youngest daughter. With her death the last light goes out in Lear's world. A heartrending outcome, all in all, and just as things had seemed to be turning for the better. I am uncomfortable with so cruel an ending to the story.

Can the fate of families and kingdoms ever be so bleak as this? Are we mere playthings of the gods? Shakespeare thinks so: "As flies to wanton boys are we to th' gods: They kill us for their sport."

4

Table Talk

As autumn came, more and more people in Charles Town were stricken with fever and ague. Duncan, however, continued to slowly recover. By early October he was able to be up and around inside the tavern, and all were heartened that he felt well enough to come down to the dining room from time to time and entertain the guests. By mid October he had recovered enough strength to venture outside the tavern, where he began assuming some of his former duties, such as dealing with the merchants of the town, though if anything heavy had to be carried back to the Packsaddle, William went along to assist him. William also continued his extra duties in and about the place. As for Crockatt's store, he had not worked there since Duncan fell ill, and he was not inclined to return. His intentions were still fixed on Mac-Donald's cowpen, and he was only waiting for Duncan's recuperation to reach a point where his aunt and uncle could manage on their own.

Meanwhile the tavern-keeping went on, and as William had suspected, it could be a boring occupation, with many tasks to be performed over and over every single day, starting with greeting the guests for breakfast and ending with closing the dining room at the end of the night. But all was not drudgery and routine. What he enjoyed most was the talk at table, especially by those who were in from the backcountry, most particularly the Indian traders, packhorsemen, and cow-hunters. They had such rich stories to tell. His memory of his year among the Cherokees was mellowing with time, and these adventurers reminded him of how much there was that was good about it. He was beginning to miss the Indian country and its people, and he grasped every opportunity to reconnect with it.

It was, therefore, a special day when two of Carolina's most notable students of the backcountry registered on the same evening for a night's lodging at the tavern. One was James Adair, a trader and self-styled Indian expert. The other was Christian Gottlieb Priber, a German who was . . . well, who knew what he was? Gossip had it that he had secured a land grant in backcountry Amelia Township, though people noted that he was more interested in philosophy than in planting. William had begun hearing stories about these two men while he himself was still out in the backcountry, but until now they had never taken lodging at the Packsaddle.

When the supper hour arrived, William saw Adair and Priber greet each other at the door of the dining room. Clearly they were well acquainted. They shared a table, and William overheard their exchange of pleasantries while they ate their supper. As they were finishing the last of their food, he walked over to their table carrying a tray that held a bottle of rum and three noggins. "Good evening, gentlemen," he said cordially. "I am William MacGregor, nephew of Duncan MacGregor, the proprietor of this establishment. I thought you might like some after-dinner rum, compliments of the house."

"By all means," said Adair. "Rum is the best dessert." He eyed the third noggin. "Perhaps you would like to join us, Mister MacGregor?"

"Ja, take a seat," said Priber, nodding genially and pointing to an empty chair.

"I don't mind if I do," said William. He sat down and poured the noggins full of rum. Adair and Priber introduced themselves to William, and they all shook hands across the table, rising a little from their seats as they did so. As they settled back, William took his measure of the two men. Adair had a head of long brown hair, a thin nose, and arresting blue eyes. He was deeply tanned, with the strongly built body of an athlete. He wore coarse clothing and an old hunting shirt that had seen hard usage in the backcountry. His was the genial face of a man who had a sense of humor. Gossip had it that he was exceptionally well educated for a trader and extremely sharp of wit.

Priber, who from his name and speech was obviously German, was broad and short in stature, with a wide forehead and a wide mouth. He was swarthy and not what you would call handsome, but he wore a merry countenance that put one at ease. He too was said to be well educated, although by all accounts he was a very odd fellow, and no one quite knew what to make of him.

"Well, MacGregor," said Adair, "how long have you been in Carolina?"

"Two years. I came here from Glasgow in 1735."

"And I came here from Ulster in that same year," said Adair, raising his cup to William.

"Ja, and a good year it was," said Priber in his thick German accent.

"You, too?" William laughed.

"Ja, in 1735! Two years ago it was. I came from London. And before London, Saxony."

"And there," said Adair, "I would expect our parallel careers diverged. After stepping ashore in Charles Town, we have no doubt taken three different paths."

"Mine is surely the most wandering path," said William. "When I first arrived, I was employed for a short while in a dry goods store. Then I worked for the better part of a year as a packhorseman and trader at the Cherokee town of Keowee. Since then I have worked at whatever I could find to do in Charles Town, mostly tending to skins and clerking at Crockatt's store. And most recently I have been working here at the tavern while my uncle recovers from a fearsome bout of ague. I am glad to say he is back on his feet again."

"Ach, is that all?" Priber exclaimed jocularly. "My path has been longer and more winding than yours. Many years ago I studied jurisprudence and philosophy in Saxony. But I spoke about my ideas too openly there, and the local authorities threatened me with arrest, and so I fled to England." This, at least, was the gist of what Priber said. William strained to understand his words. They were barely in the English language. He tended to pronounce his w's as v's—vat for what—and strung his words together in odd, Germanic ways, at times using a German word in place of the English.

"Then I came here," Priber continued. "I have a land grant in Amelia Township, but what I know about cultivating the soil would fill a very small book. A pamphlet, perhaps. Lately I have taken up residence among the Overhill Cherokees, and I am trying to learn their language and way of life. That is the long and winding path I have followed so far." He sat back and folded his arms and nodded at James Adair. "Your turn, mein friend."

"My path has been pretty straight," said Adair. "There is a brisk demand for skins and furs in Britain these days, and the Indians can lay hands on more skins and furs than they themselves can use. Straightaway upon my arrival I entered the trade that connects the one with the other. I traded first with the Catawbas, where I had the company and example of two old traders, George Haig and Thomas Brown. But the Catawba trade is now much diminished, and last year I went from there to trade with the Cherokees—in a town not so very far from Keowee, Mister MacGregor. More recently I have been getting to know the Chickasaws who live at Savannah Town, near Fort Moore. I'll be moving my trade there soon. It seems that every time I move I end up further west."

"The coincidences continue," said William. "We have all been in the Indian country, with the two of us as traders and Mister Priber as a student of the Indian way of life. Though I do not mean to elevate my own experience. I was low man in the enterprise, more a packhorseman than a trader. But I do share your interest, Mister Priber, in the manners and customs of the Indians, and I learned quite a bit on that subject in my time with them. Though in their eyes I knew less than a child."

"Then the coincidences continue even further," said Adair. "As Christian well knows, I am as interested in the Indian way of life as any man can be. He and I have exchanged several letters on the subject. But unfortunately that pleasant pastime with paper and quill has come to an end. The problem, you see, is that Indians so jealously guard their own affairs, while at the same time being so suspicious and prying into the motives of others, that they see every piece of paper that comes to me or goes out from my hand as a threat to their land and liberty. And so I must leave off conducting by mail any further conversations about them."

"Ach," said Priber, "that is a great pity. We have much to say to each other about all that we are learning. I am most interested in your experience with the Chickasaws."

"As I see it," said William, "the Chickasaws are the most unusual Indians in these parts. They have come here from so far away in the west that they seem to me to be out of place."

"Yes, it is true," said Adair. "Their homeland is less than a hundred miles from the Mississippi River, in the very lap of the French. But the Chickasaws have long been the staunchest of our Indian allies. It is the superiority of our trade over the French trade that binds them to us. Some of our traders have been among the Chickasaws so long they consider themselves to be English Chickasaws. They have married Chickasaw women and fathered a fair number of half-breeds, or breeds, as we usually say."

"Then why don't the Chickasaws stay in their own country if the British traders are going there to them?" asked Priber.

"I have wondered that, too," said William. "That Chickasaw town on the upper Savannah River is right at our back door."

"Savannah Town," nodded Adair. "The river took its name from the town."

"Any closer and they would nestle in among the planters at Goose Creek," said Priber.

"There are certainly more Chickasaws in their homeland in the west than there are in Savannah Town," said Adair. "But to understand why these have come east, you have to remember that the Chickasaws' alliance with the British causes them no end of trouble with the French. That trouble grew so great for these particular fellows that they picked up and left, put the French behind them. Their leader is Fani Miko, the 'Squirrel Chief.' Many of them are breeds."

"I have heard," said William, "that they are especially brave warriors and good fighters. The Cherokees spoke of them that way."

"You don't want to cross them," said Adair. "The French found them to be unconquerable. They tried to take them on by attacking them with two armies at once, one of them coming down the Mississippi from the north and the other up from Louisiana. But the Chickasaws routed both armies. Several French captives taken in the fight were later burned alive. That is another reason the French hate them."

"I suppose Carolina takes pains to keep our own Chickasaws happy," said William.

Priber scoffed.

"Not as they should," said Adair. "The Georgia colonists have been building a fort and town on the western side of the Savannah River, across from Fort Moore. Augusta they are calling it. And bedamned if they are not courting the Savannah Town Chickasaws to move over to their side of the river, to a place they call *New* Savannah Town. I hear that the Chickasaws are so disgruntled at how poorly Carolina is supplying them with arms that some of them are accepting Georgia's offer. So much so, our people are now falling all over themselves trying to entice them back."

"At least the colony of Georgia is not our enemy," said William. "We need not fear bloodshed over the contest."

"No, but there's money to be made and money to be lost. Enemies in commerce if not in arms."

"I have thought of getting back into the Indian trade some day," said William, "though I'll not go again as a packhorseman. There's no gain in that. I am trying to build credit at Crockatt's store, but I don't yet have nearly enough to set myself up as a trader."

"That is the right way to begin," said Adair. "A supply of credit is crucial for an Indian trader. It is a difficult occupation, though. Many try their hand at it, but few do well enough to last."

"I would like to take my turn," said William. "Some day."

The three men settled back in their chairs, and a lull came into their conversation. The room was darkening with the fading twilight. "Excuse me," said William, "while I throw more light onto our conversation." He got up and walked over to a sideboard and took a taper from a drawer. Mounting it in a candle holder, he lit it from a burning candle on the sideboard and brought it back to set in the middle of their table.

As if rallied by the light, Adair leaned forward in his chair and rested his forearms on the table. "Earlier," he said, "Priber and I were discussing the politics of the backcountry. I was saying that the southern part of America is like a marionette theater with three puppet masters—Britain, France, and Spain—all pulling at the strings of the Indian nations. At times these puppet masters work with each other—Catholic France with Catholic Spain, for example—but more commonly they wage covert or open war against each other. Spaniards in Florida are now much reduced because of the raids our Colonel Moore led against them thirty years ago. Nowadays it would not take much of a push to topple Spain from the theater entirely."

"Indian nations, too, are being toppled," said Priber. "Some of the Indians settled around and about in Carolina are no longer nations at all."

"Most of our settlement Indians are from broken nations," said Adair. "They are the ones whose numbers are small and who, for one reason or another, cannot or will not throw in their lot with an established nation. The Natchez, for example, were formerly a famous nation in the French colony, but they rose up in rebellion, killed a large number of Frenchmen, and brought a predictable outcome upon their heads: the French retaliated, crushing and scattering them to the wind. The polities of such settlement Indians among us, if they can be said to be polities at all, are too small to be of consequence. It is when they become too few in number to wage war against us that we no longer consider them to be nations."

"Earlier," William said to Adair, "you mentioned that you began your trading career with the Catawbas. Would you say that the Catawbas are settlement Indians, or do they yet remain a nation?"

"They are in between," said Adair. "They are a coalescence of scattered groups and speak several different languages amongst them. But they hold together well enough to potentially cause us trouble. Because we have to treat with them to keep the peace, they still warrant the name of nation."

"But you left off trading with them," said Priber.

"True. The trade does not flourish among the Catawbas as it used to. They are in too near us, you see. The Indian nations cannot thrive without our British trade goods, but at the same time they cannot thrive if they are too closely exposed to the world we are making. I've heard it said that to stay warm the Indians need to be near the British fire, but if they draw too close to that fire they get burned. The Catawbas have been exposed to English traders the longest of any of the Indian nations in these parts. They traded first with the men who came down from Virginia before there ever was a colony in Carolina. The Catawbas have also suffered from roving bands of northern Indian slavers, cruel fellows such as the Westos, who were formidable in their day, though they have faded now. Most recently it is French-speaking Shawnees who have come down raiding from the north. The number of Catawbas has dwindled so much that most traders who used to work among them have moved on to greener pastures."

"Where did you say you are trading now?" asked William.

"In Kanootare, a Cherokee Out Town on the Tuckasegee River. But like I say, I am moving on from there to trade with the Savannah River Chickasaws."

"And then on to the Creeks?" asked William. "If you go too far west, you will end up rubbing elbows with the French."

"Well do I know it. Some of our western traders who have ventured so far as to fall into Monsieur's lap have ended up dead or in prison in New Orleans or Mobile. I'll stick to the Savannah River for now and bide my time."

"You mean you expect the French to get out of your way?" asked Priber.

"Here is how I see it," said Adair. "Spain is all but out of the contest. That leaves only two real puppet masters in these southern colonies—Britain and France. Both are busy fanning the coals of war, and sooner or later war is bound to come. When the conflagration dies down, only one master will remain."

"Britain, I hope," said William.

"With God's help," nodded Adair.

"I see more than two contenders," said Priber. "You forget about the Indian nations. Not all of them are as weak as the Catawbas."

"These southern Indians had their chance against us in the Yamasee War of 1715," said Adair. "And they made a good fight of it. They killed and burned until they had driven most Carolinians to take refuge inside the fortifications of old Charles Town. But they could not follow through and take the city. Even then, twenty years ago, they lacked the strength for that. Instead, they grew tired of fighting, gave up, and went home. The most serious problem the Indians have, as I see it, is that they are strangers to Christian forgiveness. Because they are so vengeful against each other, they are unable to join all together and form a nation mighty enough to stand up against Britain, or against France for that matter. They would much rather seek revenge for small injuries than put their differences aside to unite into a general strategy for survival."

"Ach," said Priber. "I don't see how you can make this argument. Large nations have grown up by combining small polities in many parts of the world. The Indians are men like other men. I do not see why they could not unite if they had wise leadership. In fact, I do not see why they could not add numbers by incorporating escaped African slaves."

Aghast, Adair pulled back from the table and studied Priber. "Has that rum made you drunk, my friend? Should any Indian nation try to combine with Africans, it would raise such an alarm that the British and French would join forces together to go against them. I would not even talk about such a thing, if I were you. You could be accused of hatching such a plot. They would throw you into the darkest prison."

Priber scoffed and waved his hand dismissively.

"You do not believe me," Adair said soberly, "but I know whereof I speak. Divide and conquer. That is the one principle upon which the British and French colonists agree. Without that strategy, neither could have won an empire here in the New World. Divide the Indians from each other so that they cut each other's throats, sparing ours, and by all means divide the Indians from the Africans. I am telling you, you should keep such wild imaginings to yourself."

"But I came to the New World to speak freely," said Priber. "And I say that the Indian nations have as much right to survive as do the nations of Europe. This is a wide land with room for all. Just as the British nation lives shoulder to shoulder with the French nation in the Old World, so can it live shoulder to shoulder with the Cherokee nation in the New World. Two nations might have their quarrels, but each has the right to survive."

"But this is not the Old World," said Adair. "What manner of men do you think the Indians are?"

"The same as any other. All people everywhere are much the same."

"Wherever did you get that idea? Does that make sense to you? All men the same in everything?"

"I have got to say," said William, "that the Cherokees in Keowee did indeed remind me of Highland Scots."

"In what way?" asked Adair.

"In many ways. For example, whatever a Highlander does in life, however he makes his living, his social standing nonetheless depends upon his ability to fight, to wage war. If you cross a Highlander, he will fight you with anything that is at hand, even if it is only a stick of wood, and unless you have the soul of a warrior, he will most likely get the best of you. It is the same among the Cherokees."

"And let's not forget," said Priber, "that there are a number of philosophers in Europe who argue that all men are basically the same and have the same capabilities."

"Montaigne, for example," said William. "I have recently read Cotton's translation of Montaigne's *Essays*. Montaigne writes of a nation of Indians in Brazil who are like us in many ways. And furthermore, says he, they are not disgraced by the ways in which they are unlike us, but rather, perhaps, can be seen to be more noble. For example, they fight for honor, but they do not wage war for conquest or greed. They have no name for political superiority. They know neither riches nor poverty, no contracts, no debts of honor. The list goes on."

"Ja," said Priber. "I too have read Monsieur Montaigne. It may be that he goes too far in his admiration of the Indians, whom he has never met, but he is correct in arguing that they are not a species inferior to us."

"But it is absurd to argue that all peoples are the same," said Adair. "It is written in the Bible, is it not, that the sons of Ham were cursed with a black skin?"

"I do not agree that a black skin is a curse," said Priber. "And I would point out, for that matter, that the Indians of America are not mentioned in the Bible at all. It would seem that the Holy Ghost forgot about them when writing His account of the beginning of the world."

"I do not agree that the Indians are not mentioned there," said Adair. "As you say, they must have been present from the beginning of creation, and therefore they must be included. The challenge is to read the account properly. I have given this some thought. There are many resemblances between Indian customs and the customs of the ancient Hebrews. I would venture to say that the Indians are in fact descended from one of the lost tribes of Israel."

"Or perhaps they are a lost tribe of Scotland," said Priber, "if we go by the resemblances Mister MacGregor has noted. But tell us, my friend, how you see them resembling the Hebrews."

"We know from the Bible that the Hebrews offered up animal sacrifices. They would burn a lamb to ashes so that the smoke would ascend up to heaven. In the same way, when the Indians kill a deer, they will throw a piece of the fattest meat into the fire, sending up a plume of smoke as a gift to the gods."

"Ja," said Priber, "that is a resemblance, no doubt, and I am sure there are others. But I see one great flaw in your Hebrew-to-Indian argument."

"And what is that?"

"I have never seen nor heard of an Indian being circumcised. How do you explain the absence of a custom that was consistently practiced by the Hebrews in ancient times and is still practiced by them today?"

"Yes, I have puzzled over that. I think the answer must be that the Indians lost the ability to make steel during their long journey from the Holy Land to the New World. Here they had to make their tools from stone, and using stone knives for such a delicate cut would have been too difficult and painful. They had no choice but to give up the custom."

"Or it could be," said Priber, "that you are picking out evidence that supports your theory and explaining away that which contradicts it."

"Had we the time," said Adair, "I could give you many more examples of resemblances between the customs and beliefs of the ancient Hebrews and the Indians. You would soon be convinced of my argument."

"But there is another stumbling block that I fear would prohibit the meeting of our minds on this," said Priber.

"And what would that be?"

"Your evidence for the Hebrew side of the comparison."

"My evidence is the Bible," said Adair.

"That is just what I mean."

"Surely you do not doubt the testimony of the Bible? If we cannot trust the word of God, whose word can we trust?"

"I do not dispute that the Bible is an edifying book," said Priber. "But I find myself in agreement with those philosophers who insist that while the Bible is divinely inspired, the actual laying down of words upon paper was done by men, and men are prone to lapses of memory, transcription error, self-interest, and bias. Therefore, yes, I am saying that not every word in the Bible can be trusted. It is the duty of scholars to seek out the errors it contains so that proper allowance can be made for them."

Adair laughed. "No offence, old man, but I am beginning to see why you felt heat from the authorities in Saxony."

Priber did not find this amusing, and William took it as a cue to empty the remainder of the bottle of rum into their three cups.

"Allow me to propose a toast," said William. The others raised their cups. "To as delightful a round of conversation as I have ever been privileged to hear."

"Ever?" chuckled Adair as they clicked their cups together.

"Dare to inquire," said William, "and then dare to tolerate what comes from the mouths of men in answer to that inquiry."

"Hear, hear," said Priber, his good cheer returning.

They laughed and downed their cups to the last drop. Then, after a few more pleasantries, they called it a night and rose from the table. The two guests made their way to their beds, while William, his sense of adventure astir, went to work closing up the place.

Duncan's health was improving every day. And the backcountry was still calling to William, especially since that conversation at table with James Adair and Christian Priber. He was more convinced than ever that the road he wanted to take was to earn enough at the cowpen to stake himself as a trader to the Indians, if only in a small way. But William kept his thoughts to himself until late October, when Duncan had finally resumed almost all the tavern work. He waited until his uncle had had an especially good day, and then he broached the subject with him as they were closing the dining room.

"I've been thinking of going up to the backcountry to give John MacDonald a hand," said William. "Could you get along without me for a time?"

"To John MacDonald's, eh? Well, there's a development I didn't expect. But, aye, I am feeling strong these days. Nearly my old self again. Go on along if you wish. I'm sure John could use your help. And that daughter of his might be glad to see you, too."

William let the reference to Rosemary pass without comment. "Blood is blood, Uncle, and I wouldn't want to leave you short-handed."

"Sampson can help me carry heavy goods back from town. So long as everybody here remains healthy, we will do just fine."

"Well then, I would like to get on with it, if you don't mind. I could ready myself tomorrow and leave out the next day."

"That's mighty quick leave-taking. But if it must be so, very well. We will miss you around here. I know Mary will be sad when she hears the news."

"I'll be back often to visit," said William. "She need not think I'm deserting her."

"So the young ones always say," said Duncan. But he gave William a pat on the back. "You have my blessing," he said.

"Thank you, sir."

The next morning William saddled Viola and rode downtown to Crockatt's store, where he purchased a length of oiled linen cloth big enough to serve both as a rain slicker and as a ground cloth for himself and his blanket when he had to sleep out in wet weather. He bought two pairs of heavy, coarse stockings, and a supply of powder, bullets, and flints to last him a season. On his way back to the tavern he stopped in at the store where Duncan and Mary purchased their stored foodstuffs. He bought a parcel of coffee and a sugarloaf for MacDonald's cook and some dried peaches and figs for himself. Finally he went to the confectioner's shop on the Middle Bridge off Bay Street and bought a small parcel of sweet almond macaroons.

When he got back to the tavern, he removed Viola's bridle and saddle and carefully polished them. Up in his room he took out his musket, which had lain unused for a long time, and he cleaned and oiled it. Then he took down his canvas bag and attached two ties to it so that he could securely anchor it behind his saddle. He had decided to pack for a long stay in the hope that MacDonald would keep him on for more than a short time. Into his saddle-bags and canvas bag went his winter clothing along with the rest of his gear, including the split-cane basket with his journal, a full bottle of ink, and several quill pens. Conspicuously missing were any of his Shakespeare volumes. Superstitious or not, he did not want a repeat of the unnerving coincidences between Shakespearean tragedy and real-life tragedy. A niggling suggestion of a King Lear connection—an old man with three daughters—was already nudging at him, and he did not want it to go any further. He could do without Shakespeare on this trip. Finally, he packed the parcel of macaroons, now tied up in a bright ribbon he had begged from Aunt Mary.

William was never able to sleep well the night before a journey. He went to bed early, but his thoughts were so concentrated on what he might find at MacDonald's cowpen, it took a long time for him to fall asleep. He did sleep finally, but he awoke at the first cock's crow, the sky still dark, the morning light little more than a promise.

William arose and dressed, pulling on his hunting shirt for the first time in over a year. Around it he cinched a wide leather belt onto which he hung his dirk and through which, in the back, he stuck his hatchet. He donned his hunting pouch and powder horn and then picked up his musket, whip, and baggage and carried it all down to the stable. As he passed by the kitchen, he saw a light in the window and smoke trailing up from the chimney. He pushed open the door and stuck in his head.

"Thank you, Delilah, for helping me get an early start. After I've saddled up, I'd like to eat breakfast in the kitchen, if you don't mind. Everyone in the tavern is still sleeping. I don't want to wake them by going in there to eat."

"Yes, sir, Mister William. I don't mind. I'll have your breakfast in just a little while."

Viola nickered and tossed her head when she saw by his dress and by what he was tying onto her saddle that this was to be no ordinary day. He led her outside and over to the watering trough. After she had drunk her fill, he

39

fed her a liberal portion of shelled corn, stroking her neck and admiring her beautiful chestnut coat and flaxen mane and tail. Finally he tethered her to a rail, all ready to go. Then he went back to the kitchen.

Delilah had served up a plate of hot ham, eggs, and grits, and a cup of strong coffee lightened with cream and sweetened with sugar. William savored each bite, not knowing when he would eat so well again. As he was mixing the last of his grits with the last smear of egg yolk on his plate, Delilah came over and handed him a parcel wrapped in old newspaper with several greasy spots showing through.

"I fixed you some fried ham and bread to eat along the way," she said. "Now you take care of yourself. Tending cows can be rough, and them Indians can be mean."

"I hope to stay away from the Indians," he said, lifting the package of food to his nose and sniffing it gratefully. He smiled at her. "Thank you for looking out for me." He reached into his pocket and pulled out a coin and gave it to her. "Put this away for a rainy day."

"Thank you, Mister William. You be careful out there."

As he left the kitchen and strode over to where Viola was tethered, the sky had lightened enough for him to see that it promised to be a crisp, clear autumn day. He mounted Viola, rested his musket across the front of his saddle, and rode down the driveway past the porch to the street, where he turned left to ride north up the Charles Town neck. Viola pranced and snorted in the fresh morning air, her spirits high.

William expected to make good time on this trip, figuring he could travel each day about half again as far as he and his packhorseman mates had traveled two years earlier on their way up to Keowee. He would not have to spend time and effort each morning rounding up and packing ten horses before getting on the road, and there was little he had to attend to at the end of the day. Not to mention that a single horse could travel at a faster pace than a packtrain. He had checked back in the journal he had kept on that earlier trip and figured he had about a hundred miles to cover from Charles Town to MacDonald's cowpen. If he could make as much as thirty-three miles each day, he could cover the distance in three days. Unlike that first venture out, the Carolina landscape was familiar to him now. He had a fair idea of where he wanted to camp each night.

The sky was clear blue and the air blessedly cool as Viola trotted away from the town. The sandy wagon road took them slightly northwest to the Goose Creek bridge, at which point it swung more directly north. The day heated up as the sun rose in the sky, and before noon William took off his hunting shirt, rolled it up and tied it to his bedroll. His linen shirt was plenty warm enough. As they crossed the many little streams running into Cooper River, he stopped at each one to let Viola drink her fill. By the end of the day he had gotten some miles past James Kinloch's plantation, where he and his mates had spent their first night on that earlier trip. Confident he had made his mileage for the day, he came to a little stream where Viola could find water and good grazing, and he turned off the road and camped for the night. He hobbled Viola, and for good measure he hung a small bell around her neck, the sound of which would lead him to her if she somehow managed to stray during the night.

Early the next morning he breakfasted on a generous portion of Delilah's bread and ham. Then he set out again, continuing north at a steady pace along the road through the monotonous forest of longleaf pines. At the end of the day he camped at Eutaw Springs, where he and his mates had camped two years ago. He had traveled in two days as far as they had in three.

Next morning, his third day on the road, William awoke cold and shivering, the wind moaning through the pines. Cold air was blowing down from the north, and he was glad to find some coals still lingering in the ashes of the fire from the night before. After warming himself, he saddled Viola, and in the brisk morning air he struck out toward the northwest, spending a long day crossing the many small creeks that emptied into the Santee River. The foliage of the forest, increasingly populated by broad-leafed trees, was beginning to show the colors of early autumn. The pine trees, some of which were immensely tall, had golden brown trunks stretching a great distance upward to their lowest limbs, where the rounded clusters of long needles were an invariant dark green. In contrast, the lower-growing persimmon trees were showing a full display of their mottled, dark red leaves scattered through with orange fruit, much of which had already fallen to the ground. The dogwood leaves were turning a dark, dusty, reddish purple. Here and there were tall poplars with their bright yellow leaves showering down, and strung about like bunting were the yellow leaves of the wild muscadine grapes, some of which grew very high up in the trees. The leaves on the great-spreading oak trees were still green, but they showed the wear and tear of the past year and were starting to lighten in color. An unchanging hue on this autumn palate was the grey of the Spanish moss that hung everywhere about.

As the sun declined in the west, William entered a stand of towering poplar trees, their great trunks rising tall and straight from a carpet of yellow leaves. Exhausted from the long, cold day of travel, William pulled off the trail and allowed Viola to drink from a little stream of clear water running through the golden forest floor. He then drank his own fill from the stream and washed his hands and face. Then he sat down and leaned back against a tree while Viola grazed. He had not quite met his goal of making the trip in three days, but MacDonald's cowpen was only a few hours' ride ahead. He would be there before noon tomorrow.

When a light rain began falling, William threw up a crude lean-to shelter that would shed most of the rain. He attended to Viola, and then he wrapped himself in his blanket and lay down in the fading light, pulling up the oil cloth over the blanket. Later, as he listened to the raindrops pattering more and more loudly through the trees, he realized that this would be more than a shower. He pulled the oil cloth up over his head and lay awake for a long time, during which he began to have second thoughts about this venture of his. Now that he was well into it, the possibility of all that might go wrong became palpable. What if he was mistaken in thinking that he would still be welcome as a cow-hunter at MacDonald's cowpen? It had, after all, been more than a year since John MacDonald had invited him. This was something he had not fully considered until now, but there was nothing he could do about it at this point. He would at least pay a visit to the place and then worry about the rest if it came to pass.

5

The Cowpen

William overslept the next morning. It was still drizzling rain, but he was dry inside the cocoon of his bedroll, and he remained burrowed there long enough to get his rest. Finally, summoning his will, he got up, rolled and packed his blanket, and stuck his head through the slit in the middle of his oiled cloth, draping it around his body. Then he saddled Viola and got on his way. As he rode along, the terrain was now showing a little elevation, as witnessed in the faster flow of the small streams that ran from high ground down into the Santee River.

After making such a late start, it was mid-afternoon before he first caught a glimpse of the familiar clearing of several acres in the woods ahead. In the center of the clearing, atop a small rise, lay the cluster of buildings that were the heart of MacDonald's cowpen. William's doubts were forgotten as he remembered how this place had been an island of tranquility in the tempestuous sea he had navigated that first year in Carolina. It had seemed to him like a little piece of Scotland. His hopes rose as he spurred Viola ahead, surveying the setting where the next chapter of his life might unfold.

But as he entered the clearing, following the trail beside a small rivulet of clear water that ran through the yellow, sandy soil, the place did not seem exactly the same as it did before. The modest post-in-ground house where John and his family lived was somehow less cheery than he remembered, more unkempt and forlorn. Perhaps it was the heavy sky and the cold mist. Or perhaps John's tale of woe had changed William's perception of things. It was not that anything obvious had changed. Out behind the house there was still the detached kitchen, the spring house, and the outhouse. Beyond the house on the far side was the barn, dairy, fenced pen, chicken house, and pigsty. Plumes of smoke were rising from the chimneys of both the house and the kitchen. The ground of the clearing near the house and barn, however, was cluttered with sticks and leaf litter. William did not remember it this way. He was sure this space had always been kept clean. If a wildfire were to come blowing in from the woods, it would be too late to clear the ground, and the whole place could go up in flames. Clearly MacDonald needed more help here. The basic work was not getting done.

As William rode up toward the house, a scarred, rag-eared bulldog came running out from behind it, bristling and barking, followed by a small white dog with a cropped tail. Not to be outdone, the little dog barked furiously as he pranced stiff-legged near Viola, dodging her hooves. When William dismounted, the little dog backed off to take his measure, still barking, but sniffing the air. "Don't you remember me, Butcher Bob?" asked William, holding out his hand toward him. The dog sniffed it and tentatively began to wag his little stump of a tail. Then he wagged harder and started jumping up in the air, surprisingly high, springing with his front legs off of William to jump again. William reached down and petted him. "Hello, hello, Butcher Bob. Where is your mistress?" The little dog yapped at him in friendly reply, seeming to remember his days as a puppy in William's care, when William had brought him down from Keowee to give to Rosemary on the packtrain's return trip to Charles Town. If only his heart had not been so heavy then with loss, he might have remained here with Butcher Bob and made a place for himself. How different might his story now be?

John MacDonald came out from the house to investigate the cause of the dogs' barking, and the same commotion brought three women out from the kitchen behind the house. William recognized John's eldest daughter, Betsy, and middle daughter, Liza, and trailing behind them, the black cook, whose name William did not remember. Betsy was a tall brunette, all muscle and bone and lean as a wolf. Liza was not so tall and carried a bit more flesh. Her hair was lighter, almost blonde. Both women wore their hair clubbed in long braids, and both were wearing flour-smeared aprons, as was the cook, a small, wiry woman. Two little shirt-tail white boys riding stick horses trotted over to stand apprehensively beside Betsy.

As for John, his hair was tousled and his clothes rumpled and dirty. It now occurred to William that the heavy drinking John had done at the tavern that night was more a regular practice than a one-time occurrence.

MacDonald looked William up and down with surprise. "Billy Mac-Gregor," he said, holding out his hand. "To what do we owe this pleasure?"

"Seeing as how I'm out of work just now," said William, "I thought I'd come up this way to see what I might find."

"Are ye going up to Keowee to work for Sam Long again? I thought ye had a belly-full of packing horses."

"Actually, I was thinking about working here. You once said you would take me on if I ever wanted. I thought I'd come see if that offer is still good."

John fell silent, again looking William over from top to bottom, more slowly this time. Then he shook his head. "I wish I could help you, Billy. It's not that I couldn't use an experienced cow-hunter, but I've got no way to pay you. There's already too many hands held out to me, too many mouths to feed and backs to clothe. I don't see how I could work it."

William was stunned. He had not expected to be turned down cold. Taken on for only a short time, perhaps, but not flat turned away. "Well, then," he said, searching for words. "I had no idea. I knew things were tight, but I thought you could still use a hand. Suppose I stay around here for a day or two and help out a bit. Just for my food and a place to lay my head."

"If that's what you want to do," said John. "But things are a little out of joint at the house these days, so lay down your bedroll in the barn, if you don't mind. You can use that pile of cornshucks up in the loft."

"Good enough," said William. He had slept in that loft before.

"You'll join us for supper, then," Betsy said flatly, as if she would rather be spared the trouble.

"Thank you," said William, "but I have food in my saddlebags that needs to be finished off. A long rest in the loft would serve me well tonight. I am more than tired from my journey."

"How long do you plan to stay?" asked Liza.

William shrugged. "One day. Two. I can't say yet. I hate to turn straight around and go home."

"Och," said John. "It's doing none of us any good standing out in this cold drizzle. Let's try again tomorrow. Billy, you'll find a little corn for your horse in the crib."

"Can I ask where Rosemary might be?" asked William. The way things were going, it would be just his luck if she were off on a visit somewhere and not due home for a week.

"She is out at the pen, attending to the livestock," said John. "She can help you get that corn."

"Then I'll say good day," said William, "and go put up my horse."

They parted without further ado, John returning to the house and the women heading back to the kitchen. As William led Viola to the barn, he tried to take stock of what had just happened. That welcome was as sodden as the weather itself. He had obviously misinterpreted John's plea for loyal help. And now he could see why. It would take more than an extra hand to pull this place back together. Was it a kingdom falling in on itself? He wished he had not come.

At the barn William unsaddled Viola, opened the gate, and let her into the pen. Butcher Bob stayed close to his heels. Closing the gate, he took his gear inside the barn, and there he saw two slave girls tending to the livestock. He remembered them from his last visit and waved to them. "I am William MacGregor," he said. "I'll be spending the night in the loft. I've seen you girls before, but I don't remember your names."

The eldest of the two, perhaps fifteen years old, stopped what she was doing and smiled at him. "I remember you," she said. "My name is Venus."

"I be Daphne," said the other one, who looked to be a couple of years younger. Both girls were lighter-skinned than full-blooded Africans would be.

"Are you sisters?" asked William.

They both nodded. "Same mama and same daddy," said Venus.

"Who's your mama?" asked William, wondering if John might be their father.

"Aunt Sally," said Venus. "The cook."

"But we don't call her Aunt Sally," laughed Daphne. "She's just our mama."

"And you say you have the same father?" asked William. He knew he was prying, but at this point he wanted to know all he could about this place.

"Our daddy was a white man," said Venus. "An Indian trader. He used to come through here right often and he would stay with our mama. I remember

45

him, but Daphne don't. He died while she was still a baby. I remember him just a little."

"How'd he die?" asked William, curious now to hear the life-history of a trader.

"They say he was messin around with the wife of a Cherokee man. The man caught him at it and put a hatchet in his head. That's what Mama says."

"Och, I am sorry to hear that."

"There ain't no reason to be sorry," said Venus. "Our mama takes care of us." Venus was the prettier of the two, and you could tell that she knew it. "You must be looking for Miss Rosemary," she said.

"As a matter of fact, I am. Is she around here somewhere?"

"I saw her heading out to the corn crib," said Venus.

"Good," said William. "I need to get some corn for my horse. We have been on the trail four days, and both of us are tired out."

"We'll take care of your horse," said Venus. "We'll feed her good."

"I would appreciate that," said William.

"You gonna be cold sleeping in that loft," said Daphne.

"I've slept in worse places."

William hung up his saddle in the barn and then climbed up into the loft, making several trips to carry up his canvas bag, saddlebags, and bedroll. Butcher Bob waited patiently below while William spread the bedroll out on the thick pile of cornshucks. He was tempted to just fall into it, but instead he took the beribboned parcel of macaroons from his saddlebag, put it into the bosom of his hunting shirt, and climbed back down the ladder.

Butcher Bob trotted out in front as William walked over toward the corn crib. He had almost reached it when Rosemary came out with a bucket in her hand. The dog trotted over and sat down beside her.

"As I live and breathe," she said when she saw him. "If it's not the long lost William MacGregor."

It was a friendly enough greeting, but William again felt disappointed at a less than joyful response to his presence. But what had he expected? That she would fly into his arms? That was obviously not to be. She put down her bucket of shelled corn and rested her hands on her hips, looking at him quizzically.

"I've brought something for you," William said, reaching into his coat.

"The last time you reached into your shirt, you brought out Butch."

"Yes, I did, and he seems to have worked out well enough around here."

"He's a good little dog," she said, reaching down to pat him on the head. "He makes himself useful, keeps the rats and mice cleaned out. Last fall he

46

killed a five-foot blacksnake that had been stealing eggs from our chicken house. He just snapped it up and shook it to death. It was quite a sight. I felt sorry for that snake, though. If he had just kept to the corn crib, he would be alive today."

William nodded. "It's good to keep a blacksnake where grain is stored. To catch the mice."

"But this one wanted eggs as well," said Rosemary. "So Father let Butch get him. Butch was so proud of what he had done, he dragged that awful thing around with him for the longest time."

"I see you've shortened his name," said William. "I told you Butcher Bob was too long a name for a dog."

"I hate to say you were right about that, but you were."

"One or two syllables is about all you can hang on a dog." William pulled the parcel out of his shirt and handed it to her.

"What is this?" she asked.

"Not another dog," he chuckled.

She laughed a little as she undid the ribbon and opened it. Peering into the package, she savored the aroma. "They smell heavenly. What are they?"

"Almond macaroons. Try one."

She took one out of the parcel and bit off a piece. "Oh, this is the best thing this country girl ever tasted," she said, closing her eyes a little. "It tastes like something from the great wide world—from Charles Town or London."

She held them out to William, who took one and bit into it, reveling in the sweet almond flavor.

"They are as good as promised," he said. "Nothing else tastes like that."

"So, what brings you here?" asked Rosemary, and with that it seemed to William that the warmth was slipping out of her voice again.

"Well, I ran out of work in Charles Town, and I thought I might do better here. It seems I was wrong about that. But anyway, here I am."

"Then you won't be staying long," she said.

"A day or two, the way things stand now."

"No doubt Father has put you in the barn," she said apologetically. "He doesn't much take to visitors these days." She reached down and picked up the bucket of corn. "But we will see you at supper. I've got to go help Venus and Daphne feed the livestock. Thank you for the macaroons. They are delicious."

"I'll be dining in the barn tonight," said William. "I still have a few trail provisions left."

"In the barn? Why not with us?"

"Betsy did invite me, but the prospect of setting another place seemed to weary her."

"Och!" Rosemary said in exasperation. "Betsy! She doesn't know the meaning of the word gracious. Of course you are welcome. Come on up when you hear the bell."

"Thank you," said William, "but I'd just as soon lie low until tomorrow. I need time to take stock of my situation."

"If that's what you want, then," said Rosemary. "You'll be missing Aunt Sally's fried chicken." She went off with a little shake of her head, Butch trotting out before her.

William went up into the barn loft, and in the dimming light he wrapped himself in his blanket and sat down cross-legged in the cornshucks. This day had turned out so miserable, it put him in mind of his last days at Keowee. Like most of the other traders and packhorsemen in Indian country, he had paired off with an Indian woman while he was there. Unlike most others in that situation, he had truly loved his Otter Queen, and she had loved him. They had even married in the Cherokee way. But little did he know what he was getting into. The problem was not the marriage. It was another Indian matter he could scarcely comprehend. Before he had ever come on the scene, Otter Queen had gotten crosswise with an old woman of another clan who was determined to convince the whole town that Otter Queen was a witch. It was difficult for William to take in the seriousness of this charge, but he finally came to understand that in the Cherokee world his wife stood accused of having mysteriously caused all manner of misfortunes that had befallen various people of the old woman's clan. Because the Cherokees believe that witches work their evil in sly, unobservable ways, it was difficult to prove the charge, but equally difficult to defend against it.

So the accusation festered. In William's world he could have lived with the situation, but in Otter Queen's world she could not. She grew more and more miserable and fearful as the months wore on, until finally, to his horror and dismay, she took her own life to escape the charge. And escape it she did. After she was dead, the people of Keowee, in their own way of thinking about such things, came to the conclusion that the real witch in this sad affair was the selfsame woman who had accused Otter Queen, whereas Otter Queen, in her willingness to die, had proved her innocence, for the Cherokees believe that a witch will do anything to avoid death. But no matter that a kind of justice had been done, that the people of the town finally shunned the old woman, driving her off to a lonely death beyond the pale. It was a justice that came too late for Otter Queen. And too late for William's shattered heart. The Indian world had shaken him to his core. It was for this reason that he had quit his work as a packhorseman and spent the last year in town trying to recover from his melancholy, which, until today, he thought he had done. When John MacDonald showed up at the tavern that day, William had realized that the hope of bringing Rosemary into his life was now stronger than the pain in his heart for Otter Queen. In truth—and he had to admit it—it was the prospect of reuniting with Rosemary that was his primary motive for coming here, fool that he was. Obviously he had mistaken her earlier flirtations with him for real affection. His heart was too easily beguiled. No one had ever taught him how to navigate the waters of love.

William sighed and lay back in his rough bed. He was ever a fool when it came to women, and there was no help for it. He loved their pretty faces when they smiled, their clever word-play when they conversed, their sweet voices when they sang, their slender waists, their softly curved breasts, their shapely legs. Like many another packhorsemen who had stopped over at MacDonald's cowpen, he had admired Rosemary—her reddish blonde hair and lively blue-green eyes, the way she listened to the men's conversations at table, the quick and thorough way she carried out the work that fell to her. But from what the two of them had said to each other that year, he had thought he was more to her than just another traveler passing through. He realized now that he had always been holding onto the prospect of her, as if she were already his, as if any time he was ready, he could come back and get her. What was he thinking? That she would wait the four or five years it would yet take for him to establish himself well enough to take a wife? He scoffed at himself and hit the palm of his hand against his forehead. He could forget about that. She had not even waited this long. Today she made clear that he was no longer in her plans. So he had come here for nothing. His future lay elsewhere. But where? Where would he ever find a woman with whom to share his life?

Well, he thought, sitting up and trying to shake himself out of his melancholy, there was nothing he could do about his love life on this cold night in the loft of John MacDonald's barn. He fished around in his saddlebags and pulled out the last little bit of the ham and bread Delilah had packed for him four days ago. It was not fried chicken, but it would do.

Daylight was fading as he finished his meager meal. He glanced over at his saddlebags. He did not feel like writing in his journal, but this of all days should be recorded. If he could bear to record the dark days of Otter Queen, he could record this day. Bad as it was, he had seen worse. So he got out his journal and his pen and ink and climbed down to sit outside the barn where there was still enough light to write by.

Tuesday, November 1, MacDonald's Cowpen
This has been a day I would just as soon forget ever happened. John Mac-Donald was not especially happy to see me, and his two married daughters were even less so. But worst of all, Rosemary herself was cool toward me. I can't say she was unfriendly, but she gave me no reason to think that she has any special regard for me. On the contrary, she seemed to be encouraging me to move on. Her father certainly wants me to go. He says he has no work for me. The cowpen itself seems to be going to seed. Nothing is as it was when I was here before. And I wish I had never read King Lear. Even though I left the printed words back in Charles Town, I can't push that play out of my thoughts, and I hate the parallels I already see at this cowpen. I am sure it is the coincidence of three daughters that brings the story to mind and colors my view of this scene. Shakespeare himself would think me mad. There are many men in this world who have three daughters. I need to forget all this and come back to the rational world. In more ways than one, if ever they stage King Lear in the new theater in Charles Town, I will be the perfect one to play the Fool.

6

Topsy-Turvy

During the night William half burrowed into the pile of cornshucks and wrapped his blanket well around himself, including around his head. Come morning, he did not hear the roosters crowing nor the cows lowing. Finally he heard muffled voices out in the pen, and when he pulled the blanket from his eyes, he saw that the sun was shining brightly. From the slant of its light he could see that the morning was well along towards noon. He shook his head in dismay. Cow-hunter for hire: sleeps till noon. But then, he had not exactly been hired, had he? So far he only owed work for the feed his horse had eaten.

He arose, tidied himself up, and went to his saddlebags. He still had a few dried figs that would have to do for breakfast. He also took out the two small parcels he had brought for the cook and tucked them into his coat. Then he climbed down from the loft to the barn floor. As he walked outside, the air was pungent with the smell of livestock, wood smoke, and, surprisingly, the scent of roasting meat. The meat smelled so good he could almost taste it, and he followed his nose over to the yard behind the kitchen, where he found MacDonald's cook supervising a young black boy as he tended an open barbeque pit, over which a good sized pig was roasting on a spit. Using a miniature mop, the boy was swabbing the pig with a sauce made of vinegar and red pepper. William saw a pot of cassina tea steaming beside the fire, and on the coals there was a long-handled skillet full of sizzling pieces of fresh liver, no doubt taken from the pig on the spit.

"Good morning," he said to the cook, hesitating to call her by name in case he did not remember it correctly. "I would not mind having a piece of that liver and a cup of tea."

"I thought you might like some," said the woman as she poured tea into a cup. Then she served him up a slice of liver on a piece of bread.

"It's Aunt Sally, isn't it?" he asked.

"I ain't nobody's aunt around here, but I do answer to that name."

"I call her Mama," said the boy.

"That's cause I *am* your mama," said Aunt Sally, making a playful swipe at him. "But I ain't Mister William's mama, so he can call me Aunt Sally."

"And this is?" asked William, nodding toward the boy, who was shyly dipping his mop into the sauce.

"Tell him your name," said Aunt Sally.

"I be Mars," said the boy, looking up with a grin.

"You can call me Billy," said William.

"I thought you was Mister William," said Mars.

"That's what your mama seems to think. I don't know who told her my name."

"I knows you from before," said Aunt Sally, "when you come here with that bunch of packhorsemen. You the one that brought the little dog. I remember you, yes I do. I remember that you and Miss Rosemary was gettin sweet on each other. I expected to see you back here before now."

"It took me a while to get here," said William. He pulled the two parcels out of his hunting coat and handed them to her. "I brought along a parcel of coffee and a sugar loaf for the kitchen."

"Thank you, sir! We can make good use of this. Master John is sure enough partial to coffee in the morning, and everybody likes the taste of sugar. But he didn't bring back near enough of neither one from his last trip to Charles

Town, and we've been parceling it out like gold. This ought to put you on everbody's good side."

"If it does, that wouldn't hurt a thing."

Up at the kitchen Betsy stuck her head out of the door and yelled, "Aunt Sally!"

"I got to go," Aunt Sally said, and she turned and walked away.

William sipped on his tea and enjoyed the morning, forgetting his troubles for a time. After a few moments he looked over at the boy and the roasting pig.

"Mars," said William, "that's a powerful big hog you are cooking there. Who is going to eat all that meat?"

"We're havin us a frolic tonight," said Mars. "There'll be more people here than you can stir with a stick."

"A frolic?" William said with surprise, thinking of the lean times the cowpen was suffering through. "Is it a holiday of some kind?"

"It ain't no holiday. It's a frolic. They's gonna be lots of good barbeque."

"Maybe they'll even let me have some," said William.

"Everybody gets some."

"Good enough," said William.

He left Mars and walked over to the dairy, a small structure made of cedar that was set back into an earthen bank, with dirt piled up over its sides and roof. With this insulation it was cool in summer and protected from freezing in winter, and its heavy door could be locked to discourage pilfering. As he had hoped, he found Rosemary inside at work in the dim light. She was pouring some cream into a large stoneware jar, where she would store it until it was ready to be churned into butter. He decided to assume that all was well between them. "Mars told me there is to be a frolic tonight, but he didn't seem to know what the occasion is."

"It's a cornshucking first and foremost," said Rosemary, "but it does end with a frolic."

"Well now, I know what corn is, and if it is Indian corn we're talking about, I know what a cornshuck is. But I've never heard of a cornshucking."

"You might say it's the main event of our social season out here. But it's not like anything you have seen among the gentlefolk of Charles Town. We have a big pile of cured Indian corn harvested from our fields that's waiting to be shucked. It is tedious work, so we liven it up. The shucking proper won't start until near dark, when the rest of the day's work is done. Then everybody from the cowpen will gather here, and we will mix in some music and sport and shuck every last ear that's in that pile. And when it's all done and the corn is in the crib, we will have ourselves a banquet. It will take near most of the night."

As Rosemary bent over to put a cover on the jar, William admired the sight of her. She was muscled from her life of hard work, but she did everything with feminine grace. The beautiful lines of her body said *woman* in the strongest way, and the curve of her rump, he thought, was enough to tempt the most blinkered Puritan to relax on at least one of the Ten Commandments. William felt the same tingling glow he had felt when he first saw her, though with less hope for where it might lead. "It gladdens my heart to see you, Rosemary," he said.

"I am glad to see you too, Billy," she replied.

But not in quite the same way, he thought, or else he would feel welcome to linger for more conversation. As it was, it seemed best to move on.

William was not sure what to do with himself. He had said he would work for a few days, but everyone was busy with preparations for the evening, and he knew he would only make a pest of himself by interrupting them to ask what he might do. Finally he decided to look for John MacDonald and make one more attempt to offer his services. He went up to the house, but found no one there. He looked in the barn, and then went out to the pens. Finally he caught sight of John near the corncrib and went over to find him surveying the unshucked corn. It was piled directly in front of the crib, heaped up in a great U-shaped mound, shoulder-high in some places. Ranged around the outside of the pile of corn were several foot-high mounds of earth, each with a small stack of resinous lighter wood on top.

"That's the biggest big pile of corn I've ever seen," William said. "Does it take that much to keep the cowpen going through the winter?"

"We'll eat this down to the smallest nubbins," said John. "It's Indian corn that fuels us out here in the backcountry. It keeps body and soul together, humans and animals alike."

"It seems to me it would take several days to shuck all that."

"We'll get it done before the night is over. That's what the lighter wood is for, so we can have light to keep on working after the sun goes down."

"I'd like to help you out in any way I can," said William.

"We have plenty of hands for this," said John. "How long are you planning to stay?"

"Not long, I guess. I'll leave tomorrow if I'm in your way. I was hoping I could be of more use than that. But if there's no means for you to pay another hand, then that's the way things are, pure and simple. Not that I would need much."

"I've been thinking," said John. "We might could give you some work as a cow-hunter, if you'd be willing to take a cow or two for pay. But first I need to talk to Rufus. It would be up to him whether you would fit in with his crew."

"I would be open to such terms," William said cautiously. "When might you speak with him?"

"He'll be here for the shucking. I'll try to talk it over with him before the night is out. At the latest, we will clear it up tomorrow morning. Then if things don't work out, you can be on your way. But right now, I have things to do." John turned brusquely and headed back to his house.

Not knowing whether to feel hopeful at this development or exasperated at being strung along, William took a long walk in the woods. How long would he have to work for the pay of only one or two cows? Whatever they offered, it was not likely to be worth it. His impulse was to saddle up Viola and head back to Charles Town to save himself from further humiliation. But it would be better to spend the night and get an early start tomorrow.

His desire to be helpful rebuffed, he made himself scarce for the rest of the afternoon.

When William returned to the cowpen late in the day, he saw that people were beginning to collect around the corn crib. John and Rosemary were standing on one side of the pile of corn, and Betsy and Liza were standing on the other side. Everyone seemed to be waiting. William walked over to speak with Betsy and Liza, just in case it mattered whether or not they thought well of him. Uncertain of where he stood with these two, he felt awkward at try-ing to start a conversation. "From the smoke that's been pouring out of the kitchen chimney," he said, "I take it that the cooking for this cornshucking has fallen to you."

Liza nodded. "All this food should make everybody. . . ."

Betsy cut her off. "I don't want to hear another word about food. I'm so worn out from cooking these last three days, it makes me want to puke just thinking about it."

"At least you had the young fellow at the barbeque pit to cook the pig for you," said William.

Liza started to say something, but then she looked over at Betsy and thought better of it.

"Mars?" asked Betsy, rolling her eyes. "You have to tell that ignorant boy every single thing that needs to be done, and even then he won't do it for daydreaming. Mars is more trouble than he's worth. He's Aunt Sally's youngest and she's spoiled him."

"So Aunt Sally has three children," said William. "Venus, Daphne, and Mars."

"Those are the young ones," said Liza. "She had those two girls with a red-headed Irish trader who used to stay overnight with us. But there's also Jock and Ray. They're her older boys. She had them with Alonso. Which makes them half Indian."

"And who is Mars's father?" asked William.

"We aren't sure," said Betsy. "We think it was one of the woodcutters."

"Is Alonso another of your slaves?" asked William.

"He's one of the cow-hunters," said Betsy. She turned away from William as she spoke, making it clear that she was tired of the conversation. Liza seemed to take the cue to disengage as well, so William tipped his hat and moved on.

Circling the pile of corn, he went over to where John and Rosemary were watching the preparations. "Enjoying the spectacle?" asked William.

"I wouldn't miss it for anything," said John.

"It's a break from the routine," said Rosemary, "and God knows we have enough of that."

The festive air had infused Betsy's two little boys with excitement, and they were running and chasing about in anticipation of a night of fun in which they could stay up past their usual bedtime. Coming upon a pile of dry corncobs, they started a corncob fight, which no one bothered to break up. The cobs had just enough heft for throwing them a short distance, but not enough to cause real pain. The boys were running, throwing, and hiding behind any shelter they could find. But then the elder boy found some cobs that had soaked in a puddle of water, making them heavy enough to hurt, and in no time the younger boy was crying. Betsy grabbed the offending boy by an arm and gave him a talking-to, and soon this small rift in the cowpen was mended.

"I take it this is not all of your crew," William said to John, looking around at those who were gathered. "If it were, you would have far too much food to eat and too few hands to shuck the corn."

"The rest of them should be here any time now. The shucking won't begin until they've all arrived."

As the light began to fade, Venus and Daphne brought torches and busied themselves lighting the bonfire and the piles of lighter wood they had placed atop the mounds of dirt. The girls laughed and cavorted as they put their torches to one illumination after another. The several fires burned brightly, pleasantly scenting the air with the aroma of pitch.

As if on cue in the darkening light, voices became audible at some distance away to the northwest—men's voices, William discerned, as they drew closer. The voices grew louder and more distinct, until it could be heard that they were singing a song. A single, strong voice would call out a line:

"Oh the big black bull o' the swamp."

Then a chorus of several voices would sing out in response:

Oh don't he raaamble!

Then the lead singer:

"He rambles up and down and all around the town."

And the chorus:

Oh don't he raaamble!

Everybody strained to identify who was doing the singing. "That's Cudjo calling out," said Rosemary. "It's the cow-hunters coming in."

"He smash the cane and tremble the ground."
Oh don't he raaamble!
"He steal the cows and run em round."
Oh don't he raaamble!
"He make ole mastah cuss and frown."
Oh don't he raaamble!
"The dog trail him but he can't catch him."
Oh don't he raaamble!
"Mastah shoot, but the ball can't kill him."
Oh don't he raaamble!
"The knife be sharp, but the knife can't cut him."
Oh don't he raaamble!
"Put him on the fire, but the fire can't cook him."
Oh don't he raaamble!
"Serve him for dinner, but the boys can't eat him."
Oh don't he raaamble!
"He rambles up, he rambles down, he rambles all around the town."

Oh, don't he raaamble!
"Oh, don't he raaamble!"
Oh, don't he raaamble!

No sooner had this song ended than they heard voices coming from a distance up to the east. This would be the woodcutters. As they came in closer, the words of their song became discernable:

"All them purty gals gonna be there."
Shuck that corn before you eat!
"They gonna cook it up for us rare."
Shuck that corn before you eat!

"That has to be Obadiah calling out," said Rosemary.
"You can count on the woodcutters to sing about food," said Betsy. "They are always looking to their next meal."

"I know that supper's gonna be big."
Shuck that corn before you eat!
"I think I smell a fine roast pig."
Shuck that corn before you eat!
"Stuff that coon and roast him brown."
Shuck that corn before you eat!
"I hope they have some nice wheat bread."
Shuck that corn before you eat!
"I think I'll fill my pockets full."
Shuck that corn before you eat!
"I hope they have some whiskey there."
Shuck that corn before you eat!

The two crews had evidently paced themselves so that both would come into the light of the cornshucking ground at about the same time. A man William took to be Rufus Lyons, the husband of Betsy, rode out in front of the cow-hunters, along with a pack of mixed-breed herd dogs. Rufus was the boss William would work under if they did offer him the job and if he did decide to take it. William sized him up. Rufus looked to be a little older than himself. Though he was only of medium build, his deliberate, confident manner made him seem larger than he was. He had dark eyes and a firmly set mouth that turned down at the corners. When he dismounted, his legs were bowed from having spent so much of his life in the saddle.

The two crews mingled and said their hellos to each other, and then they came over to greet the home crew from the cowpen. The flop-eared herd dogs were lean, tired, and in no mood to be trifled with. Underfoot, they got into a spirited sniffing, barking, and snapping contest with the two home dogs, whose job it was to police the house and outbuildings. Little Butch in particular was trotting around stiff-legged, back bristling, yapping outrage at having his territory invaded by herd dogs. Rosemary had to step in and pick him up to calm him down and keep him from getting mauled.

"Butch's barking can drive a body to distraction," said Rosemary, coming over to stand beside William. The little dog squirmed until she put him down.

"Your father is thinking of offering me a job," said William. "If I take it, there are a great many names and faces here I've got to learn."

"Just start with the cow-hunters," said Rosemary.

"I've picked out Rufus," said William, "but who is that tall African fellow?"

"That is Cudjo, Rufus's main man. He grew up amongst cows in Africa. And when he was first a slave, he herded cows on Jamaica, so he knows Spanish cow-herding ways as well. Everyone says he is our best cow-hunter."

"And what about that Indian standing beside him? Walks with a limp. Would that be Alonso?"

"That's right, that's Alonso. He's one of those Apalachee slaves that got brought here many years ago from Spanish Florida. He got crippled up that way when a horse kicked him. To keep him useful after that, Aunt Sally taught him to cook. He keeps the cow camp and cooks the food."

"And those other two Africans? Are they cow-hunters too?"

"Ray and Jock? They are cow-hunters, yes, but they are only half African. The other half is Indian."

"Alonso?" asked William.

"That's right. Alonso is their father and Aunt Sally is their mother. Of the two, Ray is the good worker. He wants to get things done. Jock likes to take it easy."

"And that big red-faced fellow—he must be the boss of the woodcutters."

"Yes, that is Liza's husband, Swan Banks. He's good-hearted, and strong as an ox."

"And that older African that's with him—the one carrying the pine-knot torch?"

"That's Obadiah, Swan's main man. He can handle any job there is in timber. He can practically lift a whole tree trunk by himself."

William looked at her skeptically, but let it pass. "And the two younger black fellows are woodcutters? The ones with scars on their faces?"

"Cato and Ajax, both born in Africa. Those scars were cut into their cheeks at the ceremony that marked their entry into manhood. It's something they do back in Africa."

William looked around and could find no one else to ask about. "You've given me a good accounting of the players," he said, "though I don't know that I could name them all back to you. If I end up staying here, I'll eventually get to know them for myself."

"So has Father actually made you an offer?" asked Rosemary.

"He is thinking about it. He has to talk to Rufus first."

"Will you accept it if he does?"

"I am thinking about it."

"I would be careful if I were you," said Rosemary. "He is not likely to pay you well."

"That's exactly what has me thinking," said William.

Just then John MacDonald headed out into the crowd to assemble the crews. "We're about to start," said Rosemary.

MacDonald held up his arms for silence. "Welcome," he said in a strong voice. "Welcome to each and every one of you. We have a great pile of corn to shuck tonight, but with these two fine crews, we'll make short work of it. The womenfolk have been cooking for days. There's plenty of good food for us to eat later. When last I was in Charles Town, I bought a keg of rum that's not yet been tapped. We'll put a spigot in it tonight and see if we can't drink some of it down and have us some fun. As usual, the crew that finishes shucking their half of the pile first will get extra portions of rum. Now, let's tilt up the roof of this crib so we can toss it full of shucked corn."

Several men from each team seized up two poles, cut to length, with forks on their upper ends, and they hoisted them up so the forks caught the front edge of the corncrib's roof. Then they lifted together, tilting up the hinged roof so that a wide opening was exposed all along the upper edge of the front of the crib. When they had it high enough, they set the lower ends of the forked poles onto the ground, punching them in so they would not slip as they held the roof propped open. Next, two of the men laid a fence rail across the U-shaped pile of corn, intersecting it at the place John MacDonald estimated to be the center of the pile's curve, dividing it into equal halves.

As everyone took their places, John took up a big cow horn, and, blowing a mighty blast, he signaled the start of the contest. The cow-hunters laid into shucking the corn on the right side of the big U, Rufus taking his part as if he were one of the hands, while Cudjo served, topsy-turvy, as captain. The woodcutters started shucking on the left side of the U, and in the same fashion Swan joined in with the other workers, while Obadiah took up the post of captain.

William walked over to where Rosemary was standing. "What's going on here? It looks like the slaves are masters for the night."

"That's part of why they all love a cornshucking. It's not just the food and the rum. It's that things are turned upside down. While the corn is being shucked, the lowest among us stand highest."

"Like the carnival that comes before Lent in Catholic countries," said William.

"I guess," said Rosemary.

Some of the woodcutters, whose hands were thickly calloused, shucked their corn barehanded. But the rest of them, and all of the cow-hunters, used five-inch shucking pegs carved out of oak, their sharp points impaled through leather straps which held the peg tightly against their palms. Holding up each ear by its silk end, they would rip the shuck open, pull out the ear of corn, and break it away from the shuck. Then with one hand they would toss the shucked ear through the opening at the top of the crib, while with the other hand they would toss the shuck behind their backs. They were remarkably fast at this, and the ears of corn were soon raining into the crib in front of them, while the shucks went flying behind them to pile up on the ground. Mars, Venus, and Daphne scurried around gathering up the shucks into big split-oak baskets, taking some of them to pile in the barn loft, and emptying the rest into a square pen made of stacks of fence rails crossed at their ends. Every so often, Mars would climb up on top of the pile of shucks in the rail pen to jump up and down to compact them. The preserved shucks would be food for the dairy cows in the winter. The clean-up crew also picked up the few ears of corn that missed the opening of the crib and tossed them up to where they belonged.

The shucking never slackened. The two captains kept urging their teams to go faster, each side hoping to win the competition, the prize being an extra two fingers of rum for each man on the winning team. The two captains used songs to pace the work faster and faster. And there was a good deal of raillery and teasing in it, though without Rosemary to explain it to him, most of it would have gone over William's head. It seems that everybody knew that Venus was sweet on Cudjo, even though he was much older than she, and that this was the reason Obadiah started singing out lines about her.

"Venus, oh Venus, has pretty brown eyes."
Venus was the gal!

"He's singing this song for you, Cudjo!" called one of the woodcutters.

> "Venus, oh Venus, she was my darling."
> *Venus was the gal!*
> "Venus, oh Venus, she took to sighing."
> *Venus was the gal!*
> "Venus, oh Venus, her heart was aching."
> *Venus was the gal!*
> "Venus, oh Venus, she let me kiss her."
> *Venus was the gal!*
> "Venus, oh Venus, she said she loved me."
> *Venus was the gal!*
> "Venus, oh Venus, what's the matter?"
> *Venus was the gal!*
> "Venus, oh Venus, what's the matter?"
> *Venus was the gal!*
> "Put away the corn, boys!"
> *Put away the corn!*
> "Put away the corn, boys!"
> *Put away the corn!*

Everyone laughed to see Cudjo and Venus embarrassed. Cudjo, however, neither laughed nor smiled.

"We can do better than that," Rufus said to Cudjo. "Let's have a song for Obadiah."

"Give him the jumping song," said Alonso.

Cudjo smiled and started calling out lines while his crew sang the rhymed response.

> "Obadiah,"
> *Jumped in the fire;*
> "Fire too hot,"
> *Jumped in the pot;*
> "Pot too black,"
> *Jumped in the crack;*
> "Crack too high,"
> *Jumped in the sky;*
> "Sky too blue,"
> *Jumped in the slough;*

"Slough too deep,"
Jumped in the creek;
"Creek too shallow,"
Jumped in the tallow;
"Tallow too soft,"
Jumped in the loft;
"Loft too nice,"
Jumped in the rice;
"Rice so white,"
Stayed all night.

Everyone laughed. "That Obadiah, he's a jumping man!" one of the young cow-hunters called out. "He jumped and jumped." But Obadiah saw no humor in the song.

As the shucking proceeded, it became clear that the cow-hunters were getting the best of the contest. Rosemary went over and joined the woodcutters. Armed with a shucking peg, she began shucking corn as fast as some of the men. "I hope you boys don't mind if I even things up a little," she said to the cow-hunters across the way.

The corn and shucks flew, and in a little while the woodcutters pulled out ahead.

"This ain't fair!" Cudjo shouted. "The teams ain't equal."

William went over and joined the cow-hunters. "I'm new at this," he said, "but I'll do what I can." And he laid into it with all his might, clumsy at first, but soon he was getting the hang of it. As the cow-hunters were starting to catch up, William tore back the shucks on an ear of red-kerneled corn.

"A pokeberry ear!" called Jock, and the men laughed and slapped their legs. William started to throw it into the crib.

"Don't throw that away!" Cudjo shouted. "Don't you know what a red ear means? It means you can kiss any woman here. Ain't no one can stop you. Any woman you choose."

William grinned and held up the ear of corn and looked around. Everybody stopped shucking. "Now who will it be?" he asked as he walked slowly past Venus and Daphne. Daphne shut her eyes and puckered up her lips, but William only chuckled and patted her on the shoulder.

"She ain't looking for no pat on the shoulder," someone shouted.

"But she ain't the one," someone else said. "She ain't the one he's after."

William walked on to Betsy and Liza, circling them slowly. They looked at him as if to dare him, but he moved on.

"I see where he's going," someone said as he came to Rosemary and stopped.

"All right, mister smarty pants," she said in good humor. "You can have your kiss." But she might as well have been his sister as she turned her cheek to him. He followed her lead by giving it a chaste peck. But then she suddenly threw her arms around his neck and kissed him full on the lips as he rocked back on his heels.

Everybody laughed. "You gonna catch it now!" someone shouted. "Master John will skin you alive for carrying on with his girl!"

John MacDonald arose from his chair, grabbed up a stick of wood, and made a move toward William, who took the threat in all seriousness and was in a dither as to whether he should stand fast or run.

But MacDonald stopped, threw the stick down, and laughed. "Hold steady, Billy. Let's get back to shucking corn. Lay into it, boys!"

The corn and shucks started flying again, and the cow-hunters edged ahead.

"Luck be with us tonight, boys," shouted Cudjo. "That extra rum gonna be ours." He began singing.

> "Lookin for the last ear,"
> *Bang-a-ma-lango!*
> "Lookin for the last ear,"
> *Bang-a-ma-lango!*
> "Round up the corn boys,"
> *Bang-a-ma-lango!*
> "Round up the corn boys,"
> *Bang-a-ma-lango!*

A few moments later Rufus threw in the last ear from the cowmen's side of the pile. His crew shouted victory.

Shortly thereafter the woodcutters threw in what seemed to be their last ear.

"We're done!" proclaimed John MacDonald.

"Wait, here's one more," said Obadiah, leaning down and picking up a stray ear and ripping off the shuck. As he threw it toward the crib, he seemed to lose his footing and his throw went wild, sending the missle flying fast and hard to strike Cudjo square in the back. "It done slipped out of my hand," said Obadiah with a smirk.

"Like a lie slippin out of your mouth," said Cudjo.

"Now, what's that, cow-hunter? You callin me a liar?" Obadiah charged over and took a swing at Cudjo, and the two grappled and fell to the ground. A circle formed around them, everyone looking to see a fight.

John MacDonald pushed through the circle and held up his hands. "That's enough, you two. This is a frolic, not a dog fight. The corn has been shucked. It's time for us to eat that food and drink that rum!"

Cudjo and Obadiah got up from the ground and dusted themselves off, but neither would look at the other. William wondered if there was always bad blood between the two crews. Maybe it was the opposition of woodcutters and cow-hunters that was spoiling the cowpen so.

"Master John say its time to eat!" shouted one of the cow-hunters. "How's he gonna get to the table?"

"He gonna fly!" the men shouted.

MacDonald made a move to run away, but after only a few yards they caught him. He pretended to resist, but he quickly capitulated as the men hoisted him up above them. They fairly ran toward the house, bouncing him on their shoulders, his arms and legs sprawling. Everyone was laughing.

Carrying the master aloft, they circled all the way around his house where the feast was spread on tables in the yard, and then they deposited him on his front porch. At this point MacDonald once again resumed the dignified demeanor of the pinder of the cowpen, lord of his domain. Acknowledging this, both crews joined together in song.

> "Old MacDonald is a mighty fine man,
> A mighty fine man indeed."
> *He plants all the taters,*
> *He plants all the corn,*
> *He marks all the calves,*
> *And blows the dinner horn.*
> "Old MacDonald is a mighty fine man,
> A mighty fine man indeed."

All the topsy that had been turvy during the cornshucking came right side up again. MacDonald raised a hand for silence. "I want to thank each and every one of you for getting this corn safely into the crib," he said soberly. "Our purpose on this earth is to herd cattle and cut timber. But without Indian corn to feed us, we could not do a bit of it. You good people have labored half a year to put this corn in our crib. You burned the dead weeds off the field, put the seeds in the ground, hoed out the newly sprouted grass and weeds, kept away the crows, the squirrels, the coons, and all the other varmints that wanted to steal our food from us. You stripped the leaves off the stalks for fodder for our animals. And here tonight you have shucked all those ears and put them in the crib. And you did it with some good humor and mighty fine singing on this beautiful night. And all of it with just the least bit of a fracas. I thank you one and all. Now, let's eat and drink and have us a good time."

MacDonald came down from the porch, went over to the keg of rum, and opened the spigot for the black-and-tan ceramic cup the men held beneath it for their portions. First in line were the cow-hunters, who got the extra two fingers for winning the contest. Each man slugged down his rum without ceremony and passed the cup on to the next.

Then from blue Delftware platters and serving bowls, the men filled their wooden trenchers full of food: barbequed pork, roasted coon, hoppin john, hominy, baked sweet potatoes, buttered cornbread, pumpkin pie—and cups of cold buttermilk to wash it all down. The MacDonald women had set up several plank-and-sawhorse tables with benches around the yard so that everyone could sit to eat.

John, his three daughters, and his two sons-in-law sat around one of the tables, waiting to be served. William hesitated to join them, but they invited him over, and he squeezed in at the end of a bench. At first the company was awkwardly silent, though William was not sure why. They all seemed relieved when Venus brought trenchers heaped with food. As they filled their plates and dug in, they now had an excuse for their silence. The keg of rum was on the end of the table opposite John, with Rosemary manning the spigot, and the liquor flowed freely while they ate. But freely as it flowed, it did not lessen the tension. Rather, it increased it. William gradually discerned that the problem lay with hard feelings being nursed between Rufus and Swan, the cow-hunter and the woodcutter. Rufus on one side of the table only talked to his wife Betsy beside him, and Swan did the same with Liza on the opposite side. Though in fact they talked very little, eating and drinking in sullen silence. William expected the wives to be more sociable, but neither Betsy nor Liza made any effort to sweeten the air of the party. Finally Rufus put down his glass, pushed back his empty plate, and turned to face Swan.

"I have to say this," he said. "If your Obadiah ever attacks my Cudjo again, I will have satisfaction from you. My man was hit square in the back with a full ear of corn, and hit hard. You said not a word to your man about it."

"It was an accident," said Swan.

"Like hell it was," said Rufus. "I have eyes. I saw what happened."

"That's enough, God damn it!" John thundered, banging his fist on the table. "That's enough, do you hear me? Every time you two come within speaking distance of each other, you snarl and snap like dogs. Can you not conceive that this is a family that you two hot-heads have married into? This ship of ours will float as a family, or else we will all sink, all of us together. Each and every one of us depends on the others, and there can be no slack in our rigging. Do I make myself clear?"

"We hear you, Father," said Liza.

"We do," said Betsy. "But you need to hear us, too."

"Let's hear it then," said John. "What do I need to hear?"

An awkward silence followed.

Then Swan said, "My men are unhappy, sir, and I can't blame them. We are hopelessly short-handed. Every day they each have to do the work of two men. Cutting and squaring swamp timber and sawing planks is hard work in any season of the year, but especially in winter. If we are to have rice next year, we have got to get up that raft of timbers, planks, and shingles and float it downriver to Dubose's plantation to make the exchange. This crib of corn is all well and good, but you know it doesn't go far enough. We have to have the rice to make it through the year. And to get the rice before Dubose has sold all his away, we have to get up that raft of lumber. If I could have just one of the cow-hunters to help me for a time, things would be evened up enough to get this done."

"Evened up?" said Rufus. "I'm short-handed as it is. You should try tending six hundred head of cattle on a ten-thousand-acre range with only four cow-hunters. I ought to have a cow-hunter for every hundred head. It ain't hard for anybody to figure out how short-handed I am. The grazing hereabouts ain't what it used to be, and to make things worse, we've got a goddamned thief stealing our cattle, and there's not enough of us to cover the territory to find out how the hell he's doing it and where he's taking them. I need six men and I've got four. I sure as hell can't spare one to you."

"You've got five," said Swan.

"Alonso is too old and too stove in to work with the cows," said Rufus. "You know that. And besides, he's our cook. He has to mind the camp."

"Me and my men," said Swan, "spend our days in the muck and mire, tangled up in vines and cat-scratch briars. You don't know what hard work is. You spend your days high and dry on horseback. It shouldn't be all that hard for a few of you fellows to ride around and flush out the varmint what's taking the cows. My men would have that solved in a day."

"Then be my guest," said Rufus. "Come try your hand at finding that thief."

"Maybe what the both of you need is to try tending a dairy," said Rosemary. "You're not the only ones who work hard around here. Come do my job

66

for a while. Then you'll find that milk cows don't so much belong to you as you belong to them. They have to be brought in and milked every day—*every day*, rain or shine. Cream has to be skimmed off. Butter has to be churned. Cheese has to be made. It won't wait. And short-handed? The members of my crew are just children—Venus, Daphne, and Mars. To top it off, we have to do the lion's share of the work in the garden, and in the cornfield. And the truly bad news is that the soil in our old cornfield is starting to play out. We should be getting thirty bushels of corn to the acre, but this year we got closer to twenty. This means that before long somebody—and it's not going to be me—somebody is going to have to go in and make a big deadening and clear the trees and the bushes from some more land. Who is going to do that work, I ask you? And then tell me about being short-handed!"

"Daphne and Venus are more than children," said Betsy.

"Are they, now?" said Rosemary, her voice rising. "Then I'm sure you'd not mind if I traded them out with Rufus for Jock and Ray."

John MacDonald rose up in a fury, throwing his cup to the ground and then sweeping his hand over the table to knock away his other dishes as well. He was staggering from all the rum he had drunk. "Damn it all to hell, Rosemary!" he shouted, leaning toward her with his hands on the table, glaring furiously at her. "You, too? Is pissing and moaning all this family can do? If you think it is hard for woodcutters, cow-hunters, milkmaids, and gardeners to all work together, each of you should try making a living on your own. Then you would see what a family is for. I am coming to my wit's end with the lot of you. Has all my hard labor come to naught? Where, I ask you, is the loving family I raised? Does the father of this house get no respect?"

"Of course you do, Father," said Betsy, reaching out to put a hand on his arm. "You know how much I love you. And Rufus does, too. We have all been working so hard, that's all, and the cornshucking was just one more thing to do. It has frayed our nerves. We'll be back to ourselves after a night's rest."

"Of course we love you," said Liza. "And respect? We respect you so much, Papa. You are right about the family. We know we all need to work together. Truly we do. Swan was just trying to tell you about the rice. God only knows how he'll get up that timber in time to float it down to the plantation while there's still some rice left to be traded. But we'll do it somehow. We always have."

"That's more like it," said MacDonald. "And what about you, Rosemary? What do you have to say?"

"I say I still don't know how we'll clear the new cornfield. But that doesn't mean I am not the same daughter I have always been. I am the same today as I was yesterday, and I will be the same tomorrow."

"And what does that mean, pray tell?"

"It means what it says. You are my father. I am Rosemary, your daughter, always and forever. And I don't know how we'll clear the new cornfield."

"God damn it! That falls short even of faint praise. What is it they say? 'An ungrateful child is sharper than a serpent's tooth!' Clear the tables!" he bellowed. "This frolic is over." He turned on his heel and stormed away into the house. Everyone sat in a stunned silence.

Then Betsy finally said, "What a fool you are, Rosemary. He only wanted to hear you say that you love him. Was that too much to give him?"

"I don't know what you were thinking," said Liza. "I've never seen him so upset. You have spoiled the cornshucking for all of us."

"Just go speak to him," said Betsy. "Tell him how much you love him. That's all you have to do."

Rosemary crossed her arms and refused to answer either of her sisters.

The frolic was truly over. One by one, most of the people got up and melted away into the darkness, leaving Venus and Daphne to clear the tables. Rosemary still sat where she was, tears running down her cheeks. William understood so little of where he stood with her, let alone the significance of what had just happened, he did not know how to comfort her. He stood awkwardly aside for a few moments, trying to think of something appropriate to do or say, but then finally he turned and walked away.

Before going to his bed in the barn, he stopped in at the kitchen to see if there was a spare lantern to be had. Aunt Sally handed him one with the stump of a candle that she lit for him from the kitchen fire. He thanked her, went to the barn, and took out his journal.

Wednesday night, November 2, MacDonald's Cowpen

Now I know what a cornshucking is—part sport, part drama, part musical performance. Its purpose is to lighten everyone's mood, heal old wounds, and chirk everybody up, though it surely did not achieve its purpose tonight.

I amend what I wrote earlier about leaving King Lear behind in Charles Town. The cornshucking that was to repair the fabric of this cowpen has instead shown that it is sadly rent and torn. I have never seen John MacDonald so out of sorts. That drunken night at the tavern was nothing. Tonight he raged like a baited bear. He brought tears to Rosemary's eyes. All I could do was stand and watch. I remain puzzled by the ins and outs of this family. How are Betsy and Liza aligned? Are they spiteful to all? Only to me? My questions are many. Was this just a bad day—a very bad day—or are John's rages the usual fare around here? Even more, what is the real cause? And not to slight self-interest, is this cowpen the place I would want for my lot in life if all were to go as I have been hoping? What have I been hoping, anyhow? Have I let even myself in on that secret?

The red ear of corn I shucked entitled me to kiss any woman of my choice. Rosemary was my choice, though kissing her was like kissing a cold fish. But then to my surprise she threw her arms about me and kissed me on the lips. A long and full kiss it was, too. What am I to think of this? Was she making fun of me? As much as I would like to think otherwise, I suspect it was just a topsy-turvy cornshucking kiss. I'll not stake my hopes on it.

7

Rufus

William awoke when the first rooster crowed. He got up and packed his small belongings in his saddlebags. Everything else went into his canvas bag and bedroll. When he climbed down from the loft to make sure that Viola had been well fed, he came upon Rosemary on her way to the milk cows.

"Good morning," she said wearily. "Have you gotten over last night's corn-shucking?"

"I can't say I have. I've never seen your father so out of sorts. Being a witness to such rage is not my favorite thing."

"It's not anybody's favorite thing," she said. "Before breakfast Swan and the woodcutters picked up and headed down to the cypress tract, and Liza went with them. I don't know what will become of us all. Father is more and more in a state these days. He says he feels the cold hand of age and infirmity tugging at his sleeve. He blames his troubles on the arguing between Rufus and Swan, and now me, but it can't all be blamed on us. Anyone can see that our life here is harder than it used to be, as much for Rufus and Swan as it is for Father."

"And for you, too?"

"If he doesn't put me to clearing the new cornfield, I can't say it is altogether harder. But it is starting to wear on me more. I am seventeen now, and all that I have ever known is hard work in the dairy and cornfields. The cows do not know that Sundays are different from other days, so there is never any let-up. Tending the cornfield we already have is not supposed to fall squarely on my little crew, but it does. You have seen how my sisters treat me, with never a kind word. But I ought not complain. There are many in this world who would be glad for this life. We have food on the table and a roof over our heads. What about you, Billy? Where do you go from here?"

"Och, I wish I knew. It's up in the air right now. In the end I may go back into the Indian trade, but not as a packhorseman—that's a dead end. I'll go in as a trader next time. But for that I need credit, and to get credit I need work that pays. And there is not much of that to be found."

"Is that why you came up here? Looking for work that pays?"

"I did. It was my mistake. I did not know how much your father's fortune has changed."

"He's afraid of the future," said Rosemary, "afraid that poverty will overtake him. It makes him miserly. He won't part with a farthing he doesn't have to spend. I'm sorry you had to come all the way up here to discover that."

"Well, I have to say that hope for employment was not the sole reason I came."

"It wasn't?"

"No." It was now or never for what he wanted to say, and he searched for words. "I have not known how to bring this up, but I might as well just come out with it. I thought we two had something of an understanding when I visited here a year and a half ago. Unspoken, it is true, but still an understanding. But from what you have not said to me since I arrived, more than from what you have said, I now see that I was mistaken there, too, and that there was no such understanding."

Rosemary stood silently for a moment, as if consulting with herself. Then she said, "No, you are wrong. We did have an understanding. When you rode away, I thought you would soon be back. But there I was mistaken. And as time went on and your packhorsemen friends passed through again, I learned there is much you have never bothered to tell me about your time in Keowee. You never told me about the woman you married. Or about her death. I had to hear all of that from others. While from you I have heard not a single word about that or anything else. You could have written me a letter. At least one. From your silence I have had to draw my own conclusion, which is that once I was out of your sight, I was also out of your mind and heart. And so I have put you out of mine as well."

William looked down and shook his head. She was right about his silence, so what could he say? He had no excuse except his melancholy, which was no excuse at all. He started to speak, then fell silent, shaking his head again.

"Well, then," said Rosemary. "I need to get on to the cows."

"Wait," said William. "I have to try to explain, even if you hear it as lame and it comes too late to do me any good. I apologize, Rosemary. I regret with all my heart that you interpreted my silence in that way. You must have heard that Otter Queen's death was by her own hand, but what you could not have heard is how deep was the pit I fell into in the wake of it. It swallowed me whole, and while it had me, I had little to say to anybody about my thoughts and feelings. You did not go out of my heart and mind, but I had no words to send you. I am back to myself now, but clearly it is too late for you to accept me as a suitor. And even if it were not, I would still be burdened by my lack of prospects. I have none at this time, and that is the bitter truth of it."

Rosemary nodded, and now it was she who was silent for a while. Then at last she looked at him and said, "Thank you for explaining yourself at long last. That does give me some understanding. But now I must explain to you that I will be looking to marry one day soon. I am weary of this cowpen life, and I intend to marry someone with whom I can build a new life. From what you have said, I have to conclude that you do not yet know what your path in life will be."

"That is sad but true." He looked down and kicked slowly at the ground. What could he say? It would insult her to try to put a good face on it.

"I hope we will always be friends," she said.

"Of course, always friends," he said with a wry smile.

"So what are your plans for today?" she asked.

"After last night, it would seem I am headed back to Charles Town. Your father said he would talk to Rufus about taking me on, but I doubt he has said a word to Rufus about this or any other business."

"It might not be hopeless," said Rosemary. "If I were you, I would not leave without speaking to Father about it. He has slept off the rum and is back to his better self this morning. He and Rufus are at breakfast now, believe it or not. You should go and join them."

"I may do that," said William. "What have I to lose? I could do with a spot of breakfast, no matter where this day takes me. And I thank you for your honesty, Rosemary. At the very least, it is good that the air is cleared between us."

"Yes, that is good. Now I have a dairy to take care of, and you have a job to get." She smiled at him a little and turned to walk away.

"One more question," William said after her.

"What is it?" She looked back at him, but he could not read her face.

"Is there anyone else in your life?"

She smiled a little and gave a small shrug. "I would have to say yes and no."

"Not one or the other?"

"Both."

"I don't want to pry, but can't you say more to put my heart at ease and let me know where I stand?"

"All right then." She turned back to face him. "I met a boy—a young man—several years ago when my father took me to visit a plantation downriver. He's a planter's son and handsome enough to make any girl swoon. And he's no country bumpkin. His father has sent him out to learn something about the larger world."

"Do you see him often?"

"He has been in England."

"Does he send you letters?

"I'm afraid not. I am not sure he even remembers my name."

"Then I don't understand. I have done better by you than he has. I have come to see you, at least, late as it might be. I have brought you gifts."

"The point is this, Billy. He is the kind of man I want to spend my life with. A man with prospects, but not just any man with prospects. One who can hold up his end of a conversation. A man who's not struck dumb by a new idea, who knows the larger world. I want a husband who can provide me a better life than I have at this cowpen, but I am also romantic enough to want to marry for love. I have seen that such a man exists, although I was too young at the time to draw his attention. But the next time I encounter such a man, it will be different. It does not have to be him, but it must be someone like him."

"I have to say," said William, "that you are not shy about setting the bar higher than most men can jump."

"That may be, but for now I have to go to work. There's a churn full of clabbered cream to attend to before it curdles and spoils." She turned away again and started toward the milking pen. But after taking a few steps, she stopped, glanced back, and said, "You must think me a trollop for having kissed you on the lips last night." Before he could stammer out an answer, she continued on her way.

Despite their efforts, the air was still not entirely clear between them.

Without much hope of getting more than a breakfast, William knocked at MacDonald's door. Betsy opened it, and her baleful, hard-bitten expression did not put him at ease. He went in feeling like a lamb led to slaughter, but once inside, the slaughterhouse turned out to be pleasant enough. John and Rufus were sitting at the breakfast table with the smell of coffee and fragrant tobacco smoke in the air. John was smoking a white clay pipe and Rufus a burnished black one.

"Good morning, young MacGregor," John said cheerfully, as if his rage from the night before had been but a dream.

"The same to the both of you," William said with some relief. He walked over to where Rufus was sitting and offered his hand to him. "We have been at table together, but I have not yet shaken your hand."

"That's easy to fix," said Rufus, and he rose from his bench to exchange a handshake. His clasp was surprisingly strong.

William hoped that Betsy's exit toward the kitchen would produce some food for him, for he had not yet been offered any. "Have a seat, Billy," said John. "Betsy will bring you a trencher directly. Rufus and I were just talking about you."

"Favorably, I hope," said William.

"That remains to be seen," said John.

"I understand you have herded cows before," said Rufus.

"Back in the Highlands I lived in close amongst cattle for my first sixteen years," William said. "There's many a Mayday I helped herd our kyloes up to graze on the summer shielings in the high hills. I would spend the summer up there with my mates in a shieling hut, and at the end of the season we would drive the herd back down to graze on the lower shielings. I even went once on a MacGregor raid against neighboring clansmen who had lifted some of our cows. We got them back with a few extra to boot. So I've done most everything that has to do with herding cattle."

"I take it you were herding on foot," said Rufus.

"Yes, that is so."

"Out here we herd from horseback, and it takes a better than average rider to be equal to it when we have to round up the cattle from out of the bush."

"When I was a packhorseman, on more than one occasion we had to ride hard and rough to regain control of stampeding horses."

"What about predators?" asked Rufus. "How did you protect your cattle in the Highlands?"

"We had no predators to speak of. No big cats. The wolves have been driven out, or nearly so. Every once in a while a dog would go bad and kill a calf to fill his belly. The biggest problem was others herders who would sneak in and steal cattle."

"Well, we've got plenty of predators here. Cougars, bears, wolves, Indians, and we are hearing more and more rumors about gangs of cattle thieves coming down from the north."

Betsy came in with her mouth still set tightly, carrying a cup of coffee and a trencher of leftover food from the cornshucking. She set them on the table before William, along with a pewter spoon and a two-tined iron fork. But no kind word. No smile. What was it about this woman? Was she just mean?

"You will find," said Rufus, "that our piney woods cows are a damned sight harder to handle than those little kyloes back in Scotland. Ours are bigger, stronger, and wilder, and their horns are long enough to make a man as well as a wolf or a panther think twice about going after a calf. We have bred them with Spanish big-horned bulls that were brought into these parts from Florida and Jamaica. On a drive they are long-legged enough to keep up with the horses. Some Carolina cowmen are partial to short-horned, short-legged cattle of the British and Irish sort, but I don't think they do as well as the Spanish cattle against the varmints out here in the free range of the backcountry."

"If you ask me," said John, "the best thing about our piney-woods cows is that they can browse on bushes and low trees, almost like deer. Of course, they'll eat grass if there's any to be had, but these cows are right at home in the woods. They will eat chestnuts and sweet acorns, and if they are hungry enough they will even choke down blackberry briars. They are tough."

"Almost too tough," said Rufus. "That's their one drawback."

William looked up from his food. "How is that?"

"Any bull that will gore a panther," said Rufus, "will gore another bull, or a horse, or a man, if he takes a notion. I've heard cow-hunters say that if they are out in the woods they would rather run up against a wounded bear than a wild bull. A wild bull attacks from cover, often from behind. He comes bearing down on you with those horns lowered before you even know what's happening. Cudjo won't go out in the woods unless he has padding on his horse's flank for protection."

"Cudjo was your cornshucking captain, wasn't he?" said William. "He's from Africa, I hear. His name sounds African."

"It is," said Rufus. "He says it's a day-name. It means he was born on a Monday. Here we say that Monday's child is full of woe, but that don't exactly fit Cudjo. He does pretty well for himself. He's not one to mope. He's a doer."

"He looks different from other Africans I have seen," said William. "That copper-colored skin and straight hair, and that thin beak of a nose. And I have never seen such long legs."

"And arms," said Rufus. "He was born a Fulani. They are a race of cattle herders, and he does seem to have cattle in his blood. From what he says, the Fulani are more Moorish than most others in that land. He says they call God 'Allah' and pray to him five times a day. Cudjo himself don't do that no more,

74

but he still remembers some of it. What I like most about him is that he's a natural-born cowman. He claims to have lived right amongst cows from the time he was born. Like me. And like you, it seems."

"He herded cows in Jamaica, too," said John.

"That's right," said Rufus. "That's how he learned the Spanish way of herding. I suppose his Jamaican master needed money, otherwise I'm sure he would not have sold him. Cudjo is a steady worker, and he's smart. But he landed on the slave block here in Carolina."

"I bought him quick when I learned how much he knew about cattle," said John. "And it didn't take him long to learn our Carolina way of herding. He was a good investment."

"He is as delicate with cows as he is respectful of people," said Rufus. "He thinks some of our ways with cows are harsh, but he is as good at it as anybody I know."

William shoved his empty trencher aside and took a sip of coffee. "That Alonso fellow looks interesting, too. He's the first Indian slave I've ever seen."

"There are still a few scattered about in these parts," said Rufus.

"He came from the Spanish missions in Florida," said John. "When Carolina busted them up back years ago, Alonso and his mama got away and ran to the Lower Creeks. But later, when he was still a young man in his prime, he went out into the woods one day and got caught by Indian slave-catchers, who brought him here to Carolina. He says he spent eight years slaving on a rice plantation. If that's so, and it seems to be, I'm surprised he survived. He must have been more spirited than most. Indian slaves don't usually live very long as plantation slaves."

"I believe his story," said Rufus. "He's got scars on his back from his master's whip, and he don't bear no love a'tall for rice planters. He's a sour old feller who cusses in Spanish, and he don't have much love for anybody except Aunt Sally. Those two were thick with each other in the beginning, but even she don't have much to do with him anymore. I think she still cares something for him deep down, but he's always out at the camp. Their lives are separate."

"I got him cheap," said John. "Nobody wanted an Indian. Not after the Yamasee uprising. Indian slaves had a big hand in that, you know. But this one knew big-horned cows from his time with the Spaniards, so I took a chance. He made me a pretty fair cow-hunter until a rogue horse kicked him square on the knee. That crippled him up too much to be able to stay on a saddle, so he can't do much with cows anymore. I didn't know what to do with him after that, but Aunt Sally took him back on for a while and taught him to cook. Not fine food, mind you, but so far his cooking hasn't killed any of my cow-hunters."

William laughed. "He must have been here a long time if he's the father of those two young cow-hunters."

"Both Sally and Alonso came to this cowpen in 1718, right after the Yamassee war, when things were mighty hard. They bedded together at first and gave us the two boys. But they more or less parted ways after Jock was born."

"All in all you have an interesting crew of cow-hunters," said William. "A Fulani, an Apalachee, and two half-breeds. If you think a Scotsman would not be out of place, I would like to join up with them."

John looked at Rufus, who appeared less than enthusiastic.

"He's no beginner with cows," said Rufus, "but he doesn't know our way of herding. I'm not sure he can keep up with our cow-hunters. And if he can't keep up, then we'll be taking him on as a liability rather than an asset. That's what I'm thinking. What about you?"

"I knew his father back in Scotland and fought with him as a mate in the Jacobite cause. He was a good man, brave and true. And I can see something of him in the boy. I say we give him a chance."

"You're the pinder," said Rufus. "I'll be willing to give him a try if we can reassess after a time. I'll put him in with Cudjo. We will see whether he can pass that test."

"Good enough," said John. He looked at William. "It seems you are in. But there is still the problem of your pay. Have I mentioned that we are not having a good year?"

William smiled wryly. "Yes, I think you did. But I am hoping we can work something out."

"Here's what we can do," said John. "We can feed you and give you shelter, but beyond that I can't promise much. We'll have to see how this next year turns out."

William's hopes plummeted. A payment in cows had fallen out of the deal. "Food and shelter would be welcome," he said, "but I have got to have some kind of pay."

John clucked his tongue. "Well, let's see. I guess I could go out on a limb and promise you one of the cows that reach market in Charles Town. I've gone back and forth on whether to offer you that. I've lost so many cows this year. But I suppose I would be willing to give up one more for a good hand."

"Well, I'm not so sure one cow would be enough," said William. "The Charles Town drive is almost a year away. I don't see how I could work a year for so little gain. I'd like to help you out, Mister MacDonald. I truly would.

But I could do better for myself in Charles Town. As much as I hate to say it, it looks like I'd best go on back to town and try again to find work there."

"Just hold on for a minute," said John. "Just hold on. Let me think." He drummed his fingers on the table and seemed to be calculating things in his mind. Then he said, "How about this? You say you have had some experience retrieving stolen cows. Here's what I can offer. If you can find those cows that have been taken from us, I will add one of them to your pay. That would give you two head in all."

"Just one of all those stolen?" asked William. "Only two cows in all for a whole year's work?"

"God *damn*," said John. "You drive a hard bargain. Two of the stolen cows then, if you can find them. That would give you three in all."

"I'll do it for three," said William. "When do we leave out?"

John reached out and shook his hand, sealing their agreement. "How soon are you leaving, Rufus?" he asked his son-in-law.

"Just as soon as you can get your horse saddled and packed," Rufus said to William. "We'll be living rough, and cold weather is coming on, so come prepared. And if by spring you're not measuring up, you'll be leaving with no cows at all."

"I'm not worried about that," said William. "And as for the rest, I've lived rough most of my life." He and Rufus both pushed back from the table to get up to leave.

"Wait boys," said John, "let's get something to fortify you." He rose and went over to a cupboard and took out a bottle of Madeira and poured three fingers of wine into each of their cups. For him, evidently, it was never too early in the day to celebrate with spirits. "This seals the bargain," he said.

They raised their cups to each other and swilled down the warm, sweet wine.

8

Flea Bite Pen

It was not yet mid-morning when the cow-hunters gathered in the pen beside the barn and saddled up their horses. Jock, the youngest of the two sons of Alonso and Sally, was moving especially slowly after all the rum the night before. Finally they were all standing around waiting for him, and Rufus lost his patience.

"Jock, get your lazy arse moving," he snapped. "How long does it take to saddle a horse?"

"I'm gettin it, Master Rufus, I'm gettin it. I'm ready now."

"Then let's mount up," said Rufus.

The cow-hunters climbed into their saddles, and the herd dogs milled around excitedly. John, who had walked down from the house with Betsy, opened the gate for them to ride out of the pen. Rosemary came out from the dairy and stood a little apart from her father and sister to wave them off. William tipped his hat to John and Betsy and then to Rosemary as he rode past them, following the others out onto the dusty northern trail worn bare by livestock coming to and fro. Alonso brought up the rear, leading a string of two packhorses laden with food for the camp.

As they rode along, William soon realized that their order of march was not random. Though it was a loose formation, it was consistent with the status of each of the men. Rufus rode mostly out in front, Cudjo followed next, then came Ray and Jock, and last of all Alonso and the packhorses. Nothing had been said to William about where he should ride, but as the newest member of the crew, he took the precaution of falling back behind all of the others. The dogs appeared to have more choice than the men about where they trotted, and they moved in and out of the formation willy-nilly. The only exceptions were a yellow dog with a black mouth and a big gray dog, both of whom stayed pretty close to Cudjo. Cudjo himself was an unusual sight in that he carried, instead of a musket, a slender, twelve-foot spear with a pointed steel blade on the end.

After riding alone for a while at the rear of the train, William ventured to move up beside Alonso to make an attempt at conversation. "Did Cudjo get in the habit of carrying that spear in Africa?"

"That ain't no spear," said Alonso. "It's a Spanish lance. He learned to use it when he rode herd in Jamaica. I've seen him ride down a rabbit and stick that blade clean through it."

"What about that padded covering on his horse's flanks? Nobody else has that."

"Cudjo had a horse killed beneath him in Jamaica. A wild bull charged out of some bush, hooked his horse, and tumbled Cudjo out of his saddle. He just made it up a tree, but the bull killed his horse. He's padded his horse's flanks ever since. When Cudjo learns a lesson, he don't forget it. But except for the padding and the lance, he rides like the rest of us."

William glanced at the others and saw that it was so. Like he himself, each wore a substantial sheath knife on his belt, along with a hatchet, and each had a long braided cowhide whip looped over his shoulders and across his chest. And except for Cudjo, they all carried muskets propped across their saddles. William rode on for a time in silence and then fell back again behind Alonso, who did not seem interested in more small talk.

After a while Rufus fell back to the rear to join him. They were now deep in a forest of tall pines.

"How far are we from the cows?" William asked.

"Hard to say," replied Rufus. "Our first stop will be our camp and pen by Big Flea Bite Swamp. That's over in the northwestern part of our range, about six miles from where we started out. I doubt we'll see any cows today. The last I saw of them, they were beginning to move down into Four Hole Swamp, what with the weather cooling. As much as cows like to be near water, they don't stay in the swamp much in warm weather. Too many bugs. They start moving back down as soon as the weather cools and the grass begins giving out in the upland pastures. During the winter they mostly graze on maiden cane down in the swamp."

"How big is your range in all?"

"Right at ten thousand acres. Our cows graze mostly between Half Way Swamp and the Santee River on the east and upper Four Hole Swamp on the west. We used to go further north than we do now, but Amelia Township is cutting in on us up there. We can still manage with what's left to us, but the squeeze is on. Our range gets less every year. Move north or west is what we need to do."

"Ten thousand acres is a lot of territory," said William. "It may not be enough here in Carolina, but it would be a huge spread back in Scotland. We kept a close watch on our cows back there. That seems not to be the way you do it here."

"Cudjo makes the same complaint," said Rufus. "They keep their cows always in sight back where he came from. But we do it different, which is the very reason I like these lanky, big-horned cows. They can take care of themselves against the bears, the wolves, and the panthers. We mostly just keep our eye on them off and on through the year and keep them moving from place to place. It's the ticks that do more damage to them than anything. The longer you keep cows in one place, the thicker the ticks. Cudjo will sometimes pick them off a cow that is suffering overly much from being infested, but the rest of us don't want that job. So we try to move them on before the ticks get that bad."

"Why don't the cows just go wild out here?" asked William. "Why do they let you herd them at all?"

"Every once in a while some of them do hive off and go wild, especially the bulls. But we put out a little salt for them, and they all crave salt, so they usually come back. Our main work, outside the hunts, is to nudge the cows to better grazing ever so often. Keep watch on them when they are calving. Defend them against anything that tries to make off with them."

"And what about the hunts? What's involved in that?"

"That's when most of our hard work comes. There's a hunt in the spring and another in the fall. In the spring hunt we collect the cows together and drive all of them to a pen where we can mark the ears of all the new calves and cut the nuts off of most of the young bulls, all but the ones we select out to sire calves. Then off they go to range for the summer. In the fall we round them up again and do the same, mark and cut the new calves. But then we also select out the cows that are ready for market and drive them down to Charles Town to sell. Most of them are culls that will be butchered, salted down, and shipped to the islands. That rounds out the year, and then we come back and start over again."

"Well, that should keep us busy," said William. "I trust there will be some time in there for me to hunt up the missing cows. I intend to close out the year with three head instead of one."

"Good luck to you on that," said Rufus. "We've searched high and low for those cows and come up with nothing. If it's a wild bull taking them, he must have twenty cows in his harem by now. I don't see how he can keep them so hidden as to not leave any trace for us at all. It's as if he slips them through the veil of this world and takes them to the other side."

"They have to be around here somewhere," said William.

Rufus snorted. "Like I say, good luck." He started forward toward the front of the column. After going a little way, he turned and called back to William. "You can come up and ride with Cudjo if you want."

"I'm content back here," said William, and he stayed where he was. He didn't want to stir up resentment or jealousy in Jock and Ray before he had even gotten to know them.

They rode to the northwest through the upland forest, which was mostly tall pine trees scattered through with a few oaks. Here and there, as they rode along, William could see areas where the cows had grazed down the grass and foliage, leaving cow pies scattered about. As the morning went on, they turned more to the west and after a while came to a narrow floodplain forest with its more varied, leafy foliage. As the trail led through a burned-out patch of canebrake to the edge of a swamp, William moved up to ride with Jock and Ray. In answer to his questions, he learned that this was Big Flea Bite Swamp they were coming to, and the cow camp was nearby.

When the camp came in sight, William saw that it was not greatly different from a hunting camp he had lived in for a time in Cherokee country. The main shelter was a substantial lean-to, a large half-face camp with a good bark roof, the front side open to the weather. It was situated on a small spot of high ground above the seasonal flood waters of Big Flea Bite Creek, which ran nearby. The roof extended out in front a little way as a kind of porch. The trees and bushes had been cut to the ground for some distance around the camp to protect against a woods fire. Close to the open side of the lean-to was a large spread of ashes where a fire was kept burning for heat, light, and cooking. A spit was set up on posts planted into the ground next to the fireplace, along with a large grill for barbequing and jerking meat. Down closer to the creek was a small, crudely fenced pen where horses and cows could be put up as needed.

The men dismounted, stretched, and walked about to get the kinks out, and then they helped Alonso unpack the gear and food from the packhorses. They carried the food inside the lean-to and hung some of it from the rafters, up above reach of the herd dogs. They stored their own gear in the back of the lean-to. The dogs, tired from the journey, found shady places to lie down and rest.

Once the packhorses were unloaded, the men led all of the horses down to the creek, where they drank their fill. Then the cow-hunters lounged on the ground and rested for a while as the horses grazed on the scruffy cane.

"I'd guess the herd is at upper Four Hole," said Rufus. "Ride on over there, Cudjo, and see if you can find them. Don't spend a lot of time on it. Just look them over and try to get back here before dark."

"Yes, sir, I'll do it." Cudjo got up and mounted his horse and called out, "Samri! Bruto!" The black-mouth yellow dog and the big gray one jumped up and trotted over to him. Lance in hand, Cudjo rode across the creek and disappeared into the trees on the other side, with Samri and Bruto running out in front of him.

"So what's for supper?" Rufus asked Alonso.

"There ain't no fresh meat," said Alonso. " It's got to be bean soup. I'll put plenty of bacon in it."

"I'd appreciate it if this time you would pick the rocks and pebbles out of the beans before you put them in the pot," Rufus said. "I almost busted a tooth on that last batch."

"*Vete al inferno!*" said Alonso. "The rocks I'll take out for you, but the pebbles I'll cook to well done."

"He does his cussing in Spanish," Rufus said to William. "Cudjo understands some of it, but the rest of us don't know what he's saying, and it's just as well we don't."

William chuckled.

Alonso got up and removed the saddle from his horse and carried it up to the camp, where he set about building a new fire from a few coals that still smouldered deep inside the ashes of the fire he had left burning the day before. Once he had flames licking up through his kindling, he added more wood and started getting ready to cook up some food.

"Let's get a move on here," said Rufus. "There ain't hardly enough wood in camp for Alonso to boil a kettle of water, much less cook those beans till they're tender."

The cow-hunters rose slowly to their feet and began unsaddling their horses, slinging the saddles onto the rails of the pen. Then they hobbled and belled the horses and turned them loose to graze, all except the two pack-horses they would take out with them to carry firewood. William knew the routine from his packhorseman days.

Once the belled horses were taken care of, William took the lead ropes of the other two to set out with Ray and Jock to look for wood. "Where are we headed?" he asked them.

Ray, who had fetched a felling axe and a wedge from the camp, spoke up. "The last time we cut wood, it was to the south, down the creek a ways. There's still some down there." He seemed to appreciate that William was not lording it over them, which he could do if he chose to.

"Then that's where we will go," said William.

Ray reached out to take the lead ropes of the horses. William gave him one of them, but when Jock offered to take the other, he shook his head and said, "I have it."

They turned south from the camp, leading the horses along the edge of the creek, skirting a stand of tall oak and sweetgum trees with cane growing beneath. For quite a distance the forest floor had been picked clean of dead-wood, though eventually they came upon a few large pieces, still relatively solid, brought down by a recent storm. They chopped them into lengths of about three feet, which they bundled together and tied to one of the packsaddles. Then, going a little further, they came to a spindly oak tree that had long since given up the ghost, shaded out by tall trees towering above it. Though dead, the wood was still hard.

Ray handed the axe to Jock.

"I ain't no woodsman," said Jock.

"Just see what you can do to it," said Ray.

Jock laid into the tree with the axe, but to little good effect. The chips that came off were small ones, and he hit several glancing cuts so wild that Ray and William stepped further back.

"You swing that axe like a washer-woman," said Ray.

"I'm just gettin my rhythm," said Jock. He kept at it, landing one sorry cut for every two good ones.

Ray sighed. "We'll be all night getting a rick of wood. Here, let me have the axe."

"You ain't hurting my feelings none," Jock said as he handed it over.

Ray took a whetstone out of his pocket and dressed the edge of the axe blade evenly on both sides. Then he laid into the tree and the large chips began flying. In no time, the trunk cracked and the tree began to list. William and Jock scurried out of the way as it fell to the ground amidst a clatter of cracking limbs.

"Now," said Ray, "let's trim this genelman down to size."

He began lopping off the limbs one after another until the trunk was clear. William and Jock took out their hatchets to cut the limbs to length, while Ray went back to work on the trunk with his axe. In another hour they had reduced the little oak tree to two piles of firewood. Ray used the wedge to split the sections of the trunk into manageable pieces. They bundled up the wood, tied it to the packsaddles, and started back to camp.

It was starting to get dark as they arrived. They unloaded the horses and ricked the wood up near Alonso's cooking fire. Then they hung little bells around the necks of the packhorses and led them down to the creek to drink and graze for a while. By the time they got them back and into the pen, it was fully dark.

Alonso's kettle of soup smelled good, flavored as it was with onions and a few scraps of smoked bacon. In a large cast-iron fry pan he had cooked up a pile of cornbread cakes, made by dropping dollops of batter into sizzling lard in the hot skillet. The men served themselves, slathering the bread with fresh butter. Then they settled in around the fire and began eating hungrily.

"I swear, Alonso, I can't see nothing wrong with this cornbread," said Rufus. "But these beans ain't cooked hardly at all. I can't tell the beans from the pebbles."

"*Tu madre!*" said Alonso. "I can't cook proper beans if I don't have enough time for it."

"My mother what?" asked Rufus.

"*Tu madre es muy gatoy feo!*"

"What did he say, Cudjo?"

"Your mother is beautiful," said Cudjo.

"That's not what he said," said Rufus.

"That's what I heard."

Rufus scoffed. "Let it be, then."

"All I've got to say," said Jock, "is that it's not gonna be my fault if these beans rattle in my stomach tonight and keep everybody awake."

"*Tirato a un poso!*" said Alonso.

"That didn't sound like a compliment, either," said Rufus. "Would you say that to your own mother?"

"My mother's long gone from this earth," said Alonso.

The men heard a commotion down in the swamp, and the dogs got up and started barking. The men got to their feet with guns in hand. Then they saw Cudjo and his dogs come riding out of the darkness.

"Did you find the herd?" asked Rufus.

"Yes, sir, they are over close to upper Four Hole, but not down into the swamp yet. The skeeters is still pretty bad on warm days. The cows are waiting for a hard freeze before they go on in."

"Do they look to be in good shape?" asked Rufus.

"What I saw of them looked good. But I didn't have time to look close."

"First thing tomorrow we'll ride over and see about them," said Rufus. "All of us."

Everyone nodded, and Alonso dished up some beans for Cudjo.

After the men had finished their soup and cornbread, Alonso dug out some sweet potatoes he had baked in the ashes. They took out their knives and split the potatoes open and dressed them with butter, and then they dug in, savoring the sweet treat. Lounging back around the fire, they capped off their supper with cups of cassina tea.

Rufus took his tea and retreated to just inside the opening of the lean-to. William wondered about this, but no one else seemed to pay it any mind, so he turned his attention back to the others at the fire. He was especially curious to learn more about Cudjo, who seemed to know cowtending at least as well as Rufus did. "Cudjo," said William, "I've been told that you grew up amongst cattle herders in Africa."

"I did," said Cudjo. "My people are called Fulani."

"Tell me about them," said William. "I've never heard stories of Africa from someone who lived there."

84

"Africa is a beautiful country," said Cudjo. "We Fulani live in the dry land between the northern desert and the southern grassland and bush. There are not many who can live in such a place, so we travel about in it as we wish. Fulani country dries up for nine months of the year. That is the hard time. Both the people and the cattle suffer, and as the season goes on we keep moving further and further south, looking for water. Then it rains for three months, and that is when we drive our cattle back north to standing water and grass, and everybody has a good time. Fulani people are like birds of the bush—they never settle down."

William noted that he talked as if he were still there, still one of them.

Cudjo took a drink of his tea. "I miss the stories of my people," he said.

"Tell us one," said Ray.

"The old people say we Fulani came from Addam and Addama, who went to the ocean, and there a bull and a cow came up out of the water. Addam and Addama learned how to milk the cow, and then all of them, people and cows, went into the bush together, and there we have lived ever since. The people and the cows are one—we are all Fulani. Here in Carolina it is not so. Here the people are the people and the cows are the cows. And off to market go the cows."

"Didn't you market your cows?" asked William.

"We sell a cow or an ox from time to time, but we do not drive them to market the way you do here. A Fulani's wealth is measured in how many milk cows he owns. We herd our cows on foot, and we treat them gently. That is the Fulani way. We pick the ticks off of our cows every day. We don't whip them the way you do here. The most punishment we give them is to take a staff and rap a stubborn cow on the horns."

"But this ain't Africa," laughed Ray. "Our cows wouldn't even feel a rap on the horns."

"We can't get close enough to give them one," laughed Jock.

"Because you don't stay with them," said Cudjo. "You don't tend them and get to know them the way the Fulani do."

"Miss Rosemary knows her cows," said Alonso.

"Yes, she does," said Cudjo. "She's more like a Fulani than I now am."

"Tell us another story about your people," said William.

"At the end of the rainy season," said Cudjo, "young Fulani men dance the *Geerewol* dance to decide which of them is prettiest. When I was there, I was too young to dance with them, but I saw it done. The boys have their faces painted white—white faces, white eyes, white teeth, all shining. And they wear beads and little bells around their necks. They all stand side by side in a line and dance. Then two or three of the finest young women decide which of the young men are the prettiest. And Fulani women are *so* pretty. They wear bright colors like the birds of Africa. And when they dance in their modest, quiet way, it drives the young men crazy with lust. I remember a song about Juliyama. It is like your cornshucking songs, back and forth like that."

"Sing it for us," said Jock.

"You don't want to hear it," said Cudjo.

"We do," said Ray. "Give us a song."

"It will make me miss my people," said Cudjo.

"We are your people," said Alonso.

"That's what I mean," said Cudjo. "It will make me sad. But here it is. You take the chorus. It's the last of each line. For the first line the chorus is 'Lovely as water.'"

"Go ahead," said Jock. "We'll back you up."

Cudjo closed his eyes and began to sing.

"I sing of Juliyama, a girl as lovely as water."

The others sang the response:

Lovely as water.

Cudjo went on:

"A girl as lovely as milk."
Lovely as milk.
"A girl with eyes of a gazelle."
Eyes of a gazelle.
"She stands as straight as a tree."
Straight as a tree.
"Her teeth are white as fresh milk."
White as fresh milk.
"Her face is clear as the moon."
Clear as the moon.
"Her eyes shine like the sun."
Shine like the sun.

"That's all I remember," said Cudjo, his eyes brimming with tears. "I miss those beautiful Fulani women even more than I miss our stories." He reached over and stirred the fire with a stick, sending a burst of sparks up into the night.

The men fell silent, gazing into the fire. Cudjo's tears made them uneasy.

"What about Venus?" said Jock. "She ain't a Fulani, but she's sure enough pretty."

"She's too young," said Cudjo. "And no, she's not Fulani." He got up and walked out into the darkness.

The silence that followed was awkward. William was more aware than ever that all of the others except Rufus were slaves, with no more freedom than the cattle they were herding. "Back in Scotland," he said, hoping to lighten things, "we Highlanders also loved our cows. The hardest time for us was the winter. We didn't have the canebrakes for winter forage that we have here in Carolina. Our land was poor. We couldn't put up hardly any hay, and we only grew enough grain to scrape by. When the snow fell, and it fell heavy in the Highlands, the cows grew thin as rails. The people were hungry, too, and they would look to lift cows from their neighbors' herds that were in better shape."

"The cowpens here don't raid from each other," said Ray. "But if somebody else's cows want to stray into our range, we're glad to fold them in. And if they're not marked yet, we'll move quick to put our mark on them."

"The cattle raids in the Highlands," said William, "were a game of give and take that evened itself out over time. Every clan chief was expected to prove himself by waging a cattle raid. It made for some good stories. At our frolics, old men would sometimes recite stories in verse about great raids in ancient days."

"Tell us one of them," said Ray, as Cudjo came back and joined the fire again.

"Well," said William, "I can't do it in verse, but here's a story I once heard told by my great granduncle, Rob Roy MacGregor. It's about a vengeance raid he led after a theft of his cows. Now if Rufus was out here with us, he'd probably tell you that he's heard of Rob Roy."

"I have heard of him," Rufus called from the lean-to.

"Why don't you come out here and back me up," William called back.

"I'm fine where I am," answered Rufus.

William looked quizzically at Cudjo. "He's of the mind," Cudjo said quietly, "that if there's anyone out there in the dark that wants to shoot us, it's the firelight that makes us good targets."

"Who's out there wanting to shoot us?" asked William.

"Indians," said Jock.

"Not likely," said Ray. "But there's all manner of scoundrels in these parts."

"More than anything," said Cudjo, "he just wants to get away from us. He likes to keep his own company."

"Tell us about your granddaddy," said Ray. "This Rob Roy fellow."

"My granduncle, not my grandfather," said William.

"If he's back in your old country," said Jock, "why has Master Rufus heard of him?"

"Rob Roy's name got around," said William. "As a fighting man he gave the English overlords a run for their money. There are a great many Scotsmen in Carolina, and Rufus has heard their stories. But Rob Roy was a cowman, too. I heard this story from him more than once. The way he told it was this. The theft of his cows came in December, before much snow had accumulated on the ground, but the air was already very cold. The cattle raiders had a head start. Rob Roy got up a small party of his best men and they jogged up into the high hills with only some wheaten bannock to eat along the way. The second day out, Rob Roy woke up early and heard hungry cows lowing. He knew they were his own cows. He woke up his men and they unrolled from their plaids, dressed themselves in the Highland way, and struck out over a rise. There they saw their cows and four raiders, still wrapped in their plaids asleep, ranged around the coals of a fire. Rob Roy and his men, silent as the night, crept up to the sleeping men and laid the points of their swords at each of their necks. The raiders pissed themselves when they woke up and realized what a fix they were in. They had butchered and cooked one of the smallest cows, and the meat and bones were there for anyone to see."

"So he killed them all," said Jock.

"No, he gave them mercy. But he put the fear of God into them. They knew they could have died. He seized their swords as pay-back for the cow he had lost and the trouble he and his men had to go to get back the others. Then he sent them home without their swords, with the understanding that but for his mercy they would have lost their very lives."

"I would have killed them," said Jock.

"And no one would ever tell stories about you as they do about Rob Roy MacGregor," said Rufus, still listening from his retreat in the lean-to. "Now you boys need to turn in. We've got to get up early and go out and look after our herd."

One by one the men got up from the fire and went into the lean-to, where they laid out their bedrolls so their heads were toward the back of the shelter and their feet toward the fire. William noticed that before each man crawled into his blanket, he picked it up and shook it out pretty thoroughly.

Ray saw William eyeing this procedure. "We're snaking our blankets," he said.

"Snaking them?" asked William.

"Yes, sir. Whenever you sleep in a swamp, it's a good idea to do it. Ever once in a while a snake will crawl into a blanket to get warm, and it's an excitin thing to crawl into bed next to a snake. When it's real cold, and the snakes stay in their holes, you don't have to look out for them. But you do in the late fall like this. If the day gets warm enough, they still crawl around some."

William snaked his blanket with special care. He was beginning to feel at home amongst MacDonald's crew of cow-hunters. Whatever the complexion of their skin, or the sound of their dialect, or the philosophy or religion that shaped the world they had come from, they were members of a crew of men who had a job to do. William had worked as a crew member before—in the Highlands, in the tobacco trade, and as a packhorseman in this same backcountry. Now here he was in a new crew, but it felt familiar. Rufus was in command. Cudjo had standing because of his knowledge and experience. Ray and Jock were the beginners among them. Alonso was the butt of their jokes, but he was a canny old devil who held his own and never really bowed to anyone, even though he was a slave.

That was one understanding that eluded William. Most of the men in this crew were slaves. He could not imagine what it would be like to be enslaved. Not that slavery was new to him. It had existed in the world for all time. There were slaves in the Bible. He remembered that one of his book-club mates in Glasgow had once regaled the others with stories of how warring tribes in the ancient days of the English isles would raid each other and enslave their captives. So for all he knew, some of his own ancestors had been slaves. But how did it *feel* to be enslaved? What did it mean that one did not own one's self? Even if a slave owned himself within himself somehow, as Alonso seemed to do, he still was not free to come and go, or even to do what he wished in the place where he was. He was still enslaved. Here was a crew of men who all spoke the same language, did the same kind of work, ate the same food. But there were miles of difference between the enslaved ones and the free ones, and there was no use pretending otherwise.

Before going to sleep, William returned to the firelight and scribbled a few lines in his journal.

Thursday, November 3, Flea Bite Pen
    I find myself in another little corner of the Carolina world—a cow camp, where if not careful one can find a snake coiled up in one's bed. Rufus seems well fitted to this life. He understands very well these borderlands and this way of herding cattle. And from what I have seen so far, he seems to manage his crew well enough, though he tends to be a bit hard-nosed.

Rosemary is much in my thoughts. I have no hope of winning her. She as much as told me to give it up. If I had a drop of consideration in my veins, I would leave her alone and not bother her anymore. But if she keeps on dogging my thoughts this way, any drop of consideration I might have will be too small to save me from keeping on as a pest to her and an embarrassment to myself.

I divert myself with this philosophical question, also very much on my mind. Are we humans such flawed creatures that all our social arrangements must ultimately fall apart? Why does MacDonald's cowpen, which formerly seemed an isle of tranquility, now appear to be struggling for its very life? Why can't families, enterprises, states go on forever? Why build if nothing lasts?

9

Cut Nose

In the chill air of the next morning, the men set out early to hunt for the herd. As the sun climbed higher in the sky, they rode west about three miles through the pines and wiregrass, coming at last to the floodplain forest of upper Four Hole Swamp, bordered all along with tall cane. The cows had moved on from where Cudjo had seen them the night before, and it was impossible to tell which way they had gone, the ground being too trodden with their comings and goings to reveal a clear pattern. The crew split up, with William and Cudjo heading north, skirting the outer edge of the canebrake, and Rufus, Ray, and Jock skirting it down towards the south.

As William and Cudjo rode along, the tall cane leaned over toward them, waving lazily in the wind. William kept expecting to see the cows around each new bend, but after riding for almost half an hour, Cudjo pulled up. He used the tip of his lance to turn over a dried up cowpie. "They ain't up thisaway," he said. "We woulda come up on them by now. Let's turn back."

Returning the same way they had come, William entertained himself by watching Samri, Cudjo's black-mouth yellow cur. He seemed tireless. Standing about knee high, he was flop-eared, lanky, and looked to be able to keep up with the horses all day. "How did Samri get his name?" he asked Cudjo.

"In the Fulani language, Samri means chief." Cudjo laughed a little. "He is the chief, I can tell you. He learns quicker than any dog I've ever seen. Most any dog can trail cattle, but Samri can wind them. He sniffs the breeze and finds them when there ain't no trail. Many a time he's found a cow for me that I never could have found on my own. That comes in mighty handy in these swamps. And it don't hurt none that he is fearless, and he will go after anything or anybody that comes at me."

"Chief Samri," said William with a chuckle. "And what's the story on your big gray dog?"

"Bruto ain't that smart," said Cudjo. "But he's got some wolfhound in him, and he's so big he ain't afraid of anything either. He backs up Samri."

"The three of you make up a crew all your own."

"You could say that," said Cudjo. "I would not want to be without my dogs."

They rode southward to the place where they had begun and then rode on beyond, covering ground already covered by the other cow-hunters. Before long they came upon a group of about thirty cattle.

"Yep, they're down this way," said Cudjo.

After pausing to count them, they rode on and found more and more of the herd in similar-sized groups as they approached the mouth of Big Flea Bite Creek. Here the creek had grown much larger as it flowed into the expanse of slow, black water that was Four Hole Creek.

"I reckon Rufus and the others have done been here and gone on further," said Cudjo.

"How come the cows split up into small bunches like this?" asked William.

"They have their own pecking order, and they all know their place in it. They do better when they split up and spread out. More forage to go around. The lead cows are the ones that know where the best grazing is, and they have followers that will go with them, little herds inside the big herd. These cows have to look out for themselves. There's not enough forage in one place to keep a big herd together."

"They look well fed," said William.

"They'll skinny down before the winter is out," said Cudjo. "But then they'll fatten back up on summer forage before market time next fall."

They rode around the cows, looking them over. William could see that they were not all struck from the same mold. Far from it. They were sleek, tidy animals, short-haired, long-legged, barrel-bodied, and most of them, especially the steers, had long, upswept horns, though some few had shorter horns. Their colors were likewise varied—many were light brown to tan, while others were black, black and white, reddish brown, and brindled. They were notably larger than the shaggy little Highland cows William had herded as a boy. The full-grown cows looked to weigh as much as six hundred pounds or so, and the bulls and steers as much as twice that. All of them were notably skittish. When he and Cudjo came into view, they would stop grazing, bunch up closer to each other, and realign themselves warily to watch the mounted men. They were so alert they made William feel heedful, defensive. He wasn't sure what it would take to set them off.

Before long, Rufus came in sight, riding up to where they were.

"We've seen about a hundred head," said Cudjo. "The same ones you've seen, I'm sure. There weren't any to the north."

"That's what I figured," said Rufus. "They've already split for the winter. I expect the eastern bunch has hived off and headed over to Halfway Swamp. I want you two to go find their trail and track them down. Check em over, see what shape they're in. Count them. Then come back and we'll see what we have, all in all."

William and Cudjo turned back to the north, skirting along the cane with Samri ranging around out in front with his nose to the ground, Bruto following close behind.

"How does the herd know when to split?" asked William.

"They do it when cold weather comes," said Cudjo. "There's two main bunches, and each has its favorite swamp. Our eastern bunch is quite a bit smaller than the western bunch. Even so, we'll have plenty on our hands keepin' up with 'em."

Eventually Samri picked up the scent of the errant cattle, and William and Cudjo followed the dogs as they sniffed and tracked off toward the northeast. The trail was strong, but they had to follow it a good nine miles to lower Half Way Swamp, where they came upon the eastern bunch grazing on the young, tender cane at the edge of a vast canebrake. From the high ground where William and Cudjo sat on their horses, the canebrake looked like an endless green lake. Overhead the sky had grown dark, clouding over as evening drew near.

"It's too late to do a headcount and get back," said Cudjo. "Let's set up camp for the night. I'll show you where." He led them to a spot of high ground near a small stream where the framework of the shelter Cudjo had occupied the previous winter was still standing. The two men dismounted quickly and cut enough foliage to fashion a crude roof. It was just large enough for the two of them to lay out their bedrolls, and it would shed only some, not all, of any rain that might fall. Cudjo assured William that when they returned after reporting back to Rufus they would construct a water-tight cover that would keep them warm and dry during the coming winter. For now they built a small fire and ate some beef jerky for supper.

William was beginning to feel fortunate to be partnered with Cudjo. He already admired the man's competence. Although he did have doubts about that lance. Wouldn't a musket be better? He wondered if the lance might be some kind of affectation. As they lingered by the fire, winding down before turning in, he broached the subject. "I thought that was an African spear you are carrying," he said, "but Alonso tells me it is a Spanish lance. Can I see it?"

"Sure," said Cudjo, handing it over.

It was about twelve feet long, very light and smoothly finished, apparently made of hickory. The steel point was shaped like a long willow leaf. William touched it lightly. It was razor sharp. "Wouldn't you feel safer carrying a musket?"

"No, sir. Gun powder can get wet in these swamps."

"Do Jamaican herders use lances to drive cattle?"

"No, sir, not most of them. They mostly use a *garrocha*—a goad-stick. It is a kind of *lanza,* but a crude one, with just a little spike in the end. But if you're careful, you can use a *lanza* like this one to goad cattle. Some Jamaican herders do. And with a *lanza* you can kill just about anything."

"Even a wild bull?"

"Yes, sir, you can kill a wild bull as dead as a stone."

"Even if he's charging at you?"

"That's the only way. He's got to be charging at you."

William laughed and shook his head. "Now I don't believe you."

"You are wrong not to believe me. You just have to know how to do it. You have to anchor the butt of the *lanza* in the ground, you see, and then you can spear him in the heart when he charges you."

"You make it sound easy," William chuckled.

"It ain't easy, but it can be done. To kill a bull with a *lanza,* you need five things. If you've got those, you can do it." He fell silent.

William laughed again. "You're not going to tell me what they are?"

"I will if you want to hear it."

"I do."

"I'm not joking you," said Cudjo. "This is all you need, these five things."

"I'm listening," said William.

"One, you've got to have a strong *lanza* that will bend but won't break."

"Like this one," said William, gripping the lance in his two hands and using all his strength to bend it just a bit.

"That's right," said Cudjo. "Two, you've got to get the butt of it planted solid in the ground. Three, you've got to have the courage to kneel down and provoke the bull so he will come straight at you."

93

"That's where I fall out," said William.

"Do you want me to stop?" asked Cudjo.

"No, go on."

"Four, you've got to know where his heart is and how to aim the *lanza* right at it. And five, you've got to jump out of the way just as he hits the *lanza*. A dying bull can pile right onto you and crush you if you're not quick."

"You sound as if you have actually done it," said William.

"I did it once in Jamaica," said Cudjo.

"Then I suppose it can indeed be done. Show me what you did." William handed him the lance.

Cudjo got to his feet, and in the firelight he squatted down, stuck the end of the lance into the ground, and then he leaned it down so that the point was only about a foot off the ground. "First you got to get him to come at you in the right way." Cudjo imitated the bellow of an enraged bull. "That gets his attention. That brings him in, because, you see, this *lanza* looks like nothing to a charging bull."

William got up, walked out, and looked back to see what a bull would see. Cudjo was right. A bull would only notice the man, not the lance.

"You got to be steady while he comes charging at you," said Cudjo, "and when he gets close, you raise up the *lanza* so it's aimed at his heart when he runs up against it." Cudjo raised the lance to the height of a bull's chest, then nimbly jumped aside.

William shook his head. "I'm not at all sure I could do that."

"You could do it," Cudjo said. "You'd know that if you wavered, you would be dead."

"I'll stick to my musket," said William.

"And I'll stay with my *lanza*," said Cudjo. He got up and stretched and headed to his bedroll in the shelter.

William fetched his journal and wrote a few hurried lines beside the fire.

Thursday, November 3, Half Way Swamp Camp

Now I see why people in these parts call us cow-hunters. These piney-woods cows pretty much do as they please, and we spend all of our time out hunting for them. That is, we don't hunt them to shoot and kill them. We hunt them just to find them.

I find that my comrade in cow-hunting, Cudjo the Fulani, is a man among men.

After closing his journal, William snaked his blanket and crawled into it, shielded above and below by his oilcloth, and quickly fell asleep. But soon he awoke to the sound of wolves howling back and forth to each other in the swamp. Every so often a panther would yowl, a sound uncannily similar to that of a woman screaming. He lay there for a time. It all sounded close by. "Are you awake?" he finally asked Cudjo in the darkness.

"Yes," answered Cudjo. "Don't mind that music. Wolves and panthers hide out in the swamp by day and come out to hunt deer at night. They don't get along very well with each other."

"Like cats and dogs," said William.

"They are both after the same deer. But Samri and Bruto are on watch. We can sleep."

"If that bunch will quiet down," said William. He tried to go to sleep again, but as the wolves moved further away, a light rain began to fall, dampening their fire and dripping through the flimsy roof of their lean-to. Sleep seemed impossible.

Then next thing he knew, William was awakening at dawn to the sound of lowing cattle. He got out of his bedroll and walked a few steps into the woods to relieve himself. In the distance he heard bellowing sounds—two large animals fighting. Was it bears? Bulls? He threaded his way toward the sound through the dripping foliage, and as he drew closer he recognized the bellowing of bulls, a sound he knew from his youth. Moving cautiously, he stopped finally at a cedar thicket bordering on a small savannah. As he peeped through the foliage, he saw a large, enraged black bull goring a smaller brown bull that was down and struggling. The black bull thrust his horns again and again into the downed bull's body, humping his massive shoulders and neck, tearing muscle and cartilage, blood spurting from his victim until he ceased to struggle. The victorious bull lifted his head. Blood covered his long, narrow face, black as night, and the massive horns that crowned it. Through the cedar boughs William saw that the bull's nose had a deep, blood-smeared gash across it diagonally from side to side. It looked more like a scar than a fresh wound.

William was at a loss about what, if anything, he should do. Was this simply a contest for supremacy between two bulls in MacDonald's herd? Or was one of the bulls an invader? He was too new at the job to know their own bulls by sight. He turned and headed back to get Cudjo, but before he got far, he encountered him jogging toward him, lance in hand, to investigate. Samri and Bruto were beside him.

"Were those our bulls?" Cudjo asked.

"I don't know. One of them is down. Dead I would say."

William led the way back to the cedar trees, Samri and Bruto dashing out in front, their tails wagging excitedly. As William and Cudjo pushed through beyond the cedar trees into the savannah, they saw that the bull that had done the damage was gone. They walked over to examine the dead bull.

"That's one of ours," said Cudjo. "What did the other one look like?"

"Big, solid black. He had a scar across his nose. A big, deep scar."

"That ain't one of ours," said Cudjo. "None of our bulls is solid black. He must be a *bravo*."

"Maybe he's the one that's been stealing the cows," said William.

"Might be."

"Then let's go after him." William looked around, noting with exasperation how far he was from camp. He had no musket, no horse.

"We will," said Cudjo, "but first let's butcher this dead one and carry some of the meat down to the cowpen. We don't want it to go to waste."

"Ride clear back to the cowpen? That will take all day. I want to get my horse and gun and go after that *bravo*."

"Did he see you?"

"No."

"Then he won't be far away when we get back. There'll be plenty of time to hunt for him. But meanwhile this dead bull ain't lost to us. We can take his meat and skin back to the cowpen."

"He's lost to the market," said William.

"But he ain't lost to our stomachs."

They cut the bull's throat and bled him as best they could. Then they skinned him where he lay, and put the skin aside. They cut off the two hind quarters, as well as some generous slabs of tender meat from the back and ribs. Finally Cudjo cut open the bull's belly and took out his stomach. Emptying out its contents, he took it to the creek and carefully washed it.

"What is that for?" asked William.

"For Miss Rosemary to use when she makes cheese. A little piece of dried cow's stomach will turn the milk into curd and give the cheese a bit of a sour taste." Cudjo looked down at what remained of the bull. "That will have to do," he said. "We'll leave the rest for Samri and Bruto. What they don't eat, the wolves and buzzards can have."

They went back to their camp and saddled their horses and then led them to the butchered bull to load up the meat. Cudjo took out a small saw from his saddlebag and used it to saw off the dead bull's horns. "That skin is worth good money, and the horns are worth something too," he said.

"For the master," said William, wondering why Cudjo would take such care.

"If he's not feeling too stingy, he'll let me have the horns," said Cudjo.

They went to work and fastened the horns, rolled-up skin, and the bundled meat behind their saddles. Cudjo commanded his dogs to stay, and they were happy to obey, turning their attention to the carcass. William and Cudjo rode directly south, and after seven miles they came in sight of the cowpen.

John and Mars were at the woodpile, John chopping, Mars stacking. When John looked up and saw riders approaching, he struck the bit of his axe down into his chopping block, and he and Mars walked out to greet them. "What's the story of the meat?" John asked, looking without pleasure at their cargo as they met up.

Cudjo and William dismounted.

"We had a bull fight up at Half Way Swamp this morning," said Cudjo, "and one of our young bulls was killed. We skinned and butchered the best part of him so it won't all go to waste."

"Better this than nothing," said John with a shake of his head. "Which of the other bulls killed him? Maybe we should kill that one, too, if he's as mean as this."

"It weren't one of ours," said Cudjo. "Master William saw it happen."

"It was a big, black bull in a perfect fury," said William. "When I came up on them, he had the young bull down and was finishing him off."

"You should have shot him then and there."

"I didn't have my gun with me. I had just gotten up and was out taking a piss."

"No gun?" muttered John. "Taking a piss?"

"Yes, sir. It was dawn."

"A cow-hunter should always have his gun at hand," said John. "So what color did you say he was? A black bull?"

"The biggest I've ever seen," said William. "And he had a big scar across his nose, as if some other bull once caught him with the tip of his horn."

"Och!" said John, shaking his head. "Don't tell me this, I don't want to hear it. A big black bull with a scar on his nose? That was Cut Nose, you saw. How the hell did he get over here?"

"Who is Cut Nose?" asked William.

"He's that black monster you saw, that's who he is. He's the very devil. I once saw him myself, but I never thought I'd have to see him again. He is supposed to be on the other side of the Santee River."

"Where did you see him, Master?" asked Cudjo.

"Last summer I paddled across the river to talk to a pinder over there about trading for some Spanish cows he owns. Jenkins is his name. He told the story of a big black bull that went rogue and had everyone always looking back over their shoulders. The way Jenkins told it, this bull was damn near wild while still in the herd. What made him go rogue was that one day one of the cow-hunters got after him with a whip and laid a sharp lash across his face that cut deep into his nose. The beast turned on him, hooked a horn into his horse's side, tumbled the man off, and gored the horse to death. He tried to do the same to the cow-hunter, but the fellow managed to get to a big tree and put it between him and the bull. The tree was too big around for him to climb, so they circled around on opposite sides until a pack of dogs were brought in to distract the bull. The dogs chased him into a cane swamp, and no one, Jenkins told me, had been able to track him down since. Though now and then they would find a bull he had gored. He seemed to be hunting them down just for the sport of it. That was the story he told me. They named that bull Cut Nose."

"So you didn't actually see him," said William.

"I'm not finished telling it," said John. "Hear me out. The same day Jenkins told me that story, I rode out with him and a young boy of his family to look at his herd. Like I say, I had gone to trade for some cows. We had no more than got there when we heard a two-note call—a low and then a bellow—and right then Cut Nose came tearing out of the canebrake. Now I had just heard the story about him, mind you, not three hours before, and there he was. I like to have soiled myself. And no, I didn't have my gun. Nor did Jenkins, I'm sorry to say. It all happened so fast. There was the bull. He stopped, low-bellowed again, and began pawing the earth as he picked out his victim. But I wasn't waiting. I turned my horse and took out running. All three of us did. The boy and his pony were the slowest, and Cut Nose lit into them. He upended the pony, gored him a time or two, and then he took out after the boy. What could we do? We rode at the bull and yelled our lungs out, but we were nothings to him. He switched his tail at us, that's all. The boy screamed, and that is the last sound he ever made. I wish I had turned away so I wouldn't still have the sight of it in my mind. The bull gored him again, and then he hooked him with his horns and tossed him up in the air like a cat playing with a dead mouse. Jenkins and I pulled back so we wouldn't be next. We watched from a distance as that black devil took to the swamp. Then we went back to get the boy's body. He was Jenkins's step-son. It was a dark day for that cowpen."

"God almighty," said William.

John shook his head. "So now Cut Nose is over here in our neighborhood. He must have swum the river. I never in my wildest dreams thought he could be the one taking our cows. I thought that river stood between us. But he's our problem now, whether we like it or not. And lost cows is only the half of it. He's a killer, and it's not just bulls he kills. They say that every time he licks his nose, he gets so mad he goes looking for a man to gore."

"That's not something I want to hear," said William.

"But that's what we are up against, so keep your gun with you at all times from here on. Now let's take this meat up to the womenfolk. You don't have to tell them all that I said about the bull. Let's strike a lighter tone with them."

They led the horses to the kitchen, and as they approached it, Aunt Sally and Betsy came out to see who had come.

"Cudjo and William have brought us some fresh-killed beef," John said. "Let's set up a plank and sawhorse table out in the yard. We will butcher this meat in no time. Mars, you do the table. Aunt Sally, you get up a big fire to make coals for drying the meat. We'll dry enough jerky here to run the wood-cutters until Christmas."

As Mars was setting up the table out in the yard, Rosemary came in from the barn to see what was going on. Seeing the meat, she shook her head. "I hate to lose a cow," she said, "but I'm glad for some fresh beef."

"Then give us a hand with the butchering," said John. "And this one was a bull, not a cow."

Betsy brought out knives and trenchers. They all took up their knives and began slicing the beef into thin slivers, which they piled up on the trenchers. Soon all that was left was the tender cuts of meat.

"Before we slice the rest of this," said John, "let's cut out a steak for each of us. We might as well make the best of this misfortune."

As soon as Aunt Sally had her fire going good and hot, she got out her long-handled iron frying pan and cooked up a big stack of hoe cakes. Then she made a pot of coffee and commenced frying the meat. As it came done, they stood around the yard eating the impromptu meal with their fingers.

"Well, Cudjo," said William when they were finished, "I don't know about you, but I am fortified enough to go back and see if we can track down that rogue bull that gave us this feast." He was careful not to say "Cut Nose" in front of the women.

"Yes, sir, I'm ready if you are," said Cudjo, reaching for one more hoecake to eat as he went. They walked out to where the horses were penned.

Rosemary followed after them, coming up to walk beside William. "You be careful around that wild bull," she said. "And whatever you do, don't you be on foot when you come up on him, like you were this morning. Over the short haul, a bull can outrun a horse, but if you get a head start you can get away. Cut Nose would just as soon kill you as look at you."

"How did you know this bull is Cut Nose?" asked William.

"Mars told me. He was there when you talked with Father. There are no secrets in a cowpen."

"I have seen that bull at a distance," said William, "and at a distance is where I'd like to keep him. Musket range and no closer. If he happens to come up this way, Rosemary, don't waste a second. Get yourself to the nearest tree."

"You would be surprised at how quick I can get up amongst the squirrels," she said.

William laughed and mounted Viola. Then he and Cudjo turned their horses and headed out to try to track down the monster bull.

It was late in the afternoon before they got back to Half Way Swamp and the spot where the young bull had been killed. Samri, Bruto, and a great flock of buzzards had been at his carcass, and not much was left except the larger bones. They put Samri on the scent of Cut Nose, and he tracked along following a trail the cows had grazed down beside a little creek that ran through a gully. Bruto trotted along sniffing the ground randomly, happy to let Samri lead. They followed the trail for over a mile, with the tall canes bending over from both sides of the creek, in places touching overhead. It was like going through a green, humid tunnel, with drops of water dripping down here and there when the wind ruffled the leaves. Many animals found refuge in the canebrake, making numerous diversions for Samri's nose to investigate and sort out.

Then, where the little creek they were following joined Half Way Creek, the canebrake opened up and they could see the tree canopy and the sky overhead. Half Way Creek was ten or twelve feet wide, bordered here at the junction with the smaller creek by an open space the cows had grazed down, perhaps two acres in extent. The ground was littered with dry canes, large and small, that had been broken off, and several large trees stood widely spaced. William and Cudjo reined in their horses and listened, but there was nothing around them but dead silence. Samri tracked around the perimeter of the opening and turned up scents going both up and down Half Way Creek. He would start off on one trail and then turn back and try the other, in doubt about which scent to follow. Every so often, he would bristle and growl softly. "He's telling us that Cut Nose ain't far away," said Cudjo. "He's caught wind of him, but it's not coming in clear. We'll split up. I'll take the upstream trail and you take the down. Whichever one of us catches sight of him will crack his whip loud. But don't get in too close. Be careful. And let's hope he hasn't smelled us."

"If we crack a whip, he'll run," said William.

"If he does, it will be toward the whip's sound. So stay on your toes."

Cudjo rode away upstream following his dogs, his lance at the ready. Concerned about the dampness of the canebrake, William paused to examine the prime in his musket. It looked to be dry. Then he took his whip from his saddle and hung it coiled over his shoulder. He prodded Viola with his heels and she set out on the trail between the cane and the water. They had only gone a short distance when she snorted, stopped in her tracks and looked toward the cane. William looked, too, and saw nothing but a wall of green. He nudged Viola, but she would not go forward. Studying the canes, he craned his neck from side to side, peering carefully through them. Then his heart skipped. What were those little patches of black? And that small fluttering amongst the cane leaves? The bull's breath? Was that the tip of a horn? The hair rose up on the back of William's neck as he slowly turned Viola around to head back in the direction from whence he had come. He kept his eyes on the cane. Suddenly the pattern coalesced and he could clearly see, behind the screen of river cane, the great head of a bull, still as a statue, silently watching him like Death himself behind the veil.

His heart beating wildly, William edged away, uncoiling his whip. When he felt he had covered enough distance, he cracked the whip as loudly as he could to call Cudjo and prodded Viola smartly with his heels. As she took out running back along the trail toward the opening, he heard the bull smashing through the canes behind him, coming very fast, faster than he could have imagined. He spurred Viola, glancing back. The bull was already on their tail, lowering his head, closing the distance between them. A horn grazed Viola and she bucked and kicked the beast's head, while William held on for his life. The bull barely slowed down. Viola could not get up her speed as they entered the grazed opening in the cane, and the litter on the ground impeded her. Cut Nose ran up alongside her and hooked sideways, causing her to stagger and fall abruptly. William tumbled out of his saddle, dropping his whip but managing to hold onto his musket. Viola scrambled up quickly, apparently not badly gored. She ran one way, while William ran another. Reaching a very large tree, he put it between himself and Cut Nose. As the two of them circled the tree on opposite sides, William managed to shoulder his musket, waiting for the bull to come squarely into his sights. Then he had him, and he pulled the trigger. The gunlock snapped. Nothing—wet powder! William's mind swam from the shock of it, but then cleared. The tree was too big around for him to climb, but a large grape vine grew up alongside it, its tendrils reaching skyward into the uppermost limbs. He circled around to it, dropped his musket, and grabbed hold of the vine, heaving himself up as fast as he could, hand over hand, his feet searching for purchase, finding it, pushing higher. Cut Nose came around and butted against the big vine and thrashed about in a fury, but William was safely above his horns, clinging to the vine for dear life, climbing higher toward safety.

Then Cudjo and his dogs arrived. William tried to call out a warning, but he was too winded to do so. Nor was it necessary. Both man and dogs knew what they were coming up against. Samri ran in and nipped at the bull's hindquarters, Bruto did likewise, and Cut Nose spun around and tried to hook them. But these dogs knew bulls from long experience and easily scampered out of his way. Cut Nose chased after Samri, tossing his horns, seeming to relish the sport. But he did not know Fulani men and their dogs. Bruto ran in, jumped up, and bit down on one of Cut Nose's ears. The bull was startled and halted in his tracks. Bruto growled, holding onto the ear. But then Cut Nose bolted up into the air, shook his head, and sent Bruto flying. Cudjo rode forward, making a quick dash alongside him and thrust his lance into the bull's shoulder and quickly pulled it out again. Now with both his ear and his shoulder bloodied, Cut Nose whirled around and went after Cudjo, hooking the padded covering on his horse's flanks. But he was harried by dogs again nipping at his hindquarters. The bull came to a stop and shook his horns angrily, pawing the dirt from the ground, trying to decide whether to go after Samri, Bruto, or Cudjo. The bleeding wounds to his ear and shoulder seemed not to faze him. Cudjo dismounted. William could not believe it. He was going to try to kill him with his lance.

William slid down the grape vine to retrieve his musket. Cut Nose caught sight of him. But the bull hesitated and took his bearings: four adversaries at once. This was too much for him, and with a sudden rush he wheeled and made for the little creek that William and Cudjo had followed down to the clearing. Charging across it in a great splash of water, he set off running up the north side of Half Way Creek. Samri and Bruto commenced crossing the smaller creek to pursue him, but Cudjo called them back. "I don't want to lose a dog," he said.

"I say let's follow him," said William. "That son of a bitch tried to kill me."

"What are you going to use against him?" asked Cudjo. "Your powder is wet."

"How do you know?"

"Otherwise you would have shot him from behind that tree."

"The powder in my horn is dry, and you have your lance."

Cudjo scoffed. "We don't go looking for that kind of trouble. Cut Nose knows we're after him now. He'll go so far into the canebrake we'll never find him, or else he will hide alongside the trail and ambush us as we go by. As long as he knows we're coming, he has the advantage."

"I've got two head of cattle riding on it."

"But you've got to be alive to collect em. You need to wait until you can take him unaware. You know where to look for him now."

William relented and turned to Viola, who was coming toward him through the clearing, jittery and bleeding. The flesh over her rib cage was cut and bruised where Cut Nose had hooked her, but the horn had not penetrated to her vital organs and the bleeding had about stopped. Cudjo smeared a bear-grease ointment on the cut. Viola was able to bear William's weight, but as he hoisted himself in the stirrup, he winced with pain.

"I seem to have hurt my ankle," he said. Standing up in his stirrups, he winced again. He started to dismount, but Cudjo stopped him.

"Stay where you are. It was hard enough for you to get up there. Let me take a look." Cudjo came over to inspect the swelling that was now visible beneath his sock. He took William's foot in his hands and gingerly moved it up and down. "There ain't nothin broke," he said. "If there was, you'd be yelling instead of just gritting your teeth. It's a sprain. A bad one, I'd say."

William leaned down and felt the swelling. It was considerable.

"You'd best go on back to the cowpen," said Cudjo. "You'll not be any good out here until that ankle clears up. Back there you can take it easy and get it healed sooner." He smiled. "Miss Rosemary can nurse you."

William scoffed. "I'm afraid my nurse would be Betsy. Like as not, she'd sprain my other ankle." But he understood that he would only be a dead weight on the cow camp. He knew he had to go to the cowpen.

They rode back to their camp, where William let Cudjo pack his gear behind his saddle while he himself stayed on the horse. "We never did report back to Rufus," he said.

"I'll go tomorrow," said Cudjo.

"And I'll get back here as soon as I can," said William. "You be wary of that bull." Then he turned and headed out once again toward the cowpen.

It was past dark when he got there. Butch and the bulldog came out barking, and then the door of the house opened, soft light spilling into the darkness as John came out.

"We found Cut Nose," said William. "We didn't get him, but he damn near got me."

"Tell me you had your gun this time," said John.

"I did," said William, "but it did me no good in that swamp. The powder was damp and it misfired. Cudjo got his lance into the bull's shoulder, but that was only a pin-prick to him. He was wanting to kill something, us or the dogs, but when he realized he was outnumbered, he took off into the cane."

William dismounted. His ankle had grown so tender he had to grab hold of his saddle to keep from falling.

"What happened there?" asked John.

"Cut Nose knocked me from my saddle. I must have landed wrong on my ankle. It is worse than I thought."

"So that's why you're back," said John. "Bring in your bedroll. You can sleep by the fire tonight and for as long as it takes you to get well again. At least you were wounded in the line of duty. Though you might have taken more pains to keep your powder dry. That was an opportunity that may not come again."

Rosemary had come outside while they were talking. She came over and leaned down and felt William's swollen ankle with her hands. "I'll be right back," she said and went into the house. She returned with a corked bottle in her hand and gently removed his shoe and stocking. "This liniment will help." She sprinkled some of it onto her hands and gently rubbed it on the ankle. She then untied his bedroll from his horse and handed it to John to carry inside. "I will take Viola to the pen and attend to her," she said to William. "You need to go inside and take a load off that ankle."

She started toward the barn with Viola.

"Rosemary," her father called after her. "Look inside the barn and see if you can find that old stick of a crutch I used when I had that game leg. Billy is going to need it."

"I know where it is," she said.

Inside the house, William and John sat down at the table in the light that came from the fireplace. William propped his foot up on the bench. There were only the two of them, Betsy and her children having already gone to bed. John broke out a bottle of rum and poured William a cup of it straight. "This will help," he said.

William nursed the rum along, and the warm glow soon took his mind off of his ankle. Before long Rosemary returned from the barn. Having her sitting opposite him at the table, seemingly turned kindly toward him, was medicine all in itself. She was anxious to hear what had happened with the bull, and he replayed the scene from start to finish. The rum made him eloquent, and she and John listened with great interest.

As he finished, Rosemary put her hand on her heart. "I feel as if I were there," she said. "My heart is pounding. You were lucky, William MacGregor, to have got out of that fracas with nothing worse than a sprained ankle. That was too close for comfort."

"I have Cudjo to thank, or I'd be up in that tree still," said William. "But at least I am getting to know my foe. Mister Cut Nose and I became well acquainted today."

"Let the next meeting be in a pot of stew," said Rosemary. "And that's him in the pot, not you."

"But how to get him in the pot?" said John.

"Aye," said William. "There's the rub. But I do intend to do it."

As the fire died down, they headed for bed. Rosemary made William a pallet on the floor, and then she went up to her loft. William rolled up in his blanket, but before settling down to sleep, he wrote a few lines in his journal.

Friday, November 4, MacDonald's Cowpen
Today I had a tangle with Cut Nose—a monster of a bull—a tower of muscle, bone, horn, and vile temper. My left ankle is so badly sprained it will hardly bear any weight. The best thing about it is that I will be laid up for several days in the cowpen with Rosemary as company.

10

The Fragrance of Rosemary

William's sprain was debilitating, but the swelling, everyone agreed, was not as bad as it might have been. At first he had to hobble around the cowpen using John's old crutch. The crutch was a crude affair, made from a length of hickory with a U-shaped crotch wrapped with rags on its upper end, and with a stub of a lateral branch positioned where he could hold onto it, giving him additional support as well as a purchase on the crutch itself. Because he was a little taller than John, he had to bend over slightly to fit himself to it, which limited even more what he could do as he hobbled about, making him feel tired and that much more useless. He hated being a cripple. Here he was disabled just as he had begun to win a place for himself amongst the cow-hunters. He felt cast adrift in dead water.

The trauma of his encounter with Cut Nose was slow to abate, and he replayed it over and over in his mind. First there was the sheer terror of it. Then there was the failure of it. How much better would his standing at the cowpen now be if only he had managed to kill that bull? He had taken care to check the powder in the pan of his musket. It had seemed dry. So what had happened? Was it simply that gunpowder can never be trusted in a swamp? Or did it get wet when he rode Viola up along Half Way Creek trying to get away from the bull? And beyond all that, where had Cut Nose got to with MacDonald's cows? Finding them could make all the difference in what this year-long stint at the cowpen would profit him.

The one benefit he got from his sprained ankle was that for a while he could do as he wished each day, and this meant he could spend time around Rosemary. She had ministered kindly to the sprain, but was this simply the kindness of a friend or of a sister? Not that he was in any position to expect more. Only if he found a way to have prospects as a husband—a seemingly impossible requirement—could he expect more from her than simple kindness. But discouraged as he was by the hopelessness of his situation, he could not but think that if she were ever to turn her heart to him, they would cherish and love each other forever. Yet for now he could do nothing but bide his time.

Rosemary was most often at work in her dairy, though now in the cold season of the year she had less to do there than she did in spring and summer. In the fall the cow-hunters let most of the calves and their mothers out of the pen and onto the range to roam, keeping only a small number of them penned for Rosemary and her crew to milk. On his second morning as a cripple, William made his way out past the pens and found her in the little dairy churning butter. She was seated on a stool beside a five gallon churn, a tall vessel made of wooden staves hooped together, more narrow at the top than at the bottom. Butter churns were much the same everywhere, this one being similar to the one William's mother used in the Highlands. It had a tight-fitting lid with a hole in its center, and through this hole the butter was churned with a long stick of wood that had an X-shaped dasher attached to its bottom end. With her right hand Rosemary was thrusting the stick and dasher up and down, up and down in the clabbered cream.

"This fool clabber has gotten too cold," she said. "I've had it in the kitchen warming it by the fire, but now it's lost its heat again and the butter is not clumping." She got up and walked over to the door and shouted: "Daphne! Go to the kitchen and fetch me a kettle of hot water." William had passed

Venus and Daphne on his way to the dairy. They were out by the corncrib milling corn in a wooden mortar made from a hollowed-out section of an upright tree trunk, the two of them alternately raising and letting fall their heavy pestles into the grain-filled hollow, singing a work song to speed the task along. He was sure Daphne would not mind taking a break from this boring work.

While Rosemary waited, she sat back to exchange pleasantries with William. He noted that she seemed to be genuinely enjoying his company. A little while later Daphne came into the dairy with the kettle of hot water and handed it to Rosemary, who poured a bit of it into the churn, stirring it with the dasher and reaching in to test it repeatedly with her finger. "It can't be too cool or too warm. It's got to be just right." Satisfied, she handed off the kettle to Daphne, who carried it back to the kitchen to put it back onto the fire.

Rosemary began churning again. "You won't laugh at me, will you, if I sing to make the butter come?"

"Certainly not," said William. "I can think of nothing more pleasing." He could, but he kept that to himself and sat down on an upturned, empty keg, smiling a little as he watched her work. In a clear, strong voice she began to sing a simple song, repeating it over and over as she churned up and down in rhythm with her chant:

"Come butter come,
Come butter come,
Billy standing at the gate,
Waiting for a butter cake."

More than one interpretation of this little musical performance ran through William's mind, though he could not tell whether the song was intended for him specifically, or merely for a make-believe Billy who was always the lucky fellow in this verse.

Finally Rosemary could feel that the butter had clumped together. She removed the top and used the dasher to press most of the butter against the side of the churn, where she collected it, drew it out, and put it in a crockery bowl. Picking up a small wooden paddle, she fished out the smaller bits of butter that remained in the churn and added them to the bowl as well, pressing them into the larger mass. Then she rinsed off the whole bowl of butter with a splash of cold water, added salt, and used the paddle to mix and compact it, forcing out the remaining buttermilk. The butter made, she packed it portion by portion into a carved wooden mold, turning out each portion into a squat, cylindrical cake. Finally she poured the buttermilk from the churn into an earthenware jar and put a lid on it. This would go into the spring house to be cooled in the water trough.

"What will you do with all this butter?" asked William. "It looks like it's enough to feed the king's army."

"It's not that much. This time of year, with not many cows to milk, we eat all the butter we can make. In spring and summer we have a lot more. Then we wrap the cakes in cornshuck leaves and pack them in kegs. Salted butter will keep for quite a while, and it brings five or six pence a pound in town."

William looked up at the several cylindrical cakes that were wrapped in cloth and stored on a high shelf in the creamery. They were much larger than the ones she was making. "Those are some very large butter cakes," he said.

"Very funny. I know you know a hoop of cheese when you see one. Those are still aging, but we've cut into one of them already. It does not taste as good as it will next spring, but I'll slice you off a piece if you want."

She took down a hoop that had a V-shaped piece taken out of it, cut a hefty slice, and handed it to William. He bit into it with relish.

"This is very good," he said. "Just a hint of sour in it."

"It is nice of you to say so. It's yet too bland for my taste." She put the wheel of cheese back on the shelf and began tidying up.

"I like hearing you sing," said William. "You have a pretty voice."

"I hope it's tolerable. I'm most always either talking or singing. My mama used to say she couldn't wait until I learned to talk, and then once I did, she couldn't wait until I learned to keep quiet. Fact is, I never did manage to."

"Sing me another song."

"Well, I don't know about that."

"Don't tell me you are shy."

Rosemary laughed. "I'll sing you a song, and you can judge whether I am shy or not."

"I think I already know the answer."

"Wait and see. This song is 'The Keys of Canterbury.' I learned it from my mother. You'll have to use your imagination—it is sung in two voices." Rosemary glanced at him self-consciously and then looked away. She began the first verse, singing in an unadorned, masculine way. Hers was a big voice, and the way it welled up to fill the dairy surprised William.

> "O Madam, I will give to you
> The keys of Canterbury,
> And all the bells in London

Shall ring to make us merry,
If you will marry me,
If you will marry me."

The next verse was a response, for which she switched to a sweetly feminine voice ornamented with a fetching vibrato.

"I shall not, Sir, accept of you
The keys of Canterbury,
Nor all the bells of London
Shall ring to make us merry,
And I won't marry you,
And I won't marry you."

At times her voice would break prettily, ornamenting her words with feeling. William found the words coming directly at him as an artless art, as if to
say, "I've got a story to tell you, and here it is." Though he had no reason to
think she was singing especially for him. This seemed to be the way she would
sing for anyone. For the next verse she switched back to the masculine voice
and then kept on going back and forth:

"O Madam, I will give you
The golden keys of my heart
That we may join together
And never more may part,
If you will marry me,
If you will marry me.

I shall not, Sir, accept of you
The golden keys of your heart
That we may join together
And never more may part,
And I won't marry you,
And I won't marry you.

O Madam, I will give you
A gallant silver chest,
With keys of gold and silver

And money at your request,
If you will marry me,
If you will marry me.

I shall, Sir, accept of you
A gallant silver chest,
With keys of gold and silver
And money at my request,
And I will marry you,
And I will marry you."

William chuckled and shook his head at this turn in the song. But then came another turn:

"O Madam, I can now see
That money for you is all;
The golden keys of my heart
Mean nothing to you at all,
So I'll not marry you,
So I'll not marry you.

Alas, this seals my fate, Sir,
An old maid I will be,
I'll get myself a rocking chair
And sit me under a tree,
If you won't marry me,
If you won't marry me."

William applauded. "What a mess that turned out to be," he said. She drew back her head and looked at him. "For the lovers, I mean," he said laughingly, realizing that his words could be misinterpreted. "The song was grand. Your voice is beautiful. And no, I would not say you are shy. You don't hold back a whit when you sing."

"I don't agree that they are true lovers in the song," she said, "or it might have turned out differently for them."

William wondered what she was saying. Was there a message in that for him? If so, he could not decipher it, nor think of a clever reply. "Perhaps you could give me another song," he said.

"Not now," she answered. "I have work to do." And with that she got up and picked up the jar of buttermilk to take it to the spring house. He let her go, though everything in him wanted to follow along after her. Was he making progress with her, falling behind, or treading in place? He could not tell. But if he was not making progress, he wished he had never heard her sing. That voice of hers pierced him to the heart. Having heard it, he would never be able to forget it. The level of his misery had just been raised a notch.

By the fifth day, William's ankle had healed enough for him to limp around without using the crutch. He was still too crippled to return to the herd, but now he could get around the cowpen with less impediment and he could help out with light duties. He spent time tending the wound inflicted on Viola by Cut Nose, which was healing well enough, and he made sure she was well fed.

In the second week of his convalescence—the nineteenth of November—a cold northern wind blew through. The night temperature plunged to well below freezing and it was still very cold the next day. From past experience, John and his daughters knew that the cold was almost certainly here to stay for the winter, and that meant it was time to kill some of their hogs and cure the pork. November, William was told, was the best time for killing hogs, not only because the cold weather would keep the meat from spoiling while it cured, but because this was the season when the hogs were fat from having feasted on acorns and chestnuts. It was also good, John said, to kill them when the moon was past full and waning, so the meat would cure well. Fortunately the moon was where it should be, though if it had not been, John assured him, they would have gone ahead anyway. William was glad to have some interesting work to do. He had slaughtered cows and deer, but never hogs. Pork was a staple in Carolina, and he needed to know how to lay it in.

As the day unfolded, the cowpen went into action. Down at the timber camp, without being told, Liza realized that everything favored a hog-killing, and she walked the four and a half miles to the cowpen to lend a hand. An area near the barn was set aside for the butchering. The first thing they did was to build a fire under a big cast-iron pot full of water, heating it until it almost boiled. They all got together and dragged over an old sled to serve as a butchering platform. Venus got up a bucket of hot water and some lye soap and scrubbed it down. Everybody honed keen edges on their knives.

John selected the first hog he wanted to slaughter, and he and Mars herded it to the slaughtering stand in the pen. The bulldog and the feist did their part, barking at the hog and backing him against the fence, while John, axe in hand, positioned himself and struck the hog a killing blow to the head.

They drew out buckets of scalding water from the kettle and quickly poured it into a big rain barrel that they had set slant-wise into a shallow hole in the ground. John kept track of the temperature of the water by periodically dipping his thumb into it. Too cool and the hog's hair would not loosen; too hot and it would make the hair harder to scrape off. When the temperature was just right, John, Betsy, Liza, and William each took hold of one of the pig's legs and heaved him head first into the barrel, scalding him just long enough for the hair to loosen. Then they pulled him out and did the same to his rear end, and then pulled him out again and laid him on the sled. Working together, they quickly scraped off the scalded hair with old knives and scrapers that were sharp enough to scrape but not sharp enough to cut into the skin. This done, they slit the rear legs between the tendons and the bones, inserted a gambrel through the slits, and then hoisted up the carcass to hang upside down from an elevated pole raised up between two forked posts. Working it over, they poured small amounts of scalding water on any places where hair remained and scraped it off until all the skin was clean and smooth.

John used his knife to cut off the head. He then cut open the belly and removed the intestines, from which he cut off about a yard of the lower end and laid it aside. He also took out the bladder and put it with the length of gut.

Next the liver, heart, and kidneys came out and were set aside for the kitchen. Mars took the small intestines to the little creek and cleaned them out and left them to soak in the water. Some of these would be chittlins—not to everybody's taste, but good to some—and the rest would be used as casings for sausage. Returning from the creek, Mars picked up the piece of gut John had laid aside, carried it over to the edge of the pen, and emptied it. Then he flung it up to an overhanging limb of a tree, where it wrapped around the limb and hung there.

"What is that for?" asked William.

"It's a winter feast for chickadees," said John. "Just keep your eye on it. They wait all year for this suet."

They turned next to the butchering of the carcass. On hand were two large earthenware jars, one for lean meat trimmings for making sausage and another for fat that would be rendered into lard. From the hanging carcass they cut away the leaf lard and threw it into the lard jar. Then John used his knife to make a long cut down the hog's back in the center of the backbone, after which they took the carcass down and laid it on the sled again. John took a sharp axe and chopped down close to both sides of the backbone, which they then lifted away, leaving the carcass severed into two halves.

John and the girls began butchering out the cuts. First they sliced the tenderloin away from the backbone. Then they cut away the two sections of ribs. Finally they cut the shoulders and the hams away from the side meat, and then cut the latter into bacon and fatback.

John walked away from the crew and went over to rebuild the fire under another pot of water. The day was young, and he wanted to kill and butcher an additional hog or two before it was over. While waiting for the water to heat up, he came back over and picked up the bladder he had set aside earlier. Holding it up and waving it, he called to Betsy's boys. They came running and stood about eagerly as John washed the bladder and then used a piece of sinew to tie its larger opening to a short length of hollow cane. The smaller hole he closed with a knot. He then handed the bladder to the older boy, who grinned happily and then took a deep breath and blew into the cane with all his might until the bladder inflated. Holding his thumb over the hole in the cane, he handed it back to his grandfather, who blew more air into the balloon and then took a peg from his pocket and tightly plugged the hole. Tossing the toy to the boys, he returned to stir the fire under the pot while they ran off to play.

Betsy, Liza, Rosemary, and William remained at the butchering sled trimming the big cuts of meat, throwing the lean scraps into the sausage jar and the fat into the lard jar. Mars was here and there, running errands that needed to be done. As the big cuts of meat were finished, Mars carried each of them up to the smokehouse and laid them on the large wooden shelf built along the inside walls, where John would soon slather them with salt. At one point William looked up at the piece of gut hanging in the tree. Two little black-capped chickadees had already found the suet and were pecking at it eagerly.

The three sisters worked quietly for a time, all of them joined together in the same task. After a while Rosemary tried to lead the others into conversation. "How is it going with the woodcutters?" she asked Liza. "We've not heard anything from you since the cornshucking."

"Let's not go back to the cornshucking," said Liza. "But as for the woodcutters, things have been going as well as can be expected, I guess. Though Swan has about had his fill of cutting timber. All he talks about is building a grist mill on Poplar Creek. He is sure it would be successful if Papa would let him do it. With so many farmers and planters moving into this country, they are going to want their corn ground by a proper mill, so they can use their workers to better effect than spending all their time pounding meal in mortars. I am sure Venus and Daphne would be in favor of having a mill nearby."

"I guess most everyone at this cowpen would like to see a little light on the horizon," said Rosemary.

"Rufus talks that way, too," said Betsy. "He says that everything is closing in on the cowpen with things as they are. If it is to survive at all, it will have to find a way to a brighter future."

"I suppose we should have spoken this way at the cornshucking," said Rosemary, "instead of voicing only our complaints. Though I'm not sure it would have helped."

"What about you?" asked Betsy. "What is the light in your future? I've never even heard you speak about your hopes."

"If I did, it would be just one more thing for you and Liza to belittle."

"Oh, that is not true," said Betsy. "Look at us. Here we are working together, making sausage to carry us all through the winter."

"Well, then," said Rosemary, "I've got to say that the only light I can see for me is to leave this cowpen and get myself into some better situation."

"That is drastic," said Liza. "Just how do you propose to do it?"

"I am looking to marry."

"Well, look at us," said Betsy. "We're married, and we're still here."

"But it need not turn out that way."

"Is your husband-to-be near at hand, or far away?" asked Liza, looking for what she might see in William's face. But William kept his face carefully blank.

"I don't know where he is," said Rosemary. "But my dream is to marry a planter, a man who can afford a town house in Charles Town. I hope to have four children, and all of them will thrive and all will be educated in a real school."

Liza snickered.

"And why don't you wish for the moon while you are at it," said Betsy. "There is not a planter out there who would look twice at you. To them we are lowly cowpen people and nothing more. How do you plan to get around that? Or are you starting to think of yourself as more than a pinder's daughter, too good for the likes of us? You certainly do think you're too good for Rufus and Swan."

"I do not," said Rosemary. "You asked me what my dreams are, and I have told you. I should not have done. None of this is helping us to get this sausage meat chopped. We don't need to be falling out again."

The conversation of the three sisters faltered, and they worked on, mostly in silence. When the meat was all chopped up, they put it into a large wooden bowl and mixed it with ground-up sage, salt, a little brown sugar, and a dash of red pepper. The sausage made, they packed it into entire corn shucks, tying off the ends with pieces of string. Mars carried the sausage to the smokehouse to be hung from the rafters, bringing the work on the first hog to an end.

So it went without reprieve until sundown, as they killed and butchered two more hogs. William thought the job was over then, but Rosemary informed him that several tasks still remained to be done, though not by them. Tomorrow Venus and Daphne would fill the cast iron pot with the fat trimmings and render them down into lard, which they would dip out and store in earthenware jars. The residue from this rendering, the hard, brittle cracklin skins, would be kept and eaten as is or crumbled up and added to cornbread batter to make cracklin bread. "And then there is the smoking of the meat," she said.

"Who does that?"

"Father. He will let no one else touch it."

"Is there so much to it?"

Rosemary patiently explained that her father would treat the large cuts of meat with salt for six weeks or more and then hang them up to dangle from the smokehouse rafters. Down below the meat, on the dirt floor, he would build a small, smoky fire using green hickory wood and corn cobs, and he would keep it going for several days until the smoked meat turned amber to mahogany in color and was permeated with enough of a smokey smell to keep insects at bay. With repeated smoking to renew its protection, this meat would keep until the peach trees bloomed in the spring. "And if you put it in fly-proof cloth sacks," said Rosemary, "it will keep for a year or more."

"I take it that the reason your father won't let anyone else touch it is because only he can smoke a ham the way he thinks it should be done," said William.

"That is exactly so," said Rosemary. "You are beginning to understand him."

For dinner Aunt Sally cooked up pan after pan of sliced liver sauteed with onions, a delicacy everyone had been craving since the last hog-killing. Along with it she served baked sweet potatoes and hoe cakes. The tired crew were so hungry that they ate with little conversation, and afterward they turned in early to their beds. William managed to write a few lines in his journal.

Saturday, November 19, the Cowpen

   Today I was finally able to be of some real help to the MacDonalds as they butchered three of their hogs. Every part of the pig except the squeal and the tail went into the larder in one form or another. Even the tail is not always wasted.

They told me that sometimes they sew two little buttons as eyes on the meaty end of a pig tail, and then give it to some unsuspecting person as a prank gift. But no one seemed to be in the mood for such this year.

Betsy and Liza cajoled Rosemary into revealing her dreams for the future. It turns out she does indeed dream big. So much so, her sisters ridiculed her. Witnessing this left me divided. I have to say that I admire Rosemary for wanting more out of life than she can ever find in this cowpen. And I thought the sisters churlish for trying to drag her down to their own level. But on the other hand, I would do better to take the part of the sisters. How could I ever be a player in those high-flying dreams of hers? And yet in my heart I cannot side with the sisters against her dreams. Is this what love entails? It hardly seems right that to wish her well I must dash my own dreams at the same time.

The next day, with his smokehouse full of meat, John MacDonald turned to other things. "I'm riding out to Flea Bite pen today," he said to William at breakfast. "It's time to check on how the cow-hunters are doing. I'll be back by sundown."

"If it's only news you are needing, I could go for you," said William. "I can ride much better than I can walk."

"No, I'll go," said John. "I don't want to send a cripple out into the wilds with Cut Nose prowling about. You would need both feet if he were to get after you." And with that he left the table and went out to the pen to saddle up his horse.

William sat on at the table alone and finished his food. A cripple. Would he never get into the clear with John MacDonald? His ankle was much improved and he could have made the trip, despite the fact that he still walked with a limp.

After finishing his breakfast, he went outside to find what chores there were to do. The atmosphere at the cowpen was significantly brightened by John's departure. After working an hour or so at this and that, he decided to put his ankle to the test with a more strenuous challenge. Searching out Rosemary, he dared to ask her if she could take some time from her work to go walking with him. "I'd like to go some distance," he said. "I want to see how this ankle will do."

To his surprise, she agreed. "I'm caught up enough," she said. "We can go look at the place where Swan wants to build his grist mill, if you think you can make it that far and back."

"I can do it," said William. "How far is it?"

"More than an hour there. And the same back, of course."

"I'll be fine. The ankle is all but well."

"Perhaps you should take along the crutch, in case this much walking weakens the healing."

"I don't need the crutch," said William. "Let's get going so we can get back before your father does."

"We should take the crutch," Rosemary said decisively. "I'll carry it if you won't."

"All right, then," William said with exasperation. "I'll go get it. And I will carry it."

"Good," said Rosemary. "And let's call Butch. He would love a long walk."

With William carrying both his musket and the crutch over his shoulder, they set out on the wagon road that followed along beside Poplar Creek, Butch trotting out ahead of them. Rosemary explained that this road linked the cowpen with Swan and Liza's timber camp down at the cypress tract, where the creek ran into the Santee River. It was a cold day, but the bright sun took the edge off of the chill. Rosemary was wearing her indigo-striped dress and her grey woolen cape with the hood pushed back. She had her hair tied up in a yellow ribbon, and she had a small sprig of what looked to be lavender stuck into the ribbon. At one point William leaned close to give it a sniff. Then he sniffed again. It was not lavender. He laughed. "Are you wearing rosemary in your hair, Rosemary?"

"And what if I am?" she said. "It's one of my conceits, I admit. But even if I didn't share a name with it, I would still love the taste and fragrance of rosemary. It is the herb of remembrance, and though Father doesn't seem to know it, it's also the herb of fidelity. I have been wearing it every day since the cornshucking. Perhaps one day he will notice."

"Your father seems different from when I first met him two years ago," said William. "He was high spirited back then. The hard time he is having these days is clouding him."

"Yes, he has changed. We have never been so much on the outs as we have been since the cornshucking. Mostly he is civil to me, but he is no longer warm. I can only hope this rift between us does not last forever."

They walked along in silence. William could see that the banks of Poplar Creek had once been lined with the same dense canebrakes that grew elsewhere along Carolina streams, but this cane had been grazed down by cattle and knocked back even more by hogs, who had dug up the ground with their snouts to get at the roots. Through the little patches of remaining cane the clear water of Poplar Creek sparkled in the early winter sunlight.

"Billy," Rosemary said finally, "there is something I've been trying to understand."

"What is that?" he asked.

"I've been wondering what keeps you from choosing your calling in life and settling into it? Why are you still floundering around up here in the back-country?"

"Floundering?" said William. "That stings. Though perhaps it's a fair question. Why haven't I found my calling? Well, a calling is a calling, and I haven't yet been called. At least not so as I could hear. In the Highlands I herded cows. In Glasgow I worked in the tobacco trade. None of that felt like a calling. In Carolina I have been a dry goods clerk, a tavern-keeper, a packhorseman, an Indian trader, and now I am back to herding cows, though in a different way than when I was a boy. It is not for lack of effort that I've yet to find my place. I am always in quest of it. But the Caller, it seems to me, has been silent. I've had some fine inspirations, but no way to put them into motion."

"What would you do if you could do anything?" she asked.

"I would be an Indian trader, like Sam Long and James Adair."

"I know them both," she said. "They have taken meals with us at the cow-pen. What is it that keeps you from going into that work?"

"Money and credit," he said. "I don't have enough of either to purchase the goods for a season of trading. And who would risk credit on a beginner like me? I have been saving what little I can scrape together, but it accumulates ever so slowly."

"I don't know what I think of trading as a goal," she said. "Even if you had the means for it, you would be heading out to Indian country every fall and not coming back until spring. Your wife and children would be without husband and father for all that time."

"I've not given much thought to such as that, seeing as how I have neither wife nor child. My only consideration at this point is the money I might earn as a way of enabling me to marry. How my life as a trader might affect the keeping up of a marriage is another matter. But perhaps a trader's wife could be happy with a fine house in Charles Town and the security of a good income. I know there are handsome houses there that belong to traders, and the families in them seem to be happy. Though I've not gone to their doors to inquire about it."

"If you ever do, be sure to question the wife of the house. I have never known of an Indian trader who did not take up with an Indian woman in his trading town. Speaking for myself, I don't care how elegant a house I might have, I would not put up with infidelity. I would like a life that is comfortable in material ways, but that is not enough. I want love and trust as well."

"I've got to confess that I have not thought the trading life all the way through to that extent. But I do take your point."

"What about keeping a tavern?" she asked. "You have had some experience at that. Won't your uncle want someone to take over when he gets old?"

"I had a good dose of tavern-keeping while Duncan was down with the ague this year."

"Was it hard work?"

"Not the hard labor that packing horses or herding cattle is. But there is a lot you have to get right, things you have to think about that you don't have to think about when hunting up cows. I had to buy food and spirits for the place and keep a sharp eye on cost. I had to manage the slaves who keep the day to day operation running."

"That sounds like the cowpen," she said.

"In a way it is," he agreed. "And I had to see to the guests and handle problems that came up amongst them."

"That's like the cowpen, too, with the travelers coming through."

"Well, it is, except that travelers come through the tavern every day, for every meal as well as for the night. They all have to be managed with their different needs and peculiarities."

"So that's what really keeps you busy, then. Servicing the guests. What was it like exactly?"

"Well, the best part, as well as the worst part, is that all kinds of people come into the tavern from all walks of life, bringing in every different religion and philosophy. The conversations at table, I have to say, have been some of the most interesting I have ever heard."

"That sounds satisfying, then."

"It's good enough, but there are problems with it. It often happens that alcohol flows too copiously, and tongues wag too loosely. I've had to break up more than one fight."

"Now it truly does sound like the cowpen."

He laughed.

"So why not set your sights on the tavern rather than the Indian trade?"

"Well, for one thing, Uncle Duncan has recovered from his illness and is now back in charge. There is not enough of a living in the Packsaddle for two men with families. He pays me mostly in room and board. It's true the tavern might come down to me if I hold out for it, but Uncle Duncan could live twenty more years—ten easily. So where would I be until then?"

"I see," said Rosemary, looking down at the path in what he thought might be interpreted as disappointment. "I had not thought of it that way. If that is one thing that keeps you from setting your sights on the tavern, what is another?"

"Another is being stuck in Charles Town tending a tavern, day in and day out, after having tasted the life of the Indian trade. I might have only been a packhorseman for that one year, but it was an exciting life out there in the Indian country. It is another world. There is intrigue and sharp dealing and the political machinations of the Indian nations, and the vying interests of the colonies—not only ours, but those of Spain and France. I have tasted it, and life in Charles Town pales beside it."

"But I've heard enough talk at table to know that the trading life has its hazards," said Rosemary. "Traders get caught in uprisings and are tortured and killed. Their packhorsemen go rogue and make off with their goods. The Indians break into their storehouses and steal all their rum. Not to mention the hardship of their deserted families back home. Though that's the one thing they don't mention when they're out here on the trail relishing their freedom."

"I wouldn't call their families deserted," said William.

"Call them what you like," said Rosemary. "I call them deserted."

There was an awkward silence between them. What did she want him to say? That she was right? As if he had a choice? A life in the trade was a viable option here and now. Tavern-keeping was not. But he did not press the matter. Instead he turned the talk to her.

"Now, I'll ask the same question of you, Rosemary. What do you expect to do in life?"

"I should think that my life is the most open of books. It's father's cowpen, isn't it? Anyone who has seen one day of my life has seen the length and breadth of it. All I have ever known is the cowpen. It's like I said that night at the cornshucking, the cows don't serve me, I serve them."

"Is that it, then? A milkmaid all your life? That's not what you said to Betsy and Liza."

"They asked me my dreams. I don't dream to be a milkmaid. But I am not like a man. I cannot just set out, as you have, to seek my fortune. My only hope is to marry well. And there I have only the power of refusing, not of choosing. So yes, I might be a milkmaid all my life. Doesn't the youngest child always stay home to care for the aging parent?"

"Your aspirations seem to have plunged in the course of a day. Did your sisters pull you down? You work so hard, Rosemary. It's easy to see why you would want a different life, one with time to feed your soul. What is your favorite thing to do?"

"My very favorite thing? I can answer that in a nutshell—I love words."

"Words?"

"Yes, I love the pretty words of the English language. I like to converse. I like to sing and hear other people sing. And I love reading. Problem is, there are not many books to be had between Four Hole Swamp and the Santee River."

"Then we are kindred souls," said William. "I have always loved reading. It is the only way to fully understand the world. Simple experience is not enough. In books we can learn from those who stand at the heights and see the whole of life."

"I read as much for the moment's pleasure as for any grander purpose," she said.

"What books have you read?"

"The Bible, of course. And my mother left me her little commonplace book in which she copied down songs and poems that struck her fancy. You see, I came to my love of words honestly."

"Have you a memory for poetry?"

"Yes. I know some verses."

"Will you recite for me some of the words you love so much?"

"You know I am not shy, Billy. Be careful what you ask."

"I ask it eagerly."

"Then I will recite the prettiest words in the Bible. They are from the Song of Solomon. You have probably read them a hundred times."

"The truth is," he admitted, "I am not much acquainted with the Bible. About all I know of it is what I heard when I studied at school under my Presbyterian teachers."

"Then I doubt you have heard this after all. Presbyterians probably would not approve of it." She composed herself for a moment and then began to recite:

"I am the rose of Sharon, and the lily of the valleys.
As the lily among the thorns, so is my love among the daughters.
As the apple tree among the trees of the wood, so is my beloved among
    the sons.
I sat down under his shadow with great delight, and his fruit was sweet
    to my taste.
He brought me to the banqueting house, and his banner over me was
    love.
Stay me with flagons, comfort me with apples: for I am sick with love.

His left hand is under my head, and his right hand doth embrace me.

My beloved spoke, and said unto me, Rise up, my love, my fair one, and come away.

For, lo, the winter is past, the rain is over and gone; the fig tree has putteth forth her green figs, and the vines with the tender grapes give a good smell.

Arise, my love, my fair one, and come away.

"There," she concluded. "The prettiest words in the Bible. Though I did leave out a few words that muddy the poetry."

"Those *are* pretty words," said William, feeling a warm glow that went beyond the ordinary pleasure of poetry. "But you are right. I'm not sure the Presbyterians know about those verses. At least, I have never heard them quoted in their teachings."

After walking almost two hours, they came to a small shoal in the creek. "This is it," said Rosemary. Sitting down on a fallen tree to rest, they gazed at the stream breaking over the shoal, their thighs lightly touching as if by accident, neither of them shifting to make more distance between them. It was enough to make William forget about the pain that had arisen in his ankle from the wear and tear of the walk.

"This would be a good place for a mill," said Rosemary. "But I know it will never happen. Father goes crazy every time Swan brings it up."

"I don't see why it should be so upsetting," said William. "If there's a demand hereabouts for a mill, it would make great sense to build one. There is plenty of lumber. What is there to lose?"

"You have to think like Father. When he looks at the timber on his land, a mill is the last thing he sees. To him, timber is a crucial source of credit and exchange for the cowpen, like the load they are getting up now to trade for rice."

"I suppose he's the master," said William. "He knows the needs of the place."

"Does he?" asked Rosemary. It was clear she did not expect an answer.

Looking out at the shoal, they fell silent, thinking their own thoughts.

"I will recite you another poem," Rosemary said at last. "This one is a sonnet by Mister Shakespeare. My mother copied it down in her commonplace book." And without further ado, she launched into it.

> "Is it for fear to wet a widow's eye
> That thou consum'st thy self in single life?
> Ah, if thou issueless shalt hap to die,

The world will wail thee like a makeless wife.
The world will be thy widow and still weep
That thou no form of thee hast left behind,
When every private widow well may keep,
By children's eyes, her husband's shape in mind.
Look, what an unthrift in the world doth spend
Shifts but his place, for still the world enjoys it;
But beauty's waste hath in the world an end,
And kept unus'd, the user so destroys it.
No love toward others in that bosom sits
That on herself such murd'rous shame commits."

"Those are lovely words, Rosemary, though hard to understand. And don't mistake me. I am another who loves to read Shakespeare, even though he sometimes writes so true to actual life that he unnerves me. But his words are densely packed. Do you not find them so? It often seems he deliberately half conceals his meaning, as if he wants only the best educated, most attentive listener to understand what he is saying. He must have lived in an untrustworthy world to have been so wary of simplicity and directness."

"In short?" she asked teasingly.

"In short, your sonnet flew right past my ear. Would you mind repeating it?"

Rosemary smiled and recited it again.

"I gather that the poet is chiding a young man for holding back from marriage," said William. "Is that your sense of it?"

"Yes, but the poet is not so much chiding the young man as asking him to consider the consequences of his actions—or lack of action."

"But is it the young man's fault? A man cannot marry until he has the means."

"It is not a perfectly even world," she said. "Sometimes you just have to jump and hope to stay on your feet when you land."

"I have to say," said William, "that for a lover of poetry you seem to me to be as rational and deliberate as a carpenter's level."

Rosemary laughed.

As the afternoon light began to soften, they stood up from the fallen tree on which they had been sitting and began walking back up the road toward the cowpen. Before they were halfway there, William handed his musket to Rosemary to carry, and he put the crutch to work to lighten the load on his aching ankle.

No matter how I look at Rosemary, she is a feast for my eyes. She is beautiful when she works, when she walks, when she sings, when she recites poetry. How amazing it is to find this pearl of a woman in the midst of this rough border-land. She gave me reason today to have hope in my courting of her. But whether I can ever win her or not, it pleases me just to be in the world with her.

11

Four Hole Swamp

John did not come home that evening as promised, having chosen, evidently, to stay overnight at the cow camp. The next morning, taking his time, William packed his gear and saddled Viola. The soreness in his ankle caused by the long walk had been relieved by a night's sleep. He felt mended enough to get back to the herd.

Just as he was bidding farewell to Rosemary and Betsy, they saw John in the distance riding in. "He is in a dark mood," said Rosemary.

Betsy agreed. "You can tell from the way he is slumped in his saddle."

They waited until at last he rode into the yard, grim-faced.

"Is there trouble?" asked Betsy, going over to hold his horse as he dismounted.

"We had another loss of cattle yesterday—at least a half dozen. They were taken from the eastern bunch, near the Cherokee Trail. Cudjo is sure it was cattle thieves who took them."

"Cattle thieves?" asked William. "Not Cut Nose?"

"Human thieves says Cudjo. He is certain of it."

"Did he see them?"

"No, but he read the signs. When Cudjo claims to know something, he is usually right. He says there were three of them."

"What a piece of damned bad luck," said William. "As if Cut Nose weren't enough of a bandit."

"The worst thing about it is I have no way to track down the sons of bitches and get my cows back. I can't go after them myself. I have to go to the cypress swamp and give Swan a hand in getting up that lumber for the rice. We can't do without the rice."

"Rufus could go after them," said Betsy.

"No he can't," said John. "He's got Cut Nose on his hands. Not to mention that every man on his crew is a slave. He can't leave them out there on their own for days on end, much less send any of them out to hunt for thieves in his stead."

"I could go after the thieves," said William. "I have had some experience in hunting down men, both in Scotland and here in Carolina."

"You with a crippled ankle?" John said dismissively.

"It's healed now," said William. "There's no pain unless I walk on it a very long way."

"But you can't do it alone. The thieves would be three to your one. Neither Ray nor Jock would be of any use to you, and Alonso would just slow you down and get in your way. And we sure as hell can't spare Cudjo."

"I know someone who might go with me," said William. "If I can find him, and if he's free to come."

"There's no time for you to go back to Charles Town," said John. "Those thieves could be all the way to the Mississippi River by the time you set out after them."

"This fellow would be in Four Hole Swamp, if he's available at all."

"Are you talking about Jim Mock-Bird, from Sam Long's crew?"

"He's the one. Jim-Bird. He went with me on a manhunt two years back when we tracked down that Creek marauder, Bloody Mouth. Did you happen to notice whether Jim-Bird was with Sam's packtrain when they came through last summer on their way to Keowee?"

"It's hard for me to recollect," said John, "but I don't believe he was with them."

"He has a woman who lives in Four Hole Swamp," said William. "He could be staying there full time these days. If I can find him, and if he will come with me, three thieves against the two of us would not be bad odds. Matter of fact, I would rather have Jim-Bird with me than any two ordinary men."

"Those are big ifs," said John. "But we don't have a better choice of what to do. You had better be quick about rounding him up to join you. The trail of those thieves won't get anything but colder."

"We'll catch them," said William. "Two men on horseback can travel faster than three men herding cows. All I'm worried about is finding where the Indians are living in Four Hole Swamp. You wouldn't happen to know, would you?"

"I have heard stories about them being up in there, but I don't know exactly where they live. Probably near one of the holes. If I was looking for him, I would start with the hole directly south of here, near where Four Hole Swamp and Providence Swamp come together."

"I have ridden along the edge of Four Hole Swamp, but never down into it," said William. "I hate to sound ignorant, but what is a hole?"

"Four Hole Creek is fairly shallow for most of its course," said John. "The holes are places where there are some good-sized expanses of deep water. They are holes in the stream bed."

"That explains that," said William. "But there's one more thing."

"What's that?"

"Jim-Bird will be wanting some kind of pay. We can't expect him to up and go for the pure adventure of it."

MacDonald ran his hand through his hair. "We're only talking about six cows here. But if he does help you find them, one of them is his, I suppose. But the same doesn't go for you. I'm already paying you as many as three cows."

"I'm not expecting more," said William. "And one cow should do it for Jim-Bird. How far is Providence Swamp from here?"

"It must be twelve or fifteen miles. You can follow that strong trail that runs along the eastern side of Four Hole. There's a few hardy souls who live along there. Just stop in and ask about the Indians. They'll know how to find them."

"Then I'd better get going if I am to get there before dark."

"Good luck to you," said John, shaking his hand. William tipped his hat to Rosemary and Betsy and mounted up. "I will be back as soon as I can," he said, and he turned Viola and started out.

"Billy!" said John.

William pulled up and looked back.

"If you find those thieves, kill the bastards on the spot. We don't tolerate cow thieving around here."

William rode southwest from the cowpen to Four Hole Swamp, covering the seven-mile distance in little more than an hour. Then he swung down toward the southeast, following the trail that ran parallel to the eastern side of the swamp through a monotonous stand of tall longleaf pines, the ground underneath covered by a deep mat of pine straw. The trail was at some remove from the swamp forest of the flood plain, running along on higher ground where the creek crossings were narrower. A mile or two down this road, well into the afternoon, William caught sight of a backcountry hunter coming up out of the swamp on foot. He carried a musket in his hands, and he had a freshly taken deerskin and two haunches of venison tied together and draped across his shoulders. He was a solidly built young man, swarthy, with black hair and beard. His features reminded William of Jim-Bird. Was he Indian? White? A mixture?

William reined in his horse as he neared the man and tipped his hat. "Good day, sir. That's a mighty fine skin you've got there. From the look of those haunches, that deer must have been a big one."

"Howdy," said the man, pausing to lean on his musket. "He is a load, I'll tell you. They's some big deer in Four Hole. Good thing I ain't got fur to go."

"I'm looking for some Indians who live in these parts," said William.

"I know who you mean," said the hunter, "but I don't know that I'd call them Indians."

"It's Indians I'm looking for, not whites."

"They ain't white. They'd be the ones you are looking for, I'm right sure."

"But you said they're not Indians."

"Well, they look Indian, mostly, but they don't act Indian."

"How so?"

"Almost all of them talk English. They dress like you and me. They do some hunting, but they ain't chained to the deerskin trade like Indians are. They sell some fish and game to the planters hereabouts. Some of them are slave catchers. The planters make them out to be boogey men to try to scare their slaves into staying put."

"They do sound like the ones I'm trying to find," said William. "Can you direct me to them?"

"I don't reckon they'd want me to do that."

"I don't mean them any harm," said William. "One of them is a good friend of mine. Name of Jim Mock-Bird."

"So you know Jim-Bird, do you?" said the hunter.

"I do," said William. "I spent a year trading with him in Keowee."

"Then I guess you know his Cherokee father."

"His father was a French trader to the Natchez," said William. "And his mother was a Natchez. His woman is a Natchez, too. They all came here to-gether from the west. Except not his father. His father is long dead."

"Then you do know Jim-Bird," said the hunter. "And I'll tell you how to find him. Listen up now, it ain't easy. Go on down this road until you come near to the mouth of Providence Swamp, where it runs into Four Hole. Look sharp and you'll see a path running off to your right down into Four Hole. I'm telling you, you've got to look sharp to find it. Follow that path to a pretty good-sized hole, and right near there you will find their village. It's spread out on some high ground up above the flood stage of the creek. You'll find it if you're lucky, that is."

"Why do I need luck?"

"Those folks ain't looking to see no visitors."

"I'll take my chances," said William. "Thank ye again, and my best wishes to ye."

William rode about another five miles, when to his surprise he found himself not in an airy pine forest with needles underfoot, but in a deciduous forest whose ground was covered with a deep leaf-fall. This had to be the edge of Providence Swamp, and it could only mean that he had missed the path he had to follow to get to where Jim-Bird lived. He backtracked to upland forest, and after some distance he spotted a faint trail leading off to his left. If this was the trail to Jim-Bird's people, he thought, it was clear they did not want to draw attention to themselves.

As he entered the Four Hole swampland forest, he hurried along. The light was dimming as it slanted in through the leafless canopy and fell mottled on the ground. If he did not find Jim-Bird soon, he would have to sleep out amongst the swamp creatures. Not a welcome thought.

At first the forest around him was mostly oak, holly, sweet gum, and pines. Then, as he followed the winding path down into the swamp proper, he came to the towering bald cypress trees with their tapering trunks and reddish bark overlain with grey. Riding through the dank, spongy-earthed woods, he was aware of being dwarfed by the tallest trees he had ever seen. The faint path wound around gigantic fallen trees, some with large root balls heaved up out of the ground next to the holes where they had once stood. With these moss-covered giants lying strewn around, there was no way to travel a straight line through this forest. William kept his eye on the trail that zigzagged among them. If he lost it, it would be very hard to find his way out of here again. But even so, he looked up every now and then to see the tops of these towering trees, craning his neck to the limit. Then he would look quickly back to find the trail again. Each cypress tree was surrounded by a squad of curious, stumpy "knees" coming up from the tree's roots, like so many pointy-headed leprechauns standing sentinel to their trees. Beneath the cypress canopy grew skinny, crooked tupelo-gum trees, with their grey, blocky bark. And scattered about were stands of switch cane growing no more than four or five feet high. This was pygmy cane compared to the tall variety he had become used to. Off in the distance he heard the tense, laughing calls of several pileated woodpeckers, and from closer by came the deep double-rap of an ivory-billed woodpecker foraging for grubs. As he hurried along, the soil underfoot looked to be a dark, compacted mud with puddles of water here and there. The soft, sweet, moist swamp air filled his nostrils.

The rest of the world seemed very far away now. The swamp was mesmerizing. He passed by a small stretch of dark open water, a calm pool reflecting a crisp mirror image of all that was around it. Then he saw a sleek beaver slip into the water and slap its tail, startling Viola. William appreciated the cold air. It was too late in the season, at least, to have to worry about water moccasins.

He kept on along the faint trail for what seemed to be a very great distance. Just as he was beginning to doubt that it was even the right trail, he finally smelled a whiff of wood smoke, and then, soon after, an opening appeared in the forest ahead. As he neared it, he saw on a little rise a pretty good-sized corn field, the bedraggled stalks of last season's corn festooned with withered bean vines. Dead squash vines wound about on the ground below, all of it surrounded by a crude rail fence. As he rode along the path that passed beside the field, he heard dogs barking up ahead.

At the end of the field he came to a house that resembled the Cherokee houses he had seen at Keowee. It was square with woven wattle walls heavily plastered with clay. The peaked roof was covered with slabs of bark, and a thin column of smoke wafted up from a smoke-hole in the center. If anything, the house and its several crude outbuildings were less carefully constructed than Cherokee houses were. Perhaps, he thought, these people have a less secure right to be here than the Cherokees have to be in their own country, and so they invest less in the building of their living quarters.

These thoughts were interrupted by two mongrel dogs who came racing out with their hackles up, barking and growling, frightening Viola, who reared and threatened them with her hooves. A swarthy-skinned man slipped out of some bushes with a stick in his hand, whether cane or cudgel, William did not know. To the dogs he spoke a few words in an Indian language— it did not sound like Cherokee—and the dogs stopped barking and slunk away a few steps, their tails tucked.

"Who are you and what do you want?" the man asked in English, with an accent William had heard before. Like Jim-Bird's, it bore traces of French along with the lilt of an Indian language.

"I am William MacGregor, and I have come to find Jim Mock-Bird. Do you know him?"

"I can't say as I do."

William did not believe him. Clearly, some credentials were needed.

"I got to know Jim-Bird two years ago when we worked for the Indian trader Sam Long. We spent a year together in Keowee."

"Is that so?" the man said. He was still far from revealing anything.

William tried to think of what he could say that would convince this man that Jim-Bird was a friend of his. It probably wouldn't help to talk about the Natchez and the French, as he had done with the earlier fellow. Anyone who knew anything about Jim-Bird might know that much about him. The dogs, he thought. And just then, like a miracle, he heard the yapping of two small dogs further down the path and not yet in sight. Rising in his stirrups, he whistled loudly and called out, "Tazzie, Binkie!" The two dogs, who were just appearing in the distance, immediately stopped yapping and ran a few steps forward, but then pulled up short and yapped again. Then a man appeared on the path behind them. He carried a musket in his arms, and he was wearing a hunting coat that William recognized.

"Howdy, Jim-Bird!" William shouted.

"Well, I'll be dogged!" called Jim-Bird, raising his hand. "I'll be dogged! If it ain't Billy MacGregor!"

William looked down at the man standing alongside Viola and put out his hand. "Billy MacGregor," he said.

"I am Marcel," said the man, reaching up to shake his hand. "Jim-Bird's wife, Gloria, is my sister. In these parts we can't be too careful."

"I understand," said William. Then he prodded Viola with his heels and rode down the trail to where Jim-Bird was standing. William leaned over Viola's neck and reached down with his hand so Tazzie and Binkie could rear up on their hind legs and get a whiff of him. When they did, they remembered him and immediately began leaping up and down. "You don't know how pleased I am to see ye, Jim-Bird," said William as he climbed down off his horse. "I was afraid I was going to have to spend the night with the alligators and wolves."

"You don't have to worry much about wolves. They have just about been killed out of Four Hole. We do have alligators to watch out for, but the cool weather makes them sluggish this time of year. What brings you back in here?"

"I have recently gotten on with John MacDonald as a cow-hunter, and we have just now lost some cows to thieves of the two-legged variety. I am looking for someone to go with me to hunt them down."

"How many thieves are you talking about, and what kind?" asked Jim-Bird.

"Cudjo thinks there were three of them. And I don't have any idea of what kind. But whoever they were, they got away with about a half dozen or so of MacDonald's cattle."

"Which direction did they take?"

"I don't know that either, but I am guessing that they went north up the Cherokee Trail. Of course, that trail could lead to many destinations. What I need, Jim-Bird, is a good man to give me some backup."

"Seems to me that what you need is to learn a little more about the situation. Seems like you're going out blind."

"I have not yet been to the scene of the crime. But we will start there. I understand they left a clear trail."

"Well," said Jim-Bird, "the last thing on my mind of late has been to go out on a manhunt. But let me think it over."

"I would surely appreciate it. I shouldn't think it would take more than ten days, or two weeks at the most. There's a cow in it for you."

Jim-Bird grunted. "I'll need to talk to Gloria," he said. "Even for a cow I'm not sure I'd want to go out. But I'm glad you came. I think about you from time to time and wonder what's become of you."

"It was not easy to get in here," said William. "And then your brother-in-law nearly turned me away."

"We are not in good standing with all of the people who live outside the swamp. We have to be careful about who comes in."

"Who exactly is 'we'?" asked William. "What do you call yourselves? I tried calling you Indians to a hunter I met on my way here, and he wouldn't have it. They're not Indians, he said. Not whites, not Indians."

"Then he knows us better than most. Most of the whites around here call us settlement Indians. We answer to anything. Indians, mostly. I don't mind it. It honors my mother and my wife. But it doesn't quite cover all of who we are. We don't have an actual name for ourselves." He laughed and spread his arms to the little community around him. "We're not exactly like the Cherokee nation. Come on and let's walk down the trail. I'll show you our little settlement while we talk."

William led Viola as they ambled along the path in the darkening swamp. There were several houses strung out along the way, situated in shouting distance from each other, and all of them had resident dogs to give alarm as need be. Even though it was spread out, this was clearly a close community of people.

"They all look like Indian houses," said William. "Does that come from the Natchez influence?"

"Several of us began life as Natchez, but there are some here from other broken nations."

"How was it that the Natchez came to be a broken nation?" asked William.

"How much do you want to hear?"

"I know a little," said William. "But assume I don't know anything, and give me a simple version of the story. I can't leave out of here until tomorrow. I might as well learn a little more while I'm here."

"Well then," said Jim-Bird, "I'll tell it like this. The Natchez were once a famous nation of people who lived on the east bank of the Mississippi River. Our soil was so good it attracted French planters, who built a fort amongst us and began growing tobacco. As time went on, more and more of them came there, and they began to pressure us into working in their fields. Then they got abusive. Eventually the Natchez men got together in secret and decided what they had to do."

"I think I already know," said William.

"And you would be right. They had had enough. They sprang a surprise attack and in a short time killed almost all of the French men and enslaved their women and children. Then they looted and burned the French fort."

As he was listening to the story, William was also marveling at their surroundings. It was as if this community lay in a secret world. The path now led beside the still water of a slough, an old silted-in channel of Four Hole Creek. It was surrounded by tupelo-gum trees that grew right down to the edges of the water. Abruptly, with a splash of water and a whirr of wings, two mallard ducks flew up, a male with his garish, show-off green head and his mate wearing her modest, muted plumage. Like all wild ducks, they hurtled through the air like arrows, heading directly for another pool of water. William now became aware that the small birds of the day had stopped singing and were retiring to their roosts for the night.

Jim-Bird slowed to a stop. "We'd better head back to my house," he said.

"I thought that's where we were going," said William.

"I live back there near Marcel. I was just giving you a tour."

"Well, I do appreciate the tour," said William. "And back to your story, I suppose the French retaliated."

"Yes, it turned out there were many more Frenchmen where those came from. The next lot destroyed our town with cannon and siege warfare. We managed to flee to the western bank of the Mississippi, and we built a rickety fort there, but the French came across and attacked us again and killed and captured most everyone. A few of us evaded capture and fled to wherever we could."

"So," said William, "it was an exodus from the Natchez homeland."

"Yes, we fled to where there were no French. Gloria, Marcel, and several others ended up amongst the Cherokees. My mother and I found refuge with the Savannah Town Chickasaws. It was a comfort, at least, that they were from our same western land."

"Well, I am glad you made it to safety," said William.

"I wouldn't say we are safe. The French want all Natchez exterminated or enslaved no matter where they are. They put out a bounty on our heads, or scalps—whichever. We still feel the need to look back over our shoulder from time to time to see if anyone is coming after us. That's what Marcel was worried about. You could have been a bounty hunter."

"It would take a brave bounty hunter to get back in this swamp alone. How did you get here? And how did you get back together with Gloria, if she was up with the Cherokees?"

"A lot of Frenchmen began showing up among the Cherokees," said Jim-Bird. "They were more interested in plotting against the English than the Natchez. But they hadn't forgotten the Natchez. That was a total defeat they suffered at our hands in that uprising, and they will never forget it. When they learned that there were Natchez up there among the Cherokees, they began plotting to round them up. Gloria and Marcel caught wind of it and got out of there. They came down here to Four Hole to try to stay alive and free. That was in 1733. But there are still today about fifty Natchez living among the Cherokees, and the French still traffic in and out of that country. It feels safer to be down here with the British."

"How did you get here to Four Hole?" William asked again.

"Well, I was on my way with some Chickasaw fellows to Charles Town the next year—that was in 1734. I heard people at MacDonald's cowpen saying that some French Indians had moved into Four Hole Swamp. As soon as I could, I tracked them down, and I was mighty glad to find Gloria among them. We have lived here together ever since."

"Not ever since," said William. "You were up in Keowee with me in '35."

"But my heart was here," said Jim-Bird. "I stayed with the trade one more year and then gave it up to live with Gloria year around."

By the time Jim-Bird's story about the fall of the Natchez nation came to an end, they had gotten back to where his house stood.

"Don't you miss the adventure of being out with Sam Long's trading crew?" asked William.

"Not much," said Jim-Bird. "Come with me. I'll show you why." He led the way into his house. Standing just inside the door was a handsome young Indian woman wearing a white linen shift and a blue apron. She wore her long black hair down her back in a club, done up with strings of white beads woven into it. In her arms she held a strapping infant bound to a cradleboard. When his black eyes caught sight of William, he looked to his mother for assurance.

"Gloria," Jim-Bird said, "this is Billy MacGregor. You've heard me talk about him. He was with Sam Long's trading crew at Keowee year before last.

He's the one I went out with on the deer hunt that turned into a manhunt, when we had to go out after that Creek marauder who was on the prowl."

"I am glad to meet you, Billy MacGregor," said Gloria. "I have heard that story more than once."

"Jim-Bird, you didn't let on that you'd become a father," said William. "What's this bairn's name?"

"So far we just call him Pumpkin," said Jim-Bird. "He got that name before he was born. I thought that was how he was going to look."

Gloria laughed. "I told you he'd have arms and legs. We'll give him a proper name," she explained to William, "when we can get a better idea of what kind of little man he is."

"Right now I am thinking of naming him Horse," said Jim-Bird. "I've never seen such an appetite. He eats more than I do."

William and Gloria laughed, all eyes on the little fellow.

"Speaking of appetite," said Jim-Bird, "we were just about to eat supper. You are spending the night, aren't you? There's plenty of food in the pot."

"I don't believe I could find my way out of here in the dark," said William. "And the food smells wonderful. It has been a long day. First I need to tend to my horse, though."

"You can put her in the pen with mine," said Jim-Bird. "They ought to remember each other."

William went out and led Viola into the small pen near the house, where Jim-Bird's horse looked over at her with interest. After unsaddling her, William tied a little bell around her neck, then carried his saddle, bedroll, and gear with him as he went back inside the house.

"I hope she'll be all right," he said. "She's not used to being in a swamp at night."

"She will be fine. The dogs will let us know if anything is amiss outside."

The inside of Jim-Bird's house was similar to the houses William had lived in when he was at Keowee. Benches for sitting and sleeping were built up against three of the walls. Areas between the ends of these benches were used for storage, as were the spaces beneath them. A hearth in the center of the house was set with a small fire, mostly of coals, and in it were several cooking pots.

"So, some of MacDonald's cows have gone missing," said Jim-Bird.

"MacDonald talks of nothing else. He's lost a great number to the thieving of a wild bull that comes out and then disappears like the mist. That's bad enough, but now some human thieves have struck, and he's too short-handed to spare anyone but me to go after them. The problem is, there's just one of me and three of them. I could use your help. Like I say, MacDonald is willing to pay you a cow, but only if we can find them and get them back."

"Pumpkin's stomach is a bottomless pit," said Jim-Bird. "We could use a cow around here. If we can keep it out of the corn."

"I'll keep it out," said Gloria, who was kneeling at her cookfire, serving up their food into black mottled pottery bowls. "How long will it take you two to find the thieves?"

"I can't rightly say," said William. "They're getting a day's headstart on us. And they may not stop tonight if they really want to put some distance behind them—the moon is full. So it might take us three days to catch them, maybe four. Then we've got to drive the cows back home. I'd say we'd be out at least ten days."

"I'll be fine for that time," Gloria said to Jim-Bird. "If I need help with anything, I can call on Marcel. He has been sticking close to home lately."

"You want that cow, don't you?" said Jim-Bird.

"I do," said Gloria. "I want to make some cheese."

"That's one good thing we got from the French," said Jim-Bird. "Cheese."

"And you," said Gloria with a smile. "We got you."

"*C'est vrai,*" chuckled Jim-Bird. "*C'est très vrai.*"

Gloria handed William a bowl of thick gruel from the pot. Hominy grits. He dipped a spoon into it eagerly, blew on it to cool it, and gave it a taste. "Good," he said approvingly. "But it doesn't taste like the *ganahena* I ate in Keowee. Something is different."

"It's close to, but not the same as, *ganahena,*" said Jim-Bird. "It's a Natchez version. The French call it *sagamité.* My mother once told me that Natchez women know forty-two different ways to cook corn."

"Do you know that many ways, Gloria?" asked William.

"I've never counted," said Gloria. "But corn is what the Natchez people live on. To cook it the same way every day would gag a dog. Our Natchez life was rich when I was a child. If it had not come apart, I know I would have learned forty-two ways to cook corn."

"How much were they like the Cherokees?" asked William. "Is there a great difference among the nations?"

"It's like the hominy," said Jim-Bird. "Alike in some ways, different in others. Living as they did amongst the French, the Natchez held onto old ways of doing things longer than did the Indians in these parts. The nations around here ran up smack-dab against the English, the masters of cut-throat trade and politics. But the French were not as well set up for trading as the English were, so the Natchez way of living didn't get turned inside out so quickly. The biggest difference from the Cherokees is that Natchez chiefs all came from just one of their clans—the Sun Clan—and the Suns held themselves to be above the other clans. So much so, the French saw the Suns as nobles and all the rest of the Natchez as commoners. That wasn't quite how it was, but it was the closest those Frenchmen could come to making sense of Natchez ways. I've heard it said that in ancient times most all of the Indian nations from Carolina to the Mississippi River did things that way, but it was only the Natchez who kept up that way of life into our time. Gloria here was born a Sun. She can tell you all about it."

"Is that true, Gloria? Are you a noblewoman?"

"That's a French idea," she said. "But, yes. Like my mother I was born a *Theloël,* a Sun person. She was a priestess, a healer. The French gave her the name *La Glorieuse,* mocking her because they said she was so haughty and wanted everybody to scrape and bow to her."

"I do not believe she could have been like that," said William. "Not with a daughter like you."

"She was the sister of the Great Sun," said Gloria. "So she was special. It was true the people sometimes carried her seated on a litter. Up on the mound where we lived she always walked around on the earth like everyone else. But down below it was different. Everyone looked up to her. It was her birthright. She expected the French to look up to her as well. They were down below with the other clans, she was above. She was the matriarch of the Sun clan, granddaughter of the Sun."

"The Cherokees would never stand for one clan to set itself above the others," said William. "I cannot imagine it there."

"Yes, I know," said Gloria, "but that is how it was with the Natchez. People said it was that way from old times. Our chief—the Great Sun—was the most senior man of the Sun clan. He lived in our house high up on top of the great, four-sided mound, where the Great Suns had always lived. The Natchez believed that he and all the rest of the Sun clan were descended directly from the sun—the sun that's up in the sky. Every morning the Great Sun would come out of his house and hold his arms up to the sky, tracing an arc from east to west to tell the sun how to go."

"And your mother was his sister, not his wife?"

"Yes, his wife lived down in the village. He would visit her and her children there. The children were not Suns. They belonged to the clan of their mother."

"As with the Cherokees," said William. "And so it was his sister's children, not his own, who would be the new Suns."

"Yes, that is the Indian way everywhere I have ever been," said Gloria.

"Then what about you, the daughter of *La Glorieuse*? Are you now the matriarch of the Sun clan? Will Pumpkin be the Great Sun?"

"Things have changed," said Gloria, seemingly without regret. "The old ways are gone. They just are. But yes, if things were as they used to be, Pumpkin would grow up to be the chief of the Natchez, and he would direct the sun on its course across the sky every morning. But instead he will live out among everyone else in the world, catch as catch can. And there is no longer anyone to tell the sun where to go. It goes where it wants."

William looked at Jim-Bird. "So your son would have been a great chief."

Jim-Bird shrugged. "The Natchez nation is no more. They are scattered to the four winds. Pumpkin is just another settlement Indian, the same as his mama and daddy."

"Doesn't that make you angry?"

"I am half French as well as half Natchez. Where should my anger lie? I am making my way well enough in Carolina. This is the world I was given. Anger would be of no use."

A thought suddenly occurred to William. "If Marcel is Gloria's brother, son of *La Glorieuse*, he himself must now be the Great Sun."

Gloria smiled a little and shook her head. "That was another world."

"Marcel is a very good farmer," said Jim-Bird. "The best around here. His wife hardly has to lift a finger."

"Lucky woman," said Gloria.

"My father was a Frenchman from the city," Jim-Bird said to her lamely. "I do the best I can, but tilling the ground doesn't come naturally to me. Anyway, Indian women are supposed to be the farmers, not the men."

"So which is your excuse?" asked Gloria. "That you're French or that you're Indian?"

"I guess you could say that I'm hobbled both ways. But I'm trying to improve. Marcel sets a good example. In that way he is still highest among us."

"I am only teasing him," Gloria assured William. "Jim-Bird helps me plenty. Especially now that he is staying home instead of going out with Sam Long." Having finished eating her hominy grits, she removed Pumpkin from his cradleboard and let him settle in to play in her lap.

"I've never quite gotten used to the Indian way of tying babies on a board," said William. "It looks uncomfortable to me."

"Do you ever see them crying?" asked Jim-Bird.

"Never. It seems that they only cry when they get taken off the board."

"Pumpkin likes his cradleboard," said Gloria. "Being bound to it is not that different from how he was when he was in my belly, all wrapped up tight and held secure."

"I guess that makes sense," said William.

"And he is safer on his cradleboard," said Gloria. "Babies are bad about crawling into a fire, or into a creek or any puddle of water. It doesn't take much water to drown a baby."

"And snakes," said Jim-Bird. "The board keeps him off the ground. We can prop him up or hang him from a post or a tree, where he can see everything that is going on, just as if he was standing upright."

"It is convenient, I have to say," said William, "and the babies do seem to like it. But I'm glad to see him free for a time. That suits me better as a Scot."

Gloria smiled at Pumpkin and moved him around in her lap so that he could lean back against her and sit upright. She handed him a little rattle made of a small, dried gourd filled with a few pebbles, with a stick through it as a handle. The baby made a little rattling sound as he moved it about, but he did not yet have enough coordination to rattle it properly. Gloria reached down and folded her hand over his on the handle, and she gave it a vigorous shake. The sound startled Pumpkin, and he started laughing a laugh that was hearty beyond his age. He laughed so hard he fell over on Gloria's lap, which only made him laugh even harder. Gloria propped him up again, rattled, and he again laughed and fell over. Now the game was as much about the falling over as it was about the rattle. His laughter was infectious, and soon they were all laughing together with the merry little fellow.

When Pumpkin grew tired of this entertainment, Gloria let him nurse at her breast for a while. Soon he began to get sleepy, and Gloria murmured a lullaby to him, in French it seemed to William, though he could barely hear it. When Pumpkin finally dozed off, Gloria wrapped him tightly in a dressed deerskin and laid him down on the bed she shared with Jim-Bird.

"Was that a French song?" asked William as she came back to the fire.

"Yes, it is French. I learned it from Jim-Bird. His mother sang it to him. She learned it from his father."

"I'd ask you to sing it for me, but I wouldn't be able to understand it. What does it say?"

"It's about a little grey hen that lays her pretty little eggs in a church," Gloria said. "She lays them for the baby who is going to sleep." She smiled shyly and began to sing it softly, though loud enough now for all to hear.

When she finished, Jim-Bird yawned and stretched. "Well, that does it for me. I'm all but asleep. Let's turn in. We have a full day tomorrow."

"Then you are coming with me?" asked William.

"I guess so."

William spread out his bedroll on the floor near the hearth. Before settling down, he wrote a few lines in his journal.

Monday, November 21, Four Hole Swamp

What is an Indian? I thought I knew the answer before I came to Four Hole Swamp. Now I am not so sure. Gloria lived as a child atop a great mound where a chief directed the sun on its course each day. Now she lives in a swamp in the Carolina cow country and sings French lullabies to her child. Her name must be from the old days—Gloria, from her mother's La Glorieuse. What will Pumpkin's name be when they settle on one? Arthur? Bear Catcher? Jaques? Any of those would fit. And yet he will always be seen as an Indian. He has more Indian blood than Jim-Bird does. He'll be called an Indian, treated like an Indian. But will he also read Shakespeare? Will he get himself some farm land and buy a slave or two to work it? Or will he dress in a breechcloth and buckskin leggings and live among the Indian nations that still survive? Maybe he will be a wise man among them and explain to them what their mounds were once used for. I never knew anyone among the Cherokees who knew what Pumpkin will know about the mounds. The Cherokees told me that the spirits of dead warriors live in their mounds. That is all they know. They would never imagine that there once might have been a royal clan among them. They would never allow such a thing now, I know that.

So what is an Indian? What is a Scotsman, for that matter? It seems to me that basically we are all just people. I think I agree with Christian Priber about that.

Seeing Jim-Bird living so happily with Gloria and little Pumpkin is inexpressibly charming. It makes me wonder whether one day such pleasure might be mine.

12

Cow Thieves

William awoke early, before daylight, to the sound of a great horned owl. Its throaty call was all too familiar to him from his year among the Cherokees, who believed this owl to be a favorite of witches. He hoped that neither Jim-Bird nor Gloria were yet awake. If the Natchez were like the

Cherokees when it came to great horned owls, they would think this an ill omen for the mission he and Jim-Bird were about to undertake. Not that he thought such a fear to be unreasonable. The owl's rhythmic five-note call— *hoo, hoo-hoo, hoo, hoo*—sent terror into every small creature that knew to fear its cruel talons and silent nocturnal ways. And if one believed that owls and witches were the best of friends, one could well have a sense of foreboding at the sound of their call. Fortunately he himself was an enlightened Scotsman who only worried about ill omens that emanated from the plays of Shakespeare.

He pulled his blanket tighter against the lingering chill of the night and enjoyed the coming of the dawn. Gradually, as the earliest rays of the sun began seeping into the house, the owl's call gave way to the cheerful calls of daylight birds. A pair of wood ducks conversed in the swamp: *ooEEk,* she said; *jweep,* he replied. A flock of outraged crows cawed at an enemy, most likely the very owl that had wakened William. A wren fussed at Jim-Bird's dogs for merely existing.

Gloria got out of bed and added some small pieces of dry wood to the fire, illuminating and warming the house. Then she put the pot of last night's *sagamité* on the coals for breakfast. While it was heating, she went over and picked up Pumpkin, who was in no mood to wait in line for his breakfast, and she put him to breast.

The two men pulled on their hunting shirts, and William buckled his shoes while Jim-Bird tied on his moccasins. They made quick work of breakfast.

"We will first ride up and find Cudjo and learn what he can tell us," said William. "According to John MacDonald there were clear signs of three thieves."

"We should take Tazzie and Binkie along," said Jim-Bird. "They aren't the best dogs when it comes to tracking, but they have better noses than we do."

"I have a better idea," said William. "I'll persuade Cudjo to let us take his dog Samri with us. He is famous for his nose, and he can lope along in front of horses all day."

"Then that would be better. Tazzie and Binkie can only go so far before they give out. We would have to give them a ride half the time."

While they were fetching their horses and saddling them, Gloria came out with her arm around Pumpkin, who was bound to his cradle board. She handed each of the men a small deerskin-wrapped parcel. "I've packed some trail food. This won't feed you the whole time, but it will do when you have nothing else to eat."

They took it gratefully and mounted their horses. Gloria reached up to clasp Jim-Bird's hand. "Remember that those men are thieves. They are desperate. Be careful of them." Then she held Pumpkin up to him. Jim-Bird leaned down, picked up the cradleboard, and held the baby in his arms, rubbing his nose against his face. "I will be back as soon as I can," he told him. "I'll bring you a little cow." Pumpkin gurgled happily as Jim-Bird handed him down to Gloria.

Through the morning chill Jim-Bird and William rode out along the winding, swampy trail William had traveled the day before. Jim-Bird's two feists at first tried to follow, but Jim-Bird made them stay, pointing back sternly to the house. "You two have to guard Gloria and Pumpkin," he told them as the dogs tucked tail and trotted back home.

Once out of the swamp, they took a trail to the northwest and rode for ten miles or more through terrain that was now familiar to William. When this trail forked, they turned up to the northeast through the piney woods, towards Half Way Swamp. After about eight miles, they came upon a herd of cows grazing along the edge of a canebrake. In the distance they saw a single rider, Cudjo, with his lance. His two dogs came running out to bark at them, but when they recognized William and Viola, they calmed down. William and Jim-Bird rode on over to where Cudjo sat waiting on his horse.

"Cudjo," said William. "This here is Jim-Bird."

"Good day to you," said Cudjo. "I've seen you at the cowpen with Sam Long."

Jim-Bird tipped his hat.

"Mister MacDonald wants me and Jim-Bird to try to find out who or what made off with those cows two days ago," said William. "He says you claim they were two-legged thieves."

"It weren't Cut Nose, if that's what you're thinkin. Samri picked up the trail and we followed it north for a ways. It was men that took them—three of them. They was ridin horses."

"Can you put us onto the trail?"

"Yes, sir, I can. Come on this way."

Together with Samri they all rode out a short distance to a burned-over area on the Cherokee Trail. They dismounted and Cudjo led them across the blackened earth until they came to a wide trail of scattered prints. The cow prints were all mixed together, but easy to see. Not so easy to see were some horse prints, which Cudjo pointed out. "You see, this line of horse prints was laid down *over* the cow prints," said Cudjo. "This means the man on the horse was following along behind the herd." Then he walked over to the right side of the cow prints and pointed out a faint trail of horse prints. "That there's the second horse, out on the right side of the herd." Next, he showed them a third trail of horse prints, almost lost in the brush on the left side of the trail of cow prints.

"How many cows was it?" asked William.

"That's harder to tell. Seven, the best I can make out. We're missin about that many from the herd."

"Can you spare me Samri to use for a few days to track them down? I know you'd rather not part with him, but he would be a great help to us."

Cudjo thought it over for a moment and then nodded. "Bruto can do me for a time. But be careful with my dog. I'd rather have Samri back than any of those cows."

"Let's see if he'll work for us," said Jim-Bird. He motioned for William to come with him and for Cudjo to stay where he was. Then he called Samri over and tried to put him onto the trail, urging him to take the scent on the ground where he was pointing. Samri picked it up and trotted out before them, nose to the ground. William and Jim-Bird followed him until the trail went around a bend and Cudjo was out of sight.

"He likes to work no matter who he's with," said William.

"It helps that he knows you," said Jim-Bird. "He'll do fine. Let's go back and get our horses."

They went back to where Cudjo was waiting for them. He had mounted his horse again, and Bruto lay obediently nearby.

"They've got a better than two-day start on us," William said to Cudjo. "We've got to push our horses to the limit, else we'll never catch them. I'm sorry to keep on leaving you here alone with the herd. And now you'll be short your best dog. But we'll be back as soon as we can."

"I'll get by," said Cudjo. "Take care in comin up on those fellows. There ain't no tellin what you'll run into."

William and Jim-Bird headed out at a pretty fast clip, with Samri running along ahead, sniffing out the trail. The thieves had gone right up the Cherokee Trail with no stopping, trying to put distance between themselves and anyone who might follow. After a time, William and Jim-Bird came in sight of a familiar homestead overlooking the trail near where Ox Creek joined Half Way Swamp Creek. Near here the Catawba trail, running up towards the northeast, intersected the Cherokee Trail, running up to the northwest. This waystation was well known to all travelers in these parts. As William and Jim-Bird approached it, they saw a man out beside the house picking up hickory nuts. They rode over to the fence that surrounded the house.

"Hello, Major Russell," called William, tipping his hat. "Good day to ye."

"And good day to you," said Russell, straightening up and walking over to them. "Now let me think. I've seen you two with Sam Long's crew, haven't I? Your timing is off a mite, ain't it?"

"We are not working for Sam this year," William replied. "We're trying to catch three men who stole some of John MacDonald's cows. Did any such come through here? It would have been day before yesterday."

"I didn't know they were MacDonald's cows, but I did see a small herd come by. There were three men driving them, Indians it looked like. They were in a hurry, and I thought it was odd that they did not stop in."

"Indians, you say?" asked Jim-Bird.

"I'm pretty sure. I was out in the field, a good distance away, and like I say, they moved on through without stopping. But from where I was, they didn't look to me like they were wearing hats. So they must have been Indians. They couldn't have been white men, not without hats."

"What time of day was it?" asked William.

"About noon."

"That helps us," said William. "Thank you for the information."

"I know you're in a rush," said Major Russell, "but it could fortify you to stay for a bite to eat."

William glanced at Jim-Bird, who shook his head.

"Thank you, sir," said William. "It's kind of you to offer, but the trail is getting cold. We'd best get on."

"Then good luck to you. I hope you find your cows."

William and Jim-Bird rode up toward the northwest, and after about five more miles they came to the place where the Catawba trail forked off to the right. Samri paid the right fork no mind and went on straight ahead. Clearly the thieves had not gone to the Catawbas but had continued up the Cherokee Trail. The day was coming to an end, but William and Jim-Bird rode on through the twilight and only pulled off the trail when it became too dark to go further. For supper they ate some of the food Gloria had packed for them—jerked venison and persimmon cakes. The sky was clear, so they rolled up in their blankets and slept with no roof over their heads.

William wrote in his journal.

Tuesday, November 22, The Cherokee Trail

We traveled about 35 miles to a camp north of Major Russell's. A very long day. It would help if we knew what quarter these thieves hail from. If they are Catawbas, they missed their turn. Most likely they are Cherokees.

The next morning they got on their horses and rode hard, following the Cherokee path through rolling sandy hills with little vegetation except longleaf pines and turkey oaks. After a little over thirty miles they came to Congaree. There they went directly to Thomas Brown's store, where Jim-Bird had done some business in the past.

"What is Sam Long doing out on the trail in this season?" Brown asked.

"We ain't working for Long just now," said Jim-Bird. "We're trying to track down three Indians who stole some of John MacDonald's cows. Seven cows it was, to be exact. Have you seen a small herd come through?

"I haven't seen them, but I've heard about them. A fellow was in here just yesterday who told me that the day before that he saw some Indians driving cows north on the trail. That was on Sunday. The store was closed and I was off visiting."

"Were they Cherokees?" asked Jim-Bird.

"I have no way of knowing," Brown said. "The fellow who saw them was one of the new German settlers. He wouldn't have known a Cherokee from a Spaniard, much less another kind of Indian. Can I get you boys anything?"

"No thank you," said Jim-Bird. "After our horses catch their breath, we have to move on. They've got a two day lead on us."

Heading westward, they again rode their horses hard to make good time. Daylight was almost gone when they came to Twelve Mile Creek. Samri had his nose to the trail the whole distance, but when he got near the creek, his hackles rose and he turned off the trail and ran into a grove of trees. The reason why was soon clear. A flock of buzzards was settling down to roost in the trees around a campground littered with the remains of a butchered cow. As soon as the buzzards caught sight of William and Jim-Bird, they flew out for parts unknown. A large meat-drying hurdle stood over the remains of a large fire. Jim-Bird fished around in the deepest part of them and found some live coals. Off to one side William found a severed cow's head. He turned it over with his foot, and sure enough, the right ear bore MacDonald's markings— the tip cut off and an underbit notched out of the lower margin of the ear. He reached down and looked closely at the left ear, parting the hair on it. As expected, there was a small slit at the tip end.

"Well," he said, "that's one of MacDonald's cows we won't be able to recover."

"That may be," said Jim-Bird, "but it works in our favor. They must have spent all night and most of the next day jerking meat on this hurdle, and from these coals, I would say they left out from here this morning. We should catch up with them easily in another day."

"Why did they think they could take time out to slaughter and butcher a cow?" William wondered aloud. "It doesn't make sense." He walked around studying the long bones strewed about. Then he noticed that something was amiss with one of the hooves. He picked it up and sniffed. "Whew, this foot was in a bad way—infected and rotten. They didn't know they were stealing a lame cow. They finally killed it to make better time. But they couldn't bear to lose the meat. I'd say they are hoping we have given up the chase."

Samri was busy pulling a few scraps of meat off the ribs, but the scavengers had gotten most of it. "There's not much of that cow left for us," said Jim-Bird. "Let's build up a fire and lay the long bones on to roast." This they did, and after they had set up a quick camp, they crawled into their bedrolls to sleep.

Wednesday, November 23, Twelve Mile Creek
Another very long day of about 40 miles. These thieves are too meat hungry for their own good. Tomorrow we should discover who they are.

Next morning they got up, fished the bones out of the ashes, cracked and split them with their hatchets, and they feasted on the roasted marrow. They finished off breakfast with some of the parched corn Gloria had packed for them. "Now I'm ready to do what I've got to do today," said William. "Let's go find those thieves."

They mounted up and crossed over to the north side of Twelve Mile Creek, but they had gone only a few miles when Samri hived off to the left of the trail. Jim-Bird tried calling him back, but Samri pranced about wagging his tail, insisting that he knew where he was going.

"Well, if that don't beat all," said Jim-Bird. "Our thieves are leaving the Cherokee Trail behind. They are going westward toward Fort Moore and Savannah Town. I can't rightly comprehend it. Why would they go this round-about way to get from the lowcountry to Fort Moore? If they were coming up from Charles Town, which they seem to have been doin, why didn't they go the usual way, on the trail that crosses the Edisto River?"

"And steal cows on that route," said William, "instead of taking ours."

"I don't know the answer," said Jim-Bird. "But unless they're trying to trick us, I don't think it's Cherokees we're chasin'."

"If they're going to Savannah Town," said William, "they could be Chickasaws. You might know them from when you lived there."

"I can't think of any I know who are foolish enough to steal cows. Not this many cows. They might think they could take one and get away with it, but not seven."

"I have heard that the Savannah Town Chickasaws are having trouble getting supplies from Carolina," said William, "and that some of them are talking about moving over to the Georgia side of the Savannah River."

"I hadn't heard that," said Jim-Bird. "But I can believe it. The Carolinians enticed them to come here for safety from the French, but now that they have pulled them in, they've turned their favors to other Indians that are still out there closer to French influence. These poor fellows here are left to fend for themselves in a strange land."

"Well, they ought to fend for themselves without making use of MacDonald's cows," said William.

Continuing on, they soon came to a strong west-by-southwest trail that ran through the sandy upper fringe of the piney woods. Here the monotony of the pines was broken by oaks and hickories. They made good time, riding steadily along for the better part of a day. As the afternoon waned, the cow pies they were finding along the trail became fresher and fresher, and eventually they seemed to have issued very recently from the passing cows. They pushed on more cautiously, and as the twilight was beginning to fade toward darkness, they smelled a whiff of smoke. "Let's tether the horses and leave the dog behind," said Jim-Bird. "We'll go forward on foot and try to get a look at these fellows."

They tied their horses to a tree, and William walked over to Samri, held his hand up, and said, "Stay!" Samri sat down, hoping that would be enough, but when William did not lower his hand, he lay on down and put his chin on his paws with a little whine.

"Will that do it for him?" asked Jim-Bird.

"Cudjo has trained him to stay, and stay he will."

They eased forward in the dimming light through a grove of trees, and in a little while they saw the flicker of the campfire they had been smelling. Dropping to the ground, they waited for deeper darkness and then crawled forward through a patch of dead grass and weeds. The cows could be heard lowing softly and shifting about sleepily at the edge of a canebrake. In the firelight sat three young men eating what appeared to be beef jerky, no doubt from the cow they had slaughtered.

"We are only about three days out from Savannah Town," Jim-Bird whispered so softly William could barely hear him. "They think they are safe now."

"Let's leave them be for the night," whispered William, "and come back before dawn."

Jim-Bird nodded affirmatively.

They began backing themselves around to crawl out of the brush, but as William maneuvered, he caught a small twig under his elbow and it cracked. At the fire one of the young men looked intently in their direction, then stood up to get a better look. He said something to the others, who stood up and looked all around. All three of them picked up muskets. They began slowly moving in the direction of the sound, straining to see into the darkness.

William and Jim-Bird quietly cocked their muskets and carefully slipped them out in front of them, trained on the young Indians. They also drew their hatchets from their belts ever so slowly and hung them from their wrists, at the ready if needed. William braced himself for the fight, his heart pounding. They waited. The young fellows were nearly halfway to them when a rabbit bolted from almost beneath their feet and went bounding away into the darkness. The three boys laughed and turned back to their campfire.

William and Jim-Bird waited a long while, then crept back to Samri and the horses. After conferring together and laying their plan, they collected a few resinous pine knots from some fallen and rotted pine trees and laid them aside in a pile. They also cut six short lengths of rope. They spent the rest of the night on alert, without a fire, each taking a turn standing guard while the other slept.

Thursday, November 24, on the upper trail to Savannah Town

A mere 25 miles or so today, and our quarry is now in sight. They are three young Indians, probably Chickasaws, immigrants to Carolina the same as I am. I dread having to kill them if it comes to that.

A little before the first light of dawn, with the quarter moon still shedding its light, William and Jim-Bird crept forward to where they could barely see the thieves rolled up in their woolen matchcoats, lying side by side with their feet toward what was left of their fire. Jim-Bird crept into the camp, quiet as the very air, and laid several pine knots on the coals, and then he crept out again. William had his musket at ready in case any of the thieves awoke, but none did. Then he and Jim-Bird circled around and stood behind the heads of the sleeping men. Presently the fire flared up as the pine knots ignited and began to blaze brightly. One of the boys sat up, puzzled by the sudden burst of flame. Jim-Bird's musket clicked loud and clear as he cocked it and touched the end of the barrel to the back of the young man's head. "Do not move," Jim-Bird said quietly, "or you are dead."

The other two stirred and began to rise. William was behind them with his hatchet and dirk. "Don't move," he said, "or I'll kill you." When one of them made a sudden move to get up, William quickly clubbed him on the head with the blunt side of his hatchet, stunning him. "You aren't listening to me," said William. "Now, all of you lie down and roll onto your bellies."

The two clear-headed ones did as they were told, and William used his foot to roll the groggy one over. With Jim-Bird standing where they could see his cocked musket, William went from one to the other tying their hands behind their backs, and then he tied their feet together. Once they were trussed up, he had them roll over on their backs and sit up. They were very young, only boys really. They were dressed for the weather, wearing linen hunting shirts, blue stroud breechcloths, and deerskin leggings and moccasins. Each had a hatchet or war club beside him.

"I think I know you fellows," said Jim-Bird. "Do you remember me from Savannah Town? You have some explaining to do."

The boys were silent. They were shivering in the cold, so William went over and picked up their matchcoats and draped them about their shoulders. Then he stepped back and looked at them with his hands on his hips. "You are in worse trouble than you know," he said. "We have to decide whether to kill you or not, so you had better get busy and explain yourselves. Tell us what you are doing with our cows."

"Stealing them, it looks like to me," said Jim-Bird.

"Can they even speak English?" William asked Jim-Bird. "Maybe you should talk to them in Chickasaw."

"They know English better than I know Chickasaw," he replied. "Especially this one." He prodded one of the boys with his foot. "His father was an English trader. Still is, back out west."

"Didn't he teach you not to steal cows?" asked William.

"We didn't set out to steal them," said the boy.

"What did you set out to do?" asked Jim-Bird. "Why did you go way up north on the Cherokee Trail?"

"We were trying to get home."

"From where?"

"From Charles Town."

"That's not the way home from Charles Town. Why were you in Charles Town?"

"Some western Chickasaws came to Savannah Town on their way to Charles Town," said the boy. He was beginning to find his voice and seemed eager to explain their situation. "They were going to talk with the big men there, to ask for a supply of guns and powder and shot to help them hold out against the French back home. The French are pressing hard against the Chickasaws because they trade with the English, but the Chickasaws are trying to stand their ground. The big men in Charles Town need to help them. They need to help us in Savannah Town, too. We are the ones who guard your western border."

"Is all this to tell us that you tagged along with that crew?" asked Jim-Bird. "You went to Charles Town with them?"

"They know my father," said the boy. "They let us come along."

"Then why aren't you with them still?"

"We got hold of some rum in Charles Town," the boy said sheepishly. "We drank too much. We got into a fight with some Charles Town boys and stirred up a ruckus. The warriors turned us out, told us to get back to Savannah Town the best way we could."

"And so why didn't you go back the same way you came, across the Edisto River?"

"We tried, but the rivers and creeks were running too high from all the rain, so we decided to loop up around Four Hole Swamp and get back that way. We knew it would take longer, but it was better than crossing high water in cold weather."

"So how did that turn into cattle thieving?" asked Jim-Bird. "Going home and stealing cows are two entirely different things."

"We didn't know we were stealing. The cows were just grazing there, off to themselves beside the trail. We didn't want to go back to Savannah Town empty-handed. Everyone would laugh at us. When we left home we were in the company of those warriors. We didn't want to come back dragging our tails."

"But now look what you've gotten into," said William. "You can't go around lifting cows. They all belong to someone who is trying to make a living. The question now is what punishment you'll have to suffer for this crime. I will tell you right now that the man who owns these cows, Mister John MacDonald, wants you dead for what you have done. That was the last thing he told me when I left him. 'Kill those thieves on the spot,' he said."

The boys were visibly shaken by this news, but they did not beg for their lives.

"Let's confer," William said to Jim-Bird, motioning for him to come away out of earshot of the boys. Jim-Bird first looked around the camp and found the boys' stash of jerky and helped himself to a couple of pieces. Then he followed along after William. The three youths remained seated on the ground, securely bound, contemplating their fate.

"I don't want to kill them," said William as Jim-Bird handed him a piece of jerky. He bit into it and chewed it slowly. It had been skillfully dried, not too hard and not too moist.

"But they have to be punished," said Jim-Bird. "Cow thieving is a serious offence."

"Punished, yes, but not killed."

"So what would you do? Whip em?"

Just then they heard a sound, a faint clip-clopping of hooves on the trail in the distance. Samri stood fully alert. They listened as the sound grew louder. Soon they could hear whistling as the rider ambled along. Then the whistling stopped abruptly. After a pause they heard the rider coming cautiously through the trees toward where they stood. Evidently he had either seen smoke from the lighter-wood fire or had smelled it. William and Jim-Bird held their weapons at the ready. Over by the fire the three boys watched, transfixed on who the intruder might be. Perhaps they were hoping for some of the comrades they had left behind in Charles Town.

When the man came into view, William broke into a smile, and the traveler did the same. It was James Adair. "Hello, Mister MacGregor," said Adair, dismounting from his horse. "I never expected to find a tavern-keeper way out here on the trail to Savannah Town. What are you doing in these parts, and who have you got trussed up over there?"

"Cow thieves," said William. "James Adair, this is my partner Jim Mock-Bird. We have tracked down these three young fellows and our cows that they stole, and now we are trying to decide what their punishment should be. That's what brings us here. What brings you?"

"I am riding over to Fort Moore to talk with Richard Kent. He's the commander there now."

"Is this a friendly visit, or is there trouble?" asked William.

"Both business and pleasure. We're working on keeping the Chickasaws on our side of the river. The Georgia traders are determined to entice them over to Augusta. I'm bringing some sweet promises of our own to counter the ones our Chickasaw friends are hearing from over there."

Adair walked over to where the three boys were sitting. William and Jim-Bird followed behind. "I recognize some of you from Savannah Town," said Adair. "Are you thinking of going into the cow-herding business?"

The boys were silent.

"They went to Charles Town with some Chickasaw warriors from the west," said William, "to try to break loose some supplies of guns and ammunition. It seems they got into a drunken brawl with some Charles Town boys and their elders sent them home. They detoured north and lifted seven of John MacDonald's cows as they passed by them. They have already killed and butchered one of them. MacDonald told me to kill them on the spot."

"We didn't know they belonged to anybody," said the boy who had become their spokesman.

"Yes, you did," said Jim-Bird. "You knew you weren't in Indian country. Don't try to tell us you don't know about cowpens."

The boy fell silent again.

"So, are you going to kill them?" asked Adair.

William motioned for Adair and Jim-Bird to come back with him to finish their conference beyond hearing of the boys. "We can't kill them," said William when they got out of earshot. "They're too young. They are foolish, not evil. But they have to be punished enough to feel it. And I have to satisfy John MacDonald that justice was done."

"Why not fine them?" said Adair. "That way, MacDonald will be reimbursed for his loss, and these boys will learn their lesson. What do they have with them? Take it all."

"That would do it," said Jim-Bird. "Three horses, three muskets, a load of jerky. They'd almost rather give you their lives than lose their horses and guns."

"I feel sorry for them," said William. "I'd be willing to let them keep their guns."

"That won't do," said Adair. "You have to take away everything but their lives, or they'll feel triumphant, and the next thing you know they'll go out and steal again. The next pinder that gets robbed is not likely to be merciful. So you wouldn't be doing them a favor."

"He's right," said Jim-Bird. "They have to lose so much that they feel they've lost their very lives. So much that the next time they see a cow, their stomachs will turn."

"I'll escort them back to Savannah Town," said Adair. "Their elders aren't going to be happy with what they have done, but I'll let it be known that they've paid the price. That should get them a bit more mercy on that end."

"Let's go tell them," said William.

They returned and announced the sentence to the boys, who flinched and looked balefully at each other, but did not say a word. They were stripped to nothing, but at least they were alive.

William and Jim-Bird got the cows together along with the three horses, the muskets, and the jerky, and bidding farewell to Adair, they set out to return on the same trail by which they had come. William smiled as it occurred to him that without quite realizing it he had stolen a page out of his granduncle Rob Roy MacGregor's book. It was amusing to try to imagine himself putting this story into verse.

With the cattle to drive and the horses to string along, the return trip was a slow one. It took them five days to travel the eighty miles back to Half Way Swamp. When they got there and found Cudjo, Samri pranced over to him joyfully and pushed his head against his hand to be petted. William and Jim-Bird drove the six cows over to join the herd.

"I thought there were seven in all," said Cudjo.

"One that was lame got made into jerky by the three Chickasaws that stole them," said William. "We have what's left of the jerky."

"Did you shoot them?"

"No. They were just boys," said William. "But we did relieve them of their guns and horses, and now they have to walk back to Savannah Town and explain to their kinsmen why they are on foot and stripped of their arms."

"They were lucky," Cudjo said.

"How has it been here?" William asked.

"It's been quiet. The cows ain't complainin."

"We're going to the cowpen to report to Mister MacDonald," said William. "But first we need to cut out a cow for Jim-Bird. Mister MacDonald promised him one for his help. We need a cow that's giving milk, one with a calf ready to wean."

"I know just the one," said Cudjo. "It's a little cow whose newborn calf was taken by a cougar the other day."

They worked together to cut out from the herd a brown cow with milk in her distended udder. Jim-Bird got a rope around the cow's neck and led her away. William rode out behind Jim-Bird, leading the string of horses.

By the time they reached the cowpen, the sun was going down. John MacDonald came out to greet them. William was hoping to see Rosemary, but she was evidently busy milking.

"Well," said John. "What have we got here? I sent you after my seven cows and here you come back with three horses and one cow."

"Six cows have been put back in the herd," said William. "One of the cows they stole was crippled from the start, and the thieves butchered it for jerky. We've got what's left of the jerky. And we've got the thieves' horses, and their guns, too."

152

"Who were they? Did you kill them?"

"They were Chickasaw boys that got themselves into more trouble than they intended. We stripped them of everything, but we didn't kill them. We ran into James Adair on the trail, and he was going to Savannah Town, so he took them home, horseless and gunless. I don't think they'll steal cows again."

"You don't know an order when you hear one," said John. "I wanted them dead. But I do seem to remember a story about Rob Roy MacGregor that went something like what you have just told me. And I will say that these horses do look like good ones. I'll take one for the cow and one for the trouble I've been through, and you can take the other one, Billy, for the work you did. Jim-Bird has the cow for his pay." He looked over at Jim-Bird. "How are you, Mister Mockbird? I haven't seen you for a while."

"I am well, thank you" said Jim-Bird. "I appreciate the cow."

"I thank you for helping us out," said John. He looked back at the horses and studied them over. "I'll take the black and the bay," he said to William. "You can have the gray."

"I'd be pleased to have her," said William. "I think I might name her Cordelia."

"I'm glad you boys made it back in one piece," said John. "But you should look up 'order' in the dictionary, Billy."

"Yes, sir," said William.

"This has been all the adventure I need for a while," said Jim-Bird. "There's a little daylight left, and the moon will be up early. I'm going to push on and try to get back to my wife. She will be happy to see that I got the cow."

"Stop in the next time you come up this way," said John.

"Yes, sir, I will. I'm mighty glad to have seen you all." William, who had dismounted, shook his hand, and Jim-Bird rode off, leading the cow behind him.

"You might as well sleep here tonight," John said to William. "You can take the house or the barn to spread your blanket in."

"I'll take the barn," said William, not wanting to press his luck with Mac-Donald.

He took Viola and his new horse to the barn, wondering what he would do with the new one when he went back out to the herd. She would be one horse too many. He put the two of them in the pen and went to the corncrib to get corn. Coming back, he met Rosemary coming out of the dairy.

"Did you find the cows?" she asked, although she seemed not to have much interest or to be particularly glad to see him. She looked tired.

"We did find them," he said, "and brought back a few horses to boot."

"How many horses?"

"Three. Your father has given me one of them."

"What will you do with a second horse?"

"Sell her in Charles Town."

"But until then?"

"I don't know. I've been trying to work that out. I don't suppose you would be willing to look after her here?"

"I reckon I can if I must. But it seems like lately every little extra thing that needs to be done is falling to me."

"Should I ask Mars or one of the girls to do it?"

"No, I'll do it. I'll find the time somehow."

"Her name is Cordelia," William said.

Rosemary nodded wearily. "Cordelia. I'll see that she's cared for."

"Thank you, Rosemary," said William. He would have said more, but she seemed to want to be left alone. Feeling he had already imposed too much, he turned away and went to feed the horses.

At supper, Rosemary was still dispirited and withdrawn.

Tuesday, November 29, the Cowpen

This was a rare day when most everybody at MacDonald's cowpen ended up happy. Jim-Bird was happy going back to Gloria and Pumpkin with the cow he earned. Despite being disappointed that we didn't shoot those boys, John was happy enough to have gotten back most of those stolen cows and to have gained three muskets and two saddle horses. I am a horse to the good, and I am happy to be back in the company of Rosemary. Problem is, Rosemary seems more sad and overburdened than I have ever seen her, and I just added another burden by asking her to care for my horse. Would that I could stay on and make amends and raise her spirits in some way. But I can't. Tomorrow I've got to get back with Cudjo to help him hunt cows.

13

Tending Herd

The next morning William rode back to Half Way Swamp. It had only been a month since he had come up from Charles Town to work at the cowpen, but so much had happened during that time, it seemed much longer. Clouds had rolled in during the night, and the air, which had warmed a bit in recent days, had turned considerably cooler. He arrived at the swamp before midmorning and rode past a herd of about forty cows. Cudjo was not with them. Riding several miles further to the east, he found him near a herd of fifty or sixty cows on the edge of a canebrake by Santee Swamp.

"Well, I've finally made it back," William said. "I am sorry to have been so little help to you for so long a time."

"No need to be sorry," Cudjo said. "You got those cows back for us. If we can't keep our cows, we sure can't herd em."

"Any more excitement while I was gone?" William asked.

"Not much. The sun has been shinin, mostly, though that's left us today. The birds have been singin. The cows eatin, gettin on into the cane. There's not been a sign of Cut Nose. He must be deep in the swamp with his cows by now. He might not come out until spring. So I've just been riding here and there, from one little bunch to the next, mostly looking for cows that are calving in case any are having trouble."

"This is a cold time of year for new calves to be coming into the world."

"Our bulls run with the cows all year. We couldn't keep them separate for a single day, much less for the half of the year it would take to bring calves only in spring and summer. When a cow comes in heat, that's it. Every down-wind bull out there comes in like a hornet, his tail up and his stinger out. And he's ready to fight all comers. It can be a hoorah in any season. It's those hoorahs from nine months ago are bringing us calves today. It might be cold, but at least the calves that come in winter get spared the ticks while they're gettin their start."

"We'll remind them of that when we see them shivering in the snow," said William. He looked out over the herd. "These piney woods cows are so tough I'm surprised they need any at all help with their calving."

"They don't need much," said Cudjo. "They don't hardly ever have trouble. There might be a slow-up now and then, but the other cows will gather around to make sure nothing gets at her while she's working at it. Mostly it's only the heifers, what have never calved before, that sometimes need help. That's what we have to look out for now, and there ain't no way to do it except by riding around through the different bunches, keeping close watch. Now, there's some cows that will go off to themselves to have their calf alone, and they'll come back with it in a few days. There's not much we can do for those if they run into trouble. They're on their own, unless we happen to stumble across them."

"How many little herds are we covering?" William asked.

"Five. I've done looked at three of them today. No point in us splitting up for the last two. Let's go down the creek a ways. We'll find those last ones down there. I know there's two cows amongst them that's ready to go, one in one bunch and one in the other. One I thought would calve yesterday, but she didn't."

They rode to where the next bunch was grazing. Cudjo soon spotted the pregnant cow, nervous and pacing around, paying little attention to them as they rode over to her.

"Her water's done broke," Cudjo said. "She's into it." They dismounted and watched the cow struggle to give birth. "If it takes a long time, then we know she's in trouble," Cudjo said. "But here we don't know how long she's been at it."

Very soon, however, the calf's two front feet came out. Several of the other cows in the herd began to mill about and watch the proceedings. The cow strained and worked, and the feet gradually came out a little further.

"It ain't comin out smooth as butter," said Cudjo. "She'll make it on her own eventually, but I'd say we'd do well to give her a hand."

He walked over and grabbed hold of the emerging feet and started pulling on the calf. "You have to learn just how hard to pull," he said. "Too hard and you'll hurt the calf."

"I've pulled out calves in my day," said William.

"That's right. I forget you're not new at this."

At first the calf didn't budge, but then its nose began to appear. Cudjo pulled again, and the calf began to come on out. The cow strained again, and the little sodden lump of a calf fell out onto the ground. Cudjo peeled the afterbirth from its nose and head. William grabbed the calf's hind legs and hoisted it up, giving it a good shake to get its breathing started, while Cudjo knelt down and used his fingers to clear the fluid out of the calf's mouth and nostrils. It inhaled its first breath, alive and healthy.

William laid the calf down gently and stepped back to let the mother get to it. She looked around, and seeing her calf on the ground, she approached it, sniffed it, and began licking it clean and eating the afterbirth.

"It's the eatin of the afterbirth that gives her the smell of her calf," said Cudjo.

"I never thought about that being what starts it," said William. "But I do know you could put that calf in with the twenty others that look just like it, and she'd sniff each one and pass it by until she came to her own."

"Which is why a poor *dogi* stays an orphan," said Cudjo. "A cow don't care to nurse any calf that's not hers. You can't hardly talk her into it."

"I've never heard that word for a motherless calf," said William.

"That's what they call em in Africa, and in these parts as well. It's always sad when we get a *dogi*."

"I've seen orphaned calves get mammied up, back in the Highlands."

"With a lot of trouble you can sometimes do it," said Cudjo. "I'd most rather feed a *dogi* myself than go through all that."

As the cow licked the little calf, it tried to stand up on wobbly legs but quickly fell back in a heap. After failing several more times, it finally got itself up and found its way to a teat.

"That there's a calf and its mammy," Cudjo said. "Let's make a picture of these two in our minds."

William was already doing so. He knew from his days in the Highlands that a good cowman always knows which cow goes with which calf.

A drizzly, cold rain began falling before they found the fifth bunch of their herd. Cudjo was looking for a cow he knew was due, and he soon spotted her inside a circle of other cows that had gathered around her. The small, tan cow kept lying down and getting up again. They rode over close to her and dismounted.

"She's just a heifer," said Cudjo. "And something ain't going right here."

The little cow stayed down on the ground now and strained to push out her calf. Finally one foot and the calf's nose began to emerge. Then all progress stopped.

"One foot is turned back," Cudjo said. "That ain't good." Kneeling down at her rear, he struggled to shove the nose and foot back in and get the hoof of the other foot lined up to come out. William knew from the cow-tending days of his youth how much strength and persistence it took to reverse the course of a birth even a little way. But finally Cudjo got the errant foot situated alongside the other foot and the head. Once the calf had both feet where they should be, it came out "like a rainbow"—as William used to hear it said—in an arc of first the front legs and head, then the trunk, and finally the rear legs and tail.

"Give it a shake, Mister William."

William took hold of the hind legs, lifted the calf up off the ground, and shook it a time or two, while Cudjo cleaned the nose and mouth. But the little calf was inert. William laid it down and Cudjo pressed on its chest several times, until finally they heard the calf take air into its lungs.

"It's all right now," Cudjo said. "Good thing we got here when we did. I've had to cut some dead ones up inside the cow and take them out piece by piece. That's awful hard on the mammy."

"It is," said William. "Oft times the mother dies too."

They waited until the little heifer had licked her newborn clean. Then the calf got up, wobbled around and blundered its way to a teat, where it nursed hungrily. "It may be a cold time to be born," said Cudjo, "but this calf will be all right. The pine needles are thick hereabouts, and that will keep it up off the damp ground. At least it ain't as cold as it might be."

As William and Cudjo were riding back to their shelter, the drizzling rain stopped and the sky began to clear. The air was much colder now. "Let's ride on over to Flea Bite pen," said Cudjo. "I've been living rough for quite a while. I could use some of Alonso's food and a good night's sleep by a big fire."

"I'll not quarrel with that," William said.

They rode towards the west at the fastest choppy little trot their horses would tolerate, through tall, waving wiregrass, now turned golden by the growing grip of winter. At the end of the eight-mile trek, their horses were breathing hard and the light was beginning to dim. They found Ray, Jock, and Alonso sitting around the fire at the camp drinking hot cassina. Rufus was already in the lean-to, but he got up and came out when he saw Cudjo and William arrive, and he settled in with the others at the fire.

"I was starting to think you had headed to parts unknown," Rufus said to William.

"Cudjo and I were hoping to get here in time to eat a decent meal," said William. "Looks like we missed it."

"You fellers are dragging yourselves in here mighty late," said Rufus. "But we'll feed you." He turned to Alonso. "They look a little hungry. See if you can't find something for them."

"Something hot," said Cudjo.

"*Hijo de puta,*" said Alonso. "This ain't a tavern."

"Don't talk to me that way," Cudjo said sharply. William remembered that Cudjo had lived in Jamaica, where Spanish was spoken. "My mother was no whore and you know it."

"Of course I know it," grumbled Alonso. "It is only a manner of speaking."

"Just leave my mother out of it," said Cudjo, settling himself down by the fire. "That's all I'm sayin." Ray and Jock smiled a little, glad to see Alonso called down.

"We appreciate your trouble, Alonso," said William, standing close to the fire to get warm. "This wet cold has got inside our bones. I don't care what you give us as long as it's hot. I'm hungry enough to eat the asshole of a rotten skunk."

"Alonso's food is way better than that," said Rufus.

"*Mierda,*" said Alonso. He put some venison and cornbread cakes in a fry pan and put the pan on the coals of the fire. The cornbread was smelling burned by the time he took up two trenchers and served up the hot food. But hunger is always the best sauce, and William and Cudjo wolfed it all down to the last crumb.

"Tell us about that wild bull you tangled with," said Ray.

"Cudjo got his lance into his shoulder," said William.

"Not by much," said Cudjo. "He didn't even feel it."

"Tell us about it, Mister William," said Jock.

"I'll tell my part of it," said William. "I had the drop on him twice. The first time I found myself with no musket, and the second time my musket misfired. He got the drop on me once, wounded my horse, and ran me up a tree. Mister MacDonald is down on me for bungling both chances."

"He's down on everybody these days," said Rufus. "But at least we know now that it's Cut Nose that's raiding our herd. I've got everyone tryin to find him, but we haven't seen a trace of him. Not a trace."

"I say he's deep in Santee Swamp," said Cudjo.

"But even so," said William, "don't stop keeping a sharp eye out for him. And don't take any chances if you do find him. That bull is a killer sure enough."

"That's what I've heard," said Rufus. "We do want him dead, but we've got to be smart about how we go at it. He ain't worth anyone losing his life."

"Has Mister MacDonald been up here with the latest?" asked William. "I just got back a few days ago from hunting down some human cow thieves."

"We haven't heard about this," said Rufus, perking up with interest.

"Seven cows got stolen from the eastern bunch," William explained. "Me and my friend Jim Mock-Bird took Samri and tracked down the thieves. Turned out they were three young Savannah Town Chickasaws who were out rambling around."

"Did you get the cows back?

"Six of them."

"Did you kill the thieves?"

"We didn't have the heart. They were just boys."

"How did Father MacDonald take that?"

"Not well, I'd say. He is down on me for a long list of shortcomings, and this was just one more. He seems to stay sour all around these days."

"Sour ain't hardly the word for it," said Rufus. "The man's gonna drink himself to death if he don't wake up and see things as they are. Because the truth is, things will never again go for this cowpen as they used to, back when this country was new to cows. It's a sad fact of life that when cow-herders stay in one place for long enough, they wear out their welcome. We've been herding cows between Four Hole Swamp and Half Way Swamp for so long we know all the snakes by their first names. The winter browse in the canebrakes is not what it used to be. Ray can tell you about that. He's been struggling with it lately."

"That's right," said Ray. "Our cows has been crossin over to the western side of Four Hole Creek and gettin into the cane in Bull Swamp, and even into Little Bull Swamp."

"What's wrong with that?" asked William, pouring himself some cassina.

"What's wrong with it," said Ray, "is they's other cowpens over there that run their cows between the North Edisto River and Four Hole. They's some mighty big canebrakes in those parts, but they's already taken."

"Do the cowpens over there own that land?" asked William.

"No, they don't," said Rufus. "Just like we don't own most of the land we are on. There's an understanding amongst pinders that you run your cows in the range where you have always run them, and our range is on this side of Four Hole."

"The trouble is," said Cudjo, "cows don't have no range sense. When they get hungry, they just go to where the grazing is good."

"We've done had a go-round with some of Mister Richard Hearn's cow-hunters," said Ray. "They came across our cows about ten days ago in Bull Swamp and before we even knew anything about it, they had their muskets up in arms. I thought we was going to have to fight a war."

"It was looking like that," said Jock. "We was almost into a sure enough war. That ain't the way cow-huntin is supposed to go. No sir, it ain't."

"Did you tell Mister MacDonald about it?" asked William.

"I did," said Rufus. "But he can't seem to take it in. He thinks everything ought to work as it always has. If you ask me, he is getting too old to be running both a cowpen and a logging camp. The logging camp is up to its neck in troubles, too."

"How is that?" asked William. "I was thinking that Mister MacDonald and Swan would hardly speak, but Mister MacDonald went down there recently to help him out."

"He had to," said Rufus, "whether he wanted to or not. Here's how I understand what's going on down there. I get it from Swan when he's not trying to throw a punch at me. He says that they have already cut the best timber out of Father MacDonald's cypress tract. The way it is now, they have to go further and further into the swamp from the landing, cut the timber and snake it out to the river bank as best they can. It takes more labor than they have to give to it."

"I can't imagine that they have run out of trees along the river," said William. "There's no end to trees along the Santee from what I've seen."

"Yes, but most of them don't belong to John MacDonald."

"Who do they belong to?"

"Big landholders mostly. Speculators from down on the rice plantations. They keep an eye on those tracts, and they won't stand for anyone pirating their timber."

"So Swan's answer to this is to leave off lumbering and build a grist mill," said William.

"He keeps talking about putting one on Poplar Creek," said Rufus. "But ever time he says anything about it to Father MacDonald, the old man shuts him down. He won't hear it. For him, the cowpen and the timber cutting go together. That's what he has always known. That's been his ticket. It's the timber operation that makes the difference when it comes to paying the cowpen's bills and putting food on the table for all the mouths he has to feed."

"The mill would pay," said William.

"In time. But while it's being built and getting established, how's he gonna keep the cowpen from goin under? That's what he worries about. He worries about falling into a hole he can't climb out of."

"Then what's to be done?" asked William. "His whole operation seems close to being stalemated."

"I can only speak as a cow-hunter," said Rufus, "but I think the best thing to do would be to pick up and drive the herd towards the west, to the Savannah River, or north up the Saluda River. Our problems here will be a damn sight worse when more farmers are settled into this country. They don't have no use a'tall for free-range herders. And they're coming in more and more every year. Father MacDonald don't seem to be able to deal with it."

"But you'll run into Creek Indians if you move west," said William, "or Cherokees if you move north."

"Yes, and that will be a problem for them and for us. But it will be like it's always been. They'll have to give way. It may take a scuffle or two, but in the end they'll pick up and move further west."

William tried not to even think about what that meant for the Indians. "You'd be starting over," he said. "You would have to build an entire cowpen—a house, a barn, pens—everything."

"We would. But with everybody working hard, most of that could be put up in the course of a year. But for now we are stuck right here. Nothing will happen until Father MacDonald says so. He's the pinder—the pen belongs to him. If these cows were mine, I'd be on my way. But they're not mine."

As they had been talking, the fire had died down and the chill of the night had settled in. Calling it a day, they made their way to their shelter and crawled into their bedrolls. In weather this cold, it was no longer necessary to snake their blankets.

During the month of December, William and Cudjo settled into a routine of making frequent rounds to check out their bunches of cattle. There was little to relieve the tedium. One day they came upon a cougar dining on a newborn calf it had killed and dragged up into the crotch of a big, low-lying limb of an oak tree. No doubt the cows had given chase, and the cougar was evidently tired and hungry, judging from the oblivious, avid way it was eating. William drew down on it with his musket and killed it with a single shot. "Sorry, old cat," said William. "You should have stuck to hunting deer." The big cat fell out of the tree and the two men skinned it, leaving its carcass for scavengers.

"This skin will make you a fine saddle pad," said Cudjo.

"I was thinking that myself," said William

The only other break in the monotony came in the middle of January, when the weather turned very cold. William layered on almost every piece of clothing he owned—his linen shirt, duffle waistcoat, hunting coat, and duffle cape. But he had no gloves to wear, so his hands were cold, and the cold seeped into his legs and feet.

A deep, soft snow fell, and they had to go out and slog their way through it to make their rounds. The cattle knew the terrain well enough to take refuge in gulleys and other sheltered places. But there was no such relief for their horses, who grew tired of making their way through the snow where it had collected into deep drifts. In the last bunch of cows they visited, they found a red brindled cow with a newborn. She had cleaned it off, and the calf was nursing, but the poor little thing was shivering.

"This one won't make it through the night in this cold," said Cudjo. "We'll have to take it back with us."

They trussed up the calf and tied it on William's horse, letting the mother get a good sniff of it dangling there. She trotted along beside them as they made their way back to their camp. Whenever the cow faltered, Samri ran in and nipped at her heels to keep her moving.

When they reached the camp, they cleared the snow from in front of their lean-to and built up a large fire. The little calf soon thawed and nursed from its mother until it was full. Cudjo tethered it to a pole at the front of the lean-to, and it lay down contentedly in the glow of the fire. The mother stood nearby.

"If it gets too cold during the night," said Cudjo, "we'll bring it inside."

Around midnight, William awoke to the sound of the calf bleating. He got up and went out in the biting cold and put his hand against its body. There was not much warmth in it. It was trembling all over. Untying its tether, he led it inside. The mother followed them until she stood just outside the shelter. The little calf lay down next to William and went to sleep. William lay awake for a time and then rose up on his elbow and reached for his journal. There was just enough light from the moon reflecting on the snow for him to scratch out a short entry.

Sunday, January 15, Half Way Swamp
A cold, snowy day. The cows are on their own. The exception is a poor little newborn calf sharing our cramped quarters this night.
Would that I were in my bed at the tavern and Rosemary were in my arms.

A few days later, after the snow had melted off, William and Cudjo rode over to Flea Bite pen. Luck was with them. Rufus had shot a turkey that day and Alonso had barbequed it and roasted some sweet potatoes. After having been several weeks on the slim rations of the small game he and Cudjo had shot or trapped, Alonso's cooking tasted as good to William as that of the best tavern in Charles Town.

"Alonso," said William, "do you know how to cook turtle soup?"

"*Si*, I can cook turtle soup. But not this time of year. The turtles sleep all winter. You know that, no? I would sleep all winter, too, if I could. Come spring, you catch me a big snapping turtle out of the swamp and I will cook you some turtle soup. Sally showed me her way of making it. Hers is the best there is. Miss Rosemary likes it more than anything else from the kitchen. Now, Miss Liza and Miss Betsy, they turn up their noses. They say they ain't gonna eat no turtle. But Miss Rosemary always asks for it."

"Is that so?" said William, for it was also his favorite back at the Packsaddle.

"It is so," said Alonso. "Next time you see Miss Rosemary, you ask her how she likes Sally's turtle soup. Now, my turtle soup, maybe she would not like so much. I don't have all the spices out here that Sally has in her kitchen. But my turtle soup is very good. *Muy buena.* When spring comes, you will see."

"Speaking of Rosemary," Rufus said to William, "how does it go between you two these days? Betsy says you are sweet on her."

"I might be," said William, "but that doesn't get me very far with her. She has let me know loud and clear that I don't measure up to what she's looking for. And she doesn't seem inclined to wait until I can rise higher."

"Your education on the subject of cowpen women is just beginning," said Rufus. "You will find that they are strong-willed, hard-headed, and independent. And that's only the half of it."

"What do you mean?"

"I'm talking now about cowpen women in general," said Rufus. "There's some around here that make John MacDonald's daughters look like angels."

"This sounds like a story comin," said Alonso.

"Could be," said Rufus. "Let me tell you about a cowpen man who lived over on the other side of the Santee River. This man had a pretty young wife, and sometimes when he would come home after having been gone for several days, his suspicions would rise. He saw signs that she might be entertaining visitors in his absence. So he decided to test her. While she was out milking one day, he got under their bed and tied a string to the webbing, and he tied the other end of the string to a small stone and suspended it just above a jar of cream. In this way, he knew that if he returned home and found cream on the stone, it would prove that there had been two in the bed, enough to weigh it down that far."

"I think I know where this is going," said William with a chuckle.

"When he got back home, he crawled under the bed, and what do you think? Not only was the stone covered in cream, the cream in the jar had turned to butter."

Ray and Jock laughed as if they had never heard it before, leaning over and slapping their legs.

William laughed too. "That's where I thought that story was going," he said.

"No, the story is true," said Rufus, keeping a serious face. "These cowpen women have their ways, I'm telling you."

"They sure do," said Ray. "But I've heard a story of a worser cowpen woman than that. I heard it told by a cow-hunter in Charles Town."

"I'm not sure I want to hear it," said William.

Ray was undaunted. "There was a man married to this purty woman. He was happy with her. But after a few days, he wakes up in the night and reaches for her and she ain't there. He thinks she just out doin something, and he goes back to sleep. But this happens time and again. Finally he sets out to find where she's goin. So he pretends to go to sleep one night, and she gets up out the bed, walks over to the window, and I'm dogged if that woman doesn't climb out of her skin. Climbs right out of it. She turns into an owl and flies away. She's a witch! Before dawn she flies home, climbs back into her skin, and gets into bed.

"The next night he do the same, and when she climb out of her skin and fly away, the man sprinkles some red pepper inside the skin. She comes back and climbs into her skin, and she comes to bed. But directly she jump up and start scratching and cussing, and she climbs out of her skin in front of the man. She turns into an owl and flies away, but this time he never sees her again. A witch can't stand it if other people learn that they are witches."

"I had no idea that cowpen women were so untrustworthy and treacherous," said William with mock seriousness.

"They ain't that bad," said Jock. "They just hard to know. My mama has a saying that comes from Africa. 'People and melons are hard to know.' And women are especially hard. They ain't like us. I never know what's goin on with em."

"Just come ask your *padre,*" said Alonso. "I'll tell you everthing you need to know about women."

"He can't help you a bit," Ray said to Jock.

"Not to change the subject," said Rufus, "but we need to plan our winter burn."

"What is that?" asked William.

"We burn the grass and litter off of the woods to perk up the browse for the cows. We do it every other year, and this is the year for it."

"You set the woods on fire?"

"We surely do."

"In Scotland that can land you in jail, or worse," said William. "There are few enough trees in that land as it is, without burning some of them down on purpose."

"Well, this ain't Scotland. And these longleaf pines love a good fire. Their bark is thick and spongy and holds off the flames just fine, so all you get is a grass fire running along under them. It burns low and it don't get too hot. As a matter of fact, if we don't burn at all, the oaks and hickories will come creeping in and push out the pine trees and shade out the grass."

"But this way you've burned up the grass," said William.

"Well, that's the trick, you see. The wiregrass likes fire as much as the pines do. All it takes after a winter fire is a little stretch of spring weather, and that blackened forest floor breaks out in new grass and flowers, just as pretty as you'll ever see."

"Well, I've always wanted to set a fire I could let go wild," said William. "When do we do this?"

"We have to wait for three things," said Rufus. "We need a good rain to soak the ground and get some standing water in the swamps. That's where the cows run to get away from the fire. Then we need for the dead wiregrass to dry out from the rain. And last we need a gentle breeze from the west. When we have those three things, we'll get in motion. You and Cudjo will go out and do a burn on the eastern side of the Cherokee Trail. We will wait a day or two and make sure that goes all right, and then we'll set fire to the grass on the western side of the trail."

"Won't our fire on the east blow over to the cowpen?" asked William. "How do you keep from burning up the house and barn?."

"Father MacDonald don't keep that place as clear of litter these days as he used to, but he'll be cleaning it up before the burn. Anyone who lives in the piney woods knows to keep their yard swept clean of anything that can catch fire. When a hot grass fire comes bearing down on you, it's too late to sweep the yard."

Thursday, January 19, Flea Bite Pen
My new mates distrust women extremely. Is this the superstition of a new, rude land, or do they know something I do not?
We are waiting for just the right weather for setting the woods on fire. What is arson in one country is good husbandry in another.

A few days later the cow-hunters got their soaking rain, followed by a balmy breeze blowing in from the west. William and Cudjo got busy, each arming himself with a ten-foot cane pole with a pine knot tied to the end. By the time they had ridden over to the Cherokee Trail, the grass had dried out from the rain. They struck a small blaze and lit their pine knots, and as they ambled north, they began setting a series of fires. The litter from the pine trees— foot-long needles and large cones—ignited easily, as did the dried out clumps of wiregrass. Soon there was a sheet of fire spreading out through the pine forest, and as Rufus had promised, it was a low fire, not a conflagration.

"This must take a toll on the animals," said William.

"They know what to do," said Cudjo. "The cows head for standing water in the swamps. The deer and other four-footeds run whichever way it takes to get out of the way. The birds just fly away." Cudjo looked up in the sky and pointed to a pair of redtail hawks circling over the moving edge of the fire. "That's Old Red and his wife. You can always count on them to come over. They think we set this fire for them." One of the hawks suddenly plunged down and swept along the ground, grabbing up a small rodent that was fleeing the flames. "When the woods burn, there's winners and there's losers," said Cudjo.

"What about the slow ones like snakes and terrapins?" William asked.

"It's too early in the year for them to be out, but if they was out, there's many a burrow in the piney woods, and lots of hidey-holes for the slow-moving creatures. They just go underground until the fire burns over. Now, gopher tortoises, they're in a class by themselves. If they can't find a hole, they just dig themselves one right quick. There's enough sand in this soil that they don't have a bit of trouble."

A couple of days later, they saw a great cloud of smoke blowing their way, and they knew that Rufus and his crew were firing the western range.

Wednesday, January 25, Half Way Swamp
There is nothing like spending a few months as a cow-hunter to dispel the romance of homesteading in the New World. It is cold, wet, monotonous work. I would not want to do this for the rest of my life. The Indian trade seems to me a better prospect.
I think of Rosemary and wonder if she is happy.

14

Christian Priber

In late February there came a stretch of days that almost felt like spring. On one evening the weather had warmed up so much that a few spring peeper frogs could be heard making music ahead of the season. The next morning the sun was warm and pleasant as William and Cudjo went out to tend the herd, which was grazing in scattered bunches near the Cherokee Trail in a low area that had been too wet to burn. At noon the two of them took a break by the side of the trail to eat their midday trail rations. After they finished, they were slow to get to their feet again. Instead they lay back in the winter grass, enjoying the warmth of the sun. William was just about to shut his eyes when he saw Samri and Bruto prick up their ears and lift their heads. Cudjo saw it too, and they both sat up to see what the dogs were hearing. Before long they themselves could hear the faint sound of a traveler coming up the trail. Their respite over, they got to their feet and looked to see who might be passing by.

There soon came in view a short, fat man trudging along leading a large brown horse that had gone lame. The horse was hobbling badly, barely putting weight on its right front hoof. When the pair drew closer, William saw that the man was familiar, though for a moment he could not place him. He searched his mind and quickly found the context. At table at the Packsaddle. It was Christian Priber.

William took off his hat and waved it as he walked up the trail to meet him. "Hello, Mister Priber," he called out.

Priber strained to see who was greeting him with such familiarity. Then he took off his own hat and waved it. "Mister MacGregor," he exclaimed in his thick German accent. As the distance closed between them, he said, "I am very happy to see you. I heard from Mister MacDonald that you are working for him out in these wilds, but I never expected our paths would cross. Ja, I stayed at his cowpen last night. And such a beautiful day it was when I set out this morning. But now my horse has stepped in a rabbit hole. I am in a bad way."

"He appears to be quite lame," said William. "He can't go far in that condition." He reached out and shook Priber's hand, while Cudjo came up beside them and leaned down to feel the horse's bad leg. "I think this is not broken," said Cudjo. "But the sprain is very bad. Your horse must be off that hoof for several days."

"You need to take him back to MacDonald's cowpen," said William. Then he chuckled a little as he added, "Lately it has become a hospital for sprained ankles."

Priber did not explore the source of William's humor. He was distressed. "Ach," he said, "I must go on to the Overhill Cherokees. I will have to walk all the way, it seems."

William looked him up and down. He did not seem like a man who could make that long trek through the mountains. "That is a far piece," he said doubtfully. "Many miles to go and many mountains to climb."

"This is terrible," said Priber in English so poor William could barely understand him. "I have no choice. I must get on to the Overhills. I have urgent business there."

William wondered what business that could be, but he kept his questions to himself. "I have a proposal," he said. "It so happens I have a spare horse at MacDonald's. Perhaps you saw it, a little grey mare. I call her Cordelia. She's a Chickasaw horse. You can take her for your own, if you wish, and we will work on getting this one patched up. If the leg heals, I keep this one for myself. If not, then you will owe me for a horse, and we can settle when you return again."

"That is *sehr* generous," Priber said. "I accept your kind offer and I cannot thank you enough. But tell me, what is a Chickasaw horse?"

"They are small horses, not handsome, but they are hard-hooved, smooth gaited, and very hardy. All the traders use them for riding and packing."

"Then I will be happy to own one," said Priber.

"Do you have any paper with you, and pen and ink?"

"Ja, I always have pen and paper." He reached into his saddlebag and pulled out a bound notebook and ripped out a page. Then he took out a bottle of ink and a quill pen.

"MacDonald has three daughters," William said. "Give this letter to the youngest—to Rosemary."

"Ja, ja. I know who she is—a beautiful young woman."

"Aye," said William. "That is the one." He put the paper against the horse's saddle to write. "What is this horse's name?"

"Spinoza."

"Spinoza?" said William, turning the word over in his mind. "Haven't I heard that name? Is there a writer named Spinoza?"

"Ja, a philosopher of the first order. Though he is much vilified by the small-minded keepers of truth."

William smiled broadly. "I like having a horse named Spinoza." He turned back to the paper and began to write.

Dear Rosemary,

Priber's horse is badly lamed. I have traded him my horse for his. Please pen up his lame one and give him Cordelia to ride. I would count it a great favor if you would put your tender hand to the healing of this new horse of mine. His name is Spinoza.

I know how much you are overburdened with work. I would not ask this if I could be there myself to do it. If you can help me, I will be in your debt, and I will find a way to pay you for your trouble.

Yours most sincerely,
Billy MacGregor

"Give this letter to Rosemary and she will give you my horse. Then you must ride back out here to spend the night in our camp. Cudjo and I will cook up the best of our rations. It won't be fine food, but it will renew you after a hard day on the trail."

169

"This is so kind of you, Mister MacGregor, so kind."

"Call me Billy," said William. "And you can repay me with an evening of conversation."

"But how will I find you?" asked Priber.

"We will be out and about right around here. When you have come back to this spot, give out a loud call, and we will come meet you and lead you to the camp."

"*Danke, danke, mein* friend. I look forward to your hospitality very much, and to the great company at your fire."

And so, leading his crippled horse behind him, Priber set off down the trail in the direction from which he had come. William and Cudjo turned back to tending the herd.

It was late in the afternoon when they finally heard Priber's call. They joined up with him, and the three of them rode over to the rough little camp and soon had a fire going. Cudjo put on a pot of hominy grits flavored with small pieces of beef jerky, while William brewed up a pot of cassina tea. They were hungry and ate their food without ceremony, topping it off with some small cakes of dried persimmon pulp. The night did not require much heat from the fire, and so they fed it only a little as they sat around it drinking hot cups of tea.

"I will tell you," said William, "that my conversation with you and James Adair that night at the Packsaddle was one I will always remember. I have pondered it since, and I can't decide which of you had the better of the argument. It seems to me that Adair's idea that the Indians are descended from ancient Hebrews is worth considering. He did have some evidence to support it."

"Ja, but is it good evidence? This is a New World, and the only way Adair can explain it is by referring to knowledge from the Old World. For him, the unknown can only be explained in terms of the already known. Thus, his philosophy never truly admits an open question. Why can't we say that the Indians of America are clothed in questions that must be answered, as time permits, in their own terms?"

"I don't know how that could be done," said William.

"Neither do I. But if I remember correctly, you declared to us that evening that the motto you live by is 'Dare to inquire.'"

"Aye, so it is. I aspire to it, at least."

"My own motto is *Tempora filia veritas*. Truth is the daughter of time. There are philosophers in Europe who say that God and the world are one, and as we learn more and more about the world, we learn more and more about God."

"I have not heard that," said William, "and now that I have, I confess that I don't know what to make of it." He reached over and stirred the coals with a stick, so that the fire flared up. Then he poured each of them another cup of tea.

"I strongly believe," said Priber, "that philosophy should not limit itself to looking backward. It should look at the here and now, and also at the future."

"Speculate about the future, you mean."

"No, I mean that a philosopher must be a participant in the world in which he lives and in so doing he must try to improve the shape of things to come."

"Improve it toward his idea of what the future should be?"

"Ja, ja. Why should a philosopher submit to having his hands bound in this world of toil and trouble? To simply talk about ideas is not enough."

"Isn't Adair trying to do more than just talk?" asked William. "Surely he is a man of this world. He is trying to understand the Indians. He lives partly in the Indians' world and partly in his own. He participates in theirs."

"That is true. But in whose interest does he act? Is it not always on his own behalf and that of the British empire?"

"How could he act otherwise?"

"The Indians are in this world, too," said Priber. "If a philosopher were able to see that the cause of much of their misery is in the way they understand the world, should not that philosopher tell them about it and help them change toward a better future?"

"Are you speaking from experience? Perhaps you can give me an example of what you have in mind."

"Ja, I have been with the Overhill Cherokees. One of the foundations of their way of life is their clans. Every Cherokee belongs to the clan of his mother. A Cherokee's clan affiliation at birth is set in stone for his entire life. And the clans are fiercely jealous of their own. If a member of one clan in any way injures or insults a member of another clan, that injured clan will seek revenge, even if they have to wait the better part of a year and walk a hundred miles to do it. The chief of every Cherokee town must spend most of his time putting out small fires between clans, and he, being an outsider to most disputes, has only limited power to help out."

"I have had personal experience with trouble between Cherokee clans," said William, "and I cannot agree that any philosophical insight from outside their own world could ever have any effect on their sense of rights and justice."

"If they could only institute a single rule," said Priber, "their survival as a nation would be assured."

"And what would that rule be?"

"That every child born to a Cherokee woman belongs not to the mother's clan but to the Cherokee nation as a whole."

"In other words, you would ask them to give up their clans," said William. "They would never do that."

"The Cherokees say they want to be a nation among nations, like England or France. But they will never be a true nation until they, as an entire people, act like a nation. They will never be able to compete with England and France if they are no more than a collection of jealous clans always in conflict with each other."

"This is true," said William, "but the changing of a single rule would not be enough. Many parts of Cherokee life are interwoven with their system of clans. I don't think any philosopher in the world could be wise enough to know how to change with one wave of the hand an entire fabric of interwoven rules and laws."

Cudjo had so far remained silent, staring into the dying coals of their cookfire, seemingly oblivious to what was being said. But now he spoke up.

"I can think of a rule or two that could be changed in Carolina," he said. "But if I was to speak up about it, I would most likely be hanged."

"You mean," said William, "the rule that allows some people to purchase other people and work them as slaves for profit?"

"It was you who said that," said Cudjo. "Not me."

"Slavery spoils the claim of the New World to truly be new," said Priber. "Slavery has been practiced in the Old World from ancient times. It does not belong in the New World."

"Carolina planters cannot think of doing without it," said William, "no more than the Cherokees would ever consider giving up their clans."

"That brings us to another idea of mine that would help usher in a better future," said Priber.

"I am almost afraid to ask what that might be," said William.

"Do not be afraid," Priber said good-naturedly. "Dare to inquire."

"What is your idea, then?"

"It is simply this, that if the Cherokees were to offer asylum to escaped slaves, it would serve the interests of both the Cherokees and the enslaved Africans. The Cherokees would be able to increase their population, and the Africans would gain their freedom."

"That would change things, true enough," said Cudjo. "As it is now, if a slave tries to run—not that I would, mind you—but if any slave does try to get away, the Indians hunt him down, grab him up, and sell him back. They are slave catchers and slave traders themselves."

"Ja, and they work against their own interests," said Priber. "If they could be brought to understand another way, they would set a new example and the world could become a better place for all the peoples of the earth."

"None of this seems likely to come to pass," said William. "And I am afraid the longer we talk tonight, the more treasonous we become. I think we would be wise to get some sleep."

"Ach, these are serious matters," Priber said earnestly. "And ja, such discussions have gotten me into trouble more than once."

"Back in Saxony, you mean," said William.

"Ja, the ones in power did not want to hear my ideas about the betterment of humanity and the possibility of thinking and acting freely. They threatened me with imprisonment, and worse. So I took me to England thinking that it would surely be a place where I could thrive. England, everyone says, allows freedom of thought. But I found England is not so different from Saxony. They did not want to hear me either. So I came to Carolina."

"Well," said William, "I'd just as soon we didn't both get thrown out of Carolina. I do think it is time we went to bed."

The three of them got out their bedrolls, laid them out on the ground, and crawled in to sleep. In the dim light of the fire, William wrote a few lines in his journal.

Wednesday, February 22, Camp near the Cherokee Trail
Priber is fearless in expressing his philosophical ideas. Is it all talk? Or does he truly intend to act on what he says?

My thought is that his high ideals are in for a rude awakening. From everything I have seen, the New World is little different from the Old when it comes to human beings and their pursuit of self-interest. Within any Indian town, it is often clan against clan, while the Indian nations themselves are commonly pitted against each other, sometimes bitterly so. Within the colonies, it is rich against poor, planter against merchant, and pinder against farmer. Not to mention Anglican against dissenter. And slave against master. And then the Christian nations themselves are opposed to each other in the New World as in the Old, and here they bring their Indian allies into the contest. Especially the French and the British. Earlier the Spanish were in this mix, but now they are weak players. The game is ever afoot.

I wonder whether Cudjo would flee from this cowpen if he could find safe harbor with an Indian nation? Perhaps he would if he could be sure he could herd cattle there.

15

The Deadening

William and Cudjo continued tending herd as the winter cold returned and nipped back the early signs of spring. A cowman from birth, Cudjo seemed content with his work. For him each day was different and brought its own challenges. Not so for William. He now realized how much his years in Glasgow and Charles Town had ruined him for cow-hunting. For him the work was nothing but monotonous, and the cold made it even worse. After a particularly trying day confined to their small camp by a cold rain, the two of them rode over to the Flea Bite camp for a night of company, hoping for the best from Alonso's cooking. The rain still drizzled off and on as they rode, and the warmth of the big half-face shelter at the camp was a welcome refuge. Rufus was glad to see them. "You saved me a cold, wet ride," he said to William as they dismounted. "Father MacDonald was here yesterday and says he wants to see you down at the cowpen."

"Why would that be?" asked William.

"He didn't say. He just told me to tell you to come. He keeps counsel with none but his rum keg these days. I no longer know his mind. He didn't make it sound urgent, but just the same, if I was you I'd get over there tomorrow."

When morning came, it was still raining lightly, and it was cold and windy as well. William procrastinated, enjoying the hot cassina tea and the stories and banter of the cow-hunters. By midday the rain had slowed to an intermittent drizzle. He donned his rain slicker, saddled Viola, and set out on the long, wet ride to the cowpen. When he got there, the place was as sodden and dark as his ride had been. He walked all around, but he could not raise a soul. Not even the dogs were there to bark at him. He found no one in the house, barn, or outbuildings. No one in the pen. No one in the garden plot. Finally, he rode out to the corn field, muddy from the rain and cluttered with last year's stalks and winter-dead weeds, and there in the distance he heard the sound of axes chopping wood. He followed the sound to the nearby woods, where the dogs ran out to bark at him and he found the MacDonald women, along with Venus, Daphne, and Mars. Betsy's two little boys were there, too, cold and miserable. All three MacDonald sisters were hard at work with felling axes chopping shallow rings to girdle the bases of the larger trees. Venus was armed with an axe and Daphne with a grubbing hoe, which they used to cut down saplings and bushes, while Mars dragged away the leavings. He was stacking stout branches and small trees to one side, where they could be cut and split into rails. He piled the small brush around the bases of the large, ringed trees. William knew about deadenings. After the heat of summer, when the ringed trees were dead and dried out, the deadening crew would set the piles of brush aflame and burn as much of the standing trees as would take the fire.

The women barely looked up as William approached. He dismounted and walked over to where Rosemary was working.

"You're an unexpected sight," she said, letting her axe rest on the ground but not moving away from the tree.

"Mister MacDonald sent for me," said William, "but I can't find a sign of him anywhere. I hate to see you women out here. This is men's work. Even for men, the weather is too cold and wet to be working outside on something that can wait until later."

"You don't have to tell us that," said Betsy, who had put down her axe to listen. "Go tell it to Father. He's taken it in his head that we need to enlarge Miss Rosemary's cornfield before the planting season, and here we are at his command. All his men are tied up with cows and timber, but he looks at us and sees strong arms and declares us to be his deadening crew. We've been at this almost a week, except for yesterday when it was raining hard."

"It is still raining," said William.

"Not in Father's eyes. All he sees is planting time bearing down on us."

The deadening crew's clothing was damp from the lingering drizzle, and their hair hung forlornly lank around their faces. They had all stopped working now, taking a moment to rest and to give their support to Betsy's complaint.

"He should wait and let the cow-hunters finish this after the spring cow hunt," said Liza. "If we don't all come down sick, it will be a miracle. But Miss Rosemary will have her new cornfield this spring. Whatever she asks for, Father grants."

"Don't think for a minute," Rosemary said to her sisters, "that this extra land will be any advantage to me. Not so. It means more work for me, more field to tend. But if tend it I must, the corn and sweet potatoes that come from it will be to the advantage of all of us. So stop calling it my field. And I would appreciate it as well if you would not call me 'Miss Rosemary.'"

"You are a 'Miss' until you marry," said Betsy, "and as long as you stay a spinster, you are Father's little girl and you can work him as you wish. If you was to marry like the rest of us and bring another man to the cowpen to help us out with the work, then you might hear us change our tune."

"Where is it written," said Rosemary, "that I should marry the first lout who comes riding into the cowpen? I have told you before, I will take my time waiting for a husband with prospects."

"So Rufus and Swan are louts," said Betsy.

"Louts with no prospects," said Liza.

"That is not what I am saying," said Rosemary. "But I can give rancor for rancor if that is what you want."

There was enough rancor in the air, thought William, to offend everyone in hearing distance, including himself, though he was used to it by now and it barely fazed him. "I am a lout with no prospects who is a fair hand with an axe," he said. "Let me spell you a bit. I'll step in for each of you in turn and give you a rest."

He fetched a sharpening stone from Viola's saddlebag. Then he went over and took Betsy's axe from her, which she surrendered gladly. He used the stone to put an edge on her axe, taking care to retain the curvature of its bit.

"What about Father?" asked Betsy, as she watched him work on the axe.

"What about him?"

"I thought you said he sent for you?"

"I couldn't raise him. There wasn't a soul at the cowpen, not even Aunt Sally."

"Aunt Sally must have been in the spring house," said Betsy.

"Or the outhouse," said Liza.

"Father is likely out repairing fences," said Betsy.

"Or passed out on his bed," said Liza. "He starts his drinking early in the day."

"He's not that bad," said Rosemary. "He sleeps a lot because he's getting old."

"That's a kindly interpretation," said Liza.

"And a true one," said Rosemary, lifting her axe to get back to work.

Liza struggled to return to her work as well.

"So, must the master wait to see you?" asked Betsy.

"He's not expecting me this very moment," said William. "He can wait." Then he went to work with the sharpened axe, laying into one tree after another, cutting an eight to ten-inch girdle in each, all the way around, chopping through the bark and through the sapwood, so that all the rising sap would be cut off in the spring and the girdled tree would die. Through the coming summer all of the girdled trees in the deadening would have bare branches, allowing sunlight to reach the loamy soil of the forest floor. Rosemary and her workers would take their hoes to the soft dirt and plant hills of corn and beans among the dead trees.

After a time, William handed Betsy's axe back to her and proceeded to take Liza's, though Liza forbade him to sharpen it, implying that she lacked confidence in his ability to perform this simple act. The pride of a woodcutter's wife, no doubt. William ignored the slight and went to work with the axe as it was, girdling tree after tree while Liza rested. Then for a time he cut for Rosemary, and after her turn he started over again with Betsy.

William kept on with it, working steadily with one axe after another until it began to grow dark. Then he walked with the three sisters around the edge of the area of girdled trees. They estimated that in their several days of work they had deadened about three acres in all, which would surely be enough to satisfy their father. In the under-story there remained many small saplings and bushes that would have to be cleared out, but with hard work this could be done before planting time. As a last step, the crew would have to take down the rail fence around the margin of the old cornfield and reuse the rails to extend the fence around the deadening. This work would go quickly until they ran out of rails, after which would come the hard work of splitting new rails to finish fencing the new clearing. For that, MacDonald would surely have to bring in the woodcutters.

With their day's work behind them, the deadening crew trudged through the mud of the old cornfield back to the cowpen. Aunt Sally had supper ready, and John was already at the table, drinking black coffee and looking somewhat the worse for wear. His clothing was rumpled and his hair tousled.

"Well, Billy," he said, "I see you have come upon the deadening crew. I hope you didn't distract them from finishing the girdling."

"He was a help to us, Papa," said Liza. "We have girdled about three acres now. There's a lot more grubbing to be done, but there's still time for that before planting."

"With Billy giving us a hand today," said Betsy, "it reminded us how much deadening work is best done by men."

"That's the truth, Papa," said Liza. "You need to get some men in here to finish this. We've been willing to help, but Betsy doesn't want to neglect her boys more than she already has, and I have plenty to do at the lumber yard. Unless you can get some men in here, Rosemary and her crew are going to have to do the grubbing, and it will take them a long time to get it done."

Rosemary just shook her head and said nothing.

"All my men are busy," said John. "We have to do it any way we can. Liza can go back to the lumber camp if she needs to, but the rest of you can help me for a few more days."

Aunt Sally came in carrying a large bowl of rice and field peas. "All we got for supper tonight is hoppin john," she said. "But at least we have plenty of that."

"Hoppin john with small rice," said Betsy without enthusiasm.

"That's all there is for me to use," said Sally. "And even that's most near gone."

William had been in Carolina long enough to know that small rice was what they called the grains that got broken into pieces from being carelessly pounded in a rice mortar. It was worth only half as much as good rice, and it was mostly fed to slaves.

"We've still got some of last year's Indian corn," said John.

"Yes, sir, we do," said Sally. "I'll get Venus and Daphne to pounding up cornmeal. And they can make some of that corn into hominy. But I don't know when they'll get to it, what with having to grub out brush in the deadening, as well as milking and tending the cows."

"We can do without hominy for now," said John, "and we only need a day's worth of cornmeal at a time. We'll soon have rice again, and that will free things up." He turned toward William. "Billy, I want you to go with Rosemary in the pettiauger to follow Swan and his crew downriver as they float that raft of timber down to Dubose's plantation."

"I will do it gladly," said William. "Are we rafting lumber or logs?"

"There's some of both. Dubose wants to build a new kitchen behind his house. Swan and his men have been hard at work cutting and hewing posts and beams enough to raise it, and riving clapboards and shingles enough to cover it. Besides all this, he wants some logs for general purposes. Taken all together that ought to get us four barrels of rice, free and clear."

"What is my job to be?" asked William.

"Rosemary will oversee the exchange of the lumber for the rice. I want you there to back her up, to make sure Dubose does not short me. Check the barrels to make sure he's filled them all with good rice. And take care loading those barrels on the pettiauger. They are not very well made. The woodcutters will row the pettiauger back upstream, and you and Rosemary can paddle back in the canoe."

"Father, I'm confused," said Rosemary. "I thought it was you and I who were going down to Dubose's plantation, like we have always done before."

"I want you and Billy to do it."

"But why aren't you coming?"

"I don't feel well enough to paddle the canoe back upriver, that's why. It near killed me the last time I did it. I'm getting old, Daughter, haven't you noticed?"

"I can do most of the paddling," said Rosemary. "I'm strong enough. It's not that hard."

"No, God damn it, you will do it with Billy."

"Papa," said Liza, "why not let Swan oversee the exchange for the rice? I could go along with him. Rosemary and Billy could stay here and work on the deadening."

"Swan knows cutting and sawing wood. It's Rosemary who knows how to deal for the rice. And Billy has worked in trade. He knows buying and selling."

"If you had ever taken me with you downriver instead of her, I could do the exchange," said Liza. "I'm older than she is. I should be the one."

"Neither you nor Betsy ever wanted to go with me," said John. "Rosemary is the one who took to the job, and she's the one who has it now."

"But who will take her place with the milking?" Liza asked.

"Venus and Daphne can handle the milking. I can step in if I have to. And that's the end of the discussion. I say it is Rosemary and Billy who are going in the pettiauger, and Rosemary and Billy it will be. And that, God damn it, is the end of it."

The three sisters fell into a sullen silence. William could not have been happier with this development, though Rosemary seemed not feel the same. It was still fresh in his memory how much she had enjoyed their walk to the mill site, and he was at a loss to understand what had changed.

Friday, March 3, MacDonald's Cowpen

These backcountry people are at war with the woods. In a few days three strong-armed women have girdled all of the large trees on a three-acre piece of land. The soil in a fresh deadening is amazingly fertile, but it gives out after a few years, and then they have to deaden another area. The clearing of trees never ends.

All in all they use prodigious amounts of wood here compared to people on the other side of the ocean. Someone told me once that it takes 1,800 split rails to build a zig-zag worm fence five feet high and a quarter of a mile long. They say the fence has to be horse high, bull strong, and hog tight. Of course, they waste no wood on in-ground posts, and only the bottom rails touch the ground to rot, and even when they do rot, they can cut the spoiled rails into pieces and use them for spalty firewood. So I suppose it is not as wasteful as it seems.

Rosemary is distancing herself from me. No doubt she has given up completely on my prospects. This cow-hunting year is not getting me ahead. Were it not for the fact that Rosemary is here, I never should have come. But she is here, and, against all reason, I would rather be here than not.

William's enthusiasm for the trip dampened as he realized the degree to which Rosemary had indeed grown distant from him. The fissures in the cowpen seemed to be growing into chasms, but William feared that her reserve went beyond the general misery of the place. Hoping to find out what was amiss with her, he followed her the next morning to the milking pen, where he attended to small tasks while she and her crew milked the cows. Finally he made his way over to where she was sitting on a stool milking.

"We've been told to go down the river," he said, "but I heard nothing about when exactly we would leave. Do you know when it will be?"

"Liza told me that the woodsmen almost have the raft ready to go. I expect we will go down to the lumber camp tomorrow." She did not look up at him.

He leaned against a railing, making himself available for conversation if she wanted.

She worked on silently and finished the cow she was milking. Then she took the pail and poured the milk out into a larger collecting bucket. After that she untied the cow from the milking post and led her into the holding pen for the calves, several of whom ran over eagerly, but Rosemary brushed them aside and admitted only one calf to her udder. The hungry little thing tugged insistently at the teats to get the milk that remained.

"Let in another cow, if you please," she said, and William, glad at last to be engaged, opened the gate and let another cow into the milking pen. Rosemary tethered her to the post and again started milking.

"In the meantime," she said, as if there had not been a lull in the conversation, "we've got to work out how we are going to manage the next few days."

"I don't follow your meaning."

"We will be together in those two little boats for two days," she said tersely. "Down in the pettiauger on one day and back in the canoe on the next. Every eye will be on us."

"What is wrong with that?"

"If they see us even enjoying each other's company, we will be taken for lovers, and we are far from that. We will never hear the end of it."

"It seems to me," said William," that we could solve that problem in an instant, if only we would."

"How is that?"

"We would not be mistaken for lovers if we actually were lovers."

Rosemary pursed her lips in frustration and milked in silence, pulling the teats so hard the cow stamped a foot in protest.

"This is the problem, Billy. If I let my feelings for you show, you make too much of them. I do like you. You must know that, especially after that day we walked to the mill site. But it doesn't matter how much I like you, don't you see? I mean to get away from this cowpen, and if we were to marry, that would never happen. We would be here for the rest of our lives, and neither of us would be happy."

"I don't know whether to laugh or cry," said William. "It pleases me beyond words to know that you have actually considered whether you would marry me. But at the same time, it distresses me to have no argument to make against what you are saying. It is true that I cannot take you away from here. Not as things are now. I have no place to take you, no money to rent us even a hovel in Charles Town, and no job by which to get enough money to improve our condition. The life you have here, which you already seem to hate, is better than anything I can offer. And I know you are right that I would not be happy here either. And so we are doomed as lovers, which makes me very sad."

"I have already waited more than a year," said Rosemary, "and your prospects have not improved. All you have are dreams that would take years to bring about, if you can ever bring them about at all. I'm sorry, Billy. Perhaps I am as sad as you are. But I must think of my own future. I am not getting any younger."

"I have to say," said William, "that I am pleased that you do at least care for me. Somehow that gives me hope, though hope for what, I don't know. Perhaps just a hope that we can go forward in friendliness, that we can at least find a way to make this trip together amiably."

Rosemary stopped milking and was silent for a little while, still holding idly to the teats. The cow shifted her feet, switched her tail, and looked around at Rosemary to see what the hold-up was. "All right, how about this. I know that John MacDonald is your idea of the father you never had, and don't deny it, Billy. I know that's why you came here to work for him. You were the good son worried about his father."

"That's not the only reason," said William.

"That may be, but let me make my point. In a certain way, he is half a father to you. He was your father's friend and was with him when he died, so there is that connection. And on the other hand, in the state he is in these days he is less than a whole father to me. So he is about half a father to both of us. That means we are half-way brother and sister. So here is my proposal, Billy. I say we think of each other as brother and sister and let it be known that we regard ourselves so. As I see it, there is some truth to it."

"It is not true," William said somewhat testily, "but I do see the sense of pretending that it is. But only from your standpoint, not from mine. You are a clever girl, Rosemary. If this is what it takes to warm you to being with me, I will play my part. And now, little sister, I will leave you to your milking."

William turned and walked away, shaking his head as he left the dairy and headed out to put in the rest of the day's work grubbing in the deadening. Was he better or worse off than before that conversation? There was no way of knowing. He felt that she was giving him just enough hope to keep him dangling along. And it was working. He didn't want to lose her if there was still a chance he could have her. But it would not work forever. He was nearing the limit of his patience with Princess Rosemary.

16

The Logging Camp

Early the next morning, after Rosemary tidied up her dairy and told the milking crew what they had to attend to during her absence, she arrived at the pen where William had strapped a packsaddle on John's black Chickasaw horse. Both William and Rosemary packed their bedrolls on the horse, being unsure of where they would sleep for the next few nights. They also packed some supplies for the woodcutters, including three dozen eggs nested in a straw-lined basket, a smoked salt-cured ham, and four cornshucks filled with pork sausage.

"Most of what the woodcutters eat," said Rosemary, "is hominy grits, rice, and cornbread. They are always hungry for meat."

"This should help smooth Liza's ruffled feathers," said William.

"I wouldn't count on it. She's more likely to tell us what else we should have brought."

They set out walking the four and a half miles down the wagon road to the logging camp, traveling the same road on which they had walked together when William's ankle was still mending. Some distance beyond Swan's hoped-for mill site on Poplar Creek, they came to the outer edge of the Santee floodplain. Lower Poplar Creek, with its narrow swampland of cypress trees and cane, was to the left of their road. To their right lay the much wider swampland of the Santee River. The trees were still bare of leaves, but a little green was starting to show on the forest floor. Some of the tree buds were swelling just enough to show that spring stood at the seasons' door.

William noticed that most of the medium-sized cypress trees he saw along the way had been girdled, evidently some time ago, and they were quite dead.

"Who would make a deadening here?" he asked.

Rosemary laughed. "You would have to walk on water like Jesus to plant a field of corn here. We don't call this a deadening. But the trees are killed just the same. They are drying out, waiting to be cut. If you cut down a living cypress tree, it will sink to the bottom of the water and lie there until doomsday. They don't rot, you know. So the woodcutters kill them first and let them stand and dry out for a year or two. Then when the water is low, they cut them down, and when the water rises again, they float them out. It's not easy getting them into the river from way back in the swamp."

"I know there is a great demand for this lumber," said William. "I see cypress in use everywhere, from Charles Town to the backcountry."

"It is a wonderful wood," said Rosemary. "Light but very strong. Easy to cut down. Easy to saw into boards."

"Easy to rive into clapboards and shingles, I assume," said William. "That's how I see so much of it used."

"Yes. Insects do not bore into it, and it is wondrously slow to rot. To top it off, when it weathers it turns a pretty grey color."

"Aha, the pretty grey color," William said jokingly. "That is the best of all."

"Don't you find it attractive?" asked Rosemary

"Yes, I do. It is very attractive," said William, sounding as sincere as he could, in case she were testing him. "I find cypress to be a most admirable wood in every way."

Rosemary laughed a little and pushed against his arm with her hand. "You are humoring me for being such a champion of the cypress tree. But its lumber has helped keep the cowpen afloat, and I am thankful for it."

"As well you should be," said William.

Rounding a bend in the road, they came to a pool of black water where a male wood duck, with its red eyes and bottle-green head, suddenly bolted up from the water and flew away.

"Chances are his wife is nearby, sitting on a clutch of eggs," said Rosemary, scanning the trees for the hole in which the pair might have their nest. "That's the only kind of duck that nests up in trees and the only one that stays here the year around. Sometimes when you are walking along, minding your own business, a mama wood duck will suddenly burst like a shot out of a hole in a tree and scare the daylights out of you."

Just down the road, on a point of land, the logging camp began to come into view. It was built on high ground, above all but the highest floods of the Santee. William could see that the camp was located where it could receive timber floated down lower Poplar Creek and also from the nearby Santee swamp lands when the water was high enough. Here they could assemble rafts of lumber to be floated to buyers along the Santee River all the way down to the ocean. "It is amazing to think," he said to Rosemary, "that a cypress beam from this swamp could end up in any place in the world where the Atlantic Ocean touches the shore."

"You are becoming a cypress champion, too," she said.

The camp itself consisted of two small log houses and a long, open-sided shed that sheltered a work area. The houses were made of round logs, notched where they joined at the corners. The roofs were made of clapboards layered like shingles from the eaves up to the ridgepoles, all secured in place with weight poles running parallel to the ridgepoles. No nailed construction could be seen, the houses being mainly held together by the weight of one piece of wood upon another. Each house had a door cut through one of its gable ends, and each had a chimney on the opposite end made of small, stacked, notched pieces of wood, chinked and covered with a heavy coating of clay. The only difference between the two houses was that the one where Liza and Swan lived was more carefully finished than the other, where Obadiah, Ajax, and Cato lived. The work shed was little more than a pole building with a rough clapboard roof.

A pack of mixed-breed dogs, very similar in appearance to the MacDonald herd dogs, began barking as soon as they caught sight of William and Rosemary. It was evident that all of MacDonald's dogs came from the same litters, and William surmised that these logging camp dogs were the ones who showed no talent for herding cattle.

Liza and Swan came out to meet them as they approached their house. "The two honeymooners have arrived," said Liza.

"Very amusing," said Rosemary. "But just because we are like brother and sister does not mean we have been struck by Cupid's arrow."

"Brother and sister?" Liza said skeptically.

"Is that so hard to comprehend?" asked Rosemary. "Billy is almost a better brother to me than you are a sister."

Liza stiffened and put her hands on her hips. "Would you cut me to the heart and still expect hospitality?"

"I said 'almost.'" Rosemary smiled and gave her sister a kiss on the cheek. William could not tell whether it was sincere or not. It seemed to be. "Your simplest hospitality will do," said Rosemary. "A bite to eat and a place to sleep. And look, we have brought you some food from the cowpen—meat and eggs."

Liza's demeanor softened a little. "You two unload your horse. We can always use more food in our forgotten outpost out here. My men will especially relish the eggs. We haven't been able to do a bit of good raising chickens in this swamp. We are cursed with every kind of varmint there is—coons, possums, weasels, foxes, snakes—all of them mad for chickens. They snatch them away no matter what we try to do to guard them."

As Rosemary began unpacking the horse, William walked over to Swan and held out his hand. "We've eaten together, but we've not formally met," he said. Swan gave him a hearty handshake, while William regarded him for the first time in daylight. Swan was a little older than William, with long blonde hair and a full beard, blue eyes, and fair skin. He wore a long-sleeved linen shirt that did not hide the bulk of his neck and arms.

"Swan is an unusual name," said William. "Were you named for the bird?"

"I was christened Sven Bengtsson," said Swan.

"Would that be Swedish?"

"It is Finnish. My parents were from the Old World, but I was born in the colonies, on the Delaware River. Up there they called me Sven, but down here I am Swan. Swan Bankston." He laughed. "New World people trim Old World names to suit themselves. Some around here shorten it down to Swan Banks." He spoke perfectly intelligible English, but with a slight accent from the world of his childhood.

"How did a Finn get this far south?" asked William.

"The Finn in me is fading fast," said Swan. "Years ago two of my friends and I took our muskets and axes and set out southward from the Delaware River down through Indian country, looking for land. We were young and foolhardy. We dodged Indians all the way, and I was the only one who got here alive. It's quite a story and I can get wound up in it, but we'd best turn to other things. The raft is almost together. We'll have it loaded by tomorrow, but we still have a little more sawing and riving to be done in the wood yard today. My men are out there now, trying to finish."

"Can I give you a hand?"

"I was hoping that you would offer. We are in a bind out here."

"I am no woodsman," said William, "but I can do what you tell me to do, if it doesn't take much skill."

"A strong back is all you will need." Swan motioned for William to follow him, and they walked out to the stock pen, where Swan opened the gate to let out two very large oxen. "I have a cypress log that is ready to be trimmed and drug to the wood yard," he explained.

They hitched the oxen to a high-wheeled cart for dragging timber. It was a simple contraption, consisting of two six-foot-high spoked wheels connected by a massive square axle and pulled by means of a twelve-foot tongue. They drove the cart down to a landing on Poplar Creek, where a cypress log stripped of its limbs lay on the bank amidst a scattered pile of wood chips.

"First," said Swan, "let's cut the log to length."

"I suppose Dubose sent word for how long to cut what he's going to need," said William.

"That's right. We cut everything just a bit longer than the length they will have in the finished structure. No point in rafting down excess wood destined for the scrap heap. It's hard enough to handle it when it's trimmed down." Swan stepped off something over fifteen feet and marked the log. He took up his felling axe, which was quite different from the long-bladed, oval-socketed English felling axes with which William was familiar. Swan's axe had a short bit with a triangular socket to wed it firmly to the handle. The well-used blade flashed brightly in the sunlight, and when Swan stood on the log and swung it overhead and down into the trunk, William could see that it was sharp as a razor. With only a few strokes, Swan chopped half through the tree. Then he turned himself around, and with a few mighty strokes on the opposite side, the trunk fell asunder.

"That is an amazing axe," said William.

"The Finns make good axes," said Swan, "with weight and heft in the center of the socket where it ought to be. My father used to say that this here is the axe that will cut down the American forests. Those long-bladed ones the English use are no good. I don't ever use one if I can help it. The center of the weight is out in the blade, and it will drift on a full swing and not hit right where you aim it."

They rolled the log to rest crosswise atop two short lengths of wood. With small, accurate strokes Swan cut two tiny notches twelve inches apart into the edge of both ends of the log. He handed William one end of a long string that he had dusted with white chalk powder. The two of them stretched the string between matched notches at each end of the log, and Swan took hold of the string and snapped it against the log, leaving a white line. Then they repeated this for a second line between the other two notches, thus marking the width of a twelve-inch beam.

Swan again stood atop the log, and with his felling axe he cut a series of vertical notches, a few inches apart, into the side of the log to about the depth of one of the chalk lines. In just a few minutes he did this for the entire length of the log, and then he split off the segments of wood in between the notches until a flat surface was left. He repeated this on the opposite side of the log. Then he and William turned the log so a flat side was up, and Swan proceeded using his chalk line and his axe to slash and flatten the two remaining sides until he had a cypress beam trimmed twelve inches square.

"Now we are ready to drag it," said Swan. He maneuvered the oxen to pull the high-wheeled cart astraddle the end of the beam, and then he unhitched the oxen. Following his directions, William helped him manipulate the long tongue of the cart, and a chain and grappling tongs that were attached to it, until the tongs bit into one end of the beam and pulled it up off the ground for the wheels to bear most of the beam's weight, leaving only the trailing rear end of the beam resting on the ground. With the beam secured and the oxen hitched again, they commenced dragging the squared timber to the wood yard. Once there, they drug it up close to the sawpit, which was at one end of the work shed. William and Swan worked together to get the beam off the cart and levered up onto rollers near either end of the pit, where they anchored it solidly. Then they took a chalk line and marked up the timber into inch-wide boards.

Cato and Ajax came over to do the sawing. Cato manned the upper handle of the whipsaw while Ajax, stripped to the waist, stood down in the sawpit to man the lower end of the saw. The cutting was done only on the downward motion of the saw, with Ajax doing the hardest labor. Sawdust fell steadily downward into the pit, and though the day was cool, Ajax was soon covered with sweat and sawdust. After each cut, Cato pulled up on the saw, and it was he who made sure the saw blade was running true to the chalked mark. If it was not, he twisted the tiller handle slightly to get it precisely back on the mark the next time Ajax pulled down the blade. Each downward pull of the saw cut about one linear inch of board. According to Swan, two men working steadily could cut about a hundred board feet of lumber in a day.

With Ajax and Cato working the pit saw, Swan and William walked to the other end of the work shed where Obadiah sat on a stool riving cypress roofing shingles. He had several lengths of thick cypress logs—bolts, Swan called them—each about two feet long, resting upright on their ends. Obadiah rived the shingles off with a froe, holding the upright wooden handle of the L-shaped tool with his left hand, positioning the horizontal, bar-shaped steel blade on the end of a bolt of wood, and then striking the back of the blade with a wooden maul held in his right hand. With the blade embedded in the wood, he would twist the handle to rive off a shingle. Once he had a pile of them, he trimmed their sides with a small hatchet.

"If you don't mind," Swan said to William, "it would help us out if you would bundle up these shingles and carry them down to the raft."

"Just tell me how big to make the bundles," said William. Using cord, he tied up a bundle to Swan's specifications, and then he picked it up and carried it down to the landing. The raft was about fifteen feet wide and thirty feet long, made of poles of yellow pine lashed together parallel to each other. Most of the hewed and sawed lumber for the Dubose plantation was neatly piled aboard. A long sweep for maneuvering was affixed to the stern of the raft. Since it was only to be floated a few miles down the river, it lacked the shelter and sand-lined fire box that William had seen on other lumber rafts. Tied up in the creek nearby was the pettiauger he and Rosemary were to take downriver, a long, narrow vessel that could carry moderate amounts of freight in shallow water. William deposited his shingles on the raft and went back for another bundle, and he stayed at this work until all of the shingles were loaded.

By late afternoon, the sawing and riving were done, and all of the men worked together to finish stacking the planks and clapboards on the raft. Finally they went to supper, Swan and William to Swan's cabin, and the slaves to the other, evidently to cook for themselves.

William was famished as he lit into the supper of hominy, sausage, and fried eggs. He understood now why the timber cutters required so much food. After his hunger was satisfied, he lingered at the table to talk with the others for a time.

"It seems like another world here in this swamp," he said.

Liza shook her head wearily.

"It's a world that's about played out for us," said Swan.

"How can that be?" asked William. "The swamp is full of cypresses."

"There are plenty of big ones still standing," said Swan, "but they are too big to be cut. We can't saw into lumber a tree that's more than about eighteen inches in diameter."

"And thank God they've about cut them all," said Liza.

"She's tired of living in a swamp," said Swan, "and I can't say I blame her. I wouldn't mind moving to higher ground myself."

"In summer," said Liza, "the mosquitos make this place a living hell. I can go back to the cowpen and get away from them for a while, but Swan has to stay here with the slaves. To ward off the mosquitos, we have to keep the air full of smoke with a smudge burning day and night. It's no way to live. Even the cows have better sense than to stay down in the swamps in the summer."

"If I had my way," said Swan, "I would build a grist mill on Poplar Creek."

"Rosemary showed me the place where you want to build it," said William. "It's a beautiful spot."

"This country is going to fill up with farmers and planters," said Swan, "and all of them will want a mill close at hand to grind their corn and wheat. I like the idea of having the water of Poplar Creek turn a wheel that powers a mill. The wheel all by itself does most of a miller's work. It would free up the labor of at least one of these slaves for other work in the cowpen. All I would have to do is feed the corn and wheat into one end of the mill and collect the meal and flour as it comes out the other end."

"It sounds like a fine idea," said William. "But I hear Mister MacDonald is opposed."

"Change frightens him," said Swan. "I thought that was the whole of the problem, but now I think there is even more to it. It turns out he doesn't even trust me to trade for a few barrels of rice. No wonder he doesn't want to turn me loose with a mill. He thinks I have no talent for commerce. It's true I never learned to read or cipher, but Liza can do that. I know how to trade and get around in the world."

"You have twice the common sense my father has," said Liza. "That and your strong arms count more in getting things done than any amount of book learning."

"For my part, I have to champion books," said Rosemary, "the same as I champion cypress trees. If all that interests you is the immediate world you live in, then common sense might be enough. But our world is so much larger than the little bit of it that we see with our eyes and walk on with our feet. If we want to know about the rest of it, we have to learn it from books."

"Well, I would be happy with my small world," said Swan, "if only it had a grist mill in it. But now is not the time to go on about that. We are in for a full day tomorrow, and I for one would like to get some sleep."

William was glad for an end to the conversation, which had made him uncomfortable because of the position John MacDonald had put him in with regard to Swan. He could think of no graceful way to smooth it over, and in truth he could not imagine why MacDonald had not directed Swan to support Rosemary in her dealings instead of himself. Swan's illiteracy could not be the reason. Rosemary had all the literacy that could possibly be needed for this transaction.

Liza and Swan retired to their one-legged bed: that is, three of its corners were affixed to the walls in a corner of the house, leaving only one corner of the bed to stand on a leg. Rosemary climbed up to sleep in a small loft, and William laid his bedroll on the dirt floor. He wrote a short entry in his journal.

Sunday, March 5, Swan's Logging Camp
   Cutting, sawing, and riving lumber is another occupation that is not for me. The labor is hard and unremitting, and not a little dangerous to life and limb.

17

The Pettiauger

William stood beside Rosemary as they watched the timber raft slowly make its way out into the current of Poplar Creek and from there into the Santee River. The flat-bottomed pettiauger they were to take downriver was a very large dugout canoe carved from a cypress trunk, about three and a half feet at its widest and about thirty feet long. It drew only eighteen inches or so of water, enabling it to navigate far up the courses of many of the creeks that fed into the Santee. Up toward its prow it had four seats, one behind the other, all with single oarlocks on alternating sides. Up to four oarsmen, then, each manning a single oar, could power the boat. The pettiauger had a tiller in its stern, positioned just behind a small roofed area that was made simply of two arches of flexed wood with a piece of oiled cloth stretched between them. A steersman could sit here and maneuver the boat while protected from sun and rain. The oarsmen received no such protection.

William tied a small dugout canoe to the stern of the pettiauger, and then he and Rosemary threw in their bedrolls along with a small parcel of food, climbed aboard, and shoved off. As the long vessel looped out in the current, each of them settled in with an oar, Rosemary in the front seat manning an oar on the right side, and William just behind her, manning an oar on the left side. With the dugout canoe in tow, they propelled the boat lazily down to the mouth of the creek. As they emerged into the current of the Santee, they saw the raft about fifty yards downstream, with Swan, Obadiah, Ajax, and Cato talking and joking, happy to have a respite from their daily labors as their raft drifted in the current.

"How often have you made this trip?" William asked.

"I've come with father most every year since I've been old enough to be more a help than a hinderance. Five or six years."

"You must know Mr. Dubose then."

"Dubose senior or Dubose junior?"

"Senior, I reckon. The one who owns the plantation."

"I've seen him once or twice. But he's not often up here in the backcountry. He spends most of his time in his town house in Charles Town. Jean Dubose is his name. Perhaps you have seen him there."

"No," said William. "He would be higher and mightier than those who dine with us at the Packsaddle. The men I know are of middling rank. And some are not that high."

"Jean Dubose is a merchant as well as a planter," said Rosemary, "and they say he is as much interested in what is going on in England, the Continent, and Africa as he is in what is going on in Carolina. This plantation we are going to is not the only one he owns."

"Who is Dubose junior?"

"Jerome? He is Jean's son. I have only met him once. It was five years ago. I was a mere girl, and he was a young man heading out into the world. He seemed very old to me then, but he must have been only three or four years older than I was. So now he would be about your age, or just a little younger. His father sent him to England to be educated."

"If my father had been a rice planter, all my problems would be solved," said William. Then suddenly he had a realization. "I'll wager Jerome Dubose is the man you were talking about earlier. He's the man you want to marry."

"I don't expect to marry Jerome himself, but someone like him. I thought he was the handsomest man I ever saw, and I dreamed about him for years. But I don't think he noticed me at all. I was just a slip of a girl. No doubt he is married by now, and not to a pinder's daughter, I am sure."

"Well, if the likes of him would not take a pinder's daughter to wife, how can you keep him as an ideal husband? Shouldn't you set your sights a bit lower?"

"They are lower, Billy. I want to marry a man with prospects, that's all. I'm not asking for the moon. Now, let's not talk about this any more. It sullies the air between us."

"It does indeed," said William, feeling a growing resentment. But here he was trapped in the boat with her; no going off to the barn loft to lick his wounds. So with considerable effort he let the current wash his resentment away as they drifted in silence, dawdling at their oars, using them mainly to keep their boat aligned with the flow of the river. At times they dragged them in the water to slow themselves down, lest they come closer to the raft ahead of them than they wanted to be.

The slow river followed a course to the southeast and then it made a bold, sinuous loop to the east. They drifted through a vast forest of tall trees, still bare in the last days of winter. It was too soon for turtles to be out or for bright-colored summer birds. Both sides of the river were lined with walls of entwined branches and vines. In some places, especially on the outside of the bends where the current was strongest, trees had been uprooted and had fallen into the stream. Fortunately, the Santee was wide enough that the fallen trees did not block their passage, as so often happened when navigating smaller rivers.

Trees were, however, hazardous in other ways. At one point Rosemary spotted the merest small twig, hardly moving, coming up in the current ahead of the pettiauger, and she immediately dropped the blade of her oar deeply into the water and pulled it rightward of the course they were taking. "Pull hard, Billy! Over this way!" He helped her move the boat hard to the right, just as a mass of sodden limbs bobbed up out of the water right in the middle of the course they had been following. Had they not turned, the tree would likely have come up under them, capsizing the pettiauger.

"What the devil was that?" William asked incredulously.

"It was a sawyer," she said, "a half-buoyant tree that washed out of a bank. Sometimes when a tree comes floating down the river, its big roots will snag and hang up on the bottom, and there it stays, swaying slowly up and down like the motion of a sawyer at a sawpit. You don't want a sawyer coming up under your boat."

"Then we should be watching close," he said.

"I *am* watching," said Rosemary. "That's why I took the front seat. I'm keeping a sharp lookout."

William smiled. "It seems that you are. Carry on, madam."

A little further along, they rounded a bend and caught sight of a bear and her two small cubs coming out onto a sandbar, perhaps to fish. When the bears saw the pettiauger, they scampered back once again to the safety of the canebrake from which they had come. The cubs were comical as they flounced along trying to keep up with their mother.

Later, as the pettiauger floated close to shore, William heard a deep, coarse croaking sound—*fraaahnk*—like a great reptile rising out of the swamp. But in fact it was a crook-necked blue heron flying out of the trees with its six-foot span of arched wings beating slowly. It flew a distance downstream and landed in shallow water near the bank, where it waded slowly on stilted legs, looking for small fish.

"A blue heron is Mother Nature's poetry," said Rosemary.

"What do you mean?" asked William. He had a sense of her meaning, but he wanted to hear her explain it.

"When I see a blue heron, it makes me feel the same way I do when I hear a poem. Recite a poem for me, Billy. I recited one for you when your ankle was stove in. It's your turn now."

William smiled and shook his head. "I have a tin ear when it comes to poetry. The only ones I know are short and not fit to recite in front of a woman. But I do know some stories. I can give you a Jack tale if you want."

"Jack tales must be told everywhere," said Rosemary. "I've heard them ever since I was a babe in arms. I doubt you can tell me a Jack tale I haven't heard."

"Have you heard the story of how Jack came to America?"

"No, I haven't," said Rosemary. "I thought I had heard them all."

"There was a fellow telling this one last winter on the Charles Town docks. It was in great favor. I heard him tell it at least three different times."

"I'm listening."

William took a few moments to compose the story in his mind. Then he began to tell the tale:

One day Jack set out to do something or another, and he met a little old woman dressed in black, hobbling along with a stout cane. She was all bent over, carrying a heavy bundle of wood on her back.

"Jack," she wheezed, "would you help a poor old woman with her wood?"

Jack thought it odd that she knew his name, but he felt sorry for her, and he went over and took the load from her and leaned over to swing it up on his own back. Just then something struck him on the head, and he fell to the ground, knocked senseless. When he woke up, he found that he himself was all bound up and tied to the old woman's back. She was running very fast, lickety-split, heading for a big hole in the earth. She entered the hole and kept running down, down, down until they came to the place where she lived in the very bowels of the earth. The smell of sulphur burned Jack's nose. He saw a big iron pot on the boil—the biggest he ever saw—sitting on a hot wood fire that was fed continually by a little old man. Jack thought the old man looked familiar, but he couldn't be sure because he was covered with soot, and he was skin and bones from working so hard.

"Whatever you do, Jack, don't talk with that little old man," the old woman said as she untied him. "I want you to tend the pot. I have been working for a year collecting all the best herbs that grow up in the sunlight. I am boiling them down together to make an elixir that will impart to me all the skill and wisdom in the world. After I drink it, I will know everything and be able to do everything. Your task is to keep stirring the brew and boiling it down. If you stop stirring that pot, you will regret it."

Time after time, the old woman would run up to the world above, as fast as a swift horse, coming back with ever more herbs for the pot. One day when the old woman was up above, Jack went over to the little old man, who was piling more wood on the fire. "How long have you been here?" Jack asked him.

"Don't you recognize me? I've been here since she kidnapped me a month ago."

Hearing his voice, Jack realized that the little old man was all that was left of a young man from his village who had mysteriously gone missing a month before.

"What has happened to you?" asked Jack.

"That old witch is working me to death, and if you don't get away, she will work you to death too."

After hearing this sobering news, Jack began to look for a chance to escape.

It was becoming harder and harder up in the green world for the old woman to find herbs that she had not already collected, and one day she was gone for a very long time. The elixir in the pot had boiled down very low, and finally it was reduced to only a few drops that were popping and sizzling in the bottom of the pot. As Jack reached down in the pot to stir it, the last few drops of elixir popped up and landed on the back of his hand. They burned like blazes, and Jack licked them off. As soon as he swallowed them, the cave was lit with a flash of light and Jack realized he now possessed all the skills and wisdom of the world.

When the old woman returned, she saw immediately what had happened, and she went into a frenzy. She kicked the fire, and coals flew all over the place. With her cane she hit the little old man on the head and killed him instantly.

With that, Jack took off running up through the twisting cave until finally he came out into the world above. With the elixir inside him, he thought that he was at last the equal of the old woman. But she still pursued, and though he ran as fast as he could, she began to gain on him, her arms and legs just a-flying.

Jack snapped his fingers and changed himself into a rabbit, and soon he had raced far ahead of the old woman. But then he looked back and saw that she had changed herself into a large hound, and she was coming up right behind him, panting and showing her teeth.

Jack snapped his fingers again and changed himself into a sparrow, and he flew up into the sky. But the old woman changed herself into a falcon and flew up higher toward the clouds. Jack's heart beat faster when he looked up and saw the falcon streaking downward, its eyes fixed upon him, its talons outstretched.

Jack snapped his fingers yet again and changed himself into a grain of wheat too small for the falcon to seize, even though it tried, snatching at the air and clenching its talons furiously. Jack fell to earth in what appeared to be a wheat field, where he felt safe amongst all the other grains of wheat scattered on the ground. But then he saw a chicken nearby, and not just any chicken. It was a giant hen furiously clucking and pecking up grains of wheat. And before he could snap his fingers again, he was inside the chicken.

Jack knew that he was really in a fix when the chicken changed itself back into the old woman. What to do? If she digested him, the elixir would be hers and he would be gone. So he snapped his fingers again and changed himself into a fetus. The old woman was now pregnant with Jack!

This made her very angry. She did not want to be a mother, and especially not the mother of a child like Jack. But after a little while, he was born. The old woman vowed to get rid of Jack once and for all. But now that he was born, he was such a handsome child she couldn't bring herself to strangle him. Finally the old woman hit upon a plan. She went to where some men were killing hogs and asked them to give her a hog bladder to make into a balloon to give to her child as a play-toy. They gladly gave her what she asked.

The old woman went off to a creek, put Jack inside the bladder, blew it up, and set it into the water. The creek carried the bladder into a river, and the river carried it to the Atlantic Ocean. Jack floated on the ocean waves for a long time, years it seemed, but because he had drunk the elixir, he needed no food nor water. At last he felt the bladder wash up onto a shore.

Jack popped the bladder and stepped out into the sunlight of a vast land. There was no one to be seen, and he felt lonesome. Everything he knew anything about was back on the other side of the ocean. Here he had no family, no friends, and there were no towns to be seen. Jack had never before been downhearted, but now he sat down on a rock and cried.

But then the memory of his mother's voice came to him. She said, "You've got to have gumption, Jack. If you can't make it on your own, you can't make it at all."

Jack dried his tears, got to his feet, held out his arms to America, and said "Hurrah!" And then he was off to his next adventure.

"Whew!" said Rosemary. "That is the best Jack tale I ever heard."

"Well, I did add a few embellishments."

"My father would like to hear that story. From what I've heard him say, he felt just like Jack when he first got to these shores."

"Aye, and I felt the same," said William. "But there's no going back. We're all here now, and the world is new."

"And do you possess all of Jack's skill and wisdom?"

"Och, there's the sorrow. That bit of magic got Jack out of the Old World, but it wore off during the ocean voyage. Jack in America is just Jack again."

"Poor Jack," said Rosemary. "But he is still a clever lad."

"He keeps his spirits up," said William. "And now it's time for you to give me a tale."

"I would rather recite a poem," said Rosemary.

"As long as it's not about lovers. I don't want to go back into deep water. Jack and the hog bladder are about as deep as I want to go."

"Just remember that we are brother and sister."

"Then give me a poem about a brother and sister."

"I would if I knew one, but I don't. Jack's mother's voice made me think about my own mother. I hear her voice sometimes. She loved poetry, and this one was her favorite. It's by Master Shakespeare. She used to recite it to me when I was crying over some meanness or other from my sisters."

"Let's hear it, then," said William. "And when you are finished, we can think about why there are not more poems about brother and sister. Could it be because it is a bond between man and woman that is so fixed it does not stir the heart?"

"Don't undo us, Billy. This new way of being together is working for me."

"Then I will try to honor it. For this trip, at least."

"Thank you." She paused for a moment, gathering her thoughts. Then she began to recite:

> "Shall I compare thee to a summer's day?
> Thou art more lovely and more temperate.
> Rough winds do shake the darling buds of May.

And summer's lease hath all too short a date.
Sometimes too hot the eye of heaven shines,
And often is his gold complexion dimmed,
And ev'ry fair from fair sometimes declines,
By chance or Nature's changing course untrimmed.
But thy eternal summers shall not fade,
Nor lose possession of that fair thou ow'st,
Nor shall Death brag thou wand'rest in his shade,
When in eternal lines to time thou grow'st.
So long as men can breathe or eyes can see,
So long lives this, and this gives life to thee."

"I could almost understand that one," said William. "Say it again."

Rosemary repeated the sonnet, her voice lifting almost in song, strong and clear.

"I must say, those words are beautiful," said William. "And their meaning is not so hidden as in most of Shakespeare's knotted poetry. Do it one more time."

She laughed and recited the poem again.

"What I hear," said William, "is that the poet compares the object of his affections—his sister, no doubt—to a summer's day, but says that his sister is more comely than a summer's day, and less subject to bad turns in the weather and the changeability of nature. Then he claims she'll never die because of 'this.' What he means by 'this' went by me at first, but now I think I grasp it. 'Eternal lines' is the key. He means the very lines of his sonnet. Having captured his sister in ink on paper, time and change and even death are evaded. But who is she in truth? Is she really his sister? Or even a she? Perhaps he has captured forever his dog. Or his horse."

Rosemary laughed. "I always thought it was a pinder's daughter whose older sisters were mean to her. But maybe it was a horse."

Just then they came round a bend, and there ahead in the distance, on the right side of the river, was a landing, with the raft pulling up to it. They had arrived at Dubose's plantation. In the past three hours they had drifted close to nine miles downriver. Now they steered toward the right as they watched Swan wield the steering oar to bring the raft in close to shore. Obadiah jumped from the raft into the shallow water and pulled a mooring rope up the bank. He tied it to a tree so that the current swung the raft in alongside the shore. As William and Rosemary approached, Obadiah rang a bell that was on top of a post near the landing.

There wasn't much to the landing—a small dock and a wooden crane for loading and offloading cargo. William and Rosemary maneuvered the pettiauger to bring it alongside the dock and moor it. Then they joined Swan and walked with him up a rise to a small, strongly built warehouse. In the distance, coming down the road that led to the landing, were two men, one a white man with a whip looped over his shoulder and the other a black man dressed in tattered clothing.

"That's Conrad Mote, Dubose's overseer," Swan said to William, "and the man trailing after him is one of his drivers."

As Mote approached, Swan put out his hand. "Good to see you," Swan said as the two shook hands. "We've brung you the lumber for building the new kitchen. We can put it on the bank ourselves, but if you want it further up, we'll need some help."

"I can manage that," said Mote. He turned to his driver. "Zeus, go get me five or six of the fellows coming in from the fields."

"Yas, suh," said Zeus, and he turned and jogged up the road and out of sight.

"Conrad Mote," said Swan, "this here is William MacGregor, and you already know Rosemary MacDonald. These two will be dealing with you for the rice."

Mote shook William's hand and doffed his hat to Rosemary. "It won't be me you're dealing with this year, Miss MacDonald. Young Dubose is here for a time. He'll handle the business."

William glanced at Rosemary, but she gave nothing away as she kept her eyes on Mote.

"So nice to see you, Mr. Mote," she said to him. "Is the season going well?"

"Yes ma'am, it has gone well enough so far. The weather was too wet at first. We need it to be dry for us to get into the fields. But it finally turned our way, and the slaves have been out tilling up the ground and making rows for sowing the rice. I've had to work them hard to catch up, but the land is now ready for seeding."

"I thought rice wanted wet land," said William.

"Not in the beginning," said Mote. "The rice plants need time to get their roots down in the ground. If it turns off wet, that won't happen and we have to go back and plant it again. That makes the slaves surly, I'll tell you. We can barely keep the lid on as it is. But so far this season, I've only had one slave run away that we didn't get back. I do have one out right now, but he's not a runaway, just a slacker. He'll be back. He's done it before, and I thought I'd taught him, but I guess he needs another lesson." Mote clamped his hand around his whip.

William shifted uneasily, thinking of Alonso, who had been brutally whipped on a rice plantation.

Rosemary seemed unaffected. "It is good to hear that the season is going well," she said. "We'll be getting along up to the house to meet with Mister Dubose." And with that, she and William headed up the path to the plantation house.

"Young Dubose," William said flatly. "Imagine that."

"Let's not talk about it," said Rosemary. "I didn't know he was going to be here."

"Then we can talk about Mote and his whip," said William. "I can't get accustomed to slavery when it comes to the whipping. Though I don't imagine it bothers young Dubose."

"You talk like you've never left Glasgow," said Rosemary. "This is Carolina, don't forget, and slavery is the way in these parts. These planters think of themselves as heroes, the founders and shapers of this country. They take pride in the life they have built here and are not much interested in philosophizing or moralizing about it. They would say that philosophy belongs to them that don't have to join the fray and get things done. All they really care about is how to grow the most rice for the least cost and to what port in the wide world they can ship it to gain the highest profit."

"That's not all there is to consider," said William.

"But that's all they do consider."

"Is that all you would consider?"

"I'm not saying that it is."

"It's hard to tell which side you're on," said William.

"I'm not thinking of it as sides," she replied.

William fell silent as they passed by a small straggle of slaves dressed in ragged clothing, barefoot on this cool, early-March day and worn down from a long day's work in the great wide fields. Headed for the dock, none except the youngest of them made eye contact with William and Rosemary. Mote's driver trailed after them.

They next met up with a barefoot slave driving a team of large, mud-spattered oxen that were shod with heavy leather shoes strapped to their feet.

"What kind of country is this," said William, "where the oxen wear shoes and the workers go shoeless?"

Rosemary shook her head. "It's not Scotland, Billy. It's Carolina. The shoes give the oxen traction in the water-logged soil."

They followed on along the road, ascending to higher ground that lay above flood level. A house came into view, the overseer's, William reckoned. It was a plain house with two rooms below and two above, sided with riven

199

clapboards of yellow pine. The house was surrounded by a scatter of simple outbuildings, much like those at MacDonald's cowpen.

"Where is the main house from here?" William asked.

"This *is* the main house," said Rosemary.

"This? I expected a grand manor house like the ones on the plantations near Charles Town."

"This is a backcountry plantation," said Rosemary. "It's only purpose, pure and simple, is to produce rice. Dubose only comes out here from time to time. He doesn't live here. The overseer lives in this house. Dubose stays in it when he comes."

"Dubose senior or Dubose junior?" William asked dryly.

"Either one. But please don't give me a hard time about this, Billy. He has a wife back in Charles Town for all I know."

"I hope so," said William.

She reached out and put a hand on his arm. "I didn't know he was going to be here."

"I believe you," said William.

They reached the house, and as they walked up the steps and onto the porch, they were met at the door by a tall, light-skinned housekeeper. Dressed in a worn, but still pretty, calico shift and a white apron, she was an attractive young woman, graceful in her movements and reserved in her manner. Her chiseled nose and long limbs reminded William of Cudjo.

"I am Rosemary MacDonald," Rosemary said to her. "I have come in my father's place to see Mister Dubose about a raft of lumber he ordered for a new kitchen. We have just brought it down the river."

"Master Jerome is out back with the workers that are building the new kitchen chimney. He'll be glad to see you. He's been waitin for that wood to get here."

They followed the young woman past the central stairwell and out the back door. The present kitchen was directly behind the house, and off to one side the chimney for the new one was going up. Jerome Dubose was easily recognizable, neatly dressed and undoubtedly as handsome as Rosemary remembered him. He was conferring with the mason about the partially finished chimney, the base of which stood, with great fireplaces set into its front and back, in the middle of where the new kitchen was to be.

"Master Jerome," said the slave woman. "They's visitors here to see you."

"Thank you, Julie," said Jerome, turning to greet his guests. When he saw Rosemary, his eyebrows rose slightly in surprise.

"Do you remember me, Mister Dubose? I am Rosemary MacDonald. We met a few years ago when I was here with my father, bringing down a raft of wood."

Jerome smiled. "I do indeed remember you, Miss MacDonald. You were just a young girl, but I remember that you were quite lively and had a lot to say. Now the young girl has grown up, I see. Is this your husband?"

"No," she said, and for a moment William feared she would say he was her brother. "This is William MacGregor. He works for my father. We have come to trade lumber for rice."

"I am glad the lumber has arrived," said Jerome. "I was beginning to fear the deal had fallen through. I have your barrels of rice waiting for you down in the warehouse. If you will agree to the trade, we can winch them onto your boat. I'll send a man down."

"We'll go down and check the barrels," said Rosemary. "I'm sure all is in good order. And if you don't mind, we'll sleep in your warehouse tonight. It takes longer to get up the river than down. If we were to set out this afternoon, darkness would overtake us."

"By all means, tell your crew to settle in," said Jerome. "But you and Mister MacGregor must come back here and dine with me and sleep in the house. Our Julie is an excellent cook. Excellent for the backcountry, that is. I would very much enjoy some good company."

Rosemary glanced at William. He shrugged. He could hardly say no, though he wanted to. He already felt himself the odd man out. Rosemary had not needed him for a second in finishing the deal. He wondered whether John MacDonald had known that Jerome Dubose would be here. Perhaps he wanted to start a romance and had sent William along as a chaperone. For once he wished he were back with the cows.

18

Rice

William was not pleased when Jerome insisted on going with them to inspect the barrels of rice. Worse yet, Jerome suggested they go by a roundabout way that would give them a tour of the plantation. William would have preferred a trip straight down to the warehouse and back, but Rosemary was delighted with the prospect of a tour, and William had no choice but to go along. As they followed Jerome out of the house, Rosemary gave William a little prod with her elbow, and when he looked at her, she tightened her lips a bit and shook her head at him very slightly in disapproval. For what? he wondered in exasperation. He was going along with all this, was he not? Did he have to pretend to be happy about it as well?

"Let's start by going out back to the orchard," said Jerome, pausing to let the two of them come up beside him. As they set out strolling together, he asked, "What work do you do for MacDonald, Mister MacGregor?"

"I'm a cow-hunter," said William.

Jerome looked surprised, as if he had expected William occupy a higher position.

"Billy is like a son to my father," said Rosemary. "He helps out wherever he is needed."

William said nothing. Brother and sister again.

"And you, Mister Dubose," said Rosemary. "Are you living in Charles Town now?"

"Actually, I am living up here for a time," said Jerome. "I came just after Christmas. If I am to be master of these plantations one day, I need more knowledge of how they are run than I gained at my school in England."

William's heart began to sink. No mention yet of a wife.

Rosemary became more animated. "Tell us about your schooling in England. How wonderful it must have been to receive such a fine education."

"I wish you could have gone in my place," said Jerome.

"Surely you are joking," said Rosemary. "Tell us about your school. Was it in London?"

"No, it was to the south of London, in Kent, but connected to it by a turnpike. Sevenoaks is a very old public school."

"A public school?" Rosemary said approvingly. "I would have thought you would go to a rich man's school. Much better to mix with the public and learn the real ways of the world."

"I am sorry to disappoint," said Jerome, "but in England a public school *is* a rich man's school. A place like Sevenoaks is open to those few boys who come from wealth, power, or connections, and it is best to come from all three. The motto of the school is *Servire Deo Regnare Est*. To Serve God Is To Rule. My father had enough strings to pull to get me in. But I went there as a poorly prepared colonial boy, and my fellow students considered themselves my betters."

"But you did get a good education," said William.

"We learned mathematics—and that is a good thing. We were caned into learning Latin, the language of Romans long dead and of scholars of today, and of Papist clerics, of course, none of which I am or ever will be. We learned the literature and philosophy of ancient Greeks, which appeal to some, but not to me. I regret to say that the greatest lesson of all that I took from Sevenoaks is that tyranny is the natural order of mankind. The rules of the school were at first bewildering, but we learned them quickly, as our teachers caned us for the slightest infractions. And the tyranny did not stop there. Upperclassmen had their feet on the necks of underclassmen. We were little better than slaves to them. The older boys caned the younger boys more mercilessly than did the teachers. First I took it and then I gave it, but I hated every day I was there."

"Then surely your father did not know where he was sending you," said Rosemary.

"He did most assuredly. The boys who endure life together in a public school form attachments with each other that are life-long. One cannot have too many fast friends in this empire that Britain is a-building. I hated the school, but I value my friends and the connections they give me."

"So I suppose you were glad to come home when your studies were finished," said Rosemary.

"I did not come straight home. After Sevenoaks I went to study law at Oxford, but I only stayed there a year. The student's life was not for me, and I finally convinced my father of it. What I wanted most was to learn how money is made. So I went next to London and lived there on my own for a year, drawing on my father's connections. London was the best of my time abroad—theater, music, conversation. I learned more from the city than I ever did from books. But in the end, yes, I was glad to leave it all and return to Charles Town. In my soul of souls I truly am a colonial. And what about you, Miss MacDonald? Were you schooled by a tutor?"

"I was educated by my mother," said Rosemary. "She loved the English language and taught me to read and write it. I have a few books, though not many. Very few, in truth. But I do pay attention to the stories told by the menfolk who eat at our table at the cowpen, and I try in that way to learn about the world."

"I have seen Rosemary follow table talk better than the men who are doing the talking," said William. "I have heard her recite Shakespeare and flowery words from the Bible, improving on them all the while. And when she sings, the birds grow quiet."

Rosemary pushed against his arm in a feigned reprimand. "Hush, you are embarrassing me."

"He speaks like an admirer," said Jerome.

"We are like brother and sister," said Rosemary.

William tried to think of a clever retort, but he could not.

"So tell me about your education, Mister MacGregor," said Jerome. "You have schooling, I take it."

"My education is a bit of this, a bit of that," said William. "I learned to read, write, and do numbers in a Presbyterian mission school in the Highlands of Scotland. Since then I have schooled myself through the reading of books."

"Life itself is a school," said Jerome.

"So they say," William said dryly.

They had come to the edge of the orchard. "I wish it were a month from now," said Jerome. "Then you could see most of these trees in bloom. We have peach trees, primarily."

"I love peaches," said Rosemary. "Look at how many trees you have!"

"But even with all of these, we don't get much fruit from them. The pilferers get the greater part."

"Pilferers?" asked William.

"A troop of deer and a tribe of raccoons hereabouts keep watch on these trees and know the instant the fruit comes ripe. They come in the dark of night and gorge themselves. And the slaves sneak right in behind them. If this orchard were located anywhere near the slave quarters, we would hardly harvest a peck of peaches for the house. But let's move on now to the kitchen garden." Jerome led them along a path away from the orchard.

When they arrived at the garden, Rosemary brightened even more. "You have your garden ploughed and harrowed and some of it planted! This tells me how far behind I am in my own garden at the cowpen. I have no seeds in the ground."

"We only have the cold-hardy vegetables planted," said Jerome. "Onions. A patch of turnips. Some lettuce and coleworts."

"We call those collards," said Rosemary.

Jerome laughed. "Coleworts in England, collards in Carolina. It's all the same."

"Surely you don't feed your slaves out of this small garden," said William.

"Oh, no. They raise their own kitchen gardens in their spare time. We give them weekly rations of rice and corn, and a little salt pork. But they raise their own vegetables, and most of their meat comes from fish and small game they get on their own. They are quite resourceful."

Leaving the garden, they soon found themselves on the road leading down to the boat landing. William was glad to see the tour ending short of a trip to the rice fields. At the river they found that the slaves had unloaded the lumber, clapboards, and shingles, neatly stacking everything up near the warehouse, and they had disassembled the raft and pulled the pine poles up onto the bank.

Swan was leaning against a post talking with Conrad Mote. Obadiah, Ajax, and Cato sat on the wharf, dangling their legs over the side. The driver Zeus was sitting by the warehouse on a stack of lumber. Jerome motioned to him, and Zeus got up and came over.

"Get yourself a prybar," Jerome said to Zeus, "and go inside the warehouse with Mister MacGregor to those four barrels of rice we have for them. Pry a stave off the top of each barrel, and let him see that the barrels are full and the rice is good."

"Yas, suh," said Zeus, and he turned and walked away to the warehouse. William looked at Rosemary to see if she were coming with him to inspect the rice, but she just smiled at him, and he had no choice but to follow Zeus and leave her standing alone with Jerome.

To William the barrels appeared to be as promised. They were filled to the top. He dipped out and inspected a handful of rice from each of them, and it seemed to be of good quality. Then he plunged his arm down deeper to bring up some from further down, and it, too, seemed to be good. When he returned, Rosemary was explaining to Swan that she and William would be sleeping up at the house and that the woodcutters were welcome to bed down inside the warehouse. William wondered how Swan felt about being excluded from the company at the house, though even if he had been invited, he would not have wanted to leave his crew of slaves on their own for the whole night.

"Now we will finish our tour of the plantation," Jerome announced.

William's mood sank even lower. He had thought the tour was over.

"Mote," Jerome said to his overseer, "you and Zeus come along while we go to the rice fields. We need to take a look at what the workers accomplished today."

"Yes, sir, we do," said Mote. And so the five of them walked down along the river bank until they came in sight of the great expanse of rice fields that had been cleared out of the dense swamp forest for a considerable distance. The massive trees in the encircling swamp, festooned with a tangle of vines, spoke volumes about the water-logged, snake-infested misery of the clearing and leveling that had been done on this land by the slaves. Each rice field of ten to twenty acres was enclosed in a square earthen embankment two to three feet high. Most of the fields had been ploughed since last year's harvest. Here and there a slave was still at work with a hoe, repairing the embankments.

"I would think it would be day's end for these fellows," said William.

"Each slave has a task to complete each day," said Jerome. "Often, for instance, it is to hoe an acre of rice. Once a man hoes that acre, his day of work is over and he can do what he pleases. Some do their day's work in a hurry. Others take longer."

"These fields go on without end," said Rosemary.

"We have about 120 acres on this plantation. In a good season, each acre of rice land produces 1,000 to 1,500 pounds of rice. This is the reason the gem of Carolina shines so brightly in the British imperial crown. It is a great achievement, this rice going out to all the world. And it was the planters of Carolina who masterminded its cultivation. The original idea of the Proprietors in London was that Carolina would be a colony of large and small farmers scattered about over the countryside like those in England. That plan did not work. After much trial and error, planters like my father learned to grow rice, and we plant it on what the Proprietors took to be useless swamp land. It is through such improved agriculture that the people of Carolina prosper."

"Some people prosper this way, perhaps, but not all," said William. "A great many others must find other means. The cowpens on the northern borderlands are no small achievement."

"Yes, in the early years of our colony many of the fathers and grandfathers of today's rice planters themselves began by herding cattle, but there was a limit to the profit cattle could bring. It is only the rice plantations that have underwritten great fortunes—the greatest fortunes in the American colonies today. But that is not to say that cowherding doesn't pay. I'm sure you can testify to that, Miss MacDonald."

"Well," said Rosemary, "I can say we are getting by, but I would also have to say that all does not go as well as it used to."

"It does not go as well as it used to," said Jerome, "because the grazing of cattle wears out the land, while plantation rice improves the land. There are many rice fields in Carolina that have produced rice continuously for three decades now, and not only that, but the yield of rice per acre is greater today than it was in the past. Rice is a wonder beyond the dreams of our colony's founders. Rice planters like my father have given Carolina a secure place in the sacred order of the British Empire."

"I was unaware of any sacred order," said William.

"But you are a man of learning, MacGregor. Surely you know of the sacred chain of being by which England prospers. God in heaven bestows upon the king the right to rule. The king in turn bestows a measure of that power on Carolina's royal governor, who confers his beneficence upon the rice planters. The rice planters look after their slaves, give them food and clothing and a place to live, and the slaves repay the planters with their labor. The rice is sold, expenses are met, taxes are paid, and the Empire prospers. The links in this chain stretch from heaven to earth."

"Ah, *that* sacred order," said William. He was beginning to strongly dislike this man. He glanced at Conrad Mote and especially at Zeus to see if they were in agreement with this cosmic scheme. The two were walking quietly off to one side and seemed not to be listening, though William was sure that they were.

Very soon they came to the edge of a good-sized lake. "We dammed up this lake to supply water to flood the rice fields," said Jerome. "In late summer they must be inundated to encourage the rice to grow and to drown out the weeds and grass. The embankments around the fields hold in the water. Sometimes rainfall is sufficient to flood the fields, but when it is not, we can open the trunks in the lake's dam and let out the water we need. Mastering the flow of water on the land is the key to success with this crop. And of course the lake is stocked with fish, which serves the slaves well. Some mighty fine fish have been caught here, haven't they, Zeus?"

"Yas, suh, some mighty fine fish."

As they walked by the lake and turned to go up to the house, Mote suddenly stopped and pulled Zeus in close to him, speaking to him in a low voice and nodding toward a canebrake some distance away. Zeus peered at the canebrake and the two talked some more, Zeus nodding to what seemed to be instructions from Mote. Though William noticed this exchange, Jerome and Rosemary did not, and the three of them kept walking along.

William watched as Zeus slipped away and into some cover and then made for the canebrake. Someone in the cane yelled, and everyone stopped and looked around. They could hear the sound of men thrashing about and see the cane waving about above the fracas. A few minutes later Zeus came out driving before him a slightly-built young black man. His hands were bound with cord behind his back, and Zeus had him tethered by another cord around his neck. The young man was trembling. He was poorly clothed and soaked to the skin, but clearly it was fear that made him tremble.

"Prince, you damned rascal!" said Mote. "Did you think you could hide out in the swamp in our busiest time of the year?"

"Mercy, mastah Mote. I be hongry. I go settin snares way down river in the tall cane and couldna come out. Too late and too scahed."

"You set out to take another holiday, that's what you did. Those lashes we gave you last time weren't lesson enough. Let's give him some more, Zeus. Send him home with blood on his back for all to see."

"No, no, please, mercy," pleaded Prince, tears welling up in his eyes.

"Do it, Zeus," said Mote.

Zeus took more cord from inside his shirt and tied the man against a tree so that his arms were stretched above his head.

"No, Zeus," said Prince, "yunnah lub ma mama. Yunnah put a hurt on Prince, she mad."

"Yunah caint got no mercy wen yunnah duh run," said Zeus. "Sad we got to buhn fore we luhn."

"I won't nevah run no more," said Prince, weeping.

"Done too late. I got to der it. Most kill bird don't make no stew."

"Lay on twenty," said Mote, handing off his whip to Zeus. "Watch your aim and spare his arms. But don't spare his back." Zeus kept a strong face as he wielded the whip, the blows laying stripes on Prince's already scarred back. Prince braved the first blows in silence. But as they kept coming, he began to moan and then to cry out, louder and louder, until he lost voice and sagged in his bindings, overwhelmed by the pain.

Jerome had moved back away from the whipping, but he watched it. William averted his eyes, and so did Rosemary, the two of them frozen in place, waiting for it to be over, waiting to move along. Earlier in the day they had been floating lazily down the river telling stories, reciting poetry. But now this felt like a nightmarish dream.

"Cut him down and take him to the cabins," said Mote. "Drag him if he can't walk. This will put the other young bucks on notice that we'll have no malingering. If this plantation is to prosper, everyone must obey and do his part."

Jerome began walking on toward the house, Rosemary and William following, while Mote and Zeus struggled to get Prince on his feet and moving. William wondered what Jerome would say next, and the answer was nothing. They walked in utter silence. William considered going down to the warehouse to sleep, but he could not leave Rosemary alone with Dubose. As much as he hated this situation, he was trapped in it.

The wagon road they were following from the fields to the house led through the double row of slave cabins, five or six on each side of the road. The little cabins were made out of the same kind of materials as the Cherokee houses William had seen at Keowee and the Natchez houses in Four Hole Swamp. They were built of posts set into the earth with woven wattle walls plastered with clay and with roofs of thatch or riven boards. But these cabins were smaller than Indian houses and not so well built. It was hard to see clearly through the doors and into the darkened interiors, but William could make out that the living space was crowded. Most of the cabins had wood-and-clay chimneys, though not much smoke came up from them. After the first few houses, he averted his eyes from them and watched the path before his feet. The silence that had begun with the whipping lasted all the way back to the house.

When they arrived, they found the table spread for dinner. William was not hungry, but Jerome insisted they take their places and begin serving themselves. Jerome called for Julie to bring in a bottle of rum. She came striding in wearing her pretty calico dress, and she paused before the table and waited to be directed where to pour.

"Do you take rum, Miss MacDonald?" asked Jerome.

"Not usually. But I will today. My nerves need calming."

"I understand," said Jerome. "I myself hate to watch what we witnessed out there, but stern discipline is the only way to run a plantation. In the sacred order by which we all live, nothing is asked of the slaves but their labor. They have their part to play for the good of the whole, and they must play it. Otherwise we fail to gain the profit that turns the great wheel of commerce that provides for us all."

"Perhaps the slaves find it harder than we do to understand this idea of profit," said William. "They have not been schooled in our philosophy."

Rosemary glanced at him uneasily, but William ignored her.

Jerome appeared unruffled. "It is not a mere idea of profit," he said genially. "It is a well-established and inescapable fact. Let me explain. We presently have thirty-five slaves on this plantation, and thirty of them are good workers. If all goes well, a slave can pay for himself in four years. After that, if all goes well, a planter gets a profit of, say, ten pounds per year per slave. That provides an income of about 300 pounds per year. Of course the expenses of the plantation have to come out of that, including food, clothing, and shelter for the slaves, which is where the profit comes to them. They get their living."

"I see," said William, feeling argumentative but holding his tongue. The system of slavery was so pervasive in Carolina it was foolish to speak against it. In Glasgow further conversation could be had, but not here. He picked at his food in silence.

"Do you expect a good price for your rice this year?" asked Rosemary, trying, it would seem, to lead them to smoother ground.

"If I were able in the spring to predict the price of rice in the fall," said Jerome, "I would soon be master of all the rice fields in Carolina. The price depends upon so many things. First there is the weather—ideally it will be dry in spring and dry in the fall, with a great deal of rain in between. And come fall, no hurricanes, please. But unfortunately, ideal weather for rice comes only about one year in four, and the rest are middling to poor. And then there is the price of transport. It must be low for Carolina to make money. We also have to worry about the price of the rice crop in southern Italy, our main competitor. The merchants and planters in Charles Town keep their eyes and ears open for any scrap of information about the market for rice from their observers and agents in several Atlantic ports. And we must carefully sift through this information. Letters conveying important developments are sometimes purloined to be opened and read by others. Some planters and merchants will even circulate false information, feeding gossip that will favor their own interests."

"Goodness," said Rosemary. "I never imagined that one had to keep an eye on the whole world to be a successful rice planter. How challenging that must be."

"It is a challenge," said Jerome. "One must indeed have a grasp of conditions in a great swath of the world. That is why Father spends his time in Charles Town, with all his senses and intellect attuned to the talk of the town, while others spend their time out here where the rice is grown."

"My dream," said Rosemary, "has always been to live in Charles Town."

"Charles Town's destiny is to be a great city," said Jerome. "Rice will make it so. My British friends consider Charles Town provincial. But they are short-sighted. The future of our city is bright indeed."

"Well, for the sake of discussion," said William, "I have lived in Glasgow and I have lived in Charles Town, and if one grants that Glasgow is a great city, which I believe it is, then I wonder if Charles Town could ever truly catch up to it. Carolina has little more than rice and naval stores on which to build her future, but Glasgow has manufacturing. Even now, Glasgow imports raw tobacco from the colonies and manufactures cigars, snuff, and pipe tobacco to sell all over the world. They have factories for weaving and metalworking on a scale unimaginable in Charles Town. And so much more. Even some of the raw deerskins we ship to Glasgow come back to us as gloves and book bindings."

"That may very well be true," said Jerome, "but the people of Charles Town are not idle. Our challenge is to discover the commodities for which we are best suited. For example, some are now looking to produce indigo as a blue dye for the textile trade. Like rice, indigo requires a suitable climate, and Carolina has that climate. Our climate is our greatest advantage. Along with our system of labor."

"Again, just for the pleasure of discussion. . . ," said William.

"Billy," Rosemary said quietly, "you are contending with our host. Have a care."

"No, no," said Jerome, "let him speak. We planters are sure of where we stand. I find this conversation most interesting."

"For the sake of philosophy," said William, "I would raise a point often discussed in the coffeehouses of Glasgow. You must have heard the same in London, regarding the advantages and disadvantages of slavery. In Glasgow, for instance, I heard it argued that people who are enslaved do not advance themselves by working hard to earn more pay, as free workers do. Slaves have only to complete their tasks, with no incentive to do more. This limits the wealth, according to this argument, that this system of labor is likely to create."

"I do not agree that the effect is significant," said Jerome, "and philosophy supports me. It was Aristotle himself who famously wrote that all great civilizations have been based on slavery."

"I will not contend with Aristotle," said William, "for I have not read his works. But I have heard lectures by a Scottish philosopher of our own time—Francis Hutcheson—who himself has famously said that the standing of nations is to be judged by the degree of happiness conferred upon the greatest number of people. It might be argued that slavery raises a problem in this regard."

"Ah," said Jerome, "but surely your man Hutcheson would not contend that happiness is the only measure of a civilization. A civilization must be ordered, and the economy must be productive. Otherwise happiness is not possible. This is the value of the sacred order of the great chain of being."

"And yet, how can we be sure that we correctly understand the sacred order?" asked William.

"My goodness," said Rosemary, "can't we talk about something less contentious? Philosophy should bring light, not discord."

"Enlightenment only comes after much discussion," said William. "But we will change the subject, if you wish. Perhaps we could go back to that conversation we heard between Mote and that poor fellow, Prince."

"Billy!" Rosemary said sharply.

"No," William said to her soothingly. "I am changing the subject. Hear me out." Then he turned to Jerome. "When those two were talking, what language were they speaking? It sounded like a melodious dialect of English, but for the life of me, I could not grasp much of what they were saying."

Jerome sat back in his chair, welcoming an easier topic. "It is English, all right," he said, "but it has got some African and God knows what other languages mixed into it. The old planters say that it was brought to Carolina by the first slaves who came in from Jamaica and Barbados, and that back in those days they spoke an even stranger version of it than what we hear today. Some call it the Gullah language, after the African land of Angola, though I doubt very much it is the same language that is spoken there. After a while your ear attunes to it, and you can understand most of it, unless the slaves don't want you to. They can make it harder for us to understand if they choose to."

"How odd," said William. "A language that can both conceal and express meaning at the same time. It is not like anything else I have heard. The slaves in Charles Town and at the cowpen do speak their own dialect, but it is English through and through and no more difficult to understand than many of the dialects in Britain."

"I have made the same observation," said Jerome. "I have heard Gullah spoken only on the large plantations. Few of these slaves live in the company of their masters. They talk mostly to each other and seldom hear good English spoken."

Just then Julie returned with the jug of rum. "Does anyone want more?"

Relieved to be interrupted, they all allowed their cups to be refilled. As Julie was pouring rum into William's cup, he decided to speak to her, even though he knew it was a breach of propriety to converse with a servant at table. "Julie," he said forthrightly, "are you a Fulani girl?"

"Why—yes, suh, I am. I was born a Fulani." She did not seem shy about talking, so William pressed on.

"I know a Fulani song."

"No," she said with a wide smile. "You don't know no Fulani song."

"I do," said William. "It goes like this. *I sing of Juliyama, a girl as lovely as water. Lovely as water.*"

Julie was so startled her mouth fell open. "Juliyama? That is my Fulani name. Where did you learn that song?"

"I hunt cattle with a Fulani man," said William. "When he sings it, he gets a tear in his eye."

Julie stared at William intently. "I didn't know there was any other Fulanis around here," she said.

"This is all very interesting," said Jerome, "but we must let Julie get back to the kitchen. And as for the rest of us, morning will come early. It is time to make arrangements for the night. William, you are welcome to sleep on the floor here, or you can walk down to the landing where the rest of your crew will be sleeping. Rosemary, it would not be proper for you to sleep in my house if William goes to the landing, but you could sleep in the loft of the kitchen, where Julie lives."

William was relieved for this way out. If Rosemary could spend the night in the company of Julie, he could leave. "If it's all the same with you, Mr. Dubose," he said, "I think I will go down to the landing. A walk in the night air will do me good."

"The kitchen loft sounds fine for me," said Rosemary, trying to put the best face on an awkward situation.

"Then let us enjoy the last sip of our rum," said Jerome.

They finished off their rum with a strained interlude of small talk, and then William and Rosemary took their leave of the Dubose house. They walked along to where the path to the kitchen split off from the path to the landing. But as they were about to go their separate ways, Rosemary whirled around and confronted William.

"Damn it, Billy, you have offended Jerome. He practically threw you out of his house, telling you that you could sleep down at the landing if you wanted. And I don't blame him. Didn't your mother teach you manners?"

"Is the man of your dreams too delicate for frank conversation?"

"That's not it. That's not it at all. Whatever one thinks of the way the Duboses treat their slaves, our cowpen depends upon their rice for a great deal of what we eat. We are not the only ones who are cutting wood on the Santee River, you know."

"Where is the offense?" asked William. "I only engaged him in conversation. What is the purpose of conversation if it is not to get at the truth?"

"Conversation has many more purposes. To entertain, to put people at ease, to coordinate efforts, to find out whether you like or dislike a person, and on and on. How could you help run a tavern and not know that?"

"Conversation is also about the meeting of minds—or the not meeting."

"Let's just say good night," she said. "I will try to smooth things over with Jerome at breakfast tomorrow morning."

William sighed. "Good night, Rosemary. I am sorry if I have offended Jerome. That was not my intent."

"Good night," she said curtly and turned away toward the kitchen.

Tuesday, March 7, Dubose plantation

How to prosper in the New World: 1. Get cheap land. 2. Get cheap labor. 3. Use that labor to get from the land something that people with money in the wide world need or want. Tobacco is a wonderful discovery. People don't need it, but once they try it, they do want it and keep coming back for more. Sugar is good because it makes everything taste better and for some it becomes a necessity. Rice is good because it is a staff of life that combines well with every food there is. And better yet, the land that is good for growing rice—swampland—is worthless for any other crop, which makes it the cheapest of the cheap, just as slave labor is cheapest of the cheap.

After visiting Dubose's plantation, I see that there are slaves, and then there are slaves. I now understand what Delilah meant when she told her daughter to straighten up or risk being sold to a rice plantation. A rice slave is like a galley slave, or a prisoner in a work camp. They are held in bondage and worked to death, or close to it. How different it is for the slaves I am working with back at the cowpen. MacDonald's slaves carry arms and do the same work as their masters. They are still slaves, it is true, but they are not rice slaves. Hell, it is said, has several levels.

Tonight I not only offended Rosemary, I angered her, and her anger surprised me. Her sympathy for Jerome makes me heartsick, and not only because I want her for my own.

The next morning, William and Rosemary met at the landing. Thankfully, Jerome did not come down to see her off. While Swan and his men were loading the barrels of rice in the pettiauger and squaring it away, William and Rosemary got into their tippy little dugout canoe and set out for home, paddling upriver. Rosemary manned the front paddle and William the rear. The canoe was about fifteen feet long and just wide enough to seat a trimly proportioned person. It took the two of them some time before they adjusted their paddling and sense of balance to the severe requirements of the canoe. Once they mastered it, they went skimming along with good speed. The pettiauger behind them, loaded down with rice and four oarsmen, could only travel against the current at a fraction of their speed in the little canoe.

"I am glad you are speaking to me today," said William, as they left the pettiauger behind.

"I may be speaking to you," said Rosemary, "but if you keep on talking in public the way you were last night, you will have an unhappy career in Carolina."

"My happiness in Carolina does not depend on pleasing Jerome Dubose."

"Does it not? You have raised a question in his mind about whether you are in accord with the way the planters do business. The Dubose family includes some of the most powerful people in this colony. Their power extends from Charles Town all the way up here and into the borderlands."

"I do not care. I can do without the blessing of the Dubose family, which I never would have had anyway. I would rather keep my freedom to speak the truth as I see it than to grovel before the likes of them."

"You are a wildcat when you argue, Billy. But you should give a care lest you run up against a panther. And if you haven't guessed it, my interest in Jerome has not cooled. He was very gracious to me this morning at breakfast. I invited him to come up to the cowpen for a visit, and I think he might come. Also, he asked me to sing him a song, and I did. So I thank you for telling him that I like to sing."

"What did you sing for him?"

"The same song I sang for you when your ankle was sore: The Keys of Canterbury."

Rosemary stopped paddling and looked around at William. "I don't want you to hate Jerome. And I don't want this to put a rift between you and me."

William shook his head, trying to conceal his feelings—his great disappointment at hearing this news, the wave of jealousy sweeping over him. "It is hard for me to think well of him," he said. "I have trouble separating a person from what he stands for."

"There is more to him than just being a planter."

"Is there? I didn't see it."

"Please let's not fight, Billy."

William said nothing, and they paddled for a little time in silence.

Then Rosemary spoke. "Another thing I want to tell you about is that Julie is most interested in the Fulani man you mentioned, who is Cudjo, of course. I didn't want to reveal more to her, but when she cried, I did tell her a little bit about him."

"So?"

"I shouldn't have, that's all."

"Why not?"

"Because now the two of them may try to get together, and that could get them in trouble. They might start slipping away without permission. You saw what happened to poor Prince when he stayed away for a day. I wish you had not told her anything about Cudjo. Not that I am blameless in this myself. But I can tell you that slave-owners don't care to have their slaves passing information from one place to another. They won't stand for any sneaking around."

"They are afraid of an uprising, no doubt."

"Yes, they are. And you should be too."

Rosemary turned back around and continued paddling. All the light had gone out of the day, though the sun was still shining. They had little to say to each other for the rest of their passage up the Santee to the landing at the timber camp, nor on their walk back to the cowpen.

Wednesday, March 8, the Cowpen
It has all come to pieces. Rosemary is now as cold to me as she can be. And even worse, it looks as if her dream of Jerome is starting to come true.

19

Poke Greens

With the arrival of spring the foliage began to grow, and the cows came moseying up from the swamp to graze on the new upland grass. William could not help but be stirred by the season, by the awakening of new life and a sense of possibilities for the new year, especially after such a dismal winter. It wasn't so much the cold weather that had made it as dismal as it was, but the bad play he had made of that visit to the Dubose plantation. He did not care a whit about Jerome Dubose's opinion of him. It was Rosemary's opinion of him that mattered. If he had it to do over again, could he have done it differently? Perhaps not. He thought he might be one with King Lear's Cordelia, who lacked her older sisters' "glib and oily art" of pleasantries, empty conversation, and flattery. But most of all, what pained him to the quick was the knowledge that he had all but lost any chance he might have had for Rosemary's affections.

So the coming of spring was a balm for his pain. After the winter burn, the piney woods had seemed barren, monotonous. But now soft breezes swayed the limbs of the pines, stirring their long needles. Handsome woodpeckers with brilliant scarlet heads flew from tree to tree, pecking for insects, looking for mates, claiming territory, displaying the flashy black and white patterns on their wings. Underfoot, through the charred rubble of the forest floor, came vigorous green sprigs—not only of wiregrass but of a surprising array of herbaceous growth. The spreading greenery beneath the pines varied richly from one locale to another, depending upon soil quality and ground moisture. Most surprising of all were the flowers, a panoply of blossoms large and small bringing colorful new life to the burned-over ground. William especially loved the jewel-like blooms of the violets, which reminded him of the ones he had known in the Highlands, stirring fond memories of his mother.

He and Cudjo did their work much as before, but the warming weather made it easier for them in one respect. Their herd no longer had to scatter out in small groups to find enough grazing in the canebrake. With the grass coming in, there was plenty of forage in the upland. The herd was completely familiar with this range, and they knew where to go for the best grazing. So William and Cudjo simply followed along after them. With the weather so hospitable and the cows so easy to tend, William almost began to enjoy the work. But then came April and the spring cow hunt, and the days of ease came to an end. It began when Ray came riding over one day from Flea Bite camp with the news that Rufus wanted to start marking the calves and castrating the young bulls. This meant that William and Cudjo had to separate the calves and their mothers from the herd and drive them over to the pen.

They got up early the next day and set out on their horses to hunt up the cows that had calves. Samri, who sensed that something out of the ordinary was afoot, ran along with his tail up, prancing at times, and Bruto followed suit. William and Cudjo went coursing through the brush and cane, crossing little ravines, splashing through small creeks and branches, whooping at the top of their lungs, with William cracking his whip to move the cows along. Samri and Bruto darted hither and yon, barking and threatening, making the cows do their bidding. Cudjo's horse lived up to the maxim that a good cow-pony is three-quarters dog and one quarter horse. He could dart abruptly to head off an errant cow, or spin on a penny to make a threatening move toward a headstrong cow.

By mid-morning they had a small group of twenty-five cows with their calves gathered in a none too coherent herd, every member of it wanting to get back to the larger herd. But as they began driving them along, with Cudjo and his whip on the right side of the herd, and William with his whip on the left side, and with Samri and Bruto bringing up the rear, they soon had their little herd heading in the direction of the cow camp. They drove them gently, stringing them out. When they spotted a cow separated from her calf, they would cut her out and let her drift back along the herd until she smelled her calf. Once the two mammied up, they would rejoin the herd wherever they wanted.

Thus went the six miles to the cow camp. By the time they got there, it was too late in the afternoon to mark and castrate. Rufus and his crew had done their work for the day, so William, Cudjo, and the dogs drove their cows into the pen for the night. What might have been a tedious job was made easy by a pair of lightly built rail fences that Rufus and his crew had set up to funnel the cows into the entrance to the pen. William and Cudjo were happy to spend the night with the rest of the crew and to share in Alonso's cooking.

"How has it been for you two?" asked Rufus as they settled down.

"I'd say it has been routine," said William. "No varmints. No thieves."

"I wish that was true here," said Rufus. "We've had some cows taken from us. They have gone missing one at a time. We've never seen signs of a struggle, so it seems they are going away on their own four feet, not drug off dead. It could be Cut Nose, or it could be that crew of cow-hunters on the other side of Four Hole Creek, the ones who were ready to go to war with us."

"I'd say it was Cut Nose," said Cudjo.

"I thought his territory was on our side of the range," said William, "in Half Way and Santee Swamps. If he is over here, you need to keep a sharp lookout. You don't want to run into him unawares. He is the worst devil you'll ever meet."

"That would make him worse than my father-in-law," said Rufus, "and I'd just as soon stay clear of him."

"What do you hear from the cowpen these days?" asked William.

"Different things. Father MacDonald's mood gets meaner by the day. Betsy says he is still drinking rum and finding fault with everybody and everything. She also says that Rosemary is all aflutter over some young rice planter from down the Santee. They expect him to come visiting, though you might not want to hear that news."

"I more or less knew it already," said William. "When is he coming?"

"I don't have no idea."

William grew silent and stared into the fire. He did not even want to think about Rosemary. Instead he made himself turn his thoughts to Cut Nose. Not only had the rogue come out of Santee Swamp, but he was now ranging freely over the whole cowpen. He was becoming too bold for his own good. There would be a chance to find him now, once the spring hunt was over.

The next morning William went with the cow-hunters out to the pen, and they got to work separating the calves from their mothers. They drove the mothers outside the pen, where they milled around, lowing for their missing calves. Then the men caught each calf, one by one, threw it to the ground, and marked its ears. As a catch dog, Samri was adept at jumping up and biting down on a calf's nose, lip, or ear, stopping it in its tracks. Ray was the bulldogger who caught hold of each calf and got it to the ground by twisting its head or grabbing a front leg and throwing it off balance. If all else failed, he did as the dogs did. Amazingly, he would bite down hard on one of the calf's ears or onto its lip, an enticement to cooperate that no calf could resist.

Once a calf was down, Ray and William pinned it on the ground. Then Cudjo took a sharp knife and cut a small notch in the lower margin of the right ear and cut off the very tip of the same ear. Then he cut a very small and inconspicuous slit in the tip of the left ear. If the calf were female, she was then free to get up and run away, to be let outside the pen to mammy up.

If the calf were a male, there was one further painful step. After getting his ears marked, he was cut—that is, castrated. Cudjo would take his sharp knife and cut off the end of the calf's scrotum and pull out the testicles and the cords. He would cut the semen cord neatly and then pull on the blood cord until it broke in a jagged way, so that it would more quickly clot and stop bleeding. Even so, some of the little steers bled pretty badly. And bleeders or not, getting cut was a shock to all of them.

One of the little male calves was coal black and heftier than the others.

"Cudjo and I are thinking that bull calf might have been sired by Cut Nose," William said to Rufus.

"I say we ought to let him keep his balls," said Cudjo, "and see if he grows up to have a better temper than his daddy. He would sire strong calves."

"That's all right with me," said Rufus, "so long as he turns out to be more interested in breeding cows than he is in hooking men. If he shows the least inclination to the latter, he'll go straight into the stew pot."

After work was finished for the day, it was still early enough for William and Cudjo to ride back to their shelter. As they did, William was no longer able to keep his thoughts away from Rosemary. And in the weeks following, as they drove more little bunches of cows over to the cow camp, he kept on thinking about her. Try as he might, he could not shake her from his mind. Finally he gave up trying and resigned himself to the misery of it.

The spring cow hunt was the time to take a tally of the herd. They kept a careful count of the calves they branded, and of how many little bulls were cut to be steers and how many kept their breeding parts. This hard work went on for several weeks, until finally all of the calves had been marked and cut. In the second week of May, Rufus invited William to ride with him over to the cowpen to make his report to John MacDonald.

For William their timing could not have been worse. He spotted Jerome Dubose as soon as they rode into the yard. Dubose was out by the barn, leaning against a fence talking to Rosemary, who sat on a bench nearby. William did not try to evade the situation. While Rufus tethered his horse and went inside to talk with John, William rode directly over to the barn to put Viola in the pen.

"Good day to you, Mister Dubose," he said as he dismounted.

"Good day to you, Mister MacGregor," Dubose answered. He was dressed to the nines in a light brocaded waistcoat and a fine broadcloth coat, his boots immaculately polished.

Rosemary got up from the bench and went over to open the gate for Viola. "You-all must be done with the spring cow hunt," she said.

"We just finished," said William.

"Then you and Rufus must stay for supper," she said. "We have a big mess of poke greens I know you'll enjoy."

"Poke greens?" said William. "I know poke weed, the one that grows head high with dark red berries. I thought it was poisonous."

"It is when it's that big, but if you cut the sprouts when they first come up, only six or eight inches high, they make delicious greens. You do have to be careful to bring them to a boil and pour off the water several times, but that takes out the poison and then you can eat them."

"I am glad to be forewarned," said William. "I can't say I have ever been invited to a poisoning before."

She smiled at him, almost apologetically it seemed. "When cooked as they should be, they're safe as can be."

"Well, if you give them to Mister Dubose to eat first, then I'll eat them, too."

She laughed, trying to cover the awkward moment. She still held the gate, and as William came out of the pen, she fastened it behind him. "I hope you will stay the night," she said. "You can spread your blanket on the floor in the house or up in the barn loft. Jerome came two days ago and already has a claim to the folding cot."

"The cot? I didn't even know you had a cot."

"We don't often use it. We save it for the guests who are not accustomed to sleeping on the floor."

William glanced at Jerome, who smiled ever so slightly.

At supper John MacDonald smelled strongly of rum, though the rum punch he offered to his company was exceedingly weak, hardly more than water and sugar, and not much sugar at that. With Dubose present, John tried to be the genial host, but his underlying dark mood came through nonetheless. "Well," he said to Rufus as they settled around the table, "how is the herd these days? Are my cows still going to hell like everything else at this cowpen?"

"We haven't done too badly," said Rufus. "About eight out of ten of the new calves have survived so far. We have counted 110 of them, and that puts the herd right at 700. We now have 52 young steers and five little bulls. One of the bull calves is a big, black one. He might be a son of Cut Nose, according to William and Cudjo. If he works out, that's at least some good we've gotten from that devil to offset all the damage he's done. Which brings us to the fly in this ointment. A few more of our cows have gone missing, this time from the western herd in Four Hole Swamp."

"How many?" asked John.

"We think it's about twelve," said Rufus.

"God almighty!" For a moment John just shook his head and said no more. Then he asked, "How many does Cudjo think are gone from the eastern bunch?"

"There's about eight that went missing back in the winter," said William. "But none since spring has come."

"Twenty in all," said John, still shaking his head. "Twenty more gone. Damn it to hell! At this rate we'll hardly make a profit from our herd for this year. If it gets any worse we will have to quit herding between Four Hole and the Santee. And where will that leave us? Billy, I thought you were going to run down that thieving bull for me."

"I intend to find him," said William. "Cut Nose took to the swamps for the winter and he has only now resurfaced. With the spring hunt finished, I can turn my time to tracking him down. I'll not stop until I find him, Mister MacDonald, and I'll get you back your cows."

"I'd like to see it," said John. "That would be a hallelujah day at the cowpen. If you fail, we'll be on short rations next year."

Just then Rosemary and Betsy came in with two large bowls of poke greens topped with poached eggs, and with a heaping platter of hot corn bread. The greens tasted as good as Rosemary had said they would. After a long winter with hardly any vegetables to eat, everyone's hunger for fresh greens made them a dish for a king.

"Mister MacDonald," said Jerome, when their eating frenzy had subsided, "Rosemary and I walked down to Swan's lumber camp yesterday, and it has got me to thinking. He and his men have cut down a great many trees in that swamp, and there are few left of a size that he can harvest. Swan now considers that tract to be worthless, but of course he's not looking at it with a planter's eye. From a planter's point of view, the more trees that are cut down, the closer that land comes to being ready for rice. Have you thought about putting in a rice plantation there?"

"That tract supports Swan and Liza," said John. "All Swan really knows is cutting timber. He talks about wanting to build a grist mill on Poplar Creek, but we can't afford to do even that, much less start up a rice plantation. The initial investment is too great."

"If you are not interested in doing it yourself," said Jerome, "you ought to be thinking about selling that land to the planters downriver. They are always looking to expand, and much land along the Santee has already been taken by speculators. I am telling you, that tract is prime rice land."

"And I am telling you that Liza and Swan need that land for Swan to do his timbering. There are still trees in there he can cut. They are just further back in the swamp and harder to get out."

"Then so be it," said Jerome. "But I do find it a pity that it cannot be otherwise. The best way to wealth in Carolina is to grow rice for the world market. Not so long ago, some of us here at this table conversed on this very subject, and I made the point that it is rice more than any other commodity produced in this colony that is making Charles Town into a great city. A great city must first have wealth, and then comes the amenities and the arts: theater, music, lectures and readings, markets for fine goods, all that makes for a gracious life."

"I would be thrilled if I could enjoy only a taste of the amenities that Charles Town has to offer," said Rosemary.

"If we ever find ourselves there at the same time," said Jerome, "I would be delighted to show you the town."

"I would like that very much," she said smiling.

William was not smiling. He had sat silent for as long as he could. He knew he should keep his mouth shut, but what did he have to lose? "I was party to that earlier conversation, Mister Dubose. I've thought it over and I would like to amend something I said that evening. I said that the philosopher Francis Hutcheson tells us that the best society is the one that gives the greatest happiness to the greatest number of people. My own idea, building on his, is that the best society is the one which gives as much happiness, self-respect, and freedom to its poorest members as it does to its richest. It is surprising, perhaps, that it is I who would be the one here tonight who would say a proud word for our cowpen. But I will do it. I have heard our slaves say that the fate they fear most is enslavement on a rice plantation. The slaves at this cowpen know their place, make no mistake. They are well mannered and respectful. But they do not cower trembling and incoherent at the sight of a whip. In fact, my cow-hunter mates of every hue carry whips of their own, not to mention muskets and sharp knives, but none of us here in this cowpen fear for our lives."

"And what exactly is your point?" asked Dubose.

"My point is that you have a blinkered view of the blessedness of the kingdom of Carolina rice. One thing I learned from my year among the Cherokees is that vengeance is a powerful motive amongst people everywhere. With the floggings and scorn that are rained down on plantation slaves, I for one would be afraid of a knife at my throat in the dark of night, or a dose of poison in my soup. Answer this from your own experience, Mister Dubose. Do the planters fear being poisoned?"

"MacGregor," said Jerome, "when you spill your opinions, you spill all. Yes, in such large enterprises, with so many workers and such a wide range of trustworthiness among them, it is only natural that there is sometimes a fear of being poisoned by a disgruntled servant. But if you are not too thick to grasp it, the British Empire does not exist for the purpose of making its subjects happy. Rather, it exists for the purpose of becoming as rich and powerful among the nations of the world as it is possible for it to become. And the role of its subjects, including all of us here at this table, is to do our part in helping our nation achieve its destiny. Carolina's very existence is justified only if she brings forth products that can be sold on the world market to further the wealth of Britain. As Britain thrives, so do all of her people thrive."

"That is upside down and backwards," said William, "and self-serving to the extreme."

Rosemary rose from her chair. She looked at William as she spoke. "Gentlemen, I do not see how we can extract ourselves from this pit of argument. I am going to bed, and in the interest of peace and tranquility, I suggest that everyone else do the same. Please excuse me." She walked away from the table and climbed up to her sleeping loft. And with this, all the others, one at a time, excused themselves and went their separate ways. For William, his way led to a pile of cornshucks in the barn loft.

Thursday, May 11, the Cowpen

Tonight I burned my last bridge to Rosemary. My stand for the rights of man has left stranded my love for her. Not that she cares. Her sights are set on Jerome Dubose.

Awaking early the next morning to sounds outside the barn, William sat up in his cornshuck bed and listened. He heard voices talking in hushed tones, and he eased over to look out through a crack in the plank wall. At the gate of the pen was a horse saddled up, and nearby, as he had suspected, were Jerome and Rosemary, talking softly to each other. He could hear them plainly through the open cracks.

"I hate to go," said Jerome, and he took her in his arms and gave her a lingering kiss. "If I could stay another day, I would, but my business in Charles Town will not wait."

She sighed and leaned her head against his shoulder. "I will miss you so much. Come back to me soon."

Jerome kissed her again and then mounted his horse, and after tipping his hat to her, he turned and rode away.

William waited until Rosemary went back to the house, then he got his possessions together, saddled Viola, and rode off in the direction of the herd. It was hard for him to absorb the finality of what he had witnessed. The last of the props on which he had based a fragile vision of his future were now knocked away. But if this was the way Rosemary wanted it, this was the way it would be. He would put it completely behind him now. His first step would be to finish off the season at the cowpen the best way he could. Then back he would go to Charles Town, where it would be a new day. Anything could happen now. The world was wide open before him. Leaving the cowpen, he put his heels to Viola more vigorously than usual, and she broke into a spirited gallop.

20

A Thousand Cuts

After William returned to the herd, he threw himself into work as a way to occupy his mind and move on from Rosemary. Remembering her brought pain. Remembering Jerome brought envy. It galled him that for someone like Jerome doors were open on all sides: he had only to choose which one he wanted to enter. But in this William could also see more clearly that he himself did not have that same luxury of choice, and that if he were ever to succeed in this life, it would have to be by getting a foot into any door that cracked open. He could only get in by forcing his way through it, and then he would have to work very hard to stay there. The most important thing now was to return to Charles Town in possession of the greatest possible return for this otherwise fruitless year of work. That meant finding Cut Nose and his stolen harem, thus tripling his pay in cows from one to three.

The summer grass was plentiful, and the eastern herd still grazed on their own near the Cherokee Trail. William and Cudjo could mind them with ease, and William in fact was little needed. And so whenever he could, he went out on his own to look for the rogue bull. But search as he might, he found nothing, not the slightest sign. This went on for so long that he began to think that Cut Nose might have taken his harem back to the eastern side of the Santee River. After all, he had crossed the river once before. Cows are good swimmers, and the Santee in summer was not that wide. But if Cut Nose had taken MacDonald's cows across the river, they were lost for good, and William would go back to Charles Town a poorer man.

Late one afternoon, however, hope came a-glimmering. While searching for signs of Cut Nose in the southwestern corner of MacDonald's range, William discovered two strings of cow prints passing through a stretch of muddy soil. One set of prints was small—either a large calf or a small cow. The second set was much larger, set deeply into the ground by an animal that must have been twice as heavy as the one that laid down the small prints. Moreover, he saw several places where the larger prints were laid down over the smaller ones, just as one would expect if a bull were herding a cow.

He checked the powder in the pan of his musket, held it at half ready, and followed the tracks for over an hour. But eventually the light gave out and the prints disappeared in an area where a deep fall of pine needles covered the ground. Cudjo might have been able to track under such conditions, but William was not able to do so. He wished for Samri, or even Bruto.

He slept that night near a tree that would be easy to climb if the need arose. Near dawn a hard rain set in and kept on through the following day. All signs of the suspicious tracks were obliterated.

June and July was the slowest time for the cow-hunters. Seeking relief from the scorching sun, the cows congregated around the little creeks that were their watering holes. To cool off and while away the hours, William and Cudjo went most days to swim in one of the pools in Four Hole Swamp.

After a swim on a particularly hot day, they lingered on the bank in the shade of a big sycamore tree, letting the warm air dry them off.

"There weren't many days warm enough for swimming in Scotland," said William. "I suppose you headed for water every day in Africa."

"Only in the rainy season," said Cudjo. "In the dry season in our country there's not enough standing water to drown a mouse. But the wet season is a good time for Fulani people. Everybody enjoys it. We swim and swim. We have to watch out for crocodiles, though."

"Like our alligators," said William.

"Crocodiles are bigger and meaner. Alligators will most often get out of your way. But a crocodile will lie still under the water near a crossing or a watering place, and when anything comes near, man or beast, he will bolt up, grab it, and pull it under. Then he rolls and rolls in the water to drown his catch. A big crocodile can swallow a man whole."

"I don't believe I would go in the water at all," said William.

"Yes, you would, if you were born there. We learn to watch out. Crocodiles don't keep us from having a good time."

Cudjo's story reminded William of a bad dream his Cherokee wife once had while they were out hunting deer. In Otter Queen's dream, an *uktena*, a kind of dragon in Cherokee belief, frightened her by suddenly rearing up out of a pool of water in front of her. William had noticed that since he had put Rosemary out of his thoughts, memories of Otter Queen had begun to arise more often. Some, like her nightmare, still carried some weight of grief and regret, but now he could more easily move past those to pleasant memories of his time with her. "You once sang a song about Juliyama," he said to Cudjo.

"Yes. She was every Fulani boy's dream. Think of Juliyama and be happy, we would say."

"There is something. . . ." William caught himself, wondering whether he should be mindful of Rosemary's warning about stirring up the slaves. But why care what she wanted him to do or not do? "There is something interesting you might want to know about," said William. "When I went with Swan to take the lumber down to Dubose's plantation, there was a pretty house servant there named Julie. She was tall and thin like you. I thought she might be Fulani, and sure enough, she told me that her real name is Juliyama."

Cudjo sat up from where he was lounging. "Juliyama? You telling the truth? Then she must be Fulani."

"Yes, I asked her outright and she said she is."

"Is she a young woman?"

"Not a girl, but young enough. Tall and very pretty."

"And you told her about me?"

"I did. I said I hunted cows with a Fulani man. She was very surprised to hear there was another Fulani in these parts."

"The Dubose plantation. Where is it?" asked Cudjo.

"It's nine or ten miles down the Santee. Just before you get to it, there's a pretty good sized creek that comes in from the right. Just below the mouth of that creek there's a landing dock, and on the bank above that there's a warehouse. Not that you would ever be going down there."

"You know I can't be thinkin that way. A slave can't be travelin about without a written pass, and Master Rufus—let alone Master John—would never give me a pass to go that far. I'd get skinned if they caught me goin there without one."

"And whether you had a pass or not, you would need a boat," said William.

"A boat would come in handy, true enough," said Cudjo.

They fell silent. Cudjo stared out at the water of their swimming hole. "Juliyama," he said slowly. "Juliyama."

Later that day Mars came riding in a flurry out to where William and Cudjo were tending herd near the mouth of Flea Bite Swamp. He was bareback on Spinoza, the horse William got in the trade from Priber. With four good legs under him, Spinoza was a much better looking horse than William remembered him to be.

"Who gave you permission to ride my horse?" asked William.

"Miz Betsy did. She said Master John has taken a turn. That's what she said. And she told me to go to the cypress tract to fetch Master Swan and Miz Liza, and then to come out here and fetch you and Master Rufus."

"What do you mean, a turn? Was she upset?"

"I don't think so. I just do what she tells me. She wants everbody there in a hurry. She said to tell you not to tarry."

Mars rode on in search of Rufus, and William fetched Viola from where she was grazing and was soon on his way to the cowpen. It was too hot, however, to press Viola into more than a fast walk; he no longer cared to go to great lengths to please John McDonald. When he arrived at the cowpen, Swan and Liza were already there, standing in front of the house with Betsy. Rosemary was off to one side talking with Venus. He could see that all of them were ill at ease.

William tethered Viola and walked over to join the others. He nodded in Rosemary's direction, and she nodded back.

"Where is Mister MacDonald?" he asked. "Is he ill?"

"No, he's well," said Betsy. "He's inside the house and will be out directly. Where is Rufus?"

"He is on his way. Mars came upon me first."

"What luck have you had in tracking down that wild bull?" asked Swan.

"Not much," said William. "I believe I may have seen his tracks, but I have not seen the bull himself."

Before long Rufus came riding in on a horse that was lathered up. As he joined their company, he and Betsy exchanged a few words, and she went in to tell John that all were assembled.

In a few moments John walked out into the yard, and it seemed to William that there was more life in him than had been there for some time. He had bathed and his hair was combed.

"Thank you for coming so promptly," he said. "I've called you here to tell you that I have come to a decision, and I want all of you to hear about it at the same time. It has been hard for me to come to grips with this, but the plight of this cowpen can no longer be denied. Its life is bleeding away, and not from one cut or two, but from a thousand cuts. I've been thinking about nothing else for this past year except how to find a way to staunch the bleeding. But there is no way. I never thought it would come to this. But it has, and all of you should open your ears and pay attention to what I have to say. Here is the way it will be. After this year's herd has been culled and sold in Charles Town, I am dividing up the cowpen. I am done with it. I am too old to move and start over again. I will keep back a few beef and milk cows for myself. But all the rest of the cattle will go to you, Betsy, and you and Rufus can take them where you will. This does not include the cows that go to Billy. He gets the one promised him for his labor, and if he finds Cut Nose and his herd, he gets his reward of two more of those. Liza, as for you and Swan, twenty acres around the shoal in Poplar Creek will go to you, and the two of you can do with that what you will. Perhaps you can make a living with a grist mill, or perhaps not. Time will tell. As for me, I'll stay put right here where I am. I can support myself on the travelers who come through."

"And me, Father?" asked Rosemary.

"Until you marry, you will live with me here at the cowpen. And when I am dead, you can have it."

"How will the slaves be divided?" asked Betsy.

"I have not decided," said John. "I will work that out as we go along."

"Will Cudjo stay with my crew?" asked Rufus.

"That would make sense," said John, "but, like I said, I've made no decisions about which slaves go where."

"He's my best cow-hunter," said Rufus. "I could not replace him."

"I have said all I'm going to say today," said John.

The announcement had been made and he took no more questions. As he went back inside his house, all the others stood benumbed, trying to take in the new reality. The greater cowpen would be dissolved and all of them would have to chart new courses in life. Swan and Liza began talking quietly together, and Betsy and Rufus did the same. William untethered Viola's reins, climbed up into the saddle, and made ready to take his leave. He looked over and saw Rosemary still standing beside Venus. He again nodded in her direction, and she nodded back. No hands were waved nor words spoken. They were two people headed in separate directions in life.

As William rode along the trail back to the camp at Half Way Creek, he wondered why John had invited him to come to hear his announcement. After all, he was no more than a sojourner at the cowpen. Perhaps it was to let him know that he was back in John's good graces. Or perhaps it was to emphasize to the others that William was still to be paid his small cut of the cows when they were driven to Charles Town. But whatever it was, John's news was certainly of less importance to him than it was to the others.

When he got to Half Way camp, it was almost dark and the camp seemed oddly deserted. Samri and Bruto, who were lying beside the fire pit, got up and came out to greet William and Viola. Cudjo's horse was grazing nearby with a bell around its neck, but Cudjo himself was nowhere in sight. William went to the fire pit and felt the ashes. They were cold. There had not been a fire here since early morning.

William would have been less puzzled if the dogs had been gone. In the fading light he walked around in the woods bordering the camp and called out Cudjo's name several times. No answer came. Finally William built up a fire and ate a few pieces of venison jerky for his supper. He gave some scraps of the same to the dogs, and then he crawled into his bedroll. Where might Cudjo be? Where would he go without his horse? Was he in some kind of trouble? If so, nothing could be done about it until tomorrow. And besides, William had never known Cudjo to be in trouble. He would soon return, he was sure. Exhausted from his long ride, William quickly fell asleep.

The next morning Cudjo had still not returned. William rode around checking on the cattle and keeping an eye out for wherever Cudjo might be. From what he could see, none of the cows had been taken. Cudjo was not missing on that account. William tried to reason it through. If something had happened, it could not have been while Cudjo was out on his horse with his dogs, because even if they had come back to the camp without him, the horse would not have been belled, and the dogs would have been agitated. Nor could something have happened to him at the camp, because even though his horse seemed to have been belled for the night, no evening fire had been built. And the dogs were calm, as if they had been told to stay. And that did indeed seem to be the best theory. The dogs had been told to stay, the horse had been belled, and Cudjo had left the camp on foot, alone. To go where? William had enough of a suspicion of where he might have gone to delay notifying Rufus about his absence.

William spent an anxious night. When daylight came and there was still no Cudjo, he began to worry about what would happen if Rufus were to show up. Rufus might well be out surveying his kingdom, now that the cattle were almost his. William worked it over in his mind until he came up with a way of explaining, if need be, why Samri and Bruto were there at camp but Cudjo was not. But what about the horse? There was no way to explain that. So he tied a lead to Cudjo's horse and led him into the woods a good distance away from the camp, and he tethered him there to a tree.

These precautions were taken none too soon. After returning to camp and eating a quick breakfast, William was just mounting Viola to set out to hunt cows when he saw Rufus come riding in. William sat in his saddle and waited. "Morning," he said when Rufus drew near.

"Good morning to you," said Rufus. He looked around. "Where is Cudjo?"

"He spent the night out with the cows."

"Without his dogs? I've never known him to do that. What's he doing out with the cows?"

"He saw bear tracks the other day, and it put him on edge. He's worried we could start losing calves. So he wanted to stand guard last night and get the bear if he could. That's why he didn't take the dogs. He couldn't trust them not to spook the bear."

"It seems like he'd want the dogs to help him corner the bear."

"I thought so, too," said William, "but he said he could only kill him if he caught him by surprise. He wouldn't let me go with him, either."

"Did he take a gun?"

William shook his head. "Just his lance. You know how he is. He trusts that lance to deal with whatever might come."

Rufus's face darkened. "That's all I need, to lose my best man to a goddamned bear. Are you going out to check on him?"

"I was going right now," said William. "It's a long ride out to where he is."

Rufus looked at him hard. "You wouldn't be covering for him, would you? He hasn't gone off somewhere, has he?"

William gave a short laugh. "Where would he go? With Cudjo it's all cows and nothing else. We'll bring you the bearskin. If he gets the bear, that is."

"I'm heading up to the north a ways," said Rufus. "I want to check out some range land up there. But I'll be coming back through here, probably the day after tomorrow. Cudjo had better be here then. We only use a whip around here if a slave goes off. I'd not want to see it come to that."

"He'll be here," said William, "don't worry about that. If he had known you were coming through today, he'd be here right now."

"The day after tomorrow, then," said Rufus, and he turned his horse and rode away.

William spent another anxious night. On the third morning without Cudjo, he saddled up Viola and set out riding around the herd, making sure that everything was all right. Cudjo's horse did not like being left alone at the camp, so William let him follow along on the rounds. Several times during the day he checked back at the camp, hoping that Cudjo would be there. But he was not. William was now sure that he had gone down to Dubose's plantation. And if he didn't come back before Rufus returned the next day, William was going to be in almost as much trouble as Cudjo. It would mean the end of his cow-hunting days, and he would have nothing at all to show for it, not even the one cow. And for Cudjo it would mean the whip. William could not even think about that.

When he finally returned to camp for the evening, there was still no Cudjo. He built a fire and sat staring into it for a long time, thinking that his season as a cow-hunter was coming to as untidy an ending as his earlier season as a packhorseman. But then, just as he was getting ready to crawl into his bedroll, Samri and Bruto suddenly came alert and pricked up their ears. Springing to their feet, they ran out into the darkness, and William heard Cudjo greet them. Soon man and dogs came walking happily into the firelight. Cudjo was carrying nothing but his lance.

"Have you been where I think you've been?" asked William.

"I took a notion to paddle down the river, if that's what you are thinking."

"How did you do that? Where did you get a boat?"

"I have my own boat," Cudjo said nonchalantly.

"You do not," said William. "So did you borrow one, so to speak? That could have gotten you into even worse trouble, if you had been caught."

"I do have my own boat," said Cudjo. "I am not joking with you. It's an old cypress canoe I found floating down the river I don't know how many years ago. It's been easy to hide it. I just turn it upside down, and it looks like an old log lying in the bushes. I've never had much need to use it, but it did finally come in handy."

"Did you have any trouble finding Dubose's plantation?"

"It was right where you said it would be. Going downstream was fast and easy. Coming back was slow and hard. But the part that made me most nervous was walkin the distance from here to the river and back. I had a story to explain what I was doin if anyone had seen me, but I doubt they would have believed it. It was worth the risk of a whippin, though, to find that Juliyama."

"So you did find her," said William.

"I did."

"And were you able to talk with her?"

"Yes indeed. We talked together in the Fulani language for a day and two nights, off and on, whenever we could. She let me hide in the corn crib. The master was away and the overseer was out in the fields all day, and drunk in his bed at night."

"So, what came of it? Does she like you?"

"She says she does. We both made each other happy. But she has her master and I have mine. It won't be easy for us to meet again. We want to, but there is ten miles between us, and so much danger."

"At least you've had a taste of your former life," said William. "Rufus came looking for you, but I told him you were out trying to kill a bear. He half believed me and half didn't. He's coming back tomorrow. If you hadn't gotten back, I might have just saddled up in the morning and ridden back to Charles Town without waiting to face him."

"I thank you for this, Mister William. I will pay you back somehow."

"There's nothing to pay back," said William. "I fed your dogs and looked after your horse. Cooked up a good story. You'd do the same for me."

The two of them crawled into their bedrolls to go to sleep. Both Samri and Bruto curled up beside Cudjo.

21

The Devil's Harem

By midsummer the two herds had merged back into one, and William and Cudjo broke up their camp at Half Way Creek and returned full time to the main camp. In late August and early September the cow-hunters began nudging the herd in close to Flea Bite pen. They put out a quantity of salt on tree stumps around the camp and pen to encourage the cows to remain close by, even though most of the grass in this area had been grazed down close to the ground. Looking for stragglers one day, William and Cudjo ventured further south than was usual, some distance beyond their customary range, crossing over to the south side of Poke Spring Creek. They pushed on until they knew they had out-wandered any wandering cows. Having found nothing, they were just beginning to circle back when William caught sight of a young bull standing in some cover at the edge of the cane.

"That's not one of ours," said William. "What's he doing here all alone?"

"Don't know," said Cudjo. "He looks hurt."

Riding over to get a closer look, they saw that the bull had been gored, though perhaps not fatally. His ears were unmarked. The little bull was frightened, but he was too injured to move.

"He must be from the Roberts cowpen," said Cudjo. "Their range starts just below here."

"But suppose," said William, "he is a bull calf from a cow in Cut Nose's harem. He's old enough to be getting interested in the cows coming into heat. It was on this side of our range that I saw those tracks a while back."

"I see what you mean. It might have been Cut Nose what gored him, running him out of the herd. If so, he is lucky to be alive."

"Let's see if we can find where he came from," said William. The two of them rode up and down the edge of the cane until they came across a faint trail. With their weapons at the ready, they cautiously followed the path to a shallow crossing of Four Hole Creek and on beyond until they came out near the northern side of the mouth of Middle Pen Swamp. After proceeding for a time along the edge of this swamp, Samri suddenly bristled and gave a low growl, and they halted. Bruto sniffed the ground eagerly, his tail waving.

"They've got wind of something," said Cudjo. "Are you ready to tangle with Cut Nose?"

"If the dogs can divert him while I take aim," said William, "I believe we can kill him."

"Or him us," said Cudjo. "I don't want him to gore my dogs."

"They can handle him," said William. "Let's go in and get him."

Cudjo held his lance at ready. "I hope your powder's dry."

"It's dry. I've checked it three times."

The dogs trotted out in front on full alert, then suddenly raised their tails high. Cudjo whistled softly to bring them to his side, and he and William dismounted to creep forward on foot without raising alarm. The wind was in their favor. Cudjo kept the dogs at heel to prevent them from spoiling the surprise as they crept toward a break in the canes. From the clearing ahead they could hear cows snuffling and quietly grazing. William soundlessly cocked his musket. Easing forward, they peered through the canes. They saw cows and more cows, a small herd of them. But Cut Nose was not among them.

"He must have heard us comin and slipped away," said Cudjo. "I know most of these cows. They're ours. Let's get our horses and round them up."

"How do we know he's not right there in the cane on the other side?" asked William.

"There's too many of us," said Cudjo. "Two men, two dogs. And he's tangled with us before. I say he's long gone. But we'll check to make sure once we have horses under us."

They got their horses and rode slowly into the clearing, whistling and speaking soothingly to keep the cows calm. The young ones, who had never seen cow-hunters before, reacted skittishly, but their mothers just stopped eating and watched, and the herd stayed put. William and Cudjo rode warily around the outer edge of the clearing, peering as deeply as they could into the dense cane that surrounded them on all sides. No Cut Nose. They relaxed a bit and turned to the cows to count them. In all, there were twenty-four cows with MacDonald ear markings and fifteen unmarked calves of various sizes, thirty-nine head in all.

"This is a welcome turn," said William. "I'll get at least one feather in my cap from Mister MacDonald. But if I don't get Cut Nose, I don't know if he will give me both of my cows or just one. He'll still have the thief on his hands."

"You're not going to get Cut Nose today," said Cudjo. "He ain't waiting around for you to catch him. If you can't get him by surprise, you can't get him."

"I've come to know that's true," said William. "The son of a bitch won't even let you see a sign of him if he knows you're after him. So let's drive these cows up to Flea Bite pen and let them join their friends and relatives."

"This is a good day," said Cudjo. "I'm happy to see these cows again."

They drove the little herd as they had driven others, with William on one side, Cudjo on the other, and Samri and Bruto bringing up the rear. Cracking their whips they crossed over to the eastern side of Four Hole Creek. They looked for the little gored bull, but he was not to be seen.

"We'll come back later and look for him," said Cudjo.

Then they turned north and followed up along Poke Spring Creek.

"Cut Nose has been keeping his harem out in no-man's land," said William. "God only knows how far they've been ranging. I wonder if he'll try to come get them back."

"He knows not to come in too close," said Cudjo. "Not all the way to the pen."

In late afternoon they came in sight of Flea Bite pen. William uncoiled his whip and cracked it sharply, and Rufus and his men came out to investigate. Rufus opened the gate of the pen and they drove the herd of cattle inside.

"By God, William," said Rufus, "where on earth did you find them?"

"Over in Middle Pen Swamp. I must have looked over there half a dozen times early in the summer, after I saw tracks down that way. Never saw another sign of them. But this time, there they were."

"What is the count?"

"We've got twenty-four marked cows, plus fifteen calves. Thirty-nine in all. That ought to make Mister MacDonald rest easier. But Cut Nose is still out there, waiting for another season of thieving. The old man won't like that."

"He won't mind it a bit," said Rufus. "The cows will be mine next season, not his. I might just take them to a new range and leave old Cut Nose behind."

"Unless he follows you," said Cudjo.

"There's plenty of cows in these parts to keep him busy," said Rufus.

"But they ain't his cows," said Cudjo. "These cows are his."

Rufus shook his head and spit on the ground. "Let's not go dreaming up trouble," he said.

Rufus set Tuesday, September 12, as the day they would begin penning the new calves born since the spring cow-hunt, along with all the calves from Cut Nose's bunch. The cow-hunters mounted up early that morning, and as they penned the calves, they began marking ears and cutting the males. Cut Nose's calves were wilder than the others, but they were manageable, and the work went well enough. In good time all of the new calves were marked and cut.

This done, they began culling the herd to separate out the bunch they would drive to market in Charles Town. By their reckoning, since the fall of last year the herd had increased by about 150, bringing the total to 750, give or take a few. But various losses cut it down to 730. It was John MacDonald's practice to sell off one-tenth of his herd each year, so they had to cull out a bunch of seventy-three.

"Let's just say seventy," said Rufus.

William laughed. "You'd better not try it. John's going to know the count. He may be quitting, but not until after he's sold this last bunch."

"Seventy-three, then," Rufus said grudgingly.

They first cut out the steers that had reached mature size and weight. Then they culled cows that were no longer producing calves. And finally, they picked out cows with undesirable traits, such as runts and cows with short legs. These cows would be slaughtered in Charles Town. The prime ones would supply the local meat markets, and the rest would be packed in brine in barrels and shipped out to the sugar islands.

By dusk of September 14, they had finished selecting out the bunch for the drive, seventy-three head in all. Before stopping for the day, they mounted their horses and rode around shouting and cracking their whips, driving the rest of the herd away from the camp, dispersing them out onto the range. They wanted to keep the penned-up bunch free and clear from the rest.

The next morning they opened the gate of the pen and started moving the small herd out. They did not hurry them. The whole object of the drive was to keep weight loss to a minimum and to make the cows think that they themselves, not the cow-hunters, were in charge of the move. The herd strung out into a long formation. Rufus was the point rider out to the left, and Ray was the point rider in the lead on the right side. The point riders kept the bunch headed in the right direction. Skirting the left side of the middle of the bunch was William as a swing rider, with Bruto to help him. Jock was the swing rider on the right side with several of the herd dogs. The swing riders kept cows from straying from the sides of the herd. Cudjo, partnered with Samri, was the drag rider at the rear. Alonso came along last of all with a string of four horses—two packhorses carrying food and cooking gear, and two spare saddle horses for the cow-hunters.

The first day of the drive was always the slowest. The cows were not yet used to traveling all day at a steady pace in just one direction. The men had to push them a little, else they would not even make their modest goal for this day. The most rebellious of the cows kept trying to bolt from the herd—out front, to the side, or back in the direction from whence they had come. The cow-hunters and their dogs would ride out, intercept them, and turn them back. Usually a few cracks of a whip near their heads was enough to turn them around. After one or two attempts they would settle down in the herd. But some were especially stubborn. William had a white steer on his side of the bunch that tried repeatedly to bolt and escape the herd. The first time a mere crack was not enough to turn him. So William rode out in front where the steer could see him and then stung him smartly on the shoulder. The steer flinched and stopped, and when William cracked his whip again, he wheeled around and returned to the herd. After that, the sound of the whip alone would bring him back, but nothing seemed to settle him in for good.

As planned, they only herded the cows a distance of about eight miles by day's end, reaching the headwaters of the little creek that flowed through MacDonald's cowpen. Once there, the cow-hunters turned the herd so that they milled around into a circle and finally came to a stop. The cows took turns drinking their fill of water from the little creek. Then they grazed until they grew tired, and one after another they lay down for the night, chewing on their cuds.

Alonso served up a supper of grits and sweet potatoes.

"Where's the meat?" asked Rufus.

"Don't have no meat," grumbled Alonso. "If I ain't got it, I can't cook it."

"Wild meat would do," said Rufus. "You could do a little hunting in your spare time."

"What spare time? We're on the trail all day. I can't cook, tend camp, and hunt too. *Mierda!* Let's kill and butcher one of the steers."

"We're out here drive our cows, not to eat them. We've got to get seventy-three head to Charles Town."

"Then we will do it on grits, beans, and sweet potatoes."

"I'll send Ray and Jock out to hunt," said Rufus.

"And when will they have time to do that?"

"When they get meat-hungry enough."

The cow-hunters set up a watch to look after the cows during the night. Cudjo took the first shift from sundown until about midnight. Ray and Jock took turns with the next watch from the end of Cudjo's time through the dead of night, this being the least popular watch. William, who enjoyed seeing the dawn of a new day, took the last shift until daybreak.

As he rode around on his watch, William whistled and sang softly to assure the cows that everything was all right. They needed to know that it was one of the cow-hunters moving about in the darkness and not a bear or a pack of wolves. Nevertheless, William noticed that some of the cows were anxious. They would sniff the air and get to their feet. None of them bolted, but William was afraid they might, and he took pains to keep them calm. The last thing they needed was for a few skittish cows to start a panic at the most dangerous time—in the dark of night.

The next morning, just as they were starting to mount up, John MacDonald appeared, riding up from his cowpen to look over the herd that was on its way to market. After greeting the man, he turned his attention to the cattle and began to count. He scratched his head as he finished. "Rufus, I count seventy-one head. If that is ten percent of my herd, it's in better shape than I was led to believe."

"You shorted yourself two head. There's seventy-three in this bunch. You've got William to thank for that. He and Cudjo found Cut Nose's harem. That bumped us up nearly forty head."

John walked over to where William stood and gave him a hearty handshake. "I've been selling you short, my boy, telling the others that I didn't think you could find those cows. I'm glad I was wrong."

"I am, too," said William.

"This makes the difference between a bad season and a fair season. How on earth did you find them?"

"Luck, I suppose. Several months ago I saw some hoof prints at the south end of our range that looked like they might have been from Cut Nose, but they gave out and I could not track them properly. And I never could find another sign after that. But a few days ago, Cudjo and I found him way down to the south. He had his harem tucked back in a no-man's land between your range and the Roberts range on the other side of Four Hole."

"Did you kill him?"

"No, sir, we did not. We tried to approach quietly, but he must have heard us coming. He left his cows to us and got away. I regret that he's still out there to plague you. But at least you got your cows back with some increase. They are big, healthy calves, too."

"Well, he's Rufus's problem now," said John. "I'm happy enough with the outcome. And I can tell you that your father would have been proud of you, Billy. I'm sorry to see you go away from here."

"It has been an honor to serve you, sir," said William. "You have treated me kindly and made me feel at home."

"I wish Rosemary had done more along that line," said John. "I sent you downriver with her hoping you two would make a pair. I didn't know Jerome was going to be there. If I had, I would have sent Liza in Rosemary's stead and kept the both of you back at the cowpen."

"I thank you for that," said William in surprise. "I do fancy her, as I guess everybody knows. And I tried my best to win her over. But the truth is, I didn't have much to offer. She will have a better life with Jerome than she could have with me."

"I can't say I agree. I don't much take to that rice planter crowd. They are all gentility and good manners, but it takes a cruel man to drive slaves the way they do. They only see profit when they look out on the world. They do not see human beings."

"Well, it's Rosemary's choice," said William. "She's got backbone as well as brains. A ton of both."

"But maybe not quite enough heart," said John.

William shrugged and said nothing.

"So what will you do back in Charles Town?" asked John.

"I plan to find work and to keep saving my earnings until I have enough to get into the Indian trade," said William. "Then you might see me here again on my travels, if I go back to the Cherokees. Are you still planning to make a traveler's rest out of what's left of your cowpen?"

"I'm hoping to get enough income from that to keep me going," said John. "The traffic on this trail increases every year."

"I've been thinking about that," said William. "With all your daughters gone, as well as some of your slaves, you are going to need a capable woman to be the hostess of your inn. Aunt Sally is getting old, and even at her best she doesn't have much in the way of social graces."

John laughed.

"But I've seen just what you need in a young woman down at Dubose's plantation. She could cook, serve table, and charm any traveler who comes through your door. Her name is Julie, and, as it turns out, she's a Fulani. She would make an excellent match for Cudjo."

"I hate to hear such a good proposal when I can't do a thing about it," said John. "There was a time when such a possibility would set the wheels in my head a-turning. But I no longer have money to buy slaves. I cannot even consider it anymore. The few that I now own will have to do."

Just at that moment, out of the corner of his eye, William caught sight of an abrupt movement in the thick brush just beyond the spot where Cudjo was sitting on his horse. In the next moment there was Cut Nose, bursting into the clearing, horns lowered, and in the next second he hit Cudjo's horse squarely on its padded flank-girth, sending the horse sprawling to the ground. Cudjo fell and his lance went flying, but then he was on his feet running for the trees at the edge of the clearing. Cut Nose drove his horns into the unprotected underbelly of the downed horse, and then he looked around for another victim. William was headed for his musket. John was backing toward the trees. The other cow-hunters were yelling, and William assumed that they too were headed for the trees—none of them had their muskets in hand. All the herd dogs but Samri had turned tail. Samri was barking and circling the bull, but to no effect. Cut Nose eyed John MacDonald and started toward him.

William moved as in a dream. Time seemed to stop and all was silence. He could not hear himself as he yelled out an imitation of a bull's low-bellow and grabbed up Cudjo's lance from where it lay close by. He was not even certain he had made a sound until Cut Nose stopped in his tracks. Strangely, William was not hindered by fear. The great bull lowered his horns, shook his head, and pawed dirt in an angry spray up over his back and flanks as he caught William in his sights.

"Save yourself, Billy!" John shouted.

William heard it as if from a faraway land, another world. He bellowed again, feeling it in his throat but still not hearing it. Holding the lance, he waved his arms and squared away at the bull, then squatted down. Cut Nose lowered his head again and charged at William, his huge horns aimed directly at him. Time moved like cold molasses. With dream-like focus William anchored the end of the lance in the ground, lowered it, then raised it up a bit and aimed it at Cut Nose's chest, just where his neck joined his shoulder. Immediately the bull collided with the lance, slowing just a little as William jumped aside, the shaft penetrating deeply into the bull's chest. Time and sound righted themselves as the great beast stumbled and fell forward, William still scrambling out of the way as the great load of angry flesh slid towards him. Cut Nose thrashed and heaved and tried to get to his feet, but the lance wound was mortal, his heart pierced, and he tumbled over again, flailing his legs, and gradually breathed his last. Warily William and the others walked over and looked down on the massive body.

"By God, William, you saved my life," said John. He reached out and clasped William's hand and held it for a long time. "I've never seen a braver act," he murmured. Then he looked around for a place to sit and fairly collapsed onto a log.

"You did it the way it was supposed to be done," Cudjo said approvingly. "I knew you could."

"I don't know how I managed it," said William. "It did itself somehow. You taught me well." The full reality of what had happened was just now coming in on him, and his thoughts began to grow jangled and his knees to weaken. He moved away and walked about, attempting to recover his equilibrium. Rufus and Alonso trailed after him, patting his back, marveling at the feat. Cudjo and Jock and Ray went to work extricating the lance from the beast's chest.

William came back and sat down beside John. "This has about done me in."

"I can never repay you," said John. "Never. Never." He reached over and patted William's leg. "The least I can do is add more cows to what I promised you. Hell, take all you want. I'm done with em."

William chuckled. "You would soon regret that. But I'll take three more, if you can spare them. That would make six in all, and I could feel that this year of work has been worthwhile."

"They're yours," said John. He shook his head in wonder. "I'll never forget this day. I never will. Now I must ride back to the pen and get my little crew over here to butcher this devil. Everybody on both sides of the Santee will be glad to know that he is dead." He and William got to their feet and walked over to where Cudjo was examining his horse.

"Cut Nose got him bad," said William.

"Yes, he's breathing his last," Cudjo said sadly. "The flank girth couldn't save him from a hook to his belly. It hurts my heart to lose him. He was a good horse."

"You'll have to take one of the spare horses," said John. "I'll send Mars out with a replacement as soon as I get home."

William walked back over to look at the dead bull. The others gradually wandered over to join him.

"Old Cut Nose came to get his cows," said Cudjo. "He should have had more sense than to come in so close."

"He didn't know we had a lance with us," said Rufus with a chuckle. "I don't know how you did it, Billy."

"I was going for my musket," said William, "but it's just as well I grabbed the lance. My musket misfired the first time I drew down on him, but I knew that lance was loaded."

They all laughed. "It all happened too fast for a musket," said John. "It was the lance that saved us. And I always thought Cudjo was a fool for carrying it."

William reached out with his foot and pushed at the mountain of dead flesh. It seemed as if someone else had made the kill. "About Spinoza. . . ," he said.

"Oh yes," said John, "I meant to tell you about Spinoza. I intended to bring him with me, but when I went to the pen this morning, I found him with a bad case of colic. He was pawing the ground and then lying down and rolling around. I don't know what he ate that disagreed with him so. I've got Mars out walking him to help it pass. Aunt Sally is brewing up a tonic that we have used before on colic. He could be over it tomorrow, but that's too late for you. I'll keep him for now and send him down to you later. Or you can ride up here and fetch him. Whichever comes first."

"I can do without him for now," said William. "And he may be of some use to you while you have him."

"But he is your horse. I'll see that you get him."

"We need to move along," said Rufus. "We've got fifteen miles to make today."

John bid them farewell and watched them as they mounted up and turned their attention to rounding up the cows and getting them ready to head out. He was still watching as they started moving the herd down the trail. William looked back and waved to him, and John waved in return. As William turned back to the cows, he felt a tenderness in his heart. He wondered if it was anything like what a son would feel for a father.

22

To Market

After leaving John MacDonald and his range behind, the cow-hunters spent the entire day following along the Cherokee Trail to the southeast, paralleling the Santee River. For the most part the herd was well behaved, grazing as they ambled along at a little more than a mile an hour. They crossed over the shallow headwaters of numerous little creeks that ran down into the Santee River, and they allowed the cows and horses to stop and drink as they wished. At the end of the day they came to a wide spot in the trail with a bold creek running through it. William knew it from his earlier travels: they were now a mile or so west of Eutaw Spring. Rufus declared it a good place to spend the night, and they turned the herd and formed them up into a circle until they milled around and stopped.

For supper, it was another round of grits and sweet potatoes.

William went to his bedroll early, exhausted from the morning's excitement and the long day on the trail. A few hours before dawn Ray woke him to take the last watch. The sky was heavy with clouds. It had not yet rained, but the air felt damp, and William rolled up his oiled cloth and tied it to the back of his saddle. After riding around the herd for a time, whistling and singing, he felt a few drops of rain, and he untied the cloth and stuck his head through the slit in its middle and draped it around his body.

Perhaps it was the rain that weighed down his thoughts, or perhaps something had been shaken loose by the encounter with the bull. As a rule he tried never to think of Rosemary, but his conversation with John had stirred her up from the dark, closed-away chambers of his heart. He had lost her as surely as he had lost his beloved Otter Queen—one lost to this world, one to death, both forever out of reach. And to think that John MacDonald would have backed William in his bid for his daughter's hand. That meant that the only impediment was Rosemary herself. It was she alone who refused William's love. And why, therefore, should he grieve her loss? If she did not want him, why should he want her?

Because of her beauty, he had to admit. Because every fleeting expression on her face was charming. Because he could not think of her sprightly body without feeling aroused. Because of her sheer competence in doing what life required. Whatever she turned her hand to she did well, and without much complaint. And then there was her intellect, her ability to grasp life's meanings, to find solutions, to interpret the larger scheme of things. And her sensibility—her love of poetry and song—especially her voice when she sang. But could he not balance these tender memories of her with his memory of her cold heart? She wanted fortune, not love. So why should he waste another moment of thought on her?

He closed the door of his heart and slipped the bolt back in place. She did not deserve admittance there. He was realistic enough to see her for what she was. His relationship with her was over and done, and the road ahead stretched out free and clear before him. He turned his attention to the dawn, coming now through the drizzle of rain. He greeted it with resolve and rode over to where Alonso was starting to work on their early morning meal. More grits and sweet potatoes. William wished for meat.

By the time they headed out, pushing on toward the southeast, the rain had stopped. With no significant creek to cross, they were making good time. From where William was riding, he could see that Rufus, up ahead, was being bedeviled by the white steer, who still, after three days, had not learned that his place was with the herd. Time and again he darted out and away, making a bid for freedom. Rufus had to ride out after him, cracking his whip to drive him back. But the steer persisted, and finally Rufus rode up to him as he ran away, reached over and grabbed his tail and pulled it up sharply and broke it, causing the steer to stumble and fall. That should do it, thought William. The pain of a broken tail did wonders to dissuade a cow from misbehaving. But not always, it turned out. Before long Rufus had to go out yet again to drive the steer back to the herd.

Toward the end of this day, they came to the place where the Cherokee Trail took a more southwardly turn to run parallel to the west branch of the Cooper River. Here they settled in for the night. William was unsaddling Viola when he saw Rufus ride over to the white steer and cut him out of the herd and then drive him over to where William and the others were encamping for the night.

"I've gone huntin, boys, and look what I've found. This steer has been bedeviling me all day. He just don't want to go to Charles Town."

Alonso grinned broadly and took out a sharp knife, while Jock and Ray stepped in to still the creature. Jock held his tail while Ray caught him by the horns, twisted his head, and dropped him to the ground. Alonso put the knife to his throat.

That night, they ate their fill of barbequed beef, and merriment filled the camp at the prospect of fresh and jerked beef all the rest of the way to Charles Town. Nothing raised the spirits of the cow-hunters like good food.

After dinner they set a square of four forked posts into the ground, about three feet high, and inside the square they built a large fire and let it burn down to coals. Then they set a hurdle made of green saplings into the forks on top of the posts, and onto this they spread their thin slices of beef to dry. Alonso tended to the jerky until he went to bed. After that the tending of it was the responsibility of the men who kept watch.

Monday, September 18, near the West Branch of Cooper River
My life as a cow-hunter is nearly at an end, and my romantic follies are behind me. It is hard to believe I have spent more than three years in Carolina with so little gain in wealth to show for it. I regret nothing, but I must now turn my hand decisively to something on which I can build a future for myself. The life of an Indian trader seems to be the one door into which I can get my foot. The six cows I have earned will go some way toward building that future.

The next day was much like all the previous days on the drive. The only difference for William occurred when up the trail ahead of him he saw a succession of cows, one bunch after another, startle and lurch further into the herd from the outside edge. When he got to the spot where this was happening, he saw the reason for it: a very large rattlesnake, coiled, its tail buzzing madly. William raised his whip and cracked it, thinking he would give the snake a blow that would chase it back into the woods. To his surprise, the tip cracked around the snake's head, partly severing it, killing it instantly. Pleased with himself, he got off his horse, finished cutting off the snake's head with his dirk, and draped the whole six feet of the thick, limp body across the front of his saddle.

At the end of the day, the cow-hunters bedded the cows where the trail turned to the south as it ran down towards Goose Creek. As they were setting up camp, William took his fresh kill to Alonso. "Can you cook snake?" he asked.

"I can cook anything, but I ain't going to skin nor gut that snake."

William took out his knife and went to work skinning and gutting it.

"Only an Englishman would eat a snake," said Alonso.

"You cook it and I'll eat it," said William. "And I'm a Scotsman, not an Englishman."

Alonso did cook it, and at suppertime William offered the barbequed snake meat to his mates.

"I'll have me a bite of that rattlesnake," said Rufus. "It'll give me the strength I need to see these cows safely to the slaughterhouse."

"Not me," said Jock. "I ain't eating no snake. That thing is poison."

"No, it ain't," said Alonso. "Not the meat."

"You eat some, then," said Ray.

"I'm staying with beef," said Alonso. "But I'll give you some."

"If I was to eat the least bite of snake," said Ray, "I'd have nightmares for a month."

"Well, I'm not afraid," said William, holding out his plate. "Pile it on."

Tuesday, September 19, Cherokee Trail
We are so close to Charles Town, I can almost smell the salt water. I shall be glad to see Uncle Duncan and Aunt Mary. I am most fortunate to have family of my own in this land, a place to come home to.

The next morning the men awoke early. Only two more days to go. But they had driven the cows not more than three miles down the trail when one of the lead cows, for no obvious reason, suddenly shrieked, balked, and then bolted ahead. The other lead cows followed after her until the entire herd was in a panic, running madcap, not caring what they trampled underfoot. It was a cow-hunter's nightmare.

Every man rode hard to catch and turn them. William chopped his heels against Viola, spurring her along the flank of the panicked cattle, paying no heed to the fact that if she stumbled, he would be thrown and trampled by the herd. Rufus was ahead, cracking his whip, and it was having some effect on the terrified cattle. William uncoiled his own whip and began doing the same. The dogs at the front knew what to do and set about harassing the lead cows. Finally Rufus himself caught up with the lead cows and began cracking his whip in their faces, stinging them often as not. William followed suit, and the two of them succeeded at last in turning the lead cows to circle to the right, curving around and running back in the direction from which they had come. Soon the whole herd was turning around, and eventually they were milling in a circle.

A few cows had broken out and had run down into the Cooper River swamp. Cudjo, Jock, and Ray soon tracked them down with the dogs and brought them back to join the others, who now stood panting from their exertions. It took the cow-hunters more than an hour to get the lead cows back in front and the herd on its way again down the trail to the south.

In spite of these delays, by the end of the day they were close to Goose Creek, and this is where they bedded the cows for the night. There were plantations along the road here, and Rufus rode out to one of them and purchased some onions, potatoes, cornmeal, and butter. Alonso cooked up a hearty beef and vegetable stew and served it up along with fried corncakes. As the men savored their change of diet, they talked over their day.

"I never saw what started that panic," said William. "It looked to me like they just bolted and ran."

"It could have been anything," said Rufus. "A bear might have pissed alongside the road, and the cows smelled it. I've seen rustlers hide out and throw a rock into a herd to panic them, so that they can steal the cows that bolt away from the herd. Almost anything can set off a panic. We are lucky we have not had more trouble than we have."

"Old Cut Nose was sure enough trouble," said Cudjo.

"That was enough to last us," said Rufus.

"It will all be over tomorrow," said William.

"Yes, it will," said Rufus. "These cows will be safe at market, and we can all take a rest in Charles Town before we ride back to the cowpen. If you want to come back with us, Billy, I'd be happy to keep you on as a hand. You could come with us to the new range. I couldn't give you another six cows like Father MacDonald has done, but we could work something out."

"I thank you for the offer," said William. "I truly do. This has been a good year for me. I have learned a lot. But I believe my cow-hunting time is coming to an end. I'm going to settle in on the Indian trade."

"That's a good way to lose your scalp," said Rufus.

"So is cow-hunting out beyond the settlements."

"Don't ever say that in front of Betsy," Rufus chuckled.

As they drove the herd across the Goose Creek bridge and on down the road, William felt gladdened at the sight of the increased traffic of farm wagons hauling their contents into Charles Town. He would be happy to be back with his uncle and aunt, enjoying straightforward blood relationships, without having to worry whether he was in or out. And the amenities in Charles Town would be a pleasure. The theater, music, and tavern food. He would find some kind of work for the winter to add to his stake. The three extra cows were already a great boost. Maybe even as soon as next spring he would have enough to purchase a small load of goods to take into the Indian country to trade. He might go up to the Overhill Cherokees where Priber was. Or maybe to the country beyond Fort Moore. He could seek Adair's advice about that. With no prospect of a wife in Charles Town, there was nothing to hold him back now from spending most of his time in the Indian country. He was a free man.

Late in the afternoon the first buildings of Charles Town came into view in the far distance. William knew of a small stockyard ahead whose owner was said to have done business with pirates. Gossip had it that he had traded beef for Spanish coins.

William rode up beside Rufus. "I know you're taking these cows to your usual stockyard," William said, "but if it's all the same with you, I'd like to leave my cows at a small yard I know of that we're coming up to. I am well acquainted with this stockman—the Packsaddle buys some of its beef and pork here."

"That's fine with me," said Rufus. "The cows are yours. Take Cudjo and cut them out of the herd."

As they approached the small stockyard, William and Cudjo cut six cows away from the herd and drove them into the pen. Then Cudjo and his dogs returned to the drive, while William remained behind to arrange for the sale. After dickering for a price, the stockman offered William payment in the form of credit at a store in Charles Town.

"These cows are first rate, and I would prefer to be paid in coins," said William.

"That's not my regular way of doing business," said the stockman.

"That may be," said William, "but I am not a pinder stocking up a cow-pen. I need money, not credit. I know you appreciate the business my uncle brings you from the Packsaddle Tavern. Your stockyard is further from town than the others, and it is not so very convenient for him to come out this far. He told me to tell you that."

"I see, I see," said the stockman, hemming and hawing. "Well, it could be. . . . Let me see." He went into a back room and was gone for some time. When he returned, he had a purse in his hands. "It so happens I do have some coins," he said.

"This will help me more than you know," said William as the stockman counted out the money. William transferred the coins to his own pouch and bade the man farewell. Mounting Viola, he spurred her to a fast trot to catch up with the herd, which was now nearing the large slaughterhouse, still well out from town where the stench of decaying meat and offal would not offend the citizenry. Without much trouble, they drove MacDonald's cows into the last pen they would ever enter.

The drive was over. William shook hands with Ray and Jock. "Goodbye to you," he said. "I enjoyed working with you two." He then rode over to where Cudjo sat on his horse and shook his hand. "You are a cow-hunter among cow-hunters, old friend. I could write a book about what I learned from you. And I want you to know I put in a word with Mister MacDonald about Julie. Though I'm not sure it did much good."

"At least I had those two days with her," said Cudjo. "Maybe I can steal a few more."

"Be careful doing that," said William.

"You be careful around them Indians," said Cudjo.

Then William rode over to shake hands with Rufus. "It was a pleasure to work with you," said William. "I wish you well in building your new cowpen. Stop by the Packsaddle Tavern whenever you come to market. Perhaps I will see you there."

"I might do that," said Rufus.

William turned Viola to continue on his way. Looking back, he raised his hand in farewell to the crew, and then he rode on down the street. He had the strongest feeling that his life had taken a turn for the better.

When he came to the Packsaddle Tavern, it seemed strangely quiet, and the entrance to the drive from the street was closed off. He tethered his horse to a post beside the street and headed to the porch. As he started up the steps, he froze in his tracks. On the front door was a wreath draped in black cloth.

23

A Foot in the Door

Ordinarily William would have gone straight into the tavern without knocking, but on this occasion, not knowing what to expect inside, he did knock first. The house was silent. Finally he heard steps and someone at the door. Aunt Mary opened it, and when she caught sight of him, she broke into tears. "Oh, Billy," she wept, opening her arms to him. "I am so glad you are here."

William embraced her and held her tightly. "Is it Duncan? Is he gone?"

"Yes," Mary said, nodding and clutching him for another long moment. Then she released him and straightened herself up, drying her eyes. "It was ague again, and late in the season. He never came all the way back from that bout he had with it last year. He just wasn't strong enough to fight it off this time."

"I am so sorry, Aunt Mary," said William, shaking his head and trying to take it in. "So very sorry. I never imagined I would not see him again. I hope I am at least in time for his funeral."

Mary teared up again, shaking her head. "He died two weeks ago. Exactly two weeks. On a Wednesday. We buried him two days later. On a Friday, it was." She wiped her eyes and blew her nose. "I must tell you that things are not going well here at the tavern. I have been too distraught and distracted to take charge as I should have. I simply closed the front door. I could do nothing else. I am so glad you have come, Billy."

"I can help for as long as you need me," said William. "Until next spring at least. I am done with cow-hunting."

She smiled at him gratefully and patted his shoulder. "Duncan always praised your work here. He said you were the quickest study he ever saw."

"He never quite told me that," said William.

She shook her head. "You know how men are." Tears welled up in her eyes again. "He would want you to know how much he thought of you."

"I knew," said William, taking her hand and squeezing it reassuringly. "In a general way I knew. Now what do I need to do first to help you?"

"First," she said, "we two will take a walk. What I have to say is for your ears alone. Wait here while I fetch my shawl."

William waited while Mary went upstairs to her bedroom. She came back quickly, wearing the light shawl she wore when the weather was cool but not cold. William held open the door for her, and the two of them walked out onto King Street. They turned to their right, walking southward toward land's end.

"The servants are beside themselves with worry," said Mary, "and every scrap of information they hear becomes the germ of a wild rumor. But they are right to be worried about what will become of them."

"You won't sell them," said William. "You need them to run the tavern."

"Billy, all the wind has gone out of my sails. I can't keep on with the tavern. Duncan was my helpmate. We made a go of it by working together. Two people think better than one. And loneliness is a cross no one wants to bear. All my babies have died. I have no one depending on me, no reason to labor to leave anything to posterity. I am tired down to my very bones from working so hard for so long. Why go on with it? I could shut down the tavern, take the downstairs for myself, and take in long-term boarders in the rooms upstairs. I have a little saved, and if I were to sell most of the servants, I would have a great deal more. I could have even more if I sold the tavern—everything—and moved into a smaller house. The servants have not heard a word of any of this, but they surely know it is a possibility that could befall them."

"I hate to think that the Packsaddle might be no more," said William. "And how terrible it would be for the slaves to be broken up and sold away from each other. Could you find places for them in town? If you put them on the block, they might be sold to the rice plantations."

"I can't bear to think of it," said Mary. "But what am I to do? If I am not running a tavern, I cannot afford to keep so many servants. One or two would be enough for my needs. And of course there will always be room for you in my house, Billy. You can have the parlor bed. It will be yours whenever you are here. I only wish you were here more than you are. How long can you stay this time? Where are your plans taking you next?"

"Back into the Indian trade," said William. "Though I will go as a trader this time, not as a packhorseman. But the time for that is late spring or early summer. Until then, I can promise you that if you will let me help you, I will work as hard as I possibly can to keep the Packsaddle afloat. You need only give me room and board. I owe you so much, Aunt Mary, and I want to repay you as much as I can."

"Oh, Billy, it strengthens my heart to have a family member to talk to. I felt so vulnerable here alone. I have not had a night's sleep in the longest time, just a snatch here and there. As soon as I lie down, my mind tangles itself in problems and worry."

"You will sleep tonight," said William. "We both will. A soft bed will feel like heaven to me after a year in a cow camp. And then I will be ready to go to work. I say we dust off the tavern and see if we can't get it up and running again. You just need a new way to think about it. You've kept a tavern all your life. I know you can keep this one going."

"Ah, Billy." Mary patted his arm. "You are already raising my spirits. I think Duncan held on until he knew somehow that you were headed home."

They had walked all the way down to the end of King Street, and now they stood for a while at the Point, looking out at the broad expanse of water where the Ashley and Cooper rivers flowed together out to sea.

"Who knows," said William, putting his arm around Mary's shoulders and holding her close. "The Packsaddle Tavern may not yet have seen its best days."

As they turned and walked back up King Street, Aunt Mary's mood continued to lighten. "The first thing we need to do," she said, "is to get the servants together and tell them what our plans are. That will clear up things for them and raise their spirits. Then we will all tidy up the place, give everybody something to do. We will wind the clock and get it ticking again, so to speak."

And that is just what they did. When they returned to the tavern, Aunt Mary called the house slaves together—Delilah, Susan, and Chloe—and William went out to the stable and called in Sampson, Cuffee, and Tad. As the slaves filed into the dining room and took their seats, they were quiet and down at the mouth.

William expected Mary to address them, but she motioned to him to do it. He stood up and looked each man and woman in the eye, smiling a little, trying to instill confidence. "It's good seeing you all again, though my heart is broken with the news of Uncle Duncan's passing. I know this has been a sad time for everyone. We have had a terrible loss. Uncle Duncan was the heart and soul of the Packsaddle, and we all knew it. He is gone now, God rest his soul, but all of us are still here. So is the Packsaddle. Aunt Mary and I want to get the tavern back to where it was. If we all work hard, we may even improve the place. Mistress Mary is the one who will know how to do that, and it will be up to all of us working together to make it happen."

"Are any of us gonna be sold off?" asked Delilah.

"Of course not," said William. "If the tavern is to recover, we will need every single one of you. Our first task will be to tidy up the place. Let's all of us be up and about early tomorrow morning and start getting our house in order. I want the rooms cleaned from top to bottom, the windows washed, the rugs hung up outside and the dirt thrashed out of them. Mop all the floors. We'll open for business the day after tomorrow."

"We can do it," said Sampson.

"That's right," said William. "We can do it. Delilah, you get up your menu for the week and tell me what I need to purchase for the kitchen. Do not neglect your famous turtle soup. And put your mind to getting us up another dish or two that will bewitch the people around here so that nothing will do but to come to the Packsaddle and enjoy a bite to eat."

"Like your rice puddin," said Susan. "Nobody makes it like you do when you make it for me."

"That's what I have in mind," said William. "Sampson, you and your crew go to work on the grounds. Rake the yard and mix the leaves and litter in a heap with manure from the stable. We'll spread that on the garden next spring and have the best vegetable garden in Charles Town. Let them come to the Packsaddle for the sweetness of our melons."

"And for our collards," said Delilah. "There's nothin better in this wide world than collards cooked in wine and onions and garlic."

"There," said William. "We already have three Packsaddle specials—turtle soup, collard greens, and rice pudding. Now we all have plenty to do the next few days. You all go on and get together amongst yourselves and plan out how you will get your work done. Remember, it is up to us to help Aunt Mary get the Packsaddle on its feet again. She needs to know she is being carried along by all of us. When we do that, she will feel a lot better, and we will, too."

The slaves filed out of the kitchen talking among themselves, their mood notably elevated from what it had been before.

Mary, too, had a smile on her face. "Billy, I may know more of the ins and outs of running a tavern than you do, but I will tell you that you have the lion's share of the energy and enthusiasm it takes to be successful. Are you sure the Indian trade is the path for you?"

"I am," said William. "It has come to me of late. It's the one door I know I can get my foot through."

"You may say that, but it looks to me like you've already got it through the door of the Packsaddle. You are your uncle's nephew, a born tavern-keeper. I wish you would stay on and work with me here."

"Och, I thank you for your confidence, Aunt Mary. But I have to say, the Indian trade offers more freedom than a life tied down to a tavern. But tavern life will suit me well enough until next spring. By then you'll be going strong, and you won't need me anymore."

"We'll see," said Mary, putting an arm around his waist and giving him a hug.

Wednesday, September 21, Packsaddle Tavern
If MacDonald's cowpen was the frying pan, the Packsaddle Tavern is the fire. Rest his soul, poor Uncle Duncan is no more. His death knocked the pins out from under Aunt Mary. But I am determined to get the tavern going again. If Aunt Mary were to fold her tent now, I fear she would forfit her reason for living and would soon follow Uncle Duncan to the grave.

Judging from the next day's activities, William's talk to the household had been to good effect. The women got in motion cleaning, scrubbing down the rooms, washing windows, and freshening the linens. Sampson and his men cleaned up the grounds and the stable. By evening, the Packsaddle Tavern was shining like polished brass.

At midday William sat down with Sampson and Delilah and made up a list of everything the tavern required in the way of supplies and foodstuffs. Then he went shopping for all the items on his list, putting out the word as he went from shop to shop that beginning the next day the Packsaddle was very much on its feet again and open for business.

Soon, lodgers were again filling the beds and townspeople were coming to the tables. Besides her other featured dishes, Delilah came up with some special fruit turnovers, little folded-over pies with sugared fillings of stewed dried apples or peaches, flavored with nutmeg, cinnamon, cloves, raisins, and orange peel, and topped off with a smear of brandy-flavored icing. Word spread about "Delilah's little pies," and customers would come in at odd hours during the day to have one along with a cup of tea. The Packsaddle was doing at least as well as it had when Duncan was at the helm. Aunt Mary taught William more of the intricacies of tavern-keeping, including how to keep the books. No matter how smoothly or pleasantly the tavern operated, she emphasized, at the end of the day the books had to show a profit.

Still, there was the day-to-day routine to be endured. At such times William's mind would wander to the Indians and to the backcountry adventurers in the borderlands and beyond. On one such day, well into the evening, his chafing at the bit was soothed when James Adair showed up as a late-arriving guest at the Packsaddle.

"Well, MacGregor," said Adair, "I never know where I will run into you next, here at the tavern or out on the trail in Indian country."

"I expect to be here for quite a while," said William. "My uncle recently passed away from ague, and my aunt has needed a hand in getting the place restored."

"Yes, I was sorry to hear about Duncan. He was a fine fellow, and a great one for telling stories, as well as for listening to them."

"He left a hole here," said William, "no doubt about it. But we're doing our best to fill it. And how about you? Do you need supper? It has all been cleared away, but I can have them bring you something."

"Thank you, but no. I ate on the trail."

"Speaking of stories," said William, "what was the fate of our young cow thieves? Did their elders do as I hoped they would: punish them enough, but not too much?"

"Pull up a chair and have a drink with me," said Adair, "and I will give you the news from the backcountry."

William sat down with him and poured them each a noggin of rum.

"In answer to your question," said Adair, "the Indian way in such matters is to give a tongue lashing of sarcasm and ridicule. The Savannah Town Chickasaws now refer to the three boys as 'the Horsemen' and 'the Marksmen,' and they praise them extravagantly for their fine horsemanship and marksmanship. The boys, bereft of horse and gun, go about with stony faces. They are on the straight and narrow now."

"The Indian world is not ours," said William. "I doubt that such light chastisement would ever keep young Englishmen within bounds. In my time with the Cherokees, I found much to admire about those people. Though much also that I could neither understand nor admire."

"All in all, I prefer their way of life to ours," said Adair. "Even though I am glad to come to Charles Town, I am always gladder yet to get back to Savannah Town."

"How are things in those parts these days?" asked William.

"Not as well as we would like. The Georgians across the river are still at work trying to snake away our trade. It never ends. As soon as we achieve some kind of stability with the Indians, new schemes come along to upset it."

"That seems to be the way of the backcountry," said William. "Which reminds me, I ran into Christian Priber up on the Cherokee Trail last winter. He had been somewhere down to the south of MacDonald's cowpen, and he was on his way back to the Overhill Cherokees."

"Is that so? Do you know what was he up to?"

"He didn't say. His problem on that day was that his horse had gone lame, and he thought he was going to have to walk all the rest of the way. On foot he never would have made it over those mountains. I had a spare horse at the cowpen, and I traded it for his lame one so he could get home."

"You gave him a good horse for a lame one?"

"I was pretty sure the lame one would heal, and it did. It was a fair trade."

"How was Priber dressed?" asked Adair.

"Dressed? The usual way. Why do you ask?"

"It seems he has become the main subject in the gossip passed around by the traders. They say that our Mister Priber has gotten in with one of the Cherokee headmen at Great Tellico, and that he is becoming one of them, throwing over his Christian heritage. If these rumors are to be believed, he now dresses and does all things as the Cherokees do. He even wears an arse-cloth. Though not when he is out of their country, it seems."

"This is surprising, to be sure," said William. "But in truth I find it easy to believe. Priber is much given to lofty ideas, to philosophizing."

"Too much so," said Adair. "What especially has the traders nervous is that he is talking about establishing a so-called paradise in the old town of Coosawattee. It's right up there in the middle between the Upper Creeks and the Cherokees."

"A paradise?"

"Yes, indeed. He dreams of a new nation that will trade equally with Creeks and Cherokees, French and English. He will even admit escaped black slaves into his nation."

"Philosophizing and doing are two different things," said William.

"It depends to some degree on his skill. How much of that does he have? That is the question everyone would like to have answered. The powers that be are most interested in his affairs. They don't take kindly to such tomfoolery if it has the least chance of succeeding."

"Is he in danger, then?"

"I don't have to tell you that everyone is in danger in the Indian country."

"From the Indians, yes. But is he in danger from the Carolina men?"

"He could be."

"I would hate to see him come to harm," said William. "I confess to liking the fellow for his adventurous philosophizing."

"Perhaps the Cherokees will bring him back to earth," said Adair. "I doubt they will be interested in his paradise."

"From what I know of them," said William, "I could not agree more."

After a bit more talking about the ins and outs of the ways of the Indians and the challenges of the trade, Adair and William said good night. Adair went to his room, and after closing the dining room, William did the same.

Tuesday, October 10, Packsaddle Tavern

James Adair stopped in today with another fascinating trove of information about the backcountry. It reminds me that the tavern cannot be surpassed for interesting conversation. I am thinking I might start to keep a separate journal containing what I am able to learn about the backcountry from this vantage point. That would give my venturing spirit some work of its own while I do the day-to-day work of the tavern.

The following week, John Coleman, a good friend with whom William had worked as a packhorseman, stopped in at the tavern to visit.

"I heard you were here," Coleman said to William as he pounded him on the back in greeting.

"John Coleman!" said William, equally pleased to see him. "Where is your fiddle? You do not seem complete to me unless you have a fiddle in your hands."

"I left it back in Great Tellico. I am on a quick trip to see about my mother."

"Is she ailing?" asked William.

"Fever and ague had her, but she's on her feet again, thank God."

"The sickly season has been worse than usual this year," said William. "I suppose you've heard that it took away my Uncle Duncan."

"Yes, I was most grieved to hear of it. All of us packhorsemen enjoyed Duncan's company. He was the greater part of the pleasure of stopping in here. They tell me you are filling in for him, keeping the tavern going."

"For the present time," said William. "We are trying to make up in good food what we have lost in Uncle Duncan's banter. His death hit the Packsaddle pretty hard, but we are working hard to repair and renew, and having some success at it. How are things at Keowee?"

"It goes down a little every year. The Cherokees are out beating the bushes trying to harvest every deerskin and pelt there is. But this year it seems we've got more trade goods than they'll have skins. Next year I'm thinking of striking out on my own amongst the Overhill Cherokees."

"They say the deer are more plentiful there," said William, "and the skins weigh a bit heavier than those around Keowee."

"Yes, but it will be hard to compete with those old traders who have been amongst the Overhills for so many years. Men like Ludovic Grant. He has a good bit of that country wrapped up. What I need is a partner, Billy. Why don't you throw in with me? We could start our own trading company—Coleman and MacGregor."

"It has a nice sound to it, I've got to say," said William. "But my duty right now is to help Aunt Mary get this tavern thriving again. Next spring, if you are still thinking this way, come back again and we'll talk about it."

"I will," said John. "And in the meantime, how are you and Rosemary MacDonald getting along?"

"Not well," said William. "That's all off. She has lined herself up with a plantation lord, and the last I heard, they were making sweet music together. She aims to be his lady."

"Well, that *is* a tragedy," said John. "It's a waste of a perfectly good pinder's daughter."

William chuckled wryly. "I hate to say it, but it still breaks my heart. My head knows better, but my heart is a fool."

"I wish I had my fiddle," said John. "There must be a hundred songs on that subject."

24

The Stranger

One afternoon in early December, with the grip of winter beginning to settle on Charles Town, William walked up King Street carrying a basket filled to the top with foodstuffs for the kitchen. Coming in sight of the tavern, he noticed a large brown horse tethered to a post. It reminded him that he needed to ride out to MacDonald's cowpen to retrieve his horse Spinoza.

As he drew nearer, the horse continued to make him think of Spinoza. So great was the likeness that when he reached the tavern, he went over to examine the horse more closely. Taking a good look at the head and face, William saw to his surprise that it *was* Spinoza. He smiled. Was John MacDonald inside the tavern? Or perhaps it was Christian Priber. Perhaps Priber had come through MacDonald's cowpen on his way to Charles Town and had brought the horse to William as a favor to John. William bounded up the porch steps and hurried inside to see which it might be.

Mary was walking by as he opened the door. "Who brought my horse, Aunt Mary?" he asked.

"I don't know anything about a horse," said Mary. "But we do have a stranger in there." She nodded toward the dining room and lowered her voice. "An odd young man. He is heavily armed, and he keeps his hat on. The servants are leery of him. Something about him is not quite right. He is disagreeable, not at all civil."

"The horse I left up at John MacDonald's cowpen is tethered outside," said William. "I thought maybe Mister MacDonald had brought him, or sent him down with Christian Priber. I can't imagine who he might have sent instead, but the fellow must be trustworthy."

"Perhaps he seemed so to John MacDonald," said Mary. "But if I were you, I would be wary of him."

William peered around the door into the dining room. Only two tables were occupied, one by local people he knew. At the other table sat a slightly-built man facing toward a window, his back to William. He wore a black, broad-brimmed hat and an old hunting shirt cinched in with a wide leather belt. A dirk dangled from the belt on his left side, a pistol was stuck into it on his right side, and in the back he carried a hatchet.

It now occurred to William that this man might have stolen Spinoza, never expecting that the horse would be recognized in Charles Town. Perhaps he was a packhorseman expelled from the backcountry, an occurrence that was not uncommon. Once when William had gotten into a fight with one of his packhorseman mates, Sam Long had threatened the two of them with expulsion. Any more fighting and they could damn well get back to Charles Town the best way they could. Perhaps while getting back as best he could, this fellow, in passing by MacDonald's, had seen Spinoza and lifted him in the dead of night.

William approached the stranger from behind and addressed him. "Sir, I am William MacGregor, and I would like to thank you for the favor of bringing me my horse. What do I owe you for your trouble?"

The man did not respond. Was he deaf? William moved around to see his face, but the man turned away slightly, and William could not see around the broad brim. He said more loudly, "Sir, in case no one has shown you the courtesy, may I take your hat?"

"Bedamned! Can't you see I am having tea?" Speaking gruffly in an odd-sounding voice, the man slammed his mug of tea down on the table. Then he turned toward William and said, his voice rising, "Take my hat? Take my hat?" William caught a glimpse of a smooth oval face, still half obscured by the broad brim. "You certainly may," said the stranger and laughed as he removed his hat and a cascade of reddish blond hair tumbled out.

William fell more than sat down abruptly in a chair at the table. "Rosemary! Is it you? What on earth are you doing here? Why are you dressed as a man?" He rubbed his eyes to clear them. "I must be dreaming."

"You are not dreaming, Billy. Here I sit, and I am sorry to confuse you by the way I am dressed. But it is double dangerous for a woman to travel alone in the backcountry. I had no choice but to come as a man. And as for bringing your horse, you don't owe me a thing for the favor. I was pleased to have the use of him for my journey."

"Good God, Rosemary," said William, still in a daze. "I am so glad to see you. I thought you would be married to Jerome by now. Does your father know you have traveled here alone? I do believe you would not be afraid of Lucifer himself."

"There were times when I was afraid," she said. "I slept out of doors for two nights, and the wolves and cougars were carrying on like banshees in the swamps. I tried to keep a fire going to warn them off, but early this morning I woke up to the tinkling of my horse's bell. Spinoza was standing up close to my bedroll, between me and a wolf that had boldly come up to investigate the few coals that remained in my fire. I don't know if Spinoza meant to protect me or wanted me to protect him. But my pistol was at hand, and I drew down and shot the wolf dead. So I guess you could say we protected each other. The wolf might have been mad, coming up to the fire as it did, though maybe he was only curious."

William just shook his head and looked at her. "I am having trouble taking this in. Did your father send you to bring my horse? I can't imagine that he would do that. And how will you get back to the cowpen? I'll go with you myself to make sure you get back safely."

"I am not going back to the cowpen. I have taken matters into my own hands and gotten myself away from there. I decided to do as a man would do and come to Charles Town to make my fortune. And I will have a new life here in whatever way I can. I will hire out as a milkmaid or a kitchen servant if need be. It may be that I still must work hard, but at least I will be in town."

"Does your father know you are here?" William asked again.

"No, Billy!" Rosemary said in exasperation. "Well, he does know it now, but I did not come with his permission, if that is what you are asking. I did not need his permission. I am old enough to do as I want. I left him a letter."

"A letter?"

Rosemary smiled and reached over and shook his arm gently, as if to wake him up. "Billy, you talk like a man who's been knocked on the head with a cudgel. Yes, a letter. I informed him that I was going to take Spinoza to you in Charles Town and then find a place for myself here. I told him not to worry about me and that I would come back to visit him after I have gotten settled. You can come along with me when I go back to visit, if you want so badly to give me protection. I would enjoy your company. It would be a pleasure to travel as a woman instead of as a man."

While they were conversing, a small crowd had gathered inside the door of the dining room—Mary, Delilah, Susan, and Chloe, all trying to see what was happening. Now William noticed them and motioned to his aunt. "Aunt Mary, please come over."

Mary walked over eagerly.

"Here is someone I want you to meet," said William. "John MacDonald's youngest daughter, Rosemary."

Mary approached, followed by Delilah, Susan, and Chloe. "Oh, my dear girl!" said Mary with delight. "Dressed as a man! No wonder you seemed strange to everyone."

"I have had three days on the trail to practice my disguise," said Rosemary. "I had to appear as masculine and as forbidding as I could."

"Well, you certainly succeeded. My servants didn't want to go near you."

"I apologize for that, and for my disagreeable manner. I was uncertain how to reappear as myself."

"Even I was wary of you," said William. "I didn't know what we had on our hands until you took off your hat."

"I did bring along some clothing more proper to a woman," said Rosemary. "It is packed in a bag tied to Spinoza's saddle. It would please me no end to change out of these rough clothes. And I would give anything for a bath."

"You will stay here at the tavern, of course," said Mary.

"I will stay for a night or two," said Rosemary, "but I don't have much money. I will have to find work quickly. Perhaps a serving position with lodging. Though I can even sleep in a barn, if the grooms can be trusted."

"My dear girl," said Mary, "any daughter of John MacDonald is welcome to stay at my tavern for as long as she needs lodging. I will gladly take work for pay, if you wish."

Rosemary smiled, her face lighting up with relief. "Thank you so very much, Mistress MacGregor. I am good at milking. I can make cheese. I can change and launder linens. In truth, I can do most anything."

"We won't worry about that just now," said Mary. "Chloe, go to the kitchen and get up a hot bath for Miss Rosemary. And be sure to put out that cake of lavender soap. And Susan, you go fetch Miss Rosemary's bag from her horse. Then go up to my room and lay out a bed for her on the couch."

"I can take a public bed," said Rosemary.

"No, you will be in my room," said Mary. "Now go with Chloe and get your bath. Susan will bring you your bag."

Rosemary glanced at William with a happy smile and then followed Chloe out back to the kitchen.

Mary sat down at the table with William, who was still feeling confused. It had all unfolded so quickly.

"How would it be if we kept Rosemary on to work in the tavern?" Mary asked him. "Is she a good worker? Can she do all that she says?"

William just looked at her and shook his head. "Aunt Mary, you do not know the state I am in. I wanted her for my wife. She would not even let me court her, and before I knew it, she had chosen another. But now here she is, moving into the tavern. Yes, she is a cowpen girl, a good worker. There is none better. But I cannot believe she is here. I do not understand a thing that has happened."

"She chose another?" said Mary. "Did she marry him?"

"I don't know. It would appear not, but I have not had a chance to ask her."

"So you would not hesitate to hire her, if you were me."

"No," laughed William. "Not for a moment."

"Do you think she would be willing to work at first for only her bread and lodging?"

"Probably," said William. "But you will have to ask her. I have no idea how she plans to make her way."

"Do you think she has come here to marry you?" asked Mary.

"It doesn't seem so," said William. "But I'm glad she's no longer with Jerome Dubose. He would have ruined everything that is good about her."

Mary reached over and patted his hand. "You do love her," she said. "Don't give up hope."

When Rosemary came back to the dining room after her bath, she was transformed and glowing. She wore a blue and white striped dress that William had seen her wear before. Her hair was done up neatly, and she smelled of lavender. But her face was somber. She went over to Mary and gave her a hug. "Chloe told me about Mister MacGregor," she said. "I am so sorry he has passed away. My father will be terribly grieved. They were such good friends, all the way back to the days of their youth."

"Thank you, my dear," said Mary. "I know how grieved Duncan would have been if John had gone first. But we have survived here at the tavern. We are making our way well enough, now that we have Billy to help us."

Rosemary looked at him and smiled. "So you are back to tavern-keeping."

"Until late spring," he said. "Or early summer."

"And then?"

"I intend to join up with John Coleman and enter the Indian trade."

Rosemary sighed. "The Indian trade again. You seem determined to take that path."

"I have tried to persuade him to stay here with the tavern," said Mary. "He has tavern-keeping in his blood, the same as his uncle."

"So there it is," said Rosemary. "You have it in your blood."

"Aunt Mary thinks so, at least," said William.

"Well, I will tell you this," said Rosemary. "Any woman would favor a tavern-keeper over an Indian trader."

William smiled broadly. "Look around you. What do you see me doing here? For the moment, at least, I'm keeping a tavern."

Rosemary accepted Mary's offer to stay on at the Packsaddle and to work at first for room and board, with a wage to be added eventually, if she proved her worth. To put John MacDonald's mind at ease, Mary wrote a letter assuring him that Rosemary had landed safely in her care and was living a respectable life under her watchful eye. In the days that followed, Rosemary folded herself seamlessly into the fabric of everyday life at the tavern. She worked most particularly in the dining room, making sure that the guests were well served. She was soon getting along well with Delilah, though at first the cook was less than thrilled to have another woman in the house standing over her. But Delilah was won over when she discovered that Rosemary did not have to be asked to pitch in and help when the work load in the kitchen piled up especially high.

"Compared to the work I had to do at the cowpen," said Rosemary, "this tavern work is a song."

In no time at all she became the manager of the dining room. She saw to it that the customers were pleasantly seated and their orders filled promptly. If anything needed to be tidied up, she did so quickly and with a kind of joy. More and more customers came in, as much to enjoy the clever conversation of this handsome young woman as to savor Delilah's cooking.

Rosemary was not shy about offering her ideas for new improvements. One day she took Delilah aside. "Your fruit pies leave nothing to be desired," she said. "But there is still a great thing you could add to your menu—macaroons. Do you know how to make them?"

"It's been quite a while since I made any, but I remember how to do it."

"I have only eaten them once," said Rosemary, "but they are the best confection I have ever tasted. Tell me how they are made. I would like to know."

"The hardest thing is finding almonds," said Delilah. "But if you can get some, you take a pound or so, blanch them well, and then beat them in a mortar along with a pound of sugar. Then you take this mix and add a little rose water and the whites of three eggs beat to a froth. Then you drop it by the spoonful on tin plates and bake it in an oven not too hot. Yes ma'am, I do know how to make macaroons."

At first opportunity, Rosemary sent William in search of a pound of almonds, which he found at a store on Bay street. Delilah cooked up a batch of macaroons, and when Rosemary tasted one fresh out of the oven, she curtsied and said, "Delilah, you are a magician. From now on macaroons must be on our menu."

Mary was more than pleased to have Rosemary's help. When it became clear that the wardrobe Rosemary had brought with her from the cowpen fell short of what was needed for city life, both in variety and in style, Mary insisted on buying fabric to sew up into new gowns. Rosemary gladly accepted and was thrilled to go with her to the shops of Charles Town.

"I always had to make do with whatever cloth Father brought back from the fall cattle drive," Rosemary told William, as she showed him her new treasures. "I never got to choose anything for myself." She was especially pleased with the new pair of shoes Mary bought for her to replace the coarse country shoes she had worn at the cowpen.

As Christmas came and went, Rosemary and Mary worked together in their spare time to sew up the new gowns, three of them in all. As each was completed, Rosemary would wear it to her work in the dining room, and William would be swept off his feet anew. With the third one, she admitted to him that she was beginning to feel ill at ease. "I have so many gowns now," she said, "it feels frivolous. At the cowpen, one nice one was plenty, and even that was never so nice as any of these." The two of them were seated together in a high-backed settle by the dining room fire. It was mid-afternoon on a day in early January, and there were no guests at the moment.

"You're in the city now," said William. "Look around next time you are out. All the women above the station of servants are dressed the same as you. A great many of them have more than three gowns."

"I suppose I always expected it was my fate to be more like the serving women," said Rosemary. "Even though I hoped to be more."

"I thought Jerome was making those hopes come true," said William. "Are you ever going to tell me how things ended with him?"

"It embarrasses me to talk about Jerome," she said quietly. "But I do need to explain it to you. I truly did think I loved him, you see. But then finally I realized that what I was seeing in him was only my dream of him. It was when Father came home that day and told us about you and Cut Nose that I began to wake up. You risked your life to save my father. You killed that monster with nothing more than a lance. The meaning of it went through me like a thunderbolt. All I could think was, what would Jerome have done? And of course I knew the answer. He would have climbed the nearest tree and my father would be dead."

"I would have to agree," said William. "There are some things they don't teach in English public schools. Up against Cut Nose, my education with Cudjo served me better."

"It's not just a matter of know-how," said Rosemary. "He wouldn't have had it in him, no matter what. So that was the beginning of the end of him and me. And yet still, I am ashamed to say, I kept hoping that somehow he would prove me wrong. But then he proposed to me, and that finished us off."

"I would have thought that would have put you back up into the clouds," said William.

She laughed. "Maybe it would have if he had simply proposed that we marry. But then he proposed that we make our home at the cowpen."

William looked at her in surprise. "At the cowpen?"

"Well, not at the cowpen as it is now. He proposed that we ask Father to give us the cypress swamp so that we could clear it and start up another rice plantation. He would build a beautiful house for me, he said, with a view of the river. And I could always be near my father and sisters."

"While he was where?" asked William.

"That is exactly what I asked him," said Rosemary. "I said surely he would want to live in Charles Town. But he went on about how he loved the country more than the city and how the air is more healthful there and how he would always want to be where I was."

"I can believe his last point," said William, "but the rest of it doesn't ring true."

"Nor did it ring true to me," said Rosemary. "And it brought my foolish dream to an end. Jerome didn't know me at all. He had never listened to a word I said. If he had, he would have known not to offer me a life in the back-country, whether in a beautiful house or not. Especially not in Liza's swamp, even if it was drained and planted. So I thanked him and told him no. He was taken aback, but I stood firm."

"Is that the whole of it then?" asked William.

"I should say more," said Rosemary. "It makes me feel stupid, but I should say it anyway. You deserve to hear it."

"I thank you for that," said William. "But I leave it to your discretion."

"Here is what I came to understand about Jerome," said Rosemary. "First, he was most interested in my father's swamp. In short, he hoped to get a new rice plantation as a dowery. Second, the prospect of living with him on a rice plantation made me face up to his complicity in the cruel treatment of his father's slaves. When I thought we would live in Charles Town, I overlooked all that. I told myself it had nothing to do with him as a rice merchant in the city. Now I am ashamed of having allowed myself to think that way. And third, he turned every conversation back to the sacred order of the empire and the glory of the rice planters. His way of seeing the world is not the way I see it or know it. I had already grown weary of hearing about it. Imagine having to listen to that for a lifetime."

William beamed. "I'm glad you have told me this. I will confess I had my doubts about you when we visited his plantation. Suddenly you were not the person I thought you were."

"Now you know I am not perfect," said Rosemary. "I am no stranger to folly. And, Billy, I do thank you from my deepest heart for what you did that day for my father." She reached out and took his hand and squeezed it. "I have never heard of anything so brave. It filled me with regret about how I treated you. I never gave you a chance."

"You are doing better now," he said. He still held her hand in his and stroked it with his thumb. Just as he was thinking that he could not feel more content, the bell at the front door tinkled with the arrival of guests, and they rose reluctantly to go back to work.

"You were sweet not to bring up even more of my stupidities," said Rosemary, brushing at the skirt of her new gown to smooth the wrinkles.

"I cannot think of a single one," said William.

"Brother and sister?" she said with an apologetic smile.

"I don't seem to remember that one," he answered.

"Good," she said. The guests were locals who had come in for the dining room, and she hurried off to show them to a table.

All her life Rosemary had loved British songs and ballads, and she had committed many of them to memory. One night when the dining room was made especially lively by a boisterous table of men that included a well-known and good-humored Charles Town lawyer, Rosemary was so amused at their gaiety that she came and stood by the lawyer's chair. "Gentlemen," she said, "I will sing you a song I heard from an Indian trader who visited our cowpen. Where he learned it, I do not know."

"Let's hear it then," said the lawyer.

As Rosemary stood with her hands on her hips and sang, William thought his heart would burst with love as he watched her and listened to that big voice of hers.

"A fox may steal your hens, sir,
A whore your health and pence, sir,
Your daughter rob your chest, sir,
Your wife may steal your rest, sir,
A thief your goods and plate.
But this is all but picking,
With rest, pence, chest and chicken;
It ever was decreed, sir,
If lawyer's hand is fee'd sir,
He steals your whole estate."

Rosemary curtsied and smiled, and the table erupted in laughter. The lawyer stood up and proposed a toast to her: "To the lovely and talented *chanteuse* of the Packsaddle Tavern for that wise song from John Gay's *Beggar's Opera.*"

"I don't know what a *chanteuse* is," said Rosemary, "nor do I know what the *Beggar's Opera* is. But I will take what you said as a compliment."

After that, whenever Rosemary was moved to do so, she would take the floor and sing. Sometimes she sang old ballads running to many verses, and she never failed to hold the room of diners in rapt attention.

As if all this were not enough, William could not have been happier to have someone with whom to share his love of books. When Rosemary heard about the Book Maggots club back in Glasgow, she insisted that they institute a Charles Town chapter, with the two of them as the sole members. "And during the meetings of our club," she said, "you will be Mister Worm, and I will be Miss Worm."

"And what shall we read first, Miss Worm?" asked William.

"Shakespeare, of course," said Rosemary. "And then more Shakespeare. And then more Shakespeare until we have read everything he wrote."

This was another of the many moments when William wanted to sweep her into his arms and kiss her. But he restrained himself. Now that she was allowing him to court her, he was proceeding slowly and carefully. He did not want to spoil his chances a second time.

When their work allowed it, the two of them began taking long walks through Charles Town in the January cold. Rosemary was thrilled by the large, beautiful buildings and the bustling streets with all the people out and about, bundled up in coats and cloaks, attending to business and sharing gossip. At some point it became natural for William to reach for her hand, and she freely gave it, making their walks together all the sweeter. The way they held hands was more than a friendly gesture. It was an intimacy.

They often walked along Bay Street, where they could see the harbor with all the great ships riding at anchor and all the small craft—pettiaugers, sloops, shallops—busily plying the waters. Here in the heart of the city was the Custom House, the Council Chamber, and the Court House. They especially liked to walk through the market on the Middle Bridge, with its displays of exotic goods not to be seen elsewhere.

One day as they strolled down the southern end of Bay Street, near Granville's Bastion, Rosemary posed a question that had been on both their minds. "What I would like to know, Billy, is will it be the tavern or the Indian trade for you?"

"That is my dilemma," said William. "Until you came, I thought I had it all nailed down. I gained enough from my year's work with your father to stake myself to a small start in trade, especially if I partner with John Coleman. The Indian country has a strong pull on me. There is excitement there in the challenge of making one's way among the Indians, of establishing a trading territory, of navigating the intricacies of international intrigue. Tavern life seems tame by comparison. At least it did before you arrived."

"Are you saying that I make your life wild?" asked Rosemary, pretending to take offense.

William laughed. "Yes, you do, in a way. Not wild like Indians, but wild like Rosemary. Most everything you do is a surprise to me. I enjoy tavern-keeping when you are here. Which has put me to thinking about staying with it. If one must live in town, tavern-keeping might well be the best way to do it while still keeping in touch with the backcountry. After all, where else but in a tavern can I get the latest dispatches from the traders and packhorsemen and farmers and planters when they come into town? In truth, I might be able to gain a broader understanding of the backcountry from this vantage point than if I were immersed up to my eyebrows in the Indian trade. And so this is my dilemma. The door has opened for me to enter the Indian trade, but now you have come and made tavern-keeping so pleasant that the prospect of my being absent from here for six months at a time is becoming as unattractive to me as it may be to you."

"So," said Rosemary, "does this mean that the running of a tavern is in your future after all?"

"Aye, I think it does mean that."

Rosemary turned to him and looked deeply into his eyes, and then, before he could make a move of his own, she threw her arms around him and kissed him the way she kissed him that night at the cowpen. Full on the mouth. But this time it was no topsy-turvey cornshucking kiss, and when William kept it going, she did not pull away.

The next day they took a walk along Church Street, passing by the French Huguenot meeting house and then by St. Philip's Church of England. It was early February and the first hints of spring were in the air.

"I have always been one to ask questions," William said. "Some of my questions have wanted complicated answers. But I have one for you today that requires only a simple answer."

Rosemary stopped and looked at him. "And what might that question be, Mister MacGregor?"

"You know full well what it is."

"How can I know until you ask it?"

"My question is this. Will you, Rosemary MacDonald, do me, William MacGregor, the honor of marrying me?"

Tears welled up in her eyes. "Why am I crying?" she asked, wiping at them with her hand. "This makes me so happy, Billy. The simple answer is yes. I will marry you."

He drew her into his arms and kissed her and held her tightly. People passing on the sidewalk smiled and stared. Releasing each other, the two began to walk along again, holding hands tightly.

"There is something I want you to understand," said Rosemary.

"And what is that?" asked William, bracing himself for whatever she was about to throw his way.

"I want you to know that I am not marrying you because you say you are going to be a tavern-keeper instead of an Indian trader. I hope you will be a tavern-keeper. But I want you to know that if you ever feel that you just have to go back to the Indian country, for a season, or for several seasons, or for whatever it might be, I will not try to stop you from going. That doesn't mean I will like it. What it means is that I am not marrying you because you are this instead of that. I am marrying you because you are Billy MacGregor, and whatever Billy MacGregor is, now and in the future, that's what I am marrying."

William took a deep breath and let it out. "Rosemary, you take my breath away," he said. "Let's go home and tell the news."

Still holding hands, they ran more than walked the two blocks back to the Packsaddle. When they told Aunt Mary their plans, her eyes filled with tears and she embraced the two of them together.

The wedding was in March, a small affair in the sitting room of the Packsaddle Tavern. The guests were some of the dining room regulars. The minister, as sparing of words as any preacher William had ever heard, said all the words that were required and no more. Aunt Mary poured a round of Madeira for all assembled, congratulations were offered, and William and Rosemary were man and wife.

Mary had allocated one of the third floor rooms for them to use as their residence until they could make other arrangements. It had windows facing east and south, making it a light and cheery room for the beginning of a marriage. After all the guests had departed, Rosemary sent William up to their room to wait for her. "I will be up in a few minutes," she said and headed to her old quarters in Mary's room to ready herself.

William lit a myrtle-wax candle and climbed the two flights of stairs to their new home. Placing the candle on a table, he savored its warm, sweet scent. He wished Rosemary were there already. How long would she be? He paced the floor a few times, and then he took off his clothes and slipped under the covers. Soon he heard her coming up the stairs with a quick step. She opened the door, shut it behind her, and shimmied out of her clothing so quickly it startled him. Standing naked before him, her body glowing in the light of the candle, she held out her arms to the side and curtsied.

"Mister Worm, allow me to present Mistress Worm." She laughed at the look on his face. "My mama," she added, "always told me that I should not do this until I was married. And in case you are wondering, I almost always took her advice."

William shook his head. "Rosemary, I may never return to the backcountry, but you will always be my wild country girl."

"Billy, you are about to find out just how wild and country I really am."

William was giddy with desire as she slipped under the covers. As they embraced, he was sure he could smell the fragrance of rosemary, and love so possessed him, he was unable to put what he felt into words. But fortunately, he could express what he felt in quite another way, and he did so.

25

Will Shakespeare Should Be Here

The two members of the South Carolina chapter of the Book Maggots Club began their program of reading all of Shakespeare's works with *A Midsummer Night's Dream,* a comedy to mirror their own happiness. Lying in their bed each night, William and Rosemary took turns reading aloud by candle light. Whenever they came to a particularly lyric passage, they would read it several times so they could soak up the poetry of the words as well as their sense. Now and then, if a passage were especially beautiful or clever, Rosemary would insist they stay with it until she had memorized it. After *Midsummer,* they read *The Taming of the Shrew,* which Rosemary saw as a fitting condemnation of her cold behavior toward William at the cowpen, though William insisted there was not the least resemblance between her and Shakespeare's Katherina.

By early summer they had finished *The Shrew,* and then for a little time they left Shakespeare alone while they took in the happy prospect that was signaled by the cessation of Rosemary's monthly cycle. But once the reality of that development had settled in, Rosemary was ready for the Book Maggots to reconvene. Looking through William's collection of the master's plays, she pulled out the volume of *King Lear.* "How about this one?" she asked, standing in the light of a window and thumbing through it. "You are always quoting lines from it. You even once referred to my father as King Lear."

William came over and stood behind her, reaching around to put his hands protectively over her belly. "*King Lear* is the darkest tale I ever heard," he said. "It is a merciless story of human beings at their worst. I would not want the merest trace of it to rub off on this bairn."

"This bairn is not yet formed enough to hear or know a thing," said Rosemary.

"But if you get sad or disturbed, it could affect him. Or her."

"I have nothing but happiness in me," said Rosemary. "No story from a book can touch it. This bairn will be the happiest child in Charles Town. You'll see."

But night after night, as they read on and on about Lear's kingdom falling relentlessly asunder, until the king himself was stripped of all life's comforts and the loyal Gloucester, his eyes gouged out, was stumbling blindly about the countryside, Rosemary began to see what William had been talking about. When they finally came to the end, with poor, innocent Cordelia hanged and her pitiful father crying his words of grief to the heavens, Rosemary cast the book aside and buried herself in William's arms, pressing her face against his chest.

"Are you crying?" William asked her.

"No, but I feel devastated. I thought father and daughter were going to be together again, even though it would be in prison. Cordelia's father had come so far and learned so much. He was becoming wise. And he had finally learned how to love her. And then they snatched her up and killed her. What a cruel ending. Why did Shakespeare have to write it that way?"

"Shakespeare was the master of his own plays," said William. "He could write them any way he pleased. We'll choose a cheerier tale for the next one. *All's Well That Ends Well* would be the logical choice."

"No, I don't think so. Mistress Worm needs a rest from Master Shakespeare," said Rosemary. "I just want to live the story of Billy and Rosemary for a while."

But as summer settled in, it brought the sickly season and almost as much melancholy as could be found in Shakespeare's tragedies. Not only was there the annual return of the ague that had felled Duncan, but it was also a particularly bad summer for Barbados fever. Anyone afflicted with this terrible disease came down with high fever, yellowing skin, and black vomit. Many of the afflicted did not survive. Death carts rumbled daily along the streets. One funeral followed upon the heels of another. Many people shut themselves up in their houses, and the commercial life of the town slowed to a trickle. Preachers thundered from their pulpits about God's punishment of the sinful people of Charles Town. William was afraid for the health of both Rosemary and their unborn baby.

By late August the tavern beds were all but empty, with hardly anyone daring to venture from the good air of the backcountry into the bad air of the lowcountry. The dining room had few guests as the townspeople chose to stay home rather than risk mingling with others in public places. With fall approaching, the sickly season would soon rise to its peak, and William's fear for his new family became too much to bear.

He consulted with Mary, and she agreed with the course he wanted to take. Then he put the plan to Rosemary. "Suppose we go up and stay with your father for a few months," he said. "There's next to nothing for us to do here at the tavern, and Aunt Mary agrees that she can get along without us for a while. Your father and sisters will be glad to see you. And we can keep you and the bairn in healthier air until the weather cools and it's safe to return."

"As long as we can return to Charles Town once the cold weather comes," said Rosemary. "I would be happy to see my father. And even my sisters."

They made the three day journey in good time, but the closer they came to the cowpen, the more Rosemary dreaded the condition in which they would find it. "We've got to steel ourselves," she said. "It might be a shambles, and we can't let it weigh us down."

Late in the third day of travel they came to a familiar stand of poplar trees, the green leaves beginning to show a little yellow. The cowpen was just ahead.

"Are you ready to face it?" asked William.

"If he is still sober," said Rosemary, "nothing else matters. I can accept the whole place being overgrown. But if he has gone back to the rum, we may have to return to Charles Town."

"We will take it a day at a time," said William.

As they rode up the sandy trail to the cowpen, they were at first so amazed at what they saw that they pulled up their horses to take in the scene. The cowpen was neat as could be. The house had been patched up, and a small wing had been added to the back. Out front was a flower bed with the last of the summer flowers in bloom. The bare ground around the house and barn was swept clean of debris.

They rode to the house and tethered their horses to a new rail that had been set up for that purpose. From down at the barn a familiar yapping started up, and little Butch came running out of the barn and up the path, barking fiercely. Then out came John with a hayfork in his hand. Seeing the visitors, he propped the fork against the side of the barn and headed up the path. He appeared to be cleanly dressed, his hair combed. He had a broad smile on his face. Little Butch, charging in close enough to recognize Rosemary, became ecstatic, jumping up high in front of her several times and then running in frantic circles around her. Laughing, she reached out her arms to him and he leapt into them and licked her face as she hugged him. Then as John approached, she released Butch from her arms and held them out to her father. Butch went back to running in circles, this time around the two of them.

"He is almost as glad to see you as I am," said John, squeezing her in a tight embrace. Then he held her out at arm's length. "I see that marriage agrees with you. You have gained a little weight, and all of it around the middle. Are you. . . ?"

"Yes. By Christmas there will be two where you now see one."

"Then I am twice as happy to see you," said John, and he hugged her again.

Then he turned to William. "Congratulations to you, my boy," he said and shook his hand warmly. "Welcome to my family. I could not wish for a better match for Rosemary. And I hope you two have come to stay for a while. We have been getting reports up here about how bad the Barbados fever is in the lowcountry this year. I've worried about you no end. It would do me good if you would stay with us until the weather turns cold."

"You can rest easy," said Rosemary, "because that is just what we were hoping we could do. But we don't want to be a burden."

"You will be a boon, not a burden. You can take up residence in Betsy's old room. She and the boys are gone."

"Gone where?" asked Rosemary.

"She and Rufus have driven the herd up to the neighborhood of Ninety Six. They found a good range on a creek that runs into the Saluda River, and they are setting up a new cowpen there. I gave her Daphne to work in her kitchen and dairy, and Ajax to cut timber for the house and barn. When all has been built, they can put him to work hunting cows with the rest of the crew."

"Ninety Six," said Rosemary. "That puts them in the backyard of the Cherokees."

"Yes, it does," said John. "But that's the life of a pinder. To run your cows on a good range, you've got to go out to the borderlands. Ninety-six miles between them and the Cherokees should be buffer enough. But we have plenty of time to talk about all this. Let's take your belongings into your room and then get us some tea to enjoy while we catch up on the news."

William and Rosemary untied their baggage from behind their saddles and piled everything on the ground. As they made ready to carry it inside, a tall African woman came out of the house onto the porch. "I'll get that," she said and headed down the steps.

William and Rosemary looked at each other in surprise. It was Julie, from the Dubose plantation. Rosemary looked at her father as Julie began gathering up all the baggage she could carry. "Do you have other visitors?" she asked guardedly. "Are there any Duboses here?"

"No. Why would there be?"

"Because their Julie is here," said Rosemary, a bit exasperated to have to state the obvious.

"She's not their Julie anymore," said John. "She's ours."

Rosemary glanced at Julie heading up the steps with her load and then looked back at her father, puzzled. "But how could you afford her?"

"Questions, questions," said John. "Did you think everything would be just as you left it? Time has done its work for us the same as it has for you. Let's go get that tea and we'll tell our stories."

They all went inside the house, William carrying the rest of their belongings and following along after Rosemary to Betsy's old room. As they reached the doorway of the room, Julie was just coming out, having deposited her load.

"Welcome to my father's household," Rosemary said to her and reached out and gave her a little hug.

"Thank you, ma'am," said Julie.

"Are you happy here?" asked Rosemary. "Is it better than where you were?"

"Yes, ma'am, it is," said Julie. "But excuse me now, I need to hurry on and get the tea."

Julie went on her way and Rosemary went into the room with William. "Of course, she has to say that she is happy here," said Rosemary. "I hope that she truly is."

"If she gets to spend time with Cudjo," said William, "I know he is happy at least. And he did tell me that she liked him, too."

"Then maybe she is not sorry to be uprooted," said Rosemary. She went to their bags and began to unpack.

"Your father is waiting for us," said William.

"I know," said Rosemary, "but first I need to settle in. I have to make my nest. You go on out and talk to Father. I'll be there soon."

"I'll help you," said William, and the two of them quickly emptied their packs and put all of their things in place. William put his journal and pen and ink on the table beside the bed. The empty packs went underneath the bed.

Then they went back to the main room and sat down with John at the table. Julie was just bringing in a tray with a pot of tea and cups, a plate of bread, and some butter and blackberry jam. She poured a cup of tea for each of them, and then she buttered several slices of bread and carried the plate around the table with the pot of jam. Rosemary and William were so famished from their long ride and short rations that they concentrated on the bread and jam and let the conversation lag for a while. Julie stood by the table and refilled their cups when they emptied them. Finally John dismissed her. "We are well-fed for the time being," he told her. "But tell Aunt Sally to prepare us a feast for supper. The Prodigal Daughter has returned. We need something on the order of a fatted calf."

"What we have is chicken and rice," said Julie.

"That will be wonderful," said Rosemary, and Julie left the room. Rosemary looked at her father appreciatively. "Thank you, Father, for welcoming me home so sweetly. I would not have blamed you if you had been angry with me for leaving you the way I did. I would have asked for your blessing before going, but I didn't think I would get it."

"When I heard you were at the Packsaddle," said John, "all my anger vanished. I knew then that you had decided in favor of Billy."

"But how did you know he would still have me?" asked Rosemary. "I was not at all sure that he would."

"I had no doubt of it," said John.

"I thank you, as well, for the warm welcome, Father MacDonald," said William. "It is good to be back here, and heartening to see you looking so well."

"Yes, and the whole place sparkling," said Rosemary. "Now tell us how you got Julie. I would have thought that a new slave was the last thing you could afford at the same time you were handing over your cows and timber to Betsy and Liza."

"It was simple," said John. "I made sure she was included in the price I got for the cypress swamp."

"You sold the cypress swamp? To Jean Dubose?"

"Not to Dubose Senior. To Jerome. He could not take his eyes off that land, and evidently his father put some money in his hand. I held out for Julie to be included in the price. He didn't want to give her up, but I insisted. No Julie, no deal. Finally he gritted his teeth and we came to terms. I also stipulated that Swan and his crew be allowed to cut and saw up enough lumber to build the grist mill and to add the new wing on the back of this house. But that part of the deal was no problem. The more timber our boys clear from the swamp, the more suitable it becomes for a rice plantation."

"So Swan and Liza are getting their grist mill," Rosemary said excitedly.

"They have the mill house up, and they are using part of it for living quarters until they get up a separate house of their own. And they have put up a small house for Obadiah, who is staying on to be a mill hand. Cato is there, too, to help with the building, but soon he will go up to the new cowpen."

"Is the mill in business yet?" asked William.

"Not quite. The apparatus that transfers the power of the water wheel to the millstones is not completed. They will have to hire a millwright to help them with that. But it is certain they will be in business in a few months. I've been spending quite a bit of time down there, helping out. Running a mill is more interesting than I thought it would be."

Just then Aunt Sally and Julie came in with their dinner—chicken and rice, boiled cabbage, and fried corncakes with plenty of butter. Rosemary got up to greet Sally with an embrace, which both pleased Sally and embarrassed her. "You got to behave yourself, Miss Rosemary," she murmured. "You're a lady now. Don't be jumpin up to hug the help."

"You don't know how I've missed your cooking," said Rosemary, settling back down to the feast.

"So have I, Aunt Sally," said William. "Never let it be said that you have forgotten how to cook."

"No, sir, won't nobody ever say that. And now I have Julie to help me with cooking some dishes I never heard of. Though I do miss my girl Daphne. She got took up to the new cowpen with Miss Betsy. So I've got Daphne gone from beside me and Jock and Ray gone further than ever. But I try not to think about all that. I just keep on doin what I'm supposed to do."

Julie reached for her arm to steer her out the back door to the kitchen.

"Aunt Sally has always been one to speak her mind," said Rosemary as they left.

"She's earned the right," said John. "I let her say what she wants, as long as she keeps doing her work."

"So what is the purpose of the new wing on the house?" asked William. "Your family is smaller, not bigger. Is it for your travelers rest?"

"Aye, the improved travelers rest. MacDonald's Cattle Stand we call it. Cow-hunters driving along the trail can now pen their cattle here overnight. And with that new room for them to sleep in, packhorsemen and cow-hunters both stop in more often than before. We have four beds in there, and extra pallets for the floor. If we need more space, of course, we can still use the barn. And if gentlefolk come through on the way to and from Amelia Township, I have Betsy's room to offer them. And, Billy, I thank you for telling me about Julie. She has proven to be a great success as a hostess. She serves a gracious table and puts everyone at ease."

"So many changes," said Rosemary, "and I've not even been gone a year."

"A lot can happen in a year's time," said John. "Have I mentioned that Liza and Swan are now three?"

"No!" Rosemary exclaimed in happy surprise. "You should have told me that first thing. They have a babe? Already born?"

"A month old," said John. "A girl. Martha Ann. Named after your mother. And I have to say, after Betsy's two boys I am pleased to have a baby girl in my arms again. I got used to girls with you three."

"Father, I could not have wished for a better homecoming," said Rosemary, reaching across the table to put her hand on his. "It thrills my heart to find you happy."

"I think I have never quite been happy before," said John. "There have always been too many cares. But now that I have handed off so many of them, my life is the better for it. Especially with the mill and little Martha Ann. I find myself drawn to Poplar Creek most every day. Swan and Liza don't seem to mind. I try to make myself useful when I'm there."

He paused and looked down at Rosemary's hand on his, and then he turned his own hand palm up and closed it around hers. "I've made my apologies to the other two," he said, "but I haven't yet asked your forgiveness, Daughter, for the sour temper I visited upon you in the last year before you left. It especially pains me to think about that night of the cornshucking. I unloaded all my wrath upon you, and you did not deserve the least of it."

"I've long since forgiven it and forgotten it," said Rosemary. "Those were dark times for all of us. I myself was not exactly your little angel that night."

John smiled. "I can't say that you ever were entirely that. I like my angels with a bit of devil in them."

He released her hand, and Rosemary propped her elbow on the table, leaned her chin in her hand, and sighed contentedly. "It is good to be home," she said.

"You are looking a little tired," said John. "Why not go to your room and lie down and rest for a while?"

"That may be just the thing," she said. She got up and went around to where he sat and gave him a kiss. Then she looked at William. "Do you want to come with me?" she asked.

"As soon as I take care of the horses," said William.

William led the two horses through the warm twilight toward the barn, the late summer air loud with the song of crickets and katydids. He felt himself almost in an enchanted land, as if Puck, from *A Midsummer Night's Dream*, might be frolicking in the woods out at the edge of the clearing. The change in this place seemed magical. And yet, when he remembered his first experience of the cowpen, before the "dark times," as Rosemary put it, this was indeed a pleasant place, and John was a strong, good-natured man. And so perhaps the greatest change was not this latest turn but the dark time itself, cast like an evil spell upon the place. To break the spell, John had to release his grip on so much he had carried for so long. But how is a man to know when it is time to put down what was once right for him to take up? And how is it that so much generosity could flow from that release? Imagine John MacDonald bargaining with all his might to bring Cudjo's Julie to the cowpen. Of course, with Cudjo and the cows moved up into new territory, that situation was still not ideal. But at least both slaves were now in the same family, and Cudjo would surely be allowed to come here to visit.

When William reached the pen outside the barn, he unsaddled the horses, hung the saddles over the top rail of the pen, and then opened the gate and put the horses inside. Then he went into the barn to get some cornshucks for their feed. There was a generous pile on the floor, tossed down from the loft above, and he took up a great double armload and headed out with it. As he approached the barn door, he noticed a lance leaning against the wall nearby. Like Cudjo's lance, he thought. He stepped over to take a closer look. It *was* Cudjo's lance. What was that doing here? He went on and fed the horses, trying to puzzle it out. Cudjo would never give up his lance, or forget it and leave it here. If the lance was here, Cudjo must be here too.

William left the pen, and instead of going back to the house, he went to the milking pen. In the fading twilight, he could barely see the cows, much less the milkers. As his eyes searched the dim light, he heard a feminine voice —Venus, he was sure. Then a male voice answered her.

"Cudjo!" William called out happily.

"Over here, Mister William."

William went over and found Cudjo milking away, his pail almost full. "I don't believe my eyes," said William. "I thought you were up at Ninety Six."

"I ain't with Mister Rufus no more," said Cudjo. He looked up at William and smiled while his hands kept tugging on the teats. "Master John kept me here. In my place he gave Ajax to Master Rufus, and Cato's goin up there as well, once all the buildin gets done around here."

"So you're not herding cows anymore?"

"Ain't these cows?" asked Venus, speaking up from where she sat at the udder of another cow. William and Cudjo both laughed.

"I got these five milk cows to tend to," said Cudjo, "and twelve beef cows that range right in around the pen here. It's not like my Fulani home, but it's closer to it than the big herd was. I know all these cows by name. And they don't get driven off to market."

"But the beef cows do get eaten," said William.

"One by one, they do. But by their own people. A cow gets eaten and another cow gets born. That's more as it should be. Though back home we don't often eat our cows. We are satisfied with the milk and the cheese."

"So who is making the cheese around here now?" asked William.

"I am," said Venus. "I always helped Miss Rosemary do it. Mine is as good as hers ever was."

"It is," said Cudjo. "She makes good cheese."

"So you only have twenty cows to look after?" said William.

Cudjo laughed.

"He takes care of this whole place," said Venus. "He's the overseer now."

"Ah," said William. "Now I'm beginning to understand. That's why things are in such good order. With Father MacDonald going off to the mill every day, I was wondering how the yard had gotten so clean and the fences mended and the barn loft filled high with shucks."

"Mister John does a little around here," said Cudjo, "but mostly it seems he wants to be a miller. But I've got Mars and Venus to help me. We get along right well."

"And Juliyama," said William.

"Yes, Ju-u-ulie," said Venus in a singsong voice. "Cudjo and Julie, Cudjo and Julie. As soon as it gets dark and they finish all their work, they go into their house and close the door. We don't see them again until morning."

William laughed, and Cudjo smiled and shrugged. He had finished the milking and was getting up from the stool with the pail. "I hear you have your own missus to go home to," Cudjo said.

"I do," said William, "and I had better get home to her now. She expected me long ago."

"You gonna get in trouble," said Venus. "Miss Rosemary is particular about things. Just ask me. I know."

"I'll see you two tomorrow," said William. "We're going to be staying on for a while. Until cold weather comes."

"That's good," said Cudjo. "I'm happy to see you again."

"It's a pleasure to see you, too," said William. And then he turned and headed up through the gathering darkness to the house.

John was still up, but getting ready to retire. It was dark inside the open door of William and Rosemary's room, and John gave William a candle to light his way. When William got into the room, he saw that Rosemary was fast asleep in their bed. He quietly put the candle on the table and sat down to make an entry in his journal.

Wednesday, August 29, 1739, MacDonald's Cattle Stand

I am astonished at how much things have turned around here at the cowpen. We arrived expecting more of what before had been so hard to bear. But instead, it is as if a curtain has fallen on a tragedy and then lifted on a comedy. The gloom has been expelled; the light shines forth.

Or perhaps it is wrong to see ourselves as players on a stage, as Shakespeare is wont to do. Perhaps instead we live in a house made of history. We can see some of the walls and barriers that circumscribe us. But there are others in this house of history that we can only half see, or not see at all. When we transgress these limits, we suffer. The grazing is less than it was. The best trees for sawing lumber are all cut down and used up. The population of planters and farmers around us grows, and the free range diminishes. As problems mount, we blame each other. But it is really history that is to blame. It is the passage of time.

The question then is not why do we have these barriers and limits, or how do we get rid of them, for they are an inevitable part of life. The question is how can we learn to be sensible of them and adapt to them before they injure or overwhelm us? I do not have the answer to that, but at least I have learned to ask the question. Dare to inquire.

There is something else very much on my mind. Tonight there was a tender scene between Rosemary and her father. She more or less asked his blessing, and he answered by asking her forgiveness. It brings to mind that glowing passage at the end of King Lear, when the king speaks so lovingly to Cordelia. Rosemary memorized those words, and I will have her recite them for me when she awakes. I remember only the essence of them. Lear says something like this: "When you ask me to bless you, Daughter, I'll kneel down and ask of you forgiveness. And so we'll laugh and pray and sing and tell each other stories and happily watch the world go by."

The parallel is uncanny, except for this difference. Cordelia and Lear were on their way to prison; but Rosemary and Father MacDonald have been freed from a kind of prison and are living new lives they have each made for themselves. If only Will Shakespeare were still alive and could be here to see what has become of John MacDonald and his cowpen. It might inspire a happier ending for his play.

ACKNOWLEDGMENTS

I gratefully acknowledge:

John Gordon for providing me with hard-to-get DVD's of multiracial cowboys wrangling wild bulls in the Australian outback. In several respects they resemble the cow-hunters in this novel. I had the pleasure of getting to know John in the 1960s when he was an undergraduate and I was a novice assistant professor of anthropology at the University of Georgia.

John Jeremiah Sullivan for several stimulating phone conversations about Christian Priber, to the effect that Priber was certainly a most remarkable, and possibly the most radical, Enlightenment thinker on the early Southern frontier.

The proprietors and staff of the Coffeetree Café in Frankfort, Kentucky, for serving coffee and sausage biscuits off and on for four years to a taciturn old dude who would park himself at a table to scribble, scribble on this novel.

Leah Novak for cooking up batches of almond macaroons that gave me a taste of this delicious eighteenth-century confection.

Donald Davis for permission to quote extensively his superb story "The First Time Jack Came to America."

I thank those who read versions of my novel in manuscript and gave me useful criticism: Tad Brown read an early version while beginning a stint of anthropological fieldwork on cattle herding in West Africa; Peggy Galis, a true daughter of the South and a lifelong student of the same, read a late version of the manuscript and alerted me to a number of infelicities; Nash Cox, my Wapping Street friend and neighbor, took time out from a busy schedule to give a close reading to a later version; Richard Taylor, *primus inter pares* in the Church of Elkhorn congregation of kayakers, read a late version with a poet's sensibility, spotting some weak spots in the plot for me to strengthen; Edward R. Rogers and Bob Lancaster, fellow linemen on the 1949 Frankfort High School football team, who gave close readings to a late version; Barbara Lancaster read it with a copy editor's expertise; Robbie Ethridge, a former student and present colleague whose intelligence, knowledge, and good humor have been a delight to me in my career as a university professor, gave the manuscript a perceptive reading and made several concrete suggestions for revision; Pat Kennedy alerted me to the considerable abilities of black-mouth yellow curs; Grey Zeitz read it with a printer's eye; Kirk Somerville and Jim Gash cleared away several gaffes in matters of livestock; finally, I am most grateful to have had benefit of the criticism by the three anonymous readers for the University of South Carolina Press.

Special thanks go to my wife, but in order to do that properly I first need to say a word about the challenge of writing fiction after a lifetime of academic writing. In my long career as a university professor, I researched, taught, and wrote books about the anthropology and history of the native peoples of the southeastern United States. I was particularly interested in their history from the 1500s to the early 1700s. This work required me to assemble whatever archeological and documentary evidence I could find to reconstruct as rounded a picture as possible of these original southerners and their world. That picture, however, was necessarily limited by the incompleteness of the available evidence. It is not cricket in scholarship to use one's imagination to fill in gaps of imperfect evidence. So when I retired at the turn of the twenty-first century, having almost attained my threescore years and ten, I decided to take a turn of my own that would let me paint a fuller and more fleshed-out picture of the lives of people in the early colonial South than the strictures of academia permit. In short, I turned my hand to historical fiction.

This required a whole new set of skills, and they turned out to be more difficult to master than I had expected. Fortunately these skills come naturally to my wife, Joyce Rockwood Hudson, whose career as a novelist has brought her not only excellent reviews, but prizes—including Georgia Author of the Year in fiction for her novel *Apalachee*. Joyce and I have always edited and critiqued each others works, but whereas I was always on solid ground in writing non-fiction, I found the going to be much harder when it came to fiction. Hence I am grateful for Joyce's skill in this craft. As an exacting reader, an unsparing critic, a diligent fiction coach, and a superb editor, she has helped me flesh out my story with more craftsmanship than would have been possible without her assistance.

I am sometimes asked whether I will undertake to write a further installment in the saga of William and Rosemary MacGregor. Certainly it is easy to imagine the story going forward, but seeing as how I am now well into my eightieth year, my answer has to be: maybe so, maybe not.

NOTES

Chapter 1: Mired

For the prequel to this story, see Charles Hudson, *The Packhorseman* (Tuscaloosa: University of Alabama Press, 2009).

Chapter 4: Table Talk

For James Adair's observations about the Native Americans among whom he traded, see James Adair, *The History of the American Indians,* edited and annotated by Kathryn E. Holland Braund (Tuscaloosa: University of Alabama Press, 2005).

For more about the New World adventures of Christian Priber, see Verner W. Crane, "A Lost Utopia of the First American Frontier," *Sewanee Review* 27 (1919): 48–61; Knox Mellon, Jr., "Christian Priber's Cherokee 'Kingdom of Paradise,'" 57 (1973): 319–31; Ursula Naumann, *Priber's Paradies: Ein deutscher Utopist in der americanischen Wildnis* (Frankfurt am Main: Eichborn Verlag, 2001); and Samuel Cole Williams, *Early Travels in the Tennessee Country, 1540–1800* (Johnson City, Tennessee: Watauga Press, 1928), 147–62.

P. 36: Michel de Montaigne, *The Complete Essays,* trans. M. A. Screech (London: Penguin, 2003), pp. 228–41.

Chapter 5: The Cowpen

The physical appearance of MacDonald's cowpen is largely based on information in Richard D. Brooks, Mark D. Groover, and Samuel C. Smith, *Living on the Edge: The Archaeology of Cattle Raisers in the South Carolina Backcountry* (South Carolina Institute of Archaeology and Anthropology, Savannah River Archaeological Research Papers 10, 2000).

Chapter 6: Topsy-Turvy

Much of this chapter is based on folklore in Roger D. Abrahams's *Singing the Master: The Emergence of African-American Culture in the Plantation South* (New York and London: Penguin Books, 1993).

P. 53: Lighterwood is the resinous, highly flammable wood from the core of dead pine trees. It is also called fat lighter, heartwood, lightwood, lightered, fatwood, etc. It will ignite when put to a tiny flame.

P. 56: "The Big Black Bull of the Swamp" is partly inspired by "Rabbit in de Gyardin," *Singing the Master*, 253.

P. 57: "All them Purty gals will be There" is little changed from "All dem puty gals will be dar," *Singing the Master*, 246–47.

P. 60: "Venus has pretty brown Eyes" is adapted from "Jinny had de black eye," *Singing the Master*, 208–9.

P. 61: "Obadiah" is adapted from *Singing the Master*, 243–44.

P. 63: "Looking for the last ear" is adapted from "Lookin for de las' year [ear]," *Singing the Master*, 15.

P. 64: "Old MacDonald is a mighty fine man" is adapted from "Oh, Mr. Reid is er mighty fine man," *Singing the Master*, 16.

Chapter 8: Flea Bite Pen

P. 79: The authority on Spanish cattle, John E. Rouse, has argued in his *Cattle of North America* that Spanish and "Native American stock" (composed of mixed pre-breed northern European cows) did not interbreed in North America until 1800 in Louisiana and Texas (6–7). Nonetheless he notes that cattle were present in Spanish missions in Florida and elsewhere in the 17th century (75–76).

In contrast, Terry Jordan notes that by 1700 there were some thirty-four Spanish ranches and perhaps fifteen to twenty thousand head of cattle grown at any one time by Spanish ranchers in northern Florida. The English from Carolina destroyed these missions and ranches in 1702–6, causing the Spaniards to abandon the area and fall back to St. Augustine. The Carolina raiders took hundreds of enslaved Indians back to Carolina, and it is hard to imagine they did not drive cattle back as well. Many of the Indians they captured and enslaved had learned to tend the livestock of Spanish herders (Jordan, *North American Cattle-Ranching Frontiers*, 106–7).

In addition, Jordan cites evidence that as early as 1680 Carolina colonists possessed substantial numbers of cows that evidently came not from Barbados but from Spanish herds on Jamaica. So much so, the intrusion of these herds into Indian land was one of the causes of the Yamassee War of 1715–17. Also, some

284

of the herding techniques used by early Carolina cowmen were derived from English-Spanish herding traditions from Jamaica (109–120).

Hence it is plausible that some early Carolina herders saw an advantage in having traits of Spanish cattle amongst their stock of cattle free-ranging on the edge of Indian country.

P. 84: Cassina was a caffeinated tea made from the parched leaves of *Ilex vomitoria*, much consumed by Southeastern Indians and also by Spanish and British colonists.

P. 86: The Juliyama song is from Carol Beckwith and Marion van Offelen, *Nomads of the Niger* (New York: Harry N. Abrams, 1983), 148.

Chapter 9: Cut Nose

P. 92: On Henry Mouzon's 1775 map, Poplar Creek is named Starling Creek and Half Way Swamp Creek is named Waverick Creek. For the convenience of readers who want to locate events on maps, I have chosen to use the modern names.

P. 101: For the use of whips to drive livestock, see the movie *The Man from Snowy River*.

P. 102: Eighteenth-century cowherding dogs are thought to have resembled Texas cowdogs and the Louisiana Catahoula cur. See Terry G. Jordan, *North American Cattle-Ranching Frontiers*, 119, 181.

Chapter 10: The Fragrance of Rosemary

P. 106: Rosemary's butter making is based on folklore in: Eliot Wigginton, *The Foxfire Book* (New York: Anchor, 1972), pp. 185–88.

P. 108: "The Keys of Canterbury" is based on an old song collected by James Orchard Halliwell in the early 19th century and published in his *The Nursery Rhymes of England, 1846*, 229–30.

P. 109: I like to think of the sound of Rosemary's voice as having something of the authority of Jean Ritchie (e.g. *Jean Ritchie's Ballads from her Appalachian Family Tradition*, Smithsonian Folkways Recordings, 2003), the ornamentation of the young Iris De Ment (e.g. *My Life*, Warner Brothers Records, 1994), and the bold style of Elizabeth La Prelle (e.g. *Lizard in the Spring*, Old97wreckards, 2007).

Chapter 11: Four-Hole Swamp

For the full story of the Natchez Indians, see James A. Barnett, Jr., *The Natchez Indians: A History to 1735* (Jackson: University Press of Mississippi, 2007).

P. 128: One can see swampland like William saw by visiting Francis Beidler Forest and Congaree National Park, both in South Carolina.

Chapter 12: Cow Thieves

P. 142: Today Ox Creek is named Lyons Creek.

Chapter 13: Tending Herd

P. 157: The African word *dogi* is thought to be the origin of the American word dogie, designating a motherless calf, as in:

> Git along little dogie, git along,
> t's your misfortune and none of my own.

P. 164: The stories of the untrustworthy women are based on folklore stories in John A. Burrison's *Storytellers*, 9, 334–36.

Chapter 17: The Pettiauger

P. 190: The *pettiauger* was a dugout canoe. Sixteenth-century Spaniards first encountered them in the Caribbean, where they were named *piragua* by the Carib Indians. The French rendering of this word was *pirogue* and the English rendering of it was *pettiaugre* or *pettiauger*. These vessels ranged in size from about eighteen inches wide and eighteen feet long, to three to four feet wide and thirty to forty feet long. Loaded, the big ones drew only about eighteen inches of water. The prows could be pointed or flat. The large ones were sometimes divided up into several compartments by means of carved bulkheads.

In later times, Europeans would sometimes saw a large dugout canoe down its centerline, dividing it in two, and then they would insert fitted planks to widen the craft, allowing it to carry greater cargo and making it more stable in the water. Also, two dugout canoes could be connected parallel, a few feet apart, and then decked over, forming a kind of catamaran, which could be rowed or powered with a sail. (John A. Johnson, "Pre-Steamboat Navigation on the Lower Mississippi River," PhD dissertation, Louisiana State University, 1963, 20–54).

The Hernando de Soto expedition (1539–43) encountered very large dugout canoes at several locations in the Southeast. They were powered by single or double rows of paddlers. Often they had canopies or awnings positioned at their sterns, beneath which important persons sat. A fleet of these large canoes harried survivors of the expedition as they made their escape down the lower Mississippi River. Many of them were quite large, with double rows of as many as thirty paddlers, propelling the canoes very rapidly, and with another row of archers standing in the middle—as many as seventy men total aboard a canoe. In some of these canoes, the paddles, bows, and clothing of the occupants were all of the same color, and the crews were highly disciplined. See Charles Hudson, *Knights of Spain, Warriors of the Sun: Hernando de Soto and the South's Ancient Chiefdoms* (Athens: University of Georgia Press, 1997), 175, 284–85, 391–93.

Pirogues are still used in parts of Louisiana. They take the form of the old dugout canoes, though they are normally made of planks or plywood.

P. **193**: William's story of "How Jack Came to America" is closely based on a story collected by Donald Davis in his *Southern Jack Tales* (Little Rock: August House Publishers, 1992), 209–17.

Chapter 18: Rice

For the history of rice in South Carolina, see S. Max Edelson, *Plantation Enterprise in Colonial South Carolina* (Cambridge, Mass.: Harvard University Press, 2006).

Chapter 21: The Devil's Harem

P. **233**: Today Poke Spring Creek is known as Polk Creek.

Chapter 24: The Stranger

P. **263**: Delilah's recipe for macaroons is loosely based on one in Richard J. Hooker, ed., *A Colonial Plantation Cookbook: The Receipt Book of Harriott Pinckney Horry, 1770* (Columbia: University of South Carolina Press, 1984), 73.

P. **266**: For Rosemary's song, see John Gay, *The Beggar's Opera,* edited by Bryan Loughren and T. O. Treadwell (London: Penguin Books, 1986), 60.

SELECTED READINGS

Ackerman, Joe A. *Florida Cow Man: A History of Florida Cattle Raising.* Kissimmee: Florida Cattlemen's Association, 1976.

Beckwith, Carol and Marion van Offelen. *Nomads of Niger.* New York: Harry N. Abrams, 1983.

Burrison, John A., ed. *Storytellers: Folktales and Legends from the South.* Athens: University of Georgia Press, 1989.

Cashin, Edward J. *Guardians of the Valley: Chickasaws in Colonial South Carolina and Georgia.* Columbia: University of South Carolina Press, 2009.

Davis, Donald. *Southern Jack Tales.* Little Rock: August House Publishers, 1992.

Earley, Lawrence S. *Looking for Longleaf: The Fall and Rise of an American Forest.* Chapel Hill: University of North Carolina Press, 2004.

Edgar, Walter. *South Carolina: A History.* Columbia: University of South Carolina Press, 1998.

Gerrell, Pete. *Old Trees: The Illustrated History of Logging the Virgin Timber in the Southeastern U.S.* Crawfordville, Fla.: Southern Yellow Pine Publishing, 2000.

Guilds, John Caldwell, and Charles Hudson, eds. *An Early and Strong Sympathy: The Indian Writings of William Gilmore Simms.* Columbia: University of South Carolina Press, 2003.

Hudson, Charles. *Black Drink: A Native American Tea.* Athens: University of Georgia Press, 1979.

Hudson, Joyce Rockwood. *Apalachee: A Novel.* Athens: University of Georgia Press, 2000.

Jordan, Terry G. *The American Backwoods Frontier: An Ethnic and Ecological Interpretation.* Baltimore: Johns Hopkins University Press, 1989.

———. *North American Cattle-Ranching Frontiers: Origins, Diffusion, and Differentiation.* Albuquerque: University of New Mexico Press, 1993.

Joyner, Charles. *Down by the Riverside: A South Carolina Slave Community.* Urbana: University of Illinois Press, 1984.

Liberty, Margot, and Barry Head. *Working Cowboy: Recollections of Ray Holmes.* Norman: University of Oklahoma Press, 1995.

Meriweather, Robert L. *The Expansion of South Carolina, 1729–1765.* Kingsport, Tenn.: Southern Publishers Inc., 1940.

Moffat, Alastair, *The Highland Clans.* New York: Thames & Hudson, 2010.

Morgan, Philip D. *Slave Counterpoint: Black Culture in the Eighteenth-Century Chesapeake and Lowcountry.* Chapel Hill: University of North Carolina Press, 1998.

Olwell, Robert. *Masters, Slaves, and Subjects: The Culture of Power in the South Carolina Low Country, 1740–1790.* Ithaca: Cornell University Press, 1998.

Otto, John Solomon. *The Southern Frontiers, 1607–1860: The Agricultural Evolution of the Colonial and Antebellum South.* New York: Greenwood Press, 1989.

Rouse, John E. *Cattle of North America.* Norman: University of Oklahoma Press, 1973.

———. *The Criollo: Spanish Cattle in the Americas.* Norman: University of Oklahoma Press, 1977.

Stewart, Mart A. "From King Cane to King Cotton: Razing Cane in the Old South," *Environmental History* 12 (2007): 59–79.

Turner, Lorenzo Dow. *Africanisms in the Gullah Dialect.* First edition 1949. Columbia: University of South Carolina Press, 2002.

West, David. *Shakespeare's Sonnets.* New York: Duckworth Overlook, 2007.

Wood, Peter. *Black Majority: Negroes in Colonial South Carolina from 1670 through the Stono Rebellion.* New York: Alfred A. Knopf, 1974.